WALTER MOSLEY

A *New York Times* Notable Book of the Year

BLUE LIGHT

WARNER BOOKS

$6.99 US / $9.99 CAN.

ISBN 0-446-60692-8

9 780446 606929

50699

EAN

BLUE LIGHT

Also by Walter Mosley

Always Outnumbered, Always Outgunned
Gone Fishin'
A Little Yellow Dog
RL's Dream
Black Betty
White Butterfly
Red Death
Devil in a Blue Dress

WALTER MOSLEY

BLUE LIGHT

ASPECT®

WARNER BOOKS

A Time Warner Company

WARNER BOOKS EDITION

Copyright © 1998 by Walter Mosley

Aspect® name and logo are registered trademarks of Warner Books, Inc.

Cover design and photo illustration by Jesse Sanchez

Warner Books, Inc.
1271 Avenue of the Americas
New York, NY 10020

Visit our Web site at
www.warnerbooks.com

 A Time Warner Company

Printed in the United States of America

Originally published in hardcover by Little, Brown and Company
First Paperback Printing: November 1999

10 9 8 7 6 5 4 3 2 1

This history is dedicated to Thucydides,
the father of memory

BLUE LIGHT

PROLOGUE

The
Radiance

I didn't use a tape recorder back then, but I remember every word. Our teacher stood on a simple flat rock and told us about the blue light. What it meant—at least, as much as we could understand. Here is what he said:

I was once simple flesh like you, a man filled with meaningless words. But I was also a sleeping streak of blue light, scant seconds in length, jarred to consciousness after an age of silence. In the din of radiance rising from Neptune, I awoke and found myself leaning toward the cold gravity of that titan, rushing toward the small star it orbited. Ahead lay oblivion or the seed left on Earth eons before and, hopefully, grown to stature.

Between the graceful dance of gravities, that needle of light, no wider than a meteorite, traveled forth. Other lights—exactly the same hue—at my side, each one a perfect array unwavering in its relationship to the rest. Each one made up of a flawless matrix of thought repeated again and again in a swirl of equations that held the secrets of your deepest dreams.

As perfect and timeless as diamonds, a thousand thousand thousand brothers and sisters ignited in the silent and unfelt anticipation of breath, death, or oblivion.

Our entrance into the solar band of energies caused friction, squeals of false consciousness. Many lights drew away toward barren celestial bodies. Most of us died in the ecstasy you call the sun. The survivors passed through clouds of helium and hydrogen. The poisonous atoms turned millions of blue lights to green. Those matrices faded, as did their tainted lights upon reaching Earth's atmosphere.

Still, nearly ten thousand blue needles were destined to break the skin of air, their divine messages still intact. Hundreds sliced the ocean, cerulean knives leaving wide-eyed mackerel and barracuda with the desire to swim up onto shore.

But the rain of light moved quickly to land. Imagine a beetle contemplating infinity in his small brain, flipping forward and back trying to escape the inkling. Finally he leaps into the air, blue fire alive all around him. Then comes the merciful bat; a hiss of leathery wings, and the fire is out. Cathedrals in Rome would mourn this passing for a thousand years if they knew.

Dozens of small creatures died in the path of light that night. Each one in a terrible ecstasy of blue notions. Each one more sacred than the history of prayer. But not all died. The sleeping mosquito struck by light might have stayed at rest because the blue light has no heat. The small weed would hear the call through the slow process of photosynthesis, her roots becoming sorcerous fingers exhorting Earth to live.

The prophet always seemed smaller, weak after his sermons. But we felt elated and strong.

There were other transformations on the night that Ordé, the prophet, saw blue light. These I have gleaned from conversations, newspaper articles, interviews, obituaries, and a peculiar facility that Ordé endowed upon me—the ability to read blood.

Reggie Brown was pushing the baby carriage down Easter Street toward the Broward shelter that evening. Their uncle Barnes was drunk again and Reggie's mother was still at work, so he bundled up the twins, intending to take them to Nurse Edwards's station until their mother came home. Nurse Edwards had Fly Comics in her drawer and Baby Ruth candy bars too. She'd been their father's friend; she was at their house when the letter came from the State Department telling how Mr. Brown was missing in the police action in Vietnam. Now she helped Mrs. Brown with the children when she could.

Reggie stopped at a red light on the corner of Orchard and Easter. He peered inside the ragged double stroller to check on his two-and-a-half-year-old sisters. Brown girls, but not as dark as him, with fat faces that almost always smiled when he looked at them. Babies out of his momma like magic come to love them. Him and his mother, but not Uncle Barnes, not when he was drinking anyway.

"Hey, hey," Reggie sang. Wanita giggled but Luwanda just stared. She saw it coming.

Reggie turned his head to see the flash of blue, and then he was walking again. Up a steep path in the woods. Beneath his feet was a stream filled with blue fish. The stream was shallow and the fish were big, but they had no problem swimming and diving. The sky was bright, but it was nighttime in his vision, night with no stars. Trees grew up the side of the valley, and the bright eyes of animals watched him move along. There were whispers. Terrible things. Gouts of blood, severed limbs in the mud. And beauty beyond Reggie's poor words to say.

He traveled upward for days, it seemed. Blue smoke rose from his bare feet on the wet rocks.

A madman, who wore clothes fashioned from skins and bark decorated with bone and stone fasteners and buttons, was laughing at him. Beyond the man there was a valley. He could make out every detail—trees, leaves, and insects crawling in between. He could see single strands of spiderwebs waving lazily in the breeze. He could see the breeze too.

The trees were singing, some in a sweet alto and others in a bellowing bass.

Reggie started to run. It was a thousand miles away, but he knew that he could make it without ever stopping. He knew he could.

"Honey?" the woman said. "Honey, you okay?" It was an older brown lady with a Spanish lilt.

"Huh?" Reggie didn't remember her. He didn't remember standing there at Orchard and Easter.

The lady wasn't tall but was very round. Her glasses were framed in metal. Her teeth were edged in gold. There were big silver hoops hanging from her ears. She smiled at him the way women smile at small children.

"Are these your little sisters?" she asked. She bent over to get a closer look under the tattered hood of the stroller.

Even before she started screaming, Reggie understood that Luwanda was dead. He didn't know how he knew, but that didn't matter. His sister had passed into blue. She was in that faraway valley.

Winch Fargo had watched them all afternoon. The old couple was selling lottery tickets at the outer edge of the church bazaar. The tickets were for a drawing to help out some kind of summer camp for needy children. Propped up on a little poster card in the center of the table was a picture of a smiling blond-haired boy who needed to get away for the summer.

Mrs. and Mr. Martel were having a great time greeting their fellow churchgoers at Palm Park in South San Francisco. They didn't know that the long-haired, self-tattooed, and dangerous Winch Fargo had been watching them from behind a succession of beer bottles, hidden by the pink stucco maintenance hut, secreted between two shiny aluminum trash cans.

"If they stay till sunset," Winch whispered, "then they're mine."

The other tables began folding up at six-fifteen. The reading table. The events committee. Everybody waved, said good-bye. They offered to drive Philip and Eileen to the steering committee dinner. But the old couple was happy sitting in red nylon chairs, holding hands above the metal cashbox between them, watching the sun go down.

". . . one hundred and forty-four dollars," Eileen Martel was telling Philip. The last of the bazaar vendors were more than a hundred yards away, loading empty brownie pans, dirty dishes, and bags of trash into the back of the church van.

"And that's just how much I wan'," Fargo said.

Philip looked up with a smile on his face. The long blond hair on the man didn't bother him. It was dirty and down past his shoulders, but that was the new style, the hippie look. And so was the scruffy facial hair; you couldn't really call it a beard. Bad teeth, but rotting and discolored teeth weren't a sin—not everybody had medical and dental insurance from Hogarth's Encyclopedia and International Publishing after forty-five years without a sick day.

It was the pistol that took away Philip Martel's second-to-last mortal smile. Pitted chrome that still managed a dull shine even in the last glow of twilight.

Eileen uttered, "Oh my," and squeezed her husband's hand, her best friend's hand.

"I warned you," Winch said.

"You what?" asked Philip.

"You was fool to stay out here until dark in the park."

It rhymed, Eileen thought uselessly, *maybe everything will be all right.*

"The money," Winch said. "That's all I want. Give it."

Philip could feel his hemorrhoid throbbing, but the pain meant nothing, nothing at all. He nodded and made to reach down, but as his head moved he caught a glimpse of blue glinting off the silvery barrel of the gun. Helpless, he turned his eyes upward. Eileen, always with him, did the same.

"What the fuck . . ." Winch saw the sagging, pasty-faced old couple smiling, actually smiling, when *he* had the gun. And then Winch peeked. He caught only the last second—not the full equation, only the echo.

He guffawed, "Whoa ho!" And a blue snake the size of a python slid in through his eye socket. His head felt as if it were bulging with thoughts murmured in a foreign tongue, whispering ideas that had texture, smell, and the broken music of God.

This last thought struck Winch as odd. He had never believed in God. Where did that come from? And where was the light?

The blue light had faded and left the twilight darker than the closet in Winch's childhood apartment. Darkness so lonely that he would have done anything for light, that blue light.

He looked down and saw the old folks still sitting there—smiling.

Eileen saw her husband for the first time, it seemed. Philip Martel. Soldier. Father. Son. Lover under the covers but never so beautiful as now. A blue sheen still hanging over him like the afterglow of sex. She relived hot summer evenings, like that evening, after long days of her cooking and cleaning and his cutting the grass. After all that sweat a glass of beer . . . But that was the first time she had ever really seen him. His smile so sad that she knew, somehow, why and what he had to do.

"It was like we were in a bubble," she told me at the prophet's park many months later. "Like we felt everything the same."

Philip felt most of the blue radiance in his chest. The gun hovered somewhere beyond his sight. Sad for all those years before the light, he felt a sudden awareness in a place so far away that it was impossible to imagine. But he was there. Not him, Philip, but them—blue radiant spawn. Somehow their memories merged, and he was transported so far away and long ago that he saw the birth of Earth in a pinwheel of self-knowledge. He felt the long journey of his cells through eons of evolution. Crawling, rutting, flying, dying again and again. There was memory in his blood, quickened by the light. But also there was a call to death that formed around the weakness in his heart. His mind became part of the light as the light prepared to join the magnetic energy that flowed through the ground under his feet.

He was dying. Dying in Eileen's sad smile. Dying like the fading blue butterflies around his head.

As his heart began its final wild sprint back to blackness, he spread his arms with the strength of death and rose, knocking down the flimsy card table, to embrace his dirty half brother—the man from an eon ago with the gun.

"Whoa ho!" Winch cried out again. The light was gone, but the python still writhed in his head.

From the parking lot the Martels' fellow parishioners began yelling.

Philip was already up, hugging Winch as though he was congratulating an old army buddy back from the trenches.

The muffled shot was not intentional. It was the volatile blue light that chose Philip's fate, not the slug from Winch's gun.

"Stop! Stop!" from the parking lot.

Eileen, quickly, was up and off behind the trees.

Blue radiance rose from Philip's corpse on the ground. Winch knew somewhere that he was witnessing a miracle. The light hovered, seemed almost to hesitate, and then rose, a hundred thousand glittering pins. They hovered for a moment more and then dove into the ground beneath his feet like a frightened school of fish disappearing at the first hint of danger.

"No!" Winch yelled and then ran. The gun was in his hand, but his arms dangled awkwardly at his sides.

"He's dead," Winch said to no one. "Blue snake."

Mrs. MacMartin, the social director, screamed and threw up her hands. Winch shot her, hoping for more blue light—but none came. Roger Pliner, Felicity Burns, Bright Williams, Chas Twill—all dead by Winch's gun.

"Old lady!" he yelled. "Come on out! I don't wan' the money! I wan' the light is all!"

The snake had swallowed his mind by the time the police came. Winch knelt amid the corpses in the parking lot. It wasn't yet fully night when the flashlights hit him.

"Put down the gun!"

Winch held out the pistol in submission, thinking the voice was his mother's. But the police mistook the gesture. He didn't hear the shots. The first bullet took him in the right lung. Then one in the ankle as he rose up on one leg. In his right thigh, through his ear, in the left hand, the right shoulder, the lower intestine. Every wound a blue ember burning hot and bright. Winch Fargo smiled at the fires only he could see. They burned long after his mind closed down.

At her rented house in the Oakland Hills, in the backyard, Claudia Zimmerman was on top of Marcus. His eyes closed, a big grin on his loose lips. She moved up and down, wondering what it would be like to feel as good as he did. Her dog, Max, poked his nose into the cleft of Claudia's buttocks. It tickled. On the back porch her husband, Billy, was with Marcus's wife in the hot tub. She heard Franny yelping, *Yes, yes, yes.*

Grabbing Claudia by the wrist, Marcus groaned, "Oh, yeah."

It hurt and she swayed back against his fast thrusts, aware of Max's cold nose and lapping tongue against her rectum and of the blue light as she looked up in the sky.

Suddenly all she wanted was Marcus.

"Fuck it harder!" she yelled at the pudgy paper salesman. Max began to howl.

Claudia dug her nails into Marcus's fat shoulders and he screamed. She hunkered down on him and ground his hips into the grass.

"Harder!" she yelled.

He called out again, not from pleasure.

Lights came on in the house up the hill.

She didn't remember Billy and Franny coming down to see why Marcus was screaming. She didn't remember Marcus hitting her in the chest and face with his fists in a vain attempt to push her off. All she knew was Max's howling. His yowl a clear blue note deep in her body— a promise of rapture that the fool Marcus couldn't even imagine. There were explosions in her mind every time she thrust down on him. There was the taste of blood as she tore off his right nipple with her teeth. And then weightlessness as Billy and Franny pulled her off Marcus, and then the cold water of the unheated swimming pool. Blue water and blue cold—Marcus's spongy nipple between her back molars.

Horace LaFontaine lived for eight months and then died on the top floor of his sister's house on Laramie in West Oakland. His sister, Elza, had taken him in when he'd come down with lung cancer. She fed him and shaved him, cut his toenails, and teased the hard feces out of his rectum when he was too weak to move his own bowels. She read to him late at night in words that he had once understood. Now the words were merely sounds, unrecognizable except for the timbre of his sister's voice. That commanding voice he'd known as a youth in the black slums of Houston.

The only thing he'd known for a while was the feeling of falling out of the sky, like a lazy leaf butting up against gusts of air as it goes. The ground was his last stop, and falling was all that was left of his life.

Elza's husband, Gregory, didn't care about Horace. He was supposed to come up and see after his brother-in-law twice every night while Elza was off at work, but

Gregory stayed downstairs drinking beer and watching the TV.

Horace didn't mind. The sight of anyone moving made him dizzy. The sound of anything but his sister's voice gave him frights.

He lay there, propped up on his pillows to keep the fluid in his lungs from drowning him. The oak outside the window was full of leaves. The sky above the highest limb was a dark blue.

Late afternoon. The thought blew through Horace's mind, something he still knew between the cancer cells that crowded his brain. *When the sun goes down,* he remembered, *when the night comes and all the pretty girls put perfume on they necks and thighs.* He thought of bees then and the stinging pain. He smiled because there soon wouldn't be any pain for him to fear.

A drum was beating and he wondered if what Jimmie T had said in Attica were true; was Africa in him? Was this drum some long, long ago memory in the back of his mind? Would he awake on some vast savanna where the first men walked and made life?

But the beating was just the fast tempo of his heart, the rhythm of life pumping quickly in his veins, trying to outrun death one last time—the final act of a wasted life.

He felt the falling again. The cascading leaf now slicing the air with a downward dip. Then there came a racing toward the ground. A quick downdraft, and suddenly Horace was dead—his eyes still open but no longer seeing the tree in the window.

Human time stopped in the tiny room. The clock lost its meaning but still checked off the moments that once might have been. Horace was gone.

And then that quick shaft of blue light—a commuter minutes too late for his train—shone its full radiance into the dead stare.

Horace was gone, but the urgency of the blue light on the cells still living in his eyes coursed through his body like a seismic eruption. Life leaping from one dead synapse to another, demanding one last act. The deep breath of the corpse and his lurching leap from the bed caused a racket.

Gregory jumped out of his TV chair down below and hurried up the stairs.

The corpse that was Horace dragged itself to the lamp on the table across from his bed. He ripped the cord from the pink ceramic vase and shoved the bare wire into his mouth.

Fat Gregory took three steps with his first stride. Three hundred pounds dragging on his heart as he went.

Electricity combined with the equations of light and played through every cell in the dead man's body. The cancer withered, and the cool resolve of life enraged the lungs and bones and breath of this once-man. His skinny, naked body pocked with sores. His hair matted, eyes yellow. His forgotten cock just a lump of sagging skin.

Gregory made it to Horace's door but had to stop to catch his breath. He looked at the door and listened. All he could hear was the theme song of *The Wild Wild West* from the television two floors below. Night was close at hand, and Gregory felt a twinge of fear. He decided to go back downstairs. He decided to let Elza come home and find her brother dead in there. Gregory was sure that Horace was dead. If he wasn't dead before he fell, then the fall must have killed him.

But if Elza found him on the floor and he was cold then she would blame him. And what kind of woman could he find if she left him? He was fat *and* unemployed. All it would take was a quick look and then a call to the hospital.

Gregory opened the door.

The blue glare hovered over the zombie in an electric arc. Yellow eyes glowed from the brown skull as black lips sucked on the lamp cord.

Horace looked up, moving the cord to the side of his mouth like it was the stem of a water pipe.

"Run, Gregory," the corpse said in a voice that was like Horace but, then again, was not.

"What you say, Horace LaFontaine?"

"Run, Gregory. Run now. Enjoy your last days as a man on this rock. Run."

Gregory took a step toward his brother-in-law. He wasn't afraid, not really afraid. The man had just gone crazy with the disease. Gregory reached out to take the wire from Horace's lips, and the blue/electric shock hit him. All three hundred pounds of unemployed dock-worker went flying backward, through the doorway and down the top flight of stairs.

Gregory kept going. He ran down Laramie Street. Not running really; he was walking hard with all the force of a run in his heart. He kept up his fast pumping walk until the police stopped him, a fat man in boxer shorts screaming down the streets of Oakland. There was an article about it in that week's *Oakland Standard,* a throwaway paper. An unidentified man was detained after being stopped on the street in his BVDs raving about a zombie. He died in police custody from a heart attack, the coroner's report said.

When Elza got home that night neither man was in the house. She called the hospital, but no ambulance had been dispatched for Horace. She called the police, but they didn't identify Gregory until late the next day.

William T. Portman, burned out on hallucinogens and homeless, was living in the park at that time. Philosophy school dropout and compulsive liar, he had changed his name to Ordé and took to begging and living off young women who were temporarily fooled by his lies and handsome blond features.

Ordé had a lean-to made from a tarp in the bushes behind a large water tower. There was a woman with him then. He usually had a woman with him, until she got tired of his talk. This one's name was Adelaide.

It was late in the afternoon and Adelaide was sunbathing with Ordé atop the wooden tower. She had fallen asleep, but Ordé didn't know it.

"I can see," he was saying, "a great wrong across the city. It's like a fog, only deadly. But not smog. Not something . . . something scientific—" And then the blue light came into his eyes. He knew at once that it wasn't one of the wild hallucinogenic flashbacks. His body didn't melt, the history of his life wasn't written on the ground beneath his feet. It was his true nature repeated a trillion times. It was the whole history of something that he didn't understand—not yet.

"Did you see that, Addy?" Ordé asked sixteen seconds later.

The girl opened her eyes and sat up. She was naked and beautiful. Nineteen, with red hair and green eyes. Her eyes were small and too wide apart—which banned beauty queen contests from her life. But Ordé loved her. He'd loved her for almost a week now, and she hadn't tired of his lies yet.

"Did you hear it?" Ordé asked.

"What's wrong, honey?" She had never heard his voice without the strained notes of prophecy in it. Even when he made love, he talked in that Moses-giving-the-commandments kind of tone.

"We have to make love," he said.

She reached out to hold him.

"No," he said. "It has to, it has to—cook."

"Huh?"

Ordé touched his eyes. "The word. It has to filter down. It has to bond so I can, so we can . . . come together."

"We can do that now, honey," Adelaide said.

She reached for him again, but he held her away.

"No. No."

After a long while Ordé and Adelaide dressed and then climbed down from the water tower. Addy was a little scared of the beautiful man that she had tamed in the park. His sudden and solemn sanity, his unwillingness to lose himself in her perfect body made her think that it was time to leave.

She would have gone back to the dorms alone except that he took her to the small stream up above the tower and washed her. It was summer and the moon was three-quarters full. "The water was cold," she told me years later in the woods of Treaty. "But he was so sure of every stroke against my skin."

For once he didn't say a word, just led her, undressed her, used her T-shirt as his rag. Somewhere between the moon shimmering in the water on her skin and the fading echoes of Moses, she forgot to leave Ordé.

On the walk through the trees and then onto Derby, toward Telegraph and her dormitory, Adelaide began to think of a life with a man who lied about everything and then, in turn, believed his own lies. Maybe that wasn't so bad.

On the same walk Ordé saw great stone bodies, larger than the sun, floating in absolute darkness. These titans were dreaming, before the world, about Ordé and what he would say.

Adelaide lived with him for two weeks before they made love again. But when they did, the wild man's love had become too much for her. It burned and rasped against her insides. He slept for three days after his clawing, screaming orgasm, stretched out right there on her small dormitory cot. When he came out of his hibernation she was gone, back home to Pomona and her family.

Hundreds of lights struck that night. Most of them collapsed into inert earth. Most insects, birds, and fish that witnessed the Radiance died immediately—not because the light was poisonous but because they were so close to death as a matter of everyday existence that, blinded for the moment, they fell prey to the world around them. Claudia's dog, Max, survived the experience. A pregnant coyote in Tilden Park glimpsed blue wisdom and moved north. I know of only sixteen souls who survived the night—zygotes of the blue impregnation, children of the primal cell of life—but there may have been more.

While God's tears fell I lay in a small candlelit storage closet in a place we called the People's Warehouse, bleeding from both wrists. That was August 8, 1965. Still loaded on reds, I barely felt the blood that soaked through my jeans and spread across the floor. When Joseph Warren came in looking for paper towels, he slipped on the slick gore and fell on top of me. I saw him coming. I tried to say, "Watch it, Joe," but the words wouldn't form on my numb lips.

The impact of his weight didn't hurt. All I felt was my bones shifting. *Sack of bones,* I thought. Just a numb sack of bones.

In Tilden Park the blue-risen coyote lifted her head toward the heavens and caught the foul scent of death, which she followed like some alien explorer who had just discovered the existence of evil. At the same time Reggie Brown held his mother's head against his breast, feeling no loss at the death of his sister, and Eileen Martel identified Winch Fargo in his hospital bed. I was in the ambulance, then in my own hospital bed, under arrest for the crime of attempted suicide.

While I was recovering, Claudia Zimmerman's husband shot himself in the head. The *San Francisco*

Chronicle reported that he was despondent over his wife's leaving him for life on a hippie commune somewhere.

In the days that followed I lost my job at the Berkeley library because I didn't come in to work for two weeks. I was asked to leave the Ph.D. program in Ancient Studies because I failed to make any progress in my thesis on the Peloponnesian War. My girlfriend, Althea, went back down to LA for the weekend and never returned.

They let me stay at the People's Warehouse in the Haight, though. They said it was because my blood had claim.

I spent the next few months wandering the streets of San Francisco and Berkeley. At any other time I might have looked like a maniac. A big black man in his twenties with a mane of matted and kinky hair. I carried a large homemade book, bound in unfinished oak and leather, that I wrote in while standing on street corners or sitting on the sidewalk. I was, at that time, writing a history that I'd given the temporary title *The History of Love*.

It was a chronicle of the Bay Area at that time. Everyone back then felt the change in the air. It was the first time since the ancient city-states that a city was the center of change for the whole world. I was going to document that change. With eyewitness accounts, torn-out newspaper articles, lyrics from songs, and impressions of political speeches, I hoped to capture the sense of change from a citizen of the Haight. I attended rallies and love-ins as if I were part of the press. I experimented with a wider variety of the drugs I felt were changing the mind of the future. Instead of studying history in books, I was writing history about the real world.

That was during the day.

At night I'd curl up into a ball in my small corner and dream about my mother (her white skin somehow denying the love she claimed) and my father—his absence even blacker than me.

I'd get the night shakes. I'd wish that I were dead. It was on one such bad night that I had tried to kill myself. The head doctors told me it was the drugs that made me crazy—not my mother. They said that I was smart and that too much pressure in the Ph.D. program along with the downers and mushrooms had pushed me over the edge.

But they didn't understand. They fit inside their clothes and behind their desks. They came from places where they were recognized as members and relatives and citizens. They were never stopped on their front lawns and arrested for stealing their own bicycles the way I had been. And when my mother came to the police station, she was turned away because I was too black to have come from her.

I spoke the white man's language. I dreamed his dreams. But when I woke up, no one recognized me. No one but my mother, and I hated her for that.

All of this is why, Ordé said, I was open to the promise of blue light. My life was free from the identity *half-life* had made for itself. I was ready, the prophet said, to go further than man and his pathetic telos.

But I knew nothing of blue light as I wandered the streets scribbling and waiting for the right time to die. I had no idea that there would be a grander history for me to witness and document. I had no glimmer that I had a part to play in the future of life and in the ultimate demise of humanity.

The social worker assigned to my case was Dan Hurston. I saw him on Tuesdays on a bench at the entrance of Golden Gate Park. We met in the park because I couldn't seem to breathe right in his office.

"How's it going today?" he had asked me at our last meeting.

"It's okay," I said. "I mean, I don't feel bad or anything."

Dan had almost jet black skin, a shade or two darker than mine, and a thick mustache that reminded me of a bristle brush.

"What *do* you feel?" he asked.

I wanted to say that there was no difference between me and the air we breathed, that I was mostly dead, but instead I just shook my head.

"Have you been looking for a job?" His question seemed to be a rebuke.

"I've been walking around a lot," I said.

"How about school? Have you tried to get yourself reinstated?"

Suddenly I was exhausted. I inhaled deeply but felt little satisfaction in my lungs.

"What are you going to do?" the social worker asked.

"You know, I keep thinking," I said.

"Yeah?"

"I keep thinking that it was my father's blood on the bathroom floor. It was his blood. You know what I mean?"

Mr. Hurston shook his head at me. He looked at his watch. There were children playing on the small lawn behind our bench. I watched them scream and laugh. Their mothers were sitting on another bench, talking to each other and looking up to check on their babies now and then.

"What are you going to do?" Dan Hurston asked again.

"I'm gonna kill myself," I said. "I'm going to go over to Berkeley and kill myself in the school library."

For a few moments the social worker stared at me. I realized that I knew nothing about the man. He wore a thick gold wedding band. I was thinking that it had to be thick because his hands were so large and powerful. There were small scars on his knuckles and on the fist flats of his fingers. His eyes were dark and remote. He smiled only when he talked about football.

He stood up, expecting, I think, for me to stand also.

"Come with me, son," he said.

I made no move.

He pressed his lips out and then sucked them back in. Maybe he thought he could force me to go.

"Listen, brother," he said. "I can't stop you. And it really doesn't matter to me, or to the people down at Social Services, what happens to you. I'm going back to the office now to inform the police. So if you mean it, you better do it quick."

I never saw Mr. Hurston again. Just one of those hundreds of people who walk into your life and then walk out again. Like my father.

I got on a bus headed for Berkeley, wondering if someone might lend me a gun.

ONE

ONE

ONE

Ordé stood atop the flat stone in Garber Park—talking.

It had been four years since I'd cut my wrists. I still carried my woodbound book, but the title had changed to *The History of the Coming of Light.*

"You are but a base stock." Ordé spoke in a commanding but intimate voice. It was drizzling on and off that day, so his audience was smaller than usual—fewer than eighty of his open-air congregation were there. Winos and unemployed clerks, dark-skinned nannies and their wealthy charges, the few blue novitiates (those who learned from the light but had not witnessed it), including me. And Miles Barber.

Miles was a homicide detective who dropped by about every other week or so. He usually came after the sermon. He didn't seem to like hearing Ordé's words.

Barber was investigating the deaths of Mary Klee, Carla MacIlvey, Janet Wong, and a man whom people in the park knew only as Bruce. They were all victims of a poisoner that the police had privately nicknamed Mack the Flask. They were also regulars at Ordé's sermons, friends of mine. Among the first friends I'd ever known.

"You are but a base stock," Ordé said again. "Vegetables cooked down in an earthen pot. Soup with only the slightest hint of flavor left. One after the other there is no difference in you. You live and die, come together and fall apart, you have children and give them empty names. You are barely there and fast dissipating; like the shit in a chamber pot spilled in the sea, you are flotsam having found your way to the edge of a decaying pier."

Everyone stood close around Ordé's stumplike rock. For all Ordé's certainty, his voice was soft. His followers, acolytes, and devoted friends found that they had to push closely together to hear the words. Down in Berkeley, even in the city, they called us the Close Congregation.

We crowded together because the sermons he gave captivated us. There was something so true in his words that we clung to one another as if we were holding on to his voice. We were lulled and exalted because in some way the truth he told was him, not just some abstract idea.

"You're way out from the heart of your origin, cut off from the bloodline that could provide the nutrients of true life. You are dying, unpollinated flowers." Ordé looked around with a kindly expression. "Your death means nothing. Your lives are less important than spit on the sidewalk. I can't even call you the seeds of something larger, better. You, who call yourselves living, are really nothing but the dead flakes of skin that some great shedding beast has left in his wake. The pattern of life is in you, but it is inert and decaying. . . ."

It seemed true to me. I felt lifeless; I felt inconsequential.

Just months after his bout with the blue light, Ordé had come upon me in the quad at Berkeley. He saw my sadness, named it, and told me that it was true.

"You are born dying and so are your children. And even though your leaders claim that you are making advances through the generations, you know in your heart that it isn't true. You get better at making mechanical things, chemical things, but you can't make better art. You can't understand the real in even a stone. The stone exists, but if I were to ask you what it was, what it really was, you wouldn't even understand the question. And if you did understand, you would pull out pencil and paper, microscope and atom smasher to try and answer. You would attempt in words to explain that it would be impossible to know the nature of being stone."

A breeze kicked up just then. Ordé raised his head and smiled.

"You would be better off putting your finger to the wind, my friends. Lick your fingers, everybody," he said.

Most of us did. One old woman named Selma licked all four fingers from top to bottom.

I still remember the first time I did this exercise for Ordé. I held up my hand and felt that most familiar and exquisite sensation. The air cooling my finger, drying it and moving on into the sky with the moisture of my life.

I was desperate back then.

"It feels good, doesn't it?" Ordé asked.

Many nodded.

"It's like the cold kiss of a spirit beyond your ability to see. You can feel her only for a brief moment and then she's off."

We nodded some more.

"You are lost," Ordé said.

He stepped off his rock, walked into the crowd, cleaving the congregation, and went up into the trees. Feldman and Alexander, two of Ordé's larger acolytes, blocked the way to anybody who wanted to follow him. He would be gone for the rest of the day. He'd probably go down to San Francisco, in the secondhand brown suit I'd bought him, to look for a woman.

It was time to look for a mate again.

Many of the Close Congregation followed him up to the point of the large carob trees into which he disappeared. They pressed up against the large bodyguards and called out, "Ordé! Teacher!"

I didn't go running after him.

I had been with Ordé for nearly four years by then. I'd left everything behind me and joined the Close Congregation. Ordé and his words were my only connection left to life. The day we met I'd intended to kill myself. I'd been with him ever since. I knew he'd be back. I was one of the few who knew where he lived in town. I collected donations from the Close Congregation, kept his bank accounts, and paid his bills.

Ordé had a lot of money in the bank, the large donations he collected himself in private interviews, but he spent very little of it. I controlled the checkbook, but all I craved was his truth.

Ordé's words were the truth. You could see every image, feel every sensation he described. His metaphors (what we thought were metaphors) took on a palpable reality that hung in our nostrils, stuck in the back of our throats. Halfway through any sermon I would notice that I was no longer listening to his words but instead experiencing the phenomena he described.

"Hello, Chance," Miles Barber said.

He had come up behind me while everyone else drifted after Ordé.

"Detective Barber."

"Where's your boss gone?" the policeman asked.

"I don't know," I said. "He doesn't check in with me every time he splits."

"He go off like that often?"

"You know as well as I do," I said. "You come up here enough."

"He always go alone?" Detective Barber asked.

"We're never alone, Officer."

Barber's hair was thick and black, but his eyes were light gray. He wasn't tall and he always wore an odd-colored suit. That day it was an iridescent gray-green two-piece suit with a single-button jacket.

He looked and sounded as if his entire life were just off the second-hand rack.

"I don't care about your blue light bullshit, kid. I wanna know if your boss disappears with people from this group into the woods."

"You asked me that before," I said.

"I can arrest you anytime I want, kid."

"Yes, you can, Officer."

Barber took me in with his eyes. I had known many policemen. Ever since I was a child they'd been rousting me. I knew when a cop hated me—my big frame, my black skin. But Barber didn't have time for that kind of hatred. He had a job to do, that was all.

I would have liked to help him. But I could not.

I couldn't, because helping him would have condemned the dream. Barber was a cop, that's all. He found out who did wrong, uncovered the evidence to prove it, and sent the wrongdoers to jail. He wasn't concerned with the subtleties of truth and necessity. He couldn't see above the small laws that he worked for.

I wondered, as he interrogated me for the fifth time, if he knew how close he stood to his precious truth. Did he know that three and a half years earlier I had been summoned from my Shattuck Avenue dive by Ordé?

A man, I forget his name, who lived two floors below knocked on my door a little after 11:00 P.M.

"Phone," he said. Before I could get the door open he was already going back down the stairs.

There was a pay phone on the second floor that we all used to receive calls. I was surprised because no one ever called me. My mother never even knew the number.

"Chance?"

"Teacher?" I asked. I had never seen Ordé away from the park except for that first time we met. It had been only a short while since I'd been a member of the Close Congregation.

"Come to me," he said and then he gave me the address.

I was flattered by the call. I didn't ask why or if it could wait till morning. I just told him that it might take a while because I had no car or bike or money for the bus.

"Hurry" was his reply.

I found myself running down the nighttime streets of Berkeley.

Ordé lived in a small house about six blocks down from Telegraph. There was no path through the uncut lawn to his door. I could feel the wet blades of grass against the bare sides of my sandaled feet.

He opened the door before I reached it.

"Come in."

The small entrance area had a doorway on either side. The room to the left was empty and dark except for a single flickering flame that I thought must have been a candle. The room to the right had an electric light burning behind a half-closed door. I turned toward the brighter light.

"No," Ordé commanded. He gestured toward the flickering dark.

I obeyed him not because I felt I had to. I wanted to please him because when he spoke he seemed to understand all the pain of my life. He never blamed or made empty promises; he simply explained and left me to make my own choices.

We sat on the floor in the dark room on either side of a fat candle. He wore black slacks and a loose collarless shirt that was unbuttoned. The light played shadows on his shallow chest and gaunt face. His blond hair was in shadow, making his bronzed skin seem pale.

"You are half of a thing," he said, speaking softly and with no particular emphasis. But I felt the words wrap tightly around my mind. "The lower half," he continued. "The tripod, the foundation, the land below the stars."

I wanted to get up and run. Not to escape, but to work off the elation I felt upon receiving his words.

"You are sleep before waking, like I was before blue light. I look upon you as you would see a man who used his head to hammer nails. Poor fool."

The image was so clear in my mind, I worried that it might be a flashback to an old acid trip.

"Do you understand?" Ordé asked.

"I think so."

"What?"

"The blue light is God," I said.

"No. I don't think so," Ordé said with a little wonder in his voice. "No. Not God, but life. Not lies or hopes or dreams. Nothing that is to come later, but right now. Right now. Here."

I had never experienced anything like sitting there receiving his words. The only thing even approaching it was an early memory I had of my mother's trying to show me the San Bernardino mountain range. I was three or four, and she held me in one arm while pointing off into the distance. All I could make out was "far away" and colors. But as she kept explaining and pointing, I slowly made out the mountains she described. The elation I felt at realizing mountains for the first time was a weak emotion compared with what Ordé made me feel there in the darkness.

I'd heard him speak many times before, but it never had that kind of impact. It was as if I were transformed temporarily and for a brief moment I saw through his eyes, shared his expanded awareness.

"Do you understand?" Ordé asked again.

I nodded.

"Can you see what I'm saying?"

"It's like the whole world," I said meaninglessly. "Everything."

"Everything must change," he said, making sense out of my nonsense. "But in order for that to happen we must multiply. We must grow until every animal and fish, every rock and drop of water is one. Everything must merge."

"Like an explosion?"

"Yes. But slowly. Over thousands of years. But it will never be unless we can mate."

"Why can't you?" I asked.

"I don't know. I try," he said. "But my blood is too strong. It devours the egg."

My eyes had adjusted to the darkness by then. There was a wooden bench behind Ordé and a pile of clothes or rags on the floor.

He stood up and walked toward the door with the electric light shining behind it. I followed him into the light.

It was a small dinette separated from the kitchen by a waist-high wall of shelves. A large table, topped with red linoleum, dominated the room, but it was the small corpse slumped back in one of the chrome chairs that captured my attention. It was Mary Klee, one of the Close Congregation. Head thrown back, dark foam down her chin. One eye was wide-open while the other was mostly closed. She wore jeans and a T-shirt.

There was a bowl half filled with what looked like congealed blood on the table before her. I'm sure I would have been sick if I wasn't still stunned by the power of Ordé's words.

"I hoped that if we shared blood, her cells might have been strengthened." There was no apology in Ordé's voice. "But even just to drink some of it, she died."

He stood for a long time then, pondering, I suppose, the future of his race—the generation of blue divinity. I sat down across from Mary, looking into her cockeyed stare. I'd never seen a corpse before, but then again, I'd never believed in God before Ordé told me that there was something higher than God.

The silence continued for half an hour or more.

"Can you drive a car?" he asked finally.

I must have nodded.

"Put her in the car in the backyard and take her somewhere," he said.

There was a junkyard in Alameda I knew. No one patrolled it at night and there were no fences. All the way out I wondered why I obeyed him.

"It's only words," I said out loud. "Only words, but Mary's really dead."

But I knew the answer. Those words had transformed me, made me believe in something that I could be a part of. Ordé didn't mourn Mary. How could he? People were, at best, coma victims in his eyes. He hadn't murdered her; he had tried to elevate her life.

Detective Barber interrupted my thoughts.

"I know you think that he's your friend, kid," he said. "But you knew those people too. If you think he cares more about you than them, you're wrong. MacIlvey was his girlfriend and she's dead."

"We're all dead, Officer," I said. "Some of us just don't know it yet."

Barber shook his head at me. He was a good guy. At that moment I wanted to be like him. I wanted to forget the sad truth of Ordé's prophecies.

TWO

Phyllis Yamauchi was an astronomer working at Berkeley when the shaft of blue light came in through her laboratory window. A year later she heard about a fanatic who claimed that knives of blue cut through heaven to enlighten us. She came the following Wednesday. I had no special senses then, but I could tell that the meeting between Ordé and Phyllis Yamauchi was monumental.

The tall blond fanatic came down from his rock and took Phyllis in his arms. She was crying and he made sounds and faces that expressed no emotion that I knew.

Ordé picked up Phyllis, hoisting her with one arm as if she were a child and said, "God is not alone on this earth."

At first there was silence among us. Then I started to clap. After that the applause came, applause and cheers.

It was Ordé's power to see the past as it moved toward the future and to rouse the hearts of men with this knowledge.

But others had seen the blue light also. Gijon Diaz, a man who loved puzzles. Reggie and Wanita Brown.

Eileen Martel, who brought home dozens of wounded animals, all of whom recovered even from the worst injuries. And there was Myrtle Forché, who was a playwright before blue light and a monologist after. They, and others, showed up at Ordé's Wednesday sermons. They didn't all come to every sermon, but there was a loose association that kept most of them coming back from time to time.

They were the Blues. Men and women who had transcended the human race. Part of their mind had lived among stars so far away that our science hadn't even imagined them.

That I moved among them, shared smiles and drank from the same cups, elated me. I believed that I was privy to a pantheon of gods. Though only children in the first months after their creation, they heralded an evolution that would become the divinity their mortal lower halves had always dreamed of.

Doctor Edward Marie at the Alameda County Jail infirmary didn't expect Winch Fargo to survive his wounds. But while Ordé made his prophecies, Winch's wounds slowly healed. After seventeen months on a hospital cot Winch opened his eyes to confusion and his mind to pain.

He asked for painkillers, but Doctor Marie saw no reason to comply. The wounds were mostly healed. Edward Marie couldn't see into the half-life that infested Fargo's mind and body, the fragment of that divine equation that flitted through him like a curse from some long-forgotten victim.

* * *

Fargo had to be chained in the courtroom because he would exhibit violent spasms now and again. His defense attorneys said that he had a degenerative nerve disorder. Doctor Marie disagreed. The prosecutor dismissed the jumping agony as a ploy by the defendant to save himself from the maximum sentence.

Winch didn't care. The chains he wore were in his blood. Pain chains. Somewhere far, or near, or not at all, in his head. When the feelings converged he'd jump up, or at least try to, and scream.

Maybe the jury would have set him free. Maybe they would have sent him to a psychiatric ward, where drugs could have soothed his anticipation of eternity.

They might have except for Eileen Martel; she and the boy, Reggie, and the little girl, Wanita. They had already been to Ordé's rock.

That's how I know the tale.

Eileen had only recently found the Close Congregation when one day Reggie and Wanita were in the park with their mother. Wanita went right to Eileen and crawled into her lap.

Eileen made friends with the children's mother. She said that she'd lost her husband on the same day that Mrs. Brown's daughter Luwanda had died. She gave the family money and offered to baby-sit when Mrs. Brown needed time to work.

They were often seen at the Close Congregation—chalk white Eileen and her young brown charges. The older woman also traveled in the company of dogs wearing homemade casts, flightless birds, and all sorts of wounded wild animals that became tame in her presence. A broken leg or wing, yellowy oozing eye, or bloody gash all healed under Eileen's care. Reggie's mother told me that Reggie had gone wild after his sister died; he'd go out the window at night and sleep all day under his bed. He wouldn't listen to her or even talk until Eileen met him in the park.

"It was like magic, Chance," Mrs. Brown told me. "That old white lady stroked his forehead with her fingers, and just like that, he was my boy again. That white lady come straight from heaven."

Ordé wanted to adopt the children, but Eileen told him no. She said that she would oversee the children's well-being. It was the only time I saw Ordé back down to someone else's will.

Winch felt them as soon as they came into the courtroom. For him it was a flood of light. The Blues told me that they all could feel the presence of others like themselves. Ordé called it a tinkling. Reggie said that it sounded like a roar.

"Whoa ho!" Winch shouted when he became aware of Eileen and her charges. He leaped for her, but the chains and guards stopped him.

"Please!" he cried loudly.

Eileen was there every day after that. She had come as a witness for the prosecution but returned out of charity. Winch would nod to her at the beginning of every day and then sit back peacefully.

Ordé said that Winch was soothed by the aura of someone who had imbibed the whole light. When Eileen and Reggie explained that they felt something like a jagged tear inside them when they came near

Winch Fargo, Ordé knew, or said he knew, that Winch hadn't seen enough of the light, that the presence of someone whole eased his pain.

"The composition of light is something like the schematic structure of a computer tape," Phyllis Yamauchi explained to me one Wednesday before Ordé's talk in the park. "Do you know anything about computers?"

I did not and said so. I was eager to hear whatever she had to say. I had already begun the *History of the Coming of Light* and wanted to hear about the blue light from someone other than Ordé. I wanted to be sure that my head wasn't just fried from taking too many drugs and then brainwashed by the rantings of a fanatic.

"Every computer tape has a header," Phyllis explained, "then unique information, and finally a trailer. The header gives you information on what you are about to receive. You read the unique information in light of what preceded on the header. The trailer, on a computer tape, controls routing, count information, and other statistics gathered while processing the unique data. Does that makes sense?"

"Yes," I said. "Yes, it does."

It was a joy to talk to Phyllis. She was so calm, and calming, compared with Ordé. She was sane but still believed in the blue light.

"Blue light, as I see it, is similar to the computer tape in many ways," she said. "Only the header is repeated along the body of unique data. This header tells of our history, starting with an ancient planet and the origins of life in the universe—"

"But how did it tell you?" I asked. I felt completely comfortable interrupting her. "Didn't you have to learn the language first?"

"The language of light is in our blood, Chance," she said, smiling. "Once illuminated, we are fully aware. The middle part—our mission, our individual purpose—is most of the light, almost twelve light-seconds in length. This information is what makes us different from one another. But even if every light were exactly the same, it would become different because the information in living blood alters each one of us also."

"So you mean if you and I saw the same light, we would get different information?" I asked, willing myself not to pick up my pencil and woodbound notebook.

Phyllis Yamauchi smiled and blinked, then she put her warm fingers on my writing hand.

"Even the way you think is based on the possibility of your blood, Chance." While she waited for that truth to settle in, I noticed the Goodyear blimp floating in the sky behind her head. I thought that that flying machine would be as forgotten as some billion-year-old single-celled creature after blue light exerted its will.

"The last piece, the trailer," Phyllis continued, "is the seat of power. It releases the potential in us. For the first time in the history of this world, life evolves without dying. Ordé thinks that this Winch Fargo person saw only the last piece, the trailer. He has all of our power and sight with no understanding or purpose. That's what drives him mad."

She was wearing a green blouse with white pants that had green stains at the knees because of the lawn we knelt upon. Her skin was the color of pale honey, and her frame was small and fragile. To some passing stranger she might have been a coed talking to some way-out hippie that intrigued her.

"How do you know?" I asked.

"Know what?"

"How do you know about the light? Is it because you're a scientist?"

"I am the light," she said.

"Didn't God say that?" I asked.

Phyllis smiled at me. I had touched her somehow.

"On Earth," she said, looking deeply into my eyes, "there is science in one place and God in another. In the church or temple or synagogue there is God up above and humanity down below, forever separate. But in truth, the universe is like a vast ocean teeming with life. All of that life is related. Science and God and man all meet there and find that each of us is one becoming the other."

She came with me to my room that night and we made love. She seemed to like me, but in the morning she said that there was no possibility for me to make her pregnant. We were never together again, but I still cared for her.

Eileen's calming presence allowed the jury to sentence Fargo to 135 years. He was craning his neck, smiling at Eileen, while the foreman of the jury delivered the verdict.

Eileen took the bus out to Represa every week. He was always haggard and weak when she arrived. But after fifteen minutes, even through bulletproof glass, he revived. He told her that it was like being taken up by the wind to see her, that always the night after he saw her he was visited by gods who told him all kinds of secrets. The gods would come for two more nights, and then he would sleep on the fourth.

But for the rest of the week monsters would come to drink his blood. He had cuts and scars along his arms, Eileen could see that. But she didn't know what they meant.

The week after my fifth grilling by Miles Barber, Claudia Heart showed up. She was the last of the Blues to come to us. I didn't know her real name, Zimmerman, at the time. But her real name didn't matter, because she went by the name Heart and lived by that principle.

She was welcomed by Ordé on the first day she appeared. Like most of the Blues, she didn't seem special at first. Five feet with limp brown hair and smallish brown eyes. Her skin was neither pale nor dark. Her teeth were small. I felt the beginning of an erection coming on when I first saw her, but I figured that it came from my excitement at Ordé's recognizing her as another of the Blues.

Ordé himself was overwhelmed because Claudia's dog, he claimed, was also shot through with the first words. This was the first animal he'd seen that had been elevated above man.

Claudia accepted Ordé's embraces and the accolades of the congregation. Then she stood quietly next to me and listened to the sermon.

She was quiet but intent.

While Ordé lectured on the qualities of light, Claudia was seducing me.

I felt her shoulder nudging my arm but didn't think much of it at first. We were, after all, the Close Congregation. Even when she pressed up against me and put a finger through one of my belt loops, I thought she was just being friendly.

But then she pulled my T-shirt out at the back of my pants. Her hand found its way to the small of my back and down to the top of my buttocks. That hand was incredibly hot.

". . . the light of creation is the salvation, and also the damnation, of man," Ordé was saying. "It is the idea and the power of something beyond your notion of God. But that does not mean free will is abandoned. A scientist touched by the light will become a superscientist. That child will plumb the meaning of the universe. A craftsman . . ."

As Claudia's fingernail scratched a circle at the small of my back, I felt that the breeze blowing over me was actually her breath. I caught a glance at her. She was staring at Ordé, but her smile was for me.

". . . a craftsman will be Vulcan by earthly standards. He will make miracles with wood and stone. But not everyone who is of light can be trusted . . ."

Claudia chose that moment to shove her hand down to caress my buttocks, one finger cleaving its way through to my rectum. There were people standing behind us, and I am no exhibitionist, but I wouldn't have moved her hand for anything. Not even for Ordé.

". . . everyone that has received the light has a purpose in the divine plan but you cannot trust us all. What if a murderer looks up from his victim, into blue? A child molester, a thief, a liar, a con man? There is room for every kind of man or woman." Ordé glanced in my direction then. I wanted to moan for him to forgive me and for the teasing pleasure of Claudia's finger. But Ordé wasn't looking at me. His gaze lowered to Claudia's dog, Max. "Even a dog can ascend to the heights. . . ."

I'm a tall man. Six three and a little bit more. That's why Claudia didn't have to slouch much to get her hands down between my legs. She squeezed the hard vein below my scrotum. I could have closed my legs hard enough to stop her; I wanted to, but I couldn't.

It was as if I were a teenager again, a boy who had always wanted and never known the touch of sex.

". . . we are not here to answer your prayers," Ordé was saying. "We are here to prepare the firmament for the unification of all things. We are here to create a newer and higher order. Each of us will use the tools we have. Each of us will do what is necessary. Your desires are meaningless. We only love you if it meets our needs—"

"Come on," Claudia whispered to me. "Let's go."

She had to stand on her tiptoes and let go of my vein. I was listening closely to Ordé because that was his power. When he spoke prophecy we were enthralled. That's how I knew that sex, or passion, or love, or whatever you want to call it, was Claudia Heart's province.

No matter how much I wanted to stay and listen, I had to go with her, my erection tenting the loose work pants I wore.

She led me through the Close Congregation and down a path through the trees. We came to a small dirt road, and she stopped to kiss me.

Everything dimmed, like when lightning strikes and the electricity goes low. I could hardly see or breathe. Where our lips met became the center of a new being, that's the only way to describe it. The kiss—not the flesh, but the act of kissing itself—became the origin of something beyond me but that I was still a part of. My arms moved to embrace her but too late, she moved back and studied my eyes. Whatever it is she saw must have satisfied her, because she smiled and said, "Come on."

I didn't understand how she could bear to disengage or how she could move so quickly. The kiss seemed to go on forever, but why I couldn't get my arms around her I did not know.

We went a little ways from the park and into the street. She led me up a nameless alley, behind a machine shop. There we came to a Dodge van that was wedged between two small buildings.

She opened the back door. The carpeted back of the van was completely bare except for a canvas cot that stood against the far side.

"Get in quick," she said.

The dog, Max, ran in with me.

"Take off the clothes," she said.

She pulled off her one-piece black dress. Underneath she had well-formed small breasts and a flat stomach. Her pubic hair was plentiful and wild, like an untamed shrub. I moaned when I saw her and tore a fingernail on the knot of my bootlace.

When I had most of my clothes off she looked at me and smiled. My erection was pointing right at her.

"What do you want?" I asked. I knew that I couldn't move without her telling me to.

I was hunched down because the van wasn't big enough even for her to stand up straight.

She pulled the cot toward the center of the space.

"Here," she said, indicating that I should sit on the edge toward the bottom.

I was naked except for one boot and the pant leg I couldn't get over it.

She made me lie down and then she got herself astride my erection. I felt something so firm and warm and embracing that I gasped.

"Don't move," she said.

"But I have to."

"Does it feel good like this?"

"Yeah, but—"

"Don't move."

I was looking up into her eyes. She seemed to be asking for something, and I was trying my best to give it to her. Every now and then I'd have a spasm and a shake.

"Don't move" would be her response.

After a long time she began to move up and down slowly, leaning over a little so she could run her fingertips over my nipples. I tried to move with her, but she dug her nails into my chest and whispered, "Stop. If you feel like moving, just call out, just scream. Nobody's gonna hear you. Scream."

She started to move faster then.

I let out a yell.

The dog barked.

"Just lie there, Chance," Claudia Heart said. I wondered where she'd learned my name.

I screamed.

"How does it feel?" she asked.

"Like cashmere and steel," I said. I don't know where I found the voice or the words.

"Do you like it?"

I couldn't answer.

The dog let out a howl that echoed inside my chest and brain.

"Spread your legs," Claudia commanded.

I heard her but somehow I didn't think she was talking to me.

"Spread your legs," she said again.

I did so and instantly felt the dog's hot tongue lapping against my testicles. I tried to pull my knees together, but Claudia put her hand out to stop me.

"If you try it, Max'll snap those balls right off."

Scared as I was, I just got more excited.

"Just take it, baby," Claudia said. And she began to move fast, moving me around like rock and roll.

When I came I thought my heart would explode. Claudia let her serious gaze break for a momentary smile.

"It's just the beginning, Chance. It's just the start."

I tried to get up, but Max bit my thigh. He howled again; Claudia brought back the cashmere and steel. It was hours before she was through with me. I don't know how long it was exactly because I wasn't conscious the entire time.

* * *

After our lovemaking I slept and dreamed.

My father was there, tall and black like he'd been in the photograph Mom kept. He was wearing a suit in the dream, not the jeans and work shirt.

"Hey, Lester," he said. Lester was my given name. Ordé named me Chance through prophecy and divination. He said that the name stood for the slender thread of hope that humanity had for survival in the face of creation.

"Yeah, hey," I said to my old man.

"You still my son, boy. You still a black son to Africa too. Don't let them white folks get you down. They ain't no kinda problem less you let 'em be."

"But Mom's okay, right, Dad?" I asked.

"She's fine, fine. But just don't let her deny me in your veins. Don't let her tell you that you just the same. You're better than anybody could imagine."

I was sitting on a tiny island with Claudia. She asked me where we were, and I told her that it was my island. The island where I went to get away.

I was looking for that island when I left home to go to the University of California at Berkeley. Before that I lived in Los Angeles with my mom. She sent me to church and school and summer camp with all white kids. She told me not to listen when they made fun of me and to just ignore it when they played tricks on me. They never beat on me, because I was too big. But they could hurt my feelings anyway.

I told Mom that I'd be strong, but I couldn't be, and when I left I never went back to her or her life.

I started out in the dorms until I got my B.A., but when I entered graduate school I moved to a big warehouse in San Francisco shared by drug addicts, runaways, students, and dropouts. I kept up my studies for a year or so. I dropped acid and learned the recorder. I'd hitchhike up along the Russian River with girls I'd just met that afternoon. With the hippies I found some peace, but it was a hard peace. I felt guilty because of my mother, and so it was always difficult to sleep.

"Wake up. Wake up." Claudia was shaking me. She had her dress on again. Max was asleep in a corner of the van. "Get up."

"Hi," I said. My pants were still inside out, hanging from my left ankle and boot.

"Go on now, Chance."

"What?"

"Go. Go home."

"Can't I go in the morning?"

"No. I need to be alone now."

"But—"

"We've done whatever it was you needed, Chance. It's time for you to go."

There was no arguing with her. I pulled on my clothes. She went to the driver's seat of the van and waited while I dressed. When I was finished I tried to say good-bye but she didn't seem to hear me.

I reached out to touch her, but Max growled and leaped to his feet.

THREE

I found Ordé waiting for me when I got back to his speaking stone. It was already dark.

"You left my sermon," he said. It was neither a question nor an accusation.

"She made me."

"I know," he said. "I was trying to hold on to you with my words, but her sex was too strong."

"I knew it," I said. It felt like an unfaithful lover's confession.

"How do you feel?"

"Like I could fly but don't remember how."

"And what do you want now?"

I looked him in the eye. We were the same height. Where he was thin and golden, I was strong and the color of milk chocolate. There wasn't much of my white mother in me.

I shrugged and held back a sob. Ever since I'd left Claudia's van I wanted back in. Back into her presence. She was the only thought my mind could hold on to.

Everything else was dissolving. All my memories and desires were fading like temporary images glimpsed in the contours of a cloud.

"Would you like to hear the rest of my sermon?" Ordé asked.

I still knew how to nod on my own.

He went right into his talk just as if it were still noon.

"You are neither worm nor butterfly," Ordé said, "but only the dry husk left after the metamorphosis. If you die, it is of no consequence. Your life is only the blind bumbling of an abandoned newborn. Your pleasure is salt and sand. Your heat is tepid tea. Your life a short gust across stagnant water—"

The words came over me like a cool balm, a restorative love. The condemnation didn't bother me. He was my teacher standing on a philosopher's stone. His brutal words were only truth.

"—water that cannot flow. True life is in my veins. It is in my eyes and words. There are only two ways to become of the light. Either you see the true words or you are born of the blood of truth. You can never ascend. You have only the slight possibility of half knowledge. You may perceive that there is a truth beyond you, but you will never know it, you will never glide between the stars on webs of unity."

Not only was there truth in his words, but somehow his words themselves were true. Like Claudia's kiss, Ordé's words brought me visions of a place between things. A space that is smaller than an atom but that still encompasses everything in existence. A place that is not yet here but that is coming.

"Do you want to see it, Chance?"

"Huh?"

"Will you risk your worthless life for an inkling of the truth?" His voice was kind and concerned.

There was no choice. He was a god and I, a blind mole.

We went down toward his small house. He wore a brightly colored tie-dyed monk's cloak and habit, but nobody looked twice. This was the Bay Area in 1969 and a black man, a brother, walking with a white man who wore his hair like a woman didn't turn heads.

In the light you could see that his home was made up of four small rooms with bare floors that were scarcely furnished. We went into the kitchen. I sat down at the table, remembering Mary sitting there dead. I wondered if my other friends had died at that table. While I wondered, he switched on a glaring electric light and put a white ceramic bowl in front of me. I noticed dark remnants splattered on the floor and walls. When I looked up, Ordé was approaching me with a sharp cork-hafted knife.

"If I speak to a crowd, they listen because they suspect the truth in my words," he was saying. "One day I'll run for office."

I stared at the knife as he stood over me.

"But if I connect with the truth in words while talking to a small group, or just one person, the truth is known. I am the doorway to truth, Chance."

"Are you going to kill me?" I asked.

"I don't know," he said. "The others died, but you're different. You're . . . you're weaker than they were.

You're one of the susceptible ones. More than anyone, you hear us. You hear the music."

He handed the knife to me. "Cut a vein and cover the bottom of the bowl to about an inch or so."

I didn't want to die and I was sure that what he was going to do would kill me. But I couldn't refuse him. Death was better by far than his disappointment. I cut my wrist and the blood flowed freely. The feeling of the blood trickling down between my fingers was familiar, almost comforting. It was a sensation I associated with power—my power.

The warm dollops plopped quickly into the white bowl. I tried to stop the bleeding with my thumb, but the blood kept coming. I tried three fingers, but still it came between and around. I was beginning to panic when Ordé took my wrist and placed a large gauze pad over the cut. He pressed hard for about a minute and then produced bandage tape and wound it tightly about the gauze. A large circle of blood grew on the bandage but stopped before reaching the edges.

Then Ordé took the knife. He raised his sleeve, showing his wrist. There were many scars there along the vein. I wondered if each incision meant a death.

Ordé chose a spot between scars. He dug in the point and made a quick twist with his wrist. The blood came out in quick droplets, mixing with mine. Ordé's blood was darker, but mine was heavier. At first the droplets formed little pools across the top like dark islets in a crimson sea. But as he bled more, the islets came together to form continents.

When he was finished Ordé simply pressed his thumb against the small incision for ten seconds or so. The bleeding stopped completely, and I wondered if that had to do with his truth also.

"We have to wait for the mixture to prepare itself," Ordé said.

He sat across from me and smiled.

I remembered the first time I sat in his presence on the afternoon I'd decided to die the second time.

"How's it goin', brother?" he asked me.

"Fine."

"You at the school?"

"Uh-huh."

"What you do there?"

"I study Thucydides' *Peloponnesian War* and its impact on the idea of history. That's the general idea anyway . . ." I stopped myself from going on to explain that the general and medical observer and historian not only told history but was himself a part of that history; he *was* history. That was my thesis, simple and elegant, I believed. But no one in Ancient Studies had thought my idea was scholarly enough, and they were happy to see me gone.

"You like that?"

"It doesn't seem to matter. Maybe it did a long time ago, but not now."

"All you learn around here is how to mix up the slop," Ordé said.

"You got that right." That was the first time I felt Ordé's truth telling, but I didn't know it then.

"You know the water tower above the statue back up in Garber Park?"

"Yeah?"

"I get together with some people there at noon on Wednesdays. You'd learn a lot more up there than you ever will in a classroom."

"About what?" I asked.

Ordé turned to me then and looked in my eyes. "About everything you miss every day. About a whole world that these fools down here don't even know exists."

Back then I thought it was his eyes that convinced me to live at least until the following Wednesday.

Sitting there in his kitchen, as we stared at each other over a bowl of our blood, I wondered at how far I had drifted from my pristine studies.

"See," Ordé said. "The blood mixes itself."

He was right. The darker blood and the lighter had formed into longish clumps like fat worms. They twisted and turned against each other, sometimes slowly, sometimes fast. Every now and then two worms would collapse and fall together and then fall apart—another color completely now, almost white.

"When they're all the same color it will be ready," Ordé said.

I watched the spinning worms, thinking that this was the first time I could see Ordé's truth outside of my mind. It wasn't just Ordé's words or Claudia's love-making that dazzled me. This was proof.

My stomach began to tighten. The back of my neck trembled, and I wanted to jump up from that table. I wanted to run.

"You see," Ordé said. "They're all that milky pink color."

"Yeah," I barked.

Ordé went to a drawer in the built-in cabinets around the sink. He pulled out a small whisk and came back. The pink worms were writhing violently by then.

Ordé plunged the whisk in and mixed briskly. The worms turned back to liquid. It was as if the writhing were an illusion, a vision brought on by Ordé's suggestion.

"This is the lightest color I've ever seen," Ordé said.

"You mean like with Mary?" I asked.

"She was the first," he said. "That's what killed her and Janet Wong and Bruce too. They drank a darker fluid and died."

Ordé looked me in the eye.

I raised the bowl to my lips. The thick fluid was warm on my tongue. In my throat it seemed to change back into worms. Sinuous and twisting they went down. I tried to take the blood from my lips, but Ordé put out his hand to increase the tilt of the bowl. I drank it all down. And then threw the bowl to the floor.

Inside me the worms were on the march. Through my stomach to my intestines. Under my skin and into my heart. I screamed louder than I had for Claudia. When I jumped up Ordé tried to grab me, but I hit him and he went down. I ran to the front door and out into the street; then I took off. Every now and then the parasites in my body brought on a spasm, and I'd fall tumbling across lawns and from sidewalks into the street. A car bumped into me on Telegraph, but I kept on running.

The visions started a few blocks after the accident. Wide bands of light in which images and histories unfolded. Molecules the size of galaxies, strange-looking creatures moving in and out of multicolored lights. A flat plain appeared on one curving screen of blue. The plain, as my mind entered it, spread out in all directions. No path to follow or mountain to set my sights on . . .

"What's wrong with him, Martinez?"

"He's trippin', Sarge. Trippin' hard."

They must have been policemen. They must have arrested me. I know they did because I woke up in the drunk tank of the Berkeley jailhouse. But I was distracted by the visions and the sounds too. I imagined stars singing in a chorus; it was no mistake, no happenstance. There was meaning and the deft motions of a dance among the suns. It was then I realized that the worms had bored their way into my brain.

A pane of light opened before me. It shone like a parchment burning with alien inscriptions, equations, and hieroglyphs. I stared at the burning pages as they moved past. I took in each character but understood very little. Toward the end was the full biography of Ordé. His childhood as a liar and his adult life as a saint. I saw and felt everything he had known and done up until the moment of blue light.

There was a flash and then I was, myself, a page.

A blank sheet.

An unwritten footnote.

FOUR

Lester?"

I opened my eyes to see a tall white man dressed in a white smock that hung open to reveal a red-and-yellow-plaid shirt and blue jeans.

"Yeah."

"I'm Dr. Colby. How do you feel?"

"Where am I?"

"At Santa Teresa rest home."

"I'm tired," I said.

At some other time (it could have been later that day or another week) I awoke to find Colby standing over my bed again. He was thin. The whites of his eyes were laced with red veins, veins that seemed to be writhing.

"How do you feel?" he asked again.

"I don't know. Everything looks funny."

"Like what?"

"I don't know," I said. "Like your skin. If I look at it hard, I can see all kinds of blues and yellows that are like the negative of a photograph."

"Do you feel nausea? Headache?"

"Why?"

"Do you have any history of blood disease?"

"No."

"Any problems?" He was trying to sound nonchalant.

"Am I sick?"

"There seems to be something wrong with your blood. Not wrong really, but odd. It's not acting like we expect it to."

"So what's wrong?"

"I don't know." The doctor ran his hand over his short salt-and-pepper hair. "We've sent it out for tests."

He took my blood pressure and peered into my eyes, throat, and ears. While he examined me, I learned that I had been in the sanitarium for three and a half months.

"A fellow named Portman had you brought here," the doctor told me. "He calls every week to see how you're doing."

"I'd like to talk to him the next time he calls," I said.

"When you're strong enough to walk." Colby gave me a friendly smile. "We don't have phones in the rooms."

He gave me a dark green pill and left the room after he'd made sure that I swallowed it. I fell near to sleep, into a kind of half-dreaming, pensive state.

I was aware of new possibilities in life. Like an amoebic cell drifting in the ocean, dreaming of becoming a whale. Like a bag of cement waiting to become a part of a highway or bridge. There was anticipation in every sound and sensation.

*   *   *

Light flittered across my eyelids. A wooden flute played softly.

Ordé was sitting next to my bed, wearing that secondhand brown suit. He'd added an almost shapeless gray fedora to the ensemble—long blond hair flowed out from under the back brim. He smiled. It was a pleasant smile, a smile that a parent has for another man's child. But I could no longer have the innocent love I once felt for the prophet. I was a worker now. An adult meant for lifting and toting, building and protecting.

"I'm sorry I have to wake you up, Chance. It's almost Christmas and we have to get on with our work." Ordé smiled again and I sat up.

I was still weak, though, and fell back into the pillows of my sanitarium bed.

"You have to get back your strength, cousin. You'll need a few weeks to eat and exercise. Then you'll be ready to come back and teach us how to do the blood ritual right."

I wanted to speak but passed out instead.

When I woke up again it was night and I was alone.

The room I was in was large with a high domed ceiling. There was a big white door that must've led to some hallway, and then there were double glass doors, covered in white lace, that went outside.

The moon was shining through the curtains. I forced myself to stand up and walk to the glass doors. I didn't feel strong enough to pull them open, but I moved the curtains to the side and gazed up at the moon. I can't express the joy that I felt looking up, being filled with light. Even the comparatively sterile light of the moon is filled with wonderful truths. With my heightened senses, I could actually feel the light against my skin. The tactile sensation caused slight frictions along my nerves. It was like the diminishing strain of a classical composition that had gotten so soft a breeze could have erased it.

The music spoke of that spinning celestial body and of the sun's heat. There was a long-ago cry of free-forming gases and a yearning for silence. The universe, I knew then, was alive. Alive but still awakening. And that awakening was occurring inside my mind. I was a conduit. We were all conduits. With my mind I could reach out to the radiance that embraced me.

But I didn't understand. I wasn't blessed by light. The potion Ordé gave me opened my senses but gave me precious little knowledge. I was like the tinfoil put on a jury-rigged coat-hanger antenna—merely a convenience, an afterthought with few ideas of my own.

The universe spoke to me in a language that was beyond my comprehension. But even to hear the words, just to feel them, filled me with a sense of being so large that I couldn't imagine containing any more.

Then there came a yipping like pinching at the back of my neck. I put my hand back there but found nothing. I saw a dark blur outside the window. Two night eyes, four, six, eight.

The coyotes came slowly toward the window. I wasn't afraid. They exuded a music like the moon did, but theirs was a quartet of fast drums and a thrumming of blood.

From behind them came a larger coyote. This one, when she came into the light that carpeted the lawn, showed herself to be one-eyed. The young canines moved to their mother as she stared up at me.

I opened the doors and they all rushed in, jumping around me. In my weakened state I fell to the floor. The young coyotes pushed their forepaws against me and yipped. They nuzzled their wet snouts against my face and rubbed their bony ribs against me. They smelled of things wild and feral, but I wasn't afraid. I felt them the same way I could feel the moon. It was as if I had been a fifth cub with them in the den where they were born, as if I had run with them and suckled on my own special teat. I felt the yip in my throat and a growl too.

That's when Coyote stood before me. The cubs moved away and I looked at their mother. She whined, wanting to tell me something, I was sure. But I didn't understand. She pawed the pine floor and licked my bare feet to no avail.

At that moment the door to the hallway opened. All six faces in the room turned toward the light. A small Asian woman stood there. She threw her hands up above her head and tried to turn and run at the same time; instead, she fell to the floor, screaming.

I felt a searing pain between my left shoulder and my neck. I turned to see five coyote tails moving fast across the moonlit lawn. The nurse was hollering for all she was worth. A deep dread settled in on me and I lost consciousness again.

I was unconscious for five days. The rabies shots they administered weakened me so much that the doctor thought I might die. But Ordé said that he was never worried about that.

"You're a blue blood now," he told me. "Pale but still blue enough."

In two more weeks I was strong enough to leave Santa Teresa's. My body was strong, but my mind was full of dread.

"They were like Claudia's friend, the dog? You're sure?" Ordé asked on the bus back to Berkeley.

"I could . . . could, like, hear them, you know?"

"You mean, you felt it like that?" Ordé said rubbing the thumb and forefinger of both hands lightly together.

Somehow the gesture made sense, and I nodded.

"And so when she bit you, she was trying to communicate," Ordé said. "She was telling you something."

It was a truth waiting to come to me.

"Yeah," I said. "Ever since she bit me I've been just about ready to cry. I mean real sad crying too. Like my best friend just died in my arms."

Ordé touched the wounds on my shoulder. I turned to give him a better view of the injury and found myself looking out the bus window at the large white stones that led down to the ocean. The Pacific was singing a sonorous dirge. It was a great moving beast with flecks of life glimmering within its folds.

It was hard to control my new powers of perception. Everything I saw—grass growing, breezes darting through leafy boughs, maggots swimming in death—everything set my senses to translating. That's what Ordé called it. Reading the meaning of myself in the world and, therefore, he claimed, changing the world.

Ordé had already explained in one of his sermons that the purpose of light was to combine with the DNA molecule, to unite matter and energy into a perfect state of thought and being. The blue god, who has the only ability to know, was in me. His brilliant eyes and keen ears making and remaking the world in my particular perceptions.

I felt a sharp pain in my neck. I yanked my head around to see my teacher digging his fingernails into the half-healed wounds inflicted by Coyote. There was sympathy in his powerful gaze, sympathy and command. The blood felt as if it were mobilizing in my veins. The cells felt particular, like tiny soldiers marching toward the breach. I was shaking. Ordé touched the reopened wound with his other hand. He then brought the bloody fingers to his lips. Shock registered in his eyes, and the grip on my shoulder and neck eased.

As the pressure lessened, the despair I had felt dissipated. I was exhausted and slumped forward, putting my elbows on my knees. When I sat up I noticed a small black boy sitting across the aisle from me. He was looking fearfully at my wounded neck.

Ordé had his face buried in his hands by then. The forgotten blood on his fingers smeared the top of his forehead.

He cried all the way back to Berkeley, red drying to black across his forehead.

When we returned from Santa Teresa, Ordé went straight home. He locked himself in his house and didn't come out, as far as I knew, for days.

That was Friday.

On Wednesday he didn't show up for his sermon to the Close Congregation. The congregation was there, although smaller.

Phyllis Yamauchi was already missing. She hadn't been seen for more than two weeks, but no one in the Close Congregation was worried. It wasn't required that Blues report to anyone. Phyllis studied her charts and telescopes and every once in a while came by to let Ordé see what she theorized. Often his prophecy complemented her studies. I had been transcribing their notes into my book.

Claudia Heart had taken more than fifty of Ordé's followers to her own communal residence, not far from the People's Warehouse, in Haight-Ashbury. She would take them one by one, men and women, into her van and make love to them just as she had done with me. Most came crawling back, begging to be with her, swearing to do anything for her kiss and company.

I would have gone on my knees to her without the blood ritual. Now I felt no desire for her.

I got a ride from Feldman, Ordé's bodyguard, and went down to our teacher's house. He came to the door but didn't open up.

"Who is it?"

"It's Chance, teacher."

"Go away."

"The congregation is waiting for you."

"Tell them to go home. Tell them to go home and to say their prayers."

"What's wrong, teacher?"

"Go away, Lester."

Up until that moment, no matter how hard or frustrating life had become, I still had faith in Ordé and his Blues. I believed in the unity, perfection, and grace of the universe. I believed in what Ordé called the grand hierarchy. I was a brick in the cathedral of existence meant to support the feet of gods.

My confidence was bruised when I heard the fear in Ordé's voice, but I knew my job. I went back up to the congregation and told them that Ordé had been faced with a great mystery. I told them about the coyotes who performed their own kind of blood ritual on me, how our teacher tasted their knowledge in my blood.

I didn't tell them of my blood ritual with Ordé. I didn't trust that everyone would understand the purity of his motives.

It was a new experience for me. I had never spoken to a crowd before. But with my new powers of perception, I could read the needs of the assembly.

"You want to know something?" I asked one young acolyte.

"How did you manage to keep from going with Claudia Heart?"

"Ordé sang to me," I said.

"Will he sing to me?" There were tears in her eyes. Later I found out that her husband had tied her up when she tried to follow Claudia, that he'd drugged her for two weeks until her desire to run had changed to a deep sadness at the loss of love.

"Yes," I said.

I answered questions and soothed the nervous congregation. They accepted me as Ordé's substitute, at least for one meeting. I didn't have his power. I could perceive but could not project. What I had to offer them was passive understanding.

FIVE

After the Wednesday meeting I went back to Ordé's house, but he wouldn't even answer the door. His windows were blocked by sheets of tinfoil, and junk mail was already spilling out of the small mailbox.

I went home after that.

Ordé had paid the rent while I was in the sanitarium.

My one-room studio cost seventeen dollars a week, which I usually got in the mail from my mother even though I never answered the letters she enclosed with the checks.

Actually, I never even read those letters.

I was thinking about that on Sunday night. How I cut off my mother, and all the rest of my life. How I blamed her for bearing a black child and rearing him in a white world.

It seemed silly to be worried about race then. I had come just a few steps from something beyond race or species or life, even. Not only would I have met the maker in the coming of blue light, I would have seen myself in his radiance.

But now I was back in the mundane world. My teacher, who had been like a god to me, had become just a frightened man.

I wondered again how long it would be before I killed myself. I plugged in my radio and picked up a blues station on FM. Robert Johnson wailed that the blue light was his blues while the red one was his mind. As I fell asleep, his blues mingled with mine.

I felt a clicking around my ears and imagined that small insects were making last-minute plans before they prepared to climb into my brain. I woke up suddenly, slapping all around my head. The knock came right after that.

"Who is it?"

"It's Reggie."

"What do you want, Reggie? It's late." The windup alarm clock on the floor next to my mattress said 3:16.

"Open up, Chance, we got a problem."

I was still a member of the Close Congregation. Reggie was still one of the Blues. Even if he was only thirteen, I had to at least talk to him.

I got to my feet and opened the door. Reggie was short for his age. Five two. He had a flattop haircut and wore jeans and a buttoned-up white dress shirt with the tails out.

We just stood there because I had no chairs.

"You got to come with me, Chance."

"What's goin' on?"

"Just come on, man."

*   *   *

Even in Berkeley the streets were more or less empty at that time of morning. There were a few hippies around. A few drug deals going down. But on the whole, there was no one. We went down Shattuck to Cedar and over to La Loma; from there we got to Buena Vista, Phyllis's street. The block was lined with two- and three-story brick houses that had deep lawns and big, dark trees.

We came to one house and Reggie walked up on the lawn. He went to a redwood gate at the side and unhooked a metal latch. When he turned around he saw that I was still at the sidewalk.

"Come on."

"Come on where?"

"Come on!" Reggie shouted in an intense whisper.

We went through the gate and down the side of the house. The pathway there was yellowish cement that almost glowed in the darkness. A cold breeze met us, and I had to duck my head to make it under the low hanging branches.

At the back of the house there was a door in the ground. It was an ornate portal to the basement that had thick opaque glass panes in it. One of the panes had been broken. Reggie lifted up the door and latched it to the house. Then he stood back.

"What?" I asked the boy.

"You go on. I want you to see what's down there."

I didn't need any special powers of perception to hear the fear in Reggie's voice.

I descended into the darkness of the basement. I couldn't see a thing.

"There's a door right in front of you," Reggie called down at me. "Open it up. The light's on the right side on the wall."

I walked straight ahead until my toes kicked wood, about five steps. Then I fumbled around for the knob. The moment the door was open I smelled it. A sickly sweet odor that was cloying, like a baseball field piled high with rotting lilies.

I snapped on the light and then fell to my knees, vomiting.

Her corpse had been decapitated and then split open from pelvis to throat. Her ribs had been broken outward, and the flesh of her arms and legs had been torn open. The hands looked as if they had been lacerated by claws.

Only the bottoms of her feet were left untouched.

The head had been tossed in the corner. I was drawn to it. She was facing upward, but there was not much of a face. The maniac had destroyed her features and then discarded her.

"It's Phyllis," Reggie said.

His unexpected voice gave me such a fright that I jumped away and yelped.

"What's wrong with you, Reggie?"

Ignoring my shock, he said, "I came looking for her. Nobody'd seen her in a while, and I just thought I'd look for her."

Reggie's abilities, though still immature, were finding things and hiding. Ordé wanted to call him Scout, but Reggie liked his own name.

"I came looking for her," he said again.

I couldn't take my eyes off the remains of Phyllis Yamauchi. Her organs were spread out around the body on the dirty concrete floor. The dried blood had flowed out more or less evenly and made a kind of dark frame for the horrible sculpture.

The body was a grisly enough sight, but it was the intent behind the murder that hit me so hard. The killer not only hated her, Phyllis, but also hated her flesh and bones and blood. He'd stripped away every vestige of humanity, leaving only a tattered lump of meat.

I looked up at the ceiling, trying to blot the sight from my mind. All along the unpainted beams hung a chorus of pale spiders. Silent, spinning, waiting. They were unconcerned with the tableau on the floor. These spiders I used as beacons of sanity. Death was less to them than a spring breeze, certainly nothing compared to a frothy, juicy moth.

"What should we do?" Reggie asked me.

I had forgotten he was there.

"Can you tell what happened by tasting her blood, like Ordé?"

Reggie looked at me with big, frightened eyes.

"Well, can you?"

"Once Wanita cut her finger and I kissed it," Reggie said.

"Yeah?"

"And I saw a big ship leaving the harbor. She saw that ship the day before with my mother, but I wasn't there."

"So you can read blood," I concluded.

Reggie looked at the body and shook his head no. I understood. He might have been a god, but he was still only a boy.

I searched the basement until I found a washer and dryer in a small room. I took a sheet from a basket in there and tore it into two cloths—one larger and one smaller. Then I went back to Phyllis's body. Deep inside her chest cavity was still moist. I soaked up some of the blood in the smaller rag and then wrapped it in the larger one.

A couple of blocks away Reggie asked, "Should we call the cops?"

"Uh-uh, no, I don't think so, kid. The police would just start looking for some maniac. They'd never believe what Phyllis was. They'd probably blame us. What we should do is go to Ordé and ask him what he thinks happened."

We walked on a ways. The sun was coming up, and even though I had the blood of a murdered woman in my pocket, I was struck by the dawn's beauty. The wisps of black clouds made a grid over the orange light. There was an ancient hue to the light, something that had once known greatness. I could feel my heart and mind open up to the scrutiny of light. I felt the connection between the blood in my veins and the furnace above. I looked down after a while, seeing the afterimage of Sol in the sidewalk and passing lawns. I had walked off the sidewalk and into the street. My visions distracted me so much that I almost walked into the path of an oncoming car.

"Why'd you come to me, Reggie?" I asked the boy, partly to get the answer and partly because I wanted to concentrate on the world around me.

"Huh?"

"Why'd you come to me? You could have gone to Eileen or even Ordé."

"Eileen would have been too scared, and I don't know where Ordé lives. Anyway, I don't like Ordé too much. He so weird, always tryin' to make everything sound so big when it's all just normal."

"But you could have found Ordé if you wanted, and you know we're gonna have to go to him anyway."

"That's okay," Reggie answered. "It's okay if I go with you."

We got to Ordé's place a little bit before six. No one answered the front door, so we went around the back and knocked there. When he didn't come out I took up the metal lid of a trash can and started banging.

That got his attention.

"I told you to go away, Chance," he shouted through the closed door. "Take Scout and get as far away as you can. Run."

"Phyllis Yamauchi was murdered," I said. "I have some of her blood."

As I said it, I realized that this was the first death of a Blue other than those that died on the first night that light fell. Reggie's sister had died and so had Eileen's husband. Ordé claimed that even they had not truly died. He said that their energy, along with *who they had become,* had separated from the body to carry their life force into the energy fields of Earth. But that was dur-

ing the coming of the light. All the Blues that had lived
were healthy, never sick, and somehow had the appearance of agelessness. Even Eileen Martel looked as
though she could walk all day. Reggie and Wanita had
grown some, but they were kids.

While I was thinking about gods and death, the door
opened. Ordé stood there in an untied terry cloth
bathrobe. He was naked underneath, and Reggie stole
glances at the man's penis like any boy would.

Ordé hadn't shaved, bathed, or even pushed his hair
out of his face.

"Come on," he said.

His once sparse kitchen was now crowded. There
were boxes of powdered milk and dried soup on the
counter and a large-caliber rifle and a clip-loading pistol on the table. Under the table were boxes of ammuni-
tion.

"You going to war, teacher?" I asked, stunned at my
own brazen humor.

Ordé sat at the table and held out his hand.

"Give it to me," he said.

I took the rags from my pocket and began to unwrap
the larger from the smaller. Ordé was impatient, though,
and took them from me. He shook the tattered sheet
around until the blood packet fell to the floor. He got
down on his knees and pushed the whole thing in his
mouth.

He hiccuped once and then slumped down into unconsciousness.

Reggie and I tried to wake him, but it couldn't be
done. I pulled the rag from his mouth and made sure

that he was breathing. Then the boy and I dragged him to the cot in his bedroom.

He was unconscious for nineteen hours. Reggie went home to his mother and Wanita (they had taken up residence with Eileen Martel in San Francisco), but he came back at about six that evening.

At one the next morning Ordé gasped and scrambled to his feet.

"Oh, my God!" he yelled, maybe with some kind of relief, and then ran to the bathroom.

Reggie was sound asleep on the floor when the prophet awoke, but he was right behind me chasing Ordé to the toilet.

We found our teacher studying his face in the mirror, running his fingertips around his cheeks and eyes. He was crying and laughing.

"What is it, teacher?" I asked.

Ordé turned to me, grabbed me by my shoulders, and asked, "Do you see me?"

I nodded. He looked over at Reggie, and the boy nodded too.

"I made it back. I fought him off. I'm still alive."

Ordé went to the toilet bowl and urinated with no shame. He turned to us halfway through and said, "We have a lot to do. A lot to do."

Reggie and I went out to Ordé's living room. His couch was a long and backless wooden bench, and his chair was a piano stool. I turned on the light and then went to sit next to Reggie on the bench. There was a glistening effect to the light because of the aluminum foil Ordé had used to block out the windows.

He came in after a few more minutes, dressed in jeans with his chest still bare, his long hair at least combed, and with a look of determination and fear in his eyes.

"Thanks, Chance. You too, Scout. I was so scared after Coyote's warning that I couldn't do anything. But now I have survived." Ordé brought his hands together right between his eyes so that his fingers pointed up toward his forehead.

"Coyote's message? That's what you got out of my blood?" I asked.

"We are no longer mechanical pieces of flesh, Chance. Not just a heart to pump blood or a brain to translate primitive signals. Our blood and bone and flesh sing out the whole world that might be."

I wasn't in the mood for a sermon right then. I wanted answers but I knew that Ordé wasn't so easily pinned down.

"If I feel something," he continued, "or perceive something, if I learn something in any way—that knowledge is everywhere in me. I am more than a part of the whole; I am potentially everything. That's why I can taste what has happened in blood."

"So who killed Phyllis?" Reggie asked.

That's when Ordé told us the story of what he called Gray Man; how Horace LaFontaine died of cancer but was then resurrected in blue light. How he went out in the desert and hibernated in a cave for almost four years.

"He is Death," Ordé said. "And Death seeks its own."

"He wants to kill us?" Reggie asked.

Ordé nodded. Then he said, "It was written in Phyllis's blood because she fought Gray Man, she made him bleed that thick lifeless blood of his. She knew his story before she died."

Ordé took a small folding knife from his pocket and pricked the tip of his right forefinger. A tiny drop of red appeared from the cut. He held the finger out to me.

"Taste this and see what I've seen."

"Died?" I asked.

"Yes," Ordé replied. "It was true death. His hands ended her body's life, and his essence extinguished her light."

SIX

I was unconscious before I knew I was falling. After tasting that salty drop of blood, I was in another place. Many of Ordé's memories became my own, including the story of Gray Man.

On the night that blue light struck, the corpse that had once been Horace LaFontaine staggered, skinny as a rail and barely dressed, up into the hills. He walked through fences and over large stones, pushed down small trees when they stood in his way. His bones crackled from the electricity he'd sucked out of the wall of his once-sister's home.

The human thoughts in his mind, all the memories of the life of the man who once bore a name, were now like specimens in glass jars in a great laboratory of death.

As he made his way through dense foliage, blood-hungry night insects came at him. But before any of them could alight, cold blue electricity ignited them in the air.

He made his way like that, false fireflies dying around him as he went, perverted blue light inside and out. Walking death seeking its own company. Unbridled potential with no life to temper it.

He went north dimly aware of a coyote that stalked him. Her nose close to the ground. Her quick feet ready to run. He couldn't catch her, but then again, if she came within rock-throwing distance, she would die. Both were aware of the limits of their power. The coyote had witnessed blue light that night also. Now she smelled the unnatural odors that fumed around Horace La-Fontaine. She tracked him as a scientist might follow the path of a celestial body that has, for no known reason, altered its course.

She sniffed the air and then licked the ground he walked on. All her senses cried out. She yipped and howled, but her warnings about Gray Man went unheard.

Three days later, far up a slope that was the beginning of a long meandering decline into the northern desert, Gray Man found his cave. In some cubicle of Horace's mind he had gleaned the story of another man who died and came back to life. The man was buried in an underground chamber, behind a great boulder.

There was a stone above the cave. Gray Man climbed in, digging into the earth under the stone with hardened nails. From far off, the coyote watched, remembering the placement of the stars and the trees and the smell of the ground.

After many hours, almost in daylight, the boulder fell, sealing the dead man in.

Coyote spent the day circling, coming closer. She was skittish, frightened even by small breezes that rustled in the dead grass. It wasn't until twilight that she made it to the rockbound cave. She sniffed and studied, whimpered and barked.

When she reached the upper part of the blocking stone, she pawed the dry dirt a little and stared hard, as if maybe she could peer beneath.

The dead hand shot out of the ground faster than she could see. The long-nailed finger destroyed the right eye and curled upward to rip out the bones of her head. But she was too quick to be killed. Half blinded but still alive, crying loudly at the pain and darkness, she ran at full speed back into the hills.

And then Gray Man rested. He leaned back against the cave wall in a corpse's recline. One arm thrown carelessly beneath him, one leg at an almost impossible angle. He would lie like this for years, pondering the corpse he inhabited.

He traveled up and down the corridors of remembrance, witnessing the earliest sights forgotten by Horace: his mother bathing with him and his sister in the old iron tub in the row house in the Third Ward, a spider crawling down the banister on his first real bed, the smell of urine in the alley down at the end of the block. He remembered every word in every language that Horace had ever heard. English, Spanish, French, German, and Japanese. He remembered the numbers and their relations, as much as was taught up to the seventh grade, when Horace dropped out of school. He extended the roads of Horace's knowledge until the path of mathematics converged with the fear-laden knowledge of the big bomb. He plumbed the meaning of philosophy by comparing words that lay dormant and ununderstood. He studied crime and then ethics. He learned of prayer and of God. He learned of Satan and knew somehow that this was his deity on this planet.

Gray Man hated life.

Horace had not been a good man. As a soldier he'd killed in Europe and later in prison. He knew about God (the blue light in life's eyes) but didn't seem to care. He stole and once, in a drunken stupor, had raped a woman who he knew and lusted after.

Horace was dead but he could be recalled. He could be an ally. He would understand all those millions of word sounds and word strings repeated over and over, never meaning the same thing or sometimes meaning nothing or sometimes meaning feeling. The pinch that is good. The smile that is bad.

The joke.

What Gray Man hated most were questions asked that needed no answer and phrases repeated again and again with no purpose or resolution. There was only one answer, only one resolution—and they were both death.

Horace had understood what Gray Man needed to know.

Horace was dead, of course. He was gone when Gray Man came, but the pieces of him were still there. Like in the movie of the man named Frankenstein and the monster with the same name.

A nose, a brain.

He could be rebuilt like the old Chevrolet he once owned. The engine could take you all the way to Las Vegas and back, baby.

A dying man yells at the end of his life.

He sees the clawed hand of the Reaper reaching for his belly. Razorlike talons cut him open; blood and guts spill out like mud.

A dying man yells from a hillside grave after the end of his life.

A one-eyed coyote looks up from her four pups and sniffs the air. The coyote pups all look too. They stop their suckling and whimper from a pain they felt before birth.

Horace comes awake in the desert. The gravelly ground under him feels wonderful. The stab of small sharp stones against his cheek and ribs are things to laugh about, feelings to celebrate. He looks up and sees a moon that is ten times larger than it has ever been. Next to this moon floats a shimmering cloud of incandescent blue gas. A bright red stone, the size of the old moon, orbits the cloud crazily, like an erratic electron.

He stands up and sees that his hands are very large. But as he watches them, they shrink back to normal size.

"It's hard to keep things in place," another Horace says.

Horace looks up and sees himself approach out of nowhere.

"This thing you call desire is a powerful tool. It's easy to let it get carried away."

"Who the fuck're you s'posed t'be?" the real Horace asks.

Gray Man, in the form of his host, in the chambers of imagination, raises an eyebrow, and the true Horace—the dead Horace—feels the skin being ripped from his body.

His scream fills Gray Man's lips in the hillside crypt.

"I am your master," Gray Man says. "Grey Redstar. Recently from elsewhere."

Horace falls to the ground and rolls around until his slick-blooded body is plastered with small stones. He screams again as the second skin covers his body—a skin of pain. Then he lies still, arms and legs jutting straight out, teeth chattering.

Gray Man shrugs and Horace is standing in front of him, skin covering his flesh again. The evening breeze feels cool, but Horace no longer trusts sensation.

"I request your help, Horace LaFontaine."

"Who're you? Where am I?"

"Everything you see is mine," says the dead man. "It once was yours but you never knew it."

Horace understands these words more clearly than he has ever understood anything. He starts to wail. The cry echoes throughout the mindscape desert.

Three years later Gray Man stirred in his grave. Coyote heard the cadaver's sigh. The half-blind mother skimmed the outer edges of his tomb with four perpetually half-grown pups sniffing at her heels. Gray Man exerted his untiring strength against the great rock, and after a few days it began to give.

He was free to follow his light, which is the darkest of dark blues.

He retraced his steps, stopping now and then to break into isolated desert homes. There he sucked electricity from the walls and found money and clothes to fit him. In one house he murdered a small child who had been allowed to stay home because he was sick that day. Gray Man didn't care about humans much, but he needed to see how they died, how they clung to life, because he knew that the Blues would be similar but much stronger. The killing of little Billy Cordette was simply a science experiment, a test in the ways of half-life. He held the boy by both arms, slowly increasing the essence of death that his enhanced cells exuded. Billy struggled and screamed for his mother. He kicked and bit but finally submitted to the killing force running up and down the muscles of his body. Gray Man saw the repose of extinction as beautiful. It was as if life existed only for this beautiful moment. A cut flower, a roast suckling pig. I felt as Gray Man did and at the same time I trembled in a dark corner of our mind.

Gray Man was dressed in a green suit with a yellow shirt, brown hat, and brown shoes when he got back to Oakland. He returned to the house where Horace had died and looked up at the immense oak that Horace La-Fontaine had watched during his last days. Gray Man stood there a long time looking at the house. On the lawn there was a tiny sign that read ROOM FOR RENT.

Inside Gray Man's skull Horace LaFontaine hollered. Gray Man stood there because of his fine sense of what life is composed of—pain.

"Why do you scream, Horace?" Gray Man asked.

Inside his mind Gray Man had come to a small cell like the one Horace had lived in for seven years at Attica. Horace was in his cell, but he could see what Gray Man could see. He saw his sister's home. The large wooden house painted white and trimmed in gray.

"Let her alone!" Horace cried.

"Are you afraid for her?" Gray Man asked softly.

"Let her alone!"

"Pain is the center of life, Horace. Without pain, without anguish, there is nothing but me." Gray Man peered into the imaginary cell at the memory of a life.

Horace saw in those eyes an infinite black field at night, under no moon or star.

"I am here to give you life, Horace. You struggled so hard against me in the tomb. You tried to take your body back, to have life again. But you cannot take life from death. You cannot defeat me." Gray Man smiled. "But I can give you pain. It is similar to the gift of life. It is life's border."

"Please let her alone, man. You don't want her," Horace said. "You want them people like that coyote."

"Come on, Horace," Gray Man said. "Let's go see your sister bleed."

"No!" Horace yelled. "No, no, no, no, no, no!"

Gray Man's mind filled with the protestations of life. He enjoyed Horace's screaming. He had learned a lot from his host. He could be rid of him anytime now. There was no more need for Horace LaFontaine. But Gray Man kept the dead ex-con in his prison cell, in perpetual night, looking out at the full moon, always hungry. The only food he served him was raw, maggot-infested carrion.

Keeping Horace around made for an interesting and important game.

Horace was dead, merely an elaborate figment of Gray Man's imagination. But Horace felt alive. When Gray Man let him out of his cell, fed him decent food, let him think he was healthy and strong—then they could fight.

Death versus life.

Horace used all of his will to try and overturn Gray Man, to retake his body and freedom. In these battles Gray Man learned much of the ingenuity of life. He felt the maddening beat of life. He learned what it took to squash out flesh's pitiful molecular spasm.

"Yes?" She was young and brown, not Elza.

Somewhere inside his mind Gray Man could feel Horace sigh and then laugh. Laughter was their greatest weapon, Old Man Death knew. If life could laugh, then death had to be absolute. And if life proved anything, it was that death was not complete, not yet.

"You have a room to let, young lady?"

She hesitated a moment and then smiled again. "Sure," she said. "But I don't know if you'd like it. I mean, we usually just have a student up there."

"I've been away and I need a place to stay. I was walking down your street and noticed the sign. I'm looking for my family."

"Are you English?" the young woman asked.

Horace could see her through the window Gray Man had opened for him to witness the torture and murder of his sister. The young woman was very dark with small features that made for a plain face. Her figure was slight, not the kind of woman that he went after in life.

"Why no," Gray Man said accenting his dead words. "I'm from the Islands. Will you show me the room?"

Horace watched the slim-figured young woman as she climbed the stairs. Gray Man saw nothing. He wasn't interested in life. He wasn't interested in this girl.

"What's your name?" Gray Man asked at the door to Horace's old room. He didn't care, but he knew from Horace that this was what was called manners.

"Joclyn. Joclyn Kyle. What's yours?"

"Redstar," Gray Man said. "Grey Redstar. I'm from Trinidad originally, but I've traveled almost everywhere."

"Oh," she said as she fumbled around with the skeleton key in the door lock.

Horace's room was just as he had left it. The big brass bed was the same. The maple chest of drawers and the broken-down sofa chair. The round maroon carpet in the center of the floor was new. The oak outside the window had grown a few new branches.

"I'll take it," Gray Man said. "How much?"

"One hundred twenty-five a month," Joclyn said, obviously embarrassed by the high price. "But that includes utilities and kitchen privileges. Uncle Morris says that you can use the stove and the refrigerator as long as you clean up and don't abuse the privilege."

"Your uncle lives with you?"

"This is his house. He lets me stay here while I study at school. I'm from down in LA."

"Do I pay you now?" Gray Man asked.

"Uncle Morris wants to meet somebody before they take the place," Joclyn said. "He won't be back till six."

Gray Man stood there in the small room, staring at Joclyn. He considered killing her because he didn't know what to do next. But he couldn't find anywhere in Horace's memories an excuse for such an act. And Gray Man wanted to be normal. He would have liked to kill Elza, to savor Horace's pain, but more than that he needed a place to stay. He needed to be where the light struck. He needed to find his brethren.

"May I wait for him?" Gray Man asked.

"Well, not really, I have to go soon. To school, you know."

Gray Man became angry then. He wasn't used to waiting or to someone telling him no. He had no patience with the girl Joclyn or her absent uncle and so he receded, back into the dark cave of his mind.

Horace's cell melted away, and suddenly he stood there before the plain girl.

"Uh," stalled Horace. "Uh, well, maybe, I mean, I'll go back out and come back around six. Six, right?"

Horace turned to leave but then turned back again.

"What part' a LA you from?" he asked. His voice was the same but the accent had become Southern.

Joclyn frowned and said, "On Compton Boulevard. I was born in Mississippi, in Greenwood, but I don't remember it."

"I lived on Slauson once," Horace said. "A long time ago. Long time. But I used to go to a barbecue place on Compton. It was called . . . lemme see now . . . It was called, um, Bolger's. Yeah, that's it—Bolger's."

"I know Bolger's. We used to go there all the time." The happy smile on Joclyn's face, the smile of a lonely girl who has found a displaced kindred spirit, might have sparked some interest in Horace, when he was alive.

"I gotta go," he said.

Horace hurried down the stairs with the young landlady in his wake.

He was out the front door and walking away when Joclyn called out from the door, "Nice to meet you, Mr. Redstar."

Horace waved but didn't say anything more.

Gray Man allowed Horace to walk until he found a place for them to wait.

Horace savored each moment. It wasn't an hallucination. It wasn't a lie. Somehow he knew that he'd been given a day pass from death. He found a bus stop on Peralta. While Gray Man lay dormant, Horace sat there watching pigeons peck, fly, and fornicate. The traffic moved. Every now and then an airplane or jet passed overhead. A breeze felt chilly on Horace's face. He realized that there was no temperature in hell, not unless Gray Man wanted it.

Horace sat for more than an hour running the fingers of his left hand over the back of his right. His light touch, passing from wrist to fingertip, was more life than all of his drunken binges and back-alley brawls.

On his mumbling lips was a prayer, a hope that he had paid his penance and that God would let him live out a few weeks on this bench before he passed on to eternal rest.

But Gray Man was through with his plans. He could feel how peaceful and happy Horace LaFontaine was, and he didn't like it, but the dark recesses of his mind were so pure that he decided to stay for a while.

In his mind there were no crazy, jangly, fleshy feelings. No monotonous pumping, hungering, snuffling around. In his inner cave Gray Man could ponder the infinite. He could send his mind outward past all things physical, past the limits of logic. He could bask in the glow of the giant blue eye of energy—the first thought. Basking in this pure notion of reality, Gray Man wondered how any true sentient being could think that mixing with flesh could be an improvement. It would be like a butterfly turning back into a worm, like a tree trying to press itself back down to a seed, like a sun worshiping dust.

Gray Man wanted to be freed from the flesh. He imagined ripping off the old coat called Horace LaFontaine and flooding up from the earth toward home. That infinite journey from which he could return and tell them that it was all a mistake, that perfection had already been obtained, that he was the ultimate.

But before that could happen there would have to be much death. Many lights would have to be extinguished. Many lights.

Horace LaFontaine gagged and tried to rise up from his bus stop bench. He wanted to throw himself in front of the truck rushing down the street. He almost made it, but Gray Man reached up and stopped him dead in his tracks.

It was time to go see Uncle Morris and Joclyn.

"So you wanna room?" Morris Beakman asked Grey Redstar, recently from elsewhere.

"Yes, Mr. Beakman," Gray Man answered. "I'm looking for work at the university and I have some cousins who live somewhere around here. I'd like to find them also."

"What's their names?" Beakman asked. He was a tall brown man with a broad stomach. His hair was gray and his nose had been broken more than once. He towered over Death.

"Azure," Gray Man said and smiled. "The Azures."

"Never heard that name before," Beakman offered. His eyes seemed to be searching the prospective tenant for something.

"I'm willing to pay you three months in advance, Mr. Beakman. I'll be very quiet and I won't have any visitors, I give you my word." Gray Man stifled his desire to kill the landlord. He knew there would be no profit and little pleasure in the act.

"I don't take no mess, Mr. Redstar," the large man said. "I don't want no problems."

"All I need is a place to sleep and study, sir," Death said. "I'll take my meals out and I don't listen to your music."

"What do you mean *my* music?"

"Just a way of speaking, sir. I don't own a radio, that's what I meant."

"Well, you know, I usually only rent to students. But you got problems with your students too. Girls just seem to want to take advantage, and the boys all wanna get into Joclyn's panties. . . ."

"I just need a place to sleep and study, sir," Gray Man said again.

In the weeks to follow Gray Man took long walks around San Francisco, Oakland, and Berkeley. He didn't go into the parks much because fewer people were there. He wandered down streets both rich and poor, tasting the air and listening with ears that could hear the music of light.

When Gray Man wasn't searching he burrowed down under consciousness. While he slept, Horace was free to wander in the body that was no longer his. At these times there was nothing of Gray Man in Horace's mind, but he still felt as if he were being held prisoner in his bones. He was rarely hungry, and even though Gray Man had money in his pockets, Horace dared not spend it. Mainly because the money came from the corpses of men and women that Gray Man had killed and robbed.

Horace was sick of violence and blood. He never wanted another soul to feel pain because of him.

With no money he could spend, no real freedom, and Gray Man liable to reappear and torture him at any time,

Horace stayed around his sister's home. He wandered up and down the stairs and out into the backyard under the big oak. Morris Beakman was a construction foreman in the daytime and a cook at Logan's Bar and Grill most evenings. Horace rarely saw Morris, and when they did meet, few words passed between them.

But Joclyn was always home when she wasn't at nursing-school classes. Her parents paid room and board at Morris's house, and the construction foreman/cook paid her twenty dollars a week to keep the place clean.

Joclyn liked Mr. Redstar when he wasn't putting on airs. That's what she told Horace one day when he was counting blades of grass in the backyard.

"I don't ever say more than hi when you got airs, Mr. Redstar," she said. "I know that you must be thinkin' somethin' or wonderin' where your family might be."

Horace explained that he had a mental condition, that when his face looked cold she should leave him alone because that's when he was crazy.

"Real crazy?" the nursing student asked.

"Yeah," Horace responded gravely. "Sometimes so crazy that I think everybody might be better off if I was dead."

"Oh, don't say that, Mr. Redstar," Joclyn complained. "You're a real nice man. So sensitive and quiet-like. Sometimes all that craziness is just in your mind. You know, I feel like that sometimes. I get real lonely, you know? Even if I'm wit' people and I'm laughin' or dancin'. I mean, I could even be kissin' some boy an' I still feel all by myself."

Horace didn't say a word. He just stared. For him the heartfelt chatter of her life was like a doorway out from his own misery. The smile on his face felt rare, almost alien.

Joclyn noticed his queer smile and ducked her head, mumbling, "I guess I shouldn'ta said that, about kissin', I mean."

Horace pressed his fingers lightly on the girl's forearm. He didn't even know that he was touching her until she looked up.

"That's okay, girl. I know about kissin'."

She smiled and a rumble went off in Horace's chest.

For months after that he had a schoolboy crush on Joclyn. Whenever Gray Man sank into his dark realm of reflection, Horace ran down the stairs, looking for his new friend. What he loved was to listen to her talking about her courses and parents, her *sometimes* dates and her dreams. Horace even helped in the cleaning to spend time with her. They mopped and washed and talked and talked.

They never let her Uncle Morris find them together. It was like an illicit affair, some secret liaison that they maintained under strictest secrecy.

Whenever Morris came home, Horace sprinted up the stairs with a gait that defied his age. He never spoke more than two words to the landlord because he couldn't make himself sound like the articulate Gray Man. He worried that the landlord might become suspicious and try to evict Death.

"You ever wonder about evil?" Horace asked Joclyn one day when they were drying dishes together.

"I don't know," she replied. The happiness in her voice was common when she spent time with her friend. "I mean, there's a lotta bad in the world. But somebody bad can always come to be good too. That's what they say in my church."

"What I mean is way past church. Way past."

Joclyn put down the glass she was drying.

"You talkin' 'bout that mental illness again?"

Horace looked into his only friend's eyes.

"It's okay, Mr. Redstar," Joclyn said. "You're a good man. You just get a little stiff sometimes. I know you ain't evil, 'cause evil destroys itself. My minister says that too. Evil has to lose 'cause he hate everything, even himself."

Horace smiled as he began stacking dishes on the light blue doorless shelves above the sink. Just outside the window, in a dwarf lemon bush, he could see a huge black-and-yellow garden spider waiting in the center of her web.

When Joclyn left for school that afternoon, Horace saw her to the door.

"Thank you," he said.

"For what?"

"For helping me. For showing me the truth. And you don't have to worry about the downstairs toilet, I'm gonna clean it up real good."

Horace took Joclyn's cleaning bucket to the small water closet next to the kitchen. In the yellow bucket was a scrub towel, ammonia, some detergent and scouring powder, and a small plastic bottle of bleach.

Gray Man stirred as Horace closed the toilet door. He stretched his mind to semi-wakefulness as Horace got down on his knees before the bowl. For so long Gray Man had considered the crystalline equations of light that he found it difficult to attach meaning to a simple chemical reaction. Before Gray Man could arouse himself, Horace had poured the ammonia into the bowl. Before Death could reach into his glove, Horace's hand, the corpse laced the ammonia with bleach. Before Death could restrict his lungs, Horace inhaled deeply the mustard gas.

As Horace lost consciousness, I was thrown fully into the mind of Death. Everything in that consciousness was disintegrating, falling into dust. Horace dying, already dead. His last act was that of a hero killing his inner demon.

But then Gray Man screamed. He would not leave without fulfilling his self-proclaimed mission. And for a second time he resurrected the husk of Horace LaFontaine. Reassembling shattered cells and broken capillaries, he writhed there before the toilet bowl until finally he began to vomit. Black bile and poisons gushed from the dead man's lips into the tainted water. Gray Man pushed himself out into the kitchen and staggered up the stairs. In his room he took out a special plug that ran a bare wire from the wall socket. He sat on the brown sofa chair, sucking on electricity.

The light within him remembered the internal workings of Horace's body. The hatred within him recalled Horace the man.

Again they were on an open plain under a crazy sky. Horace found himself on his knees before a towering Grey Redstar.

"Fool!" Death shouted.

Horace, his courage gone, trembled.

"I warned you!" Death declared. "Didn't I warn you?"

There were no thoughts or words within Horace. All he had left was the anticipation of pain.

The following weeks passed like centuries. Writhing in his Attica hole, skinless and demented, Horace La-Fontaine could not scream, because his lips were sewn; he could not breathe, but suffocation did not bring death.

While Horace suffered in the recesses of his own mind, Gray Man finally caught the scent of one of the Blues. On one of his long walks he heard the ripple of a complex strain, music that spoke a language far beyond the range of life. He followed that melody until it led him to Phyllis Yamauchi's empty home. He broke in through a side window and then walked down a long corridor to the memory of a prison cell and the recollection of a man.

"Horace." Gray Man smiled at his prisoner. "You've been bad and you have to suffer for it."

Horace looked up at his captor without recognizing him as the source of his pain. He had come to believe that his sins in life had made this hell. Gray Man was just the executor of the sentence. That's why he could not be killed.

"Would you like to go back for a while again, Horace?"

His skin grew back and his mouth sucked air. Horace appeared on the desert plain with Gray Man.

"You would have to promise not to try and kill me, though," Gray Man said. "You can't kill me, you know, but you could cause me a great deal of grief and delay."

Horace could speak but did not.

"Would you like to go back?" Gray Man asked again.

"Yes."

Sitting on the edge of Phyllis Yamauchi's sofa chair in her living room, Horace simply enjoyed the rhythm of his breath. It reminded him of waves at the shore. He wondered then if the ocean was actually breathing, soaking up the sun and stars in its heart and thinking about those long-ago times that sang in Gray Man's soul.

Gray Man had a soul, but Horace did not. Horace was, he knew, just like a thinking rock, a mechanical doll that made a mistake and thought he had a heart.

Hours later Phyllis Yamauchi opened the door and walked in. Gray Man was deep in his solitary cave, and Phyllis did not know him to be there.

She looked at the stranger with no fear.

Horace stared back at her, wondering why his executor cared about her.

"Who are you?" Phyllis asked.

"My name is Horace."

"What do you want here? Are you going to rob me?"

"I just wanna die," Horace said. He sobbed and then choked as if he were experiencing a bout of nausea.

Gray Man leaped into his consciousness like a pouncing lion. And in that brief fraction of a second before he was exiled again, Horace saw the true nature of Phyllis Yamauchi. She was blue, all blue, and sparkling. Tendrils and spikes and curving wings of light spread from her body. Somewhere over her shoulder was an orb of maddeningly dark blue.

The presence of Gray Man, as he rose in the corpse's body, struck at her like a gale. The blue in her was tinged with yellow for a moment, and then Horace was in his grave. Dead and buried far below the consciousness of Gray Man.

It took less than five seconds to squash the life from Phyllis Yamauchi. Gray Man used his inhuman strength and his claws and his teeth and the electricity that flowed in him. But in those few seconds all the force of life in the small woman exploded outward. Horace felt the vibrations in his grave.

Gray Man fell back from the small body weak and in pain. He dragged her down to the basement. He stripped himself naked and stripped her too. Then he performed a ritual of death that he had created long before in the northern California desert, all the while singing a long, whining dirge.

SEVEN

When I woke up, the dirge was still in my ears. I had passed out on the floor. Gray Man and Horace were still alive in my senses, but I didn't feel afraid. Somehow Ordé had passed his newfound courage on to me.

Ordé and Reggie were gone. I went to the front door and opened it on a beautiful Bay day. The sun was bright but the air was cool. My heightened senses were more in order. I could look deeply into things if I wanted, but I had to push it. And somehow the plain grass and simple concrete took on a special beauty for me.

I didn't know where to go, so I made it up to Ordé's rock. None of the Close Congregation was there, as it was a Tuesday. There were people in the park, of course. Baseball players, old men on their constitutionals. There was a young woman holding a red-haired child about three or four years of age. She was slight, in her mother's arms, gazing into my face with all the amazement of a newborn. It was a little disconcerting to have a small child stare so intensely, almost as if she were interrogating me. Her eyes were so dark and unwavering that I could almost feel the weight of their intent. That's when I looked closer. I could sense in her face something blue.

The mother, who had been looking around, noticed the child's fixed stare and looked at me. She tried to turn the girl, to talk to her, but the child kept moving her head to look at me. She was saying something to her mother that I couldn't hear.

So I walked the seventeen steps it took me to reach them, realizing as I walked that every fact and action I took from then on would be of interest to generations that follow. Up until then I had been a follower and an acolyte. I was writing a history about something I was seeing unfold. But now it came to me that I was a piece of that history. Like my hero Thucydides, I was a part of some of the most important events in the history of the world. Those seventeen steps might be remembered as were Job's trials and Socrates' hemlock.

There was nothing special about the mother. Just another hippie. Young but with strands of premature gray shot through her long red hair. Her skin was very tanned and red underneath the tan. The tiny wrinkles around her eyes and jaw were from long hours spent out of doors.

The child wore a homemade dress cut from a purple tie-dyed sheet. It was just a sack with arms and neck cut into it. The woman wore boy's jeans and a shirt of Indian fabric that was made from blue, red, and dull orange cloths that had been pieced together. There were tiny mirrors and patches of dark lace nested here and there throughout the garment.

Both she and the girl smelled strongly of patchouli oil.

"Hi," I said to the mother and child.

The girl jumped out of her mother's arms and into mine. The quickness of her movements shocked me.

"Do you know Bill Portman?" the woman asked while her daughter dug both hands into my unkempt natural and tugged. The child laughed.

"I don't think so," I said, stalling.

"You're beautiful," the child said as she rubbed her hand across my nose and mouth. Her fingers smelled of peanut butter.

I was surprised that her mother didn't take her back or make her stop. But then I thought that this was just another hippie who wasn't afraid to let her child explore the world around her.

"They also called him"—the mother stalled and pressed her fingers between her eyes—"Ordé."

The child started laughing. She wrapped her arms around my head and squeezed. She was strong for her age, but I had a hard head, hard enough to take police sticks when they raided squatters in the Haight. My head was as hard as it needed to be, but I wasn't stupid.

"Are you Adelaide?" I asked the woman.

She nodded and said, "And this is Julia."

"That's not my name," the child whispered.

"And you're looking for Ordé?" I asked.

"I need him," Adelaide said. "He has to help me with her. Every night she's been waking up terrified. And she keeps talking about things I don't get, only I kinda remember Bill saying the same things."

"What does she say?"

"Hey," the little girl in my arms said.

Adelaide looked directly into my eyes and said, "I know it sounds crazy, but she's always talking about planets that don't have suns that planted people here. That's the kind of stuff Bill used to say, but lately she's been saying something different, that everyone will die. And somehow I feel like maybe she's right." A shudder went through the hippie mother's shoulders.

There were no other offspring from the Blues that were known, though Coyote was pregnant before she saw the light. Ordé went out once every six months or so, when everything was right, he said, to try and impregnate some woman. It had never worked, to our knowledge. The women usually got sick, and none of them ever came up pregnant.

Ordé had asked me to go down to Pomona to look for Adelaide, to see if she had taken his seed.

"She was sitting right next to me, Chance," Ordé said. "When the light struck. She was sleeping and so she wouldn't be transformed, but her skin might have taken in something—she was naked. I don't know, maybe a little got in through her eyelids. It wouldn't take much. Find her. Maybe she has our firstborn of Earth."

I did find her family, but by then their daughter had come and gone. She'd left because her father said that if she came up pregnant, he'd want her to get an abortion.

I got all that from her little sister, Ada, who also told me that if her father found a black man asking after his daughter, he'd take out his shotgun and kill him.

I took her word, on all counts, and left. I didn't think that Adelaide had actually gotten pregnant. I asked Ada, who was nice enough, and she said that as far as she knew, Adelaide was not pregnant. No one else among Ordé's peers had managed to conceive. Ordé said that it was because of their potency. He believed that it was more likely for a woman of his kind to take the sperm from a normal man than for a Blue male to impregnate a normal woman. He believed that sperm from the blue light would devour the ova. But Claudia Heart hadn't conceived either.

There had been a few attempts to intermingle between the Blues, but the effect was quite toxic. Gijon Diaz and Phyllis Yamauchi tried once. The result was a skin rash that spread all over Diaz's body, and Phyllis developed a fever from which she almost died. Ordé said that it wasn't a chemical reaction that caused the maladies. He said that the Blues suffered because of something that arose from the original radiance of blue light. Once one had experienced the light in his own eyes, Ordé said, he could not share another's vision.

"I asked around, and some people said that I might find him around here. Do you know where he is?" Adelaide asked me.

"Tomorrow," I said. "But you better get away from here until then."

"Why?"

"Maybe what Julia's scared about isn't so crazy. There's some bad shit goin' down," I said, my adopted street tongue slipping in with fear.

"What do you mean?" Adelaide asked. "What are you talking about?"

"Let's just go," I said. "I'll tell you on the way down."

And I did tell her. I told her about what I knew of Ordé. I told her about his visions and dreams of unity. It sounded ridiculous coming out of my mouth, but I knew the truth of my words and hoped that Addy (that's what she asked me to call her) would hear that truth.

I didn't say anything about blood or blood rituals. I didn't say anything about Ordé reading people's minds by tasting their blood. But I did tell her about Grey Redstar. I told her that he had already killed Phyllis Yamauchi.

On the walk I carried Julia. She climbed up my arm and onto my back. She once stood up on top of my head and then leaped down, grabbing on to me about the waist.

She was an amazing child.

We walked along the street toward my flophouse room. I was thinking that Addy trusted me with no reason, really. I could have been lying to her about everything. Or I could have been crazy. But that wasn't a time of distrust. We had our long hair and our drugs and our music. Everything about us, young people, was revolutionary. The way we made love, whom we loved. The best plans were laid in seconds; our greatest leaders denied the history praised in schools.

What was so wonderful about Addy was something that I couldn't use my newfound sight to see; she trusted me. She took that walk, her daughter in my arms, believing that I wouldn't harm her.

I thought about Ordé and his light. I had seen his visions, traveled among the stars back to those primal molecules that wound through time and around the universe. I was a drone in a cosmic game larger than anything ever imagined by priest or zealot. I was a half-aware particle in a light much greater than any star. I was life becoming a higher matter.

I was, as Ordé once said, a pool on whose surface shimmered the image of God.

But still Addy offered me something more delicate than a flake of ash rising from a campfire flame. It wasn't her but her trusting me that said something that couldn't be felt before it was known.

When we reached my street, Julia stopped playing and jumping around. She wrapped her arms around my neck and held on with all her strength—and she was strong.

The front door of my apartment building led to a shattered green-and-black-tile floor with a bank of tin mailboxes to the right and a stairway straight ahead. There was always a slight smell of urine under the stairway, and no real mail was ever delivered because of theft.

I tried to loosen Julia's grip as we made it up the stairs, but she only held on more tightly. It was actually getting hard for me to breathe, but I didn't pay much attention because of the fear emanating from the child.

"Don't be afraid," I said.

"Don't be afraid," she repeated.

We went up the stairs, me choking, Julia shivering, and Addy bringing up the rear.

Up four flights and we were finally at my door. Filtered sunlight streamed in through a half-closed dirty window at the end of the hall.

I put my key into the lock and turned it. The door blew outward because of a draft caused by an open window inside. I didn't remember leaving a window open, but I could have; I didn't have anything worth stealing.

He was looking out the window. His back turned to us. A smallish man, well dressed as far as I could see.

I fell back into the visions I got from Ordé's blood for a moment. I was looking out of Grey Redstar's eyes into the bloody entrails of Phyllis Yamauchi. When Death's hardened hands kneaded and crushed the organs and flesh, small sparks of blue surfaced and extinguished, leaving behind traces that held images of Phyllis's consciousness. One of these images was me and a trail of footsteps leading to my door.

I hollowed out my stomach and pushed backward, using my toes. Addy grunted and Julia released her grip. The man turned around as I yelled, "Run!"

He was a black man with two large fleshy bumps on his face, one above his left eye and one on his right cheek. For a moment there was sorrow in his eyes, almost an apology. By then I was back out across the threshold. As I slammed the door, my new sight picked up an explosion of deep blue hues.

"Oh, my God!" Addy cried as if she had shared my sight.

"Not that way!" I yelled at her.

She was running toward the window, not the stairs. Our fire escape had rotted away, but the landlord was waiting for the city to make him fix it.

The door behind me flew off its hinges, and Gray Man, in the body of Horace LaFontaine, fell into the hall. I ran down to the window to protect the child and mother, various hues of blue flickering around my second sight.

Julia screamed.

I heard the window open behind me but I couldn't turn to warn them, because Gray Man was on me. I reached out to stop him; that's probably what saved my life. He was excited and there was an electrical field around him. The shock threw me on the floor at Addy's feet. I looked up to see her throw her child through the open window. Before I could rise to help them Gray Man ran up, stepped on my chest, and leaped after the girl.

I raised myself to the sill, fully expecting to see the corpses of both man and child. But what I saw was Gray Man running down the alley behind my building holding a tree branch and looking up at the sky. I followed his gaze until I saw the tiny figure of Julia climbing to the roof of the building across the street. She ran along the edge of the building at great speed and then disappeared.

"Come on!" Adelaide cried.

She was running for the stairs. I limped behind her as well as I could. The electrical shock had turned my muscles to spaghetti. I had to hold on tight to the handrails as I went down the stairs.

"Wait for me, Addy!" I shouted.

When I reached the door she was nowhere that I could see.

When I stepped outside someone grabbed me by the arm. I knew it wasn't Gray Man, so I said, "It's all right. I can make it."

"Lester 'Chance' Foote?" someone asked.

I looked up to see Miles Barber standing there. He was wearing a two-piece maroon suit and a stained powder blue shirt. There were five uniformed policemen behind him. Three of them were restraining Addy.

"Let me go!" she screamed.

I tried to hit Barber. I balled my fist and threw it, but he sidestepped and I was so weak that the punch dragged me down until I was on the ground.

They cuffed me while Barber said something about murder and arresting me. Addy was yelling about her daughter, but the cops didn't seem to care.

I couldn't bring myself to care either. Touching Gray Man had sent shock waves of death up and down my nerves. I was shaking all over, wishing that I had never been born.

EIGHT

Miles Barber wasn't a bad cop. That is to say, he didn't hate Negroes. He didn't enjoy other people's suffering either, I'm sure. But that didn't mean he'd shrink from violence if it would bring some justice to the situation. He didn't mind inflicting a little unconstitutional pain.

"Why did you kill Phyllis Yamauchi?" he asked after his friend, Officer Harlan Castro, had hit me on the side of the head with a short length of sand-filled rubber hose.

I felt the pain and heard the question, but I couldn't react to either. The cool slither of death was still moving along my nerves. It was as if I had died by just touching Gray Man. The feeling of death stayed with me, its images playing over and over in my mind.

I was in a coffin, aware, with no ability to breathe. Days passed like seconds as the coffin deteriorated and the worms ate my eyes.

"Phyllis Yamauchi," someone said.

I imagined that Gray Man was waiting downstairs. Castro hit me down the center of my forehead with the hose. I fell off the chair, terrified that they would release me into the arms of Death. I wanted to confess, to be put in jail. Maybe in prison I could be free of his touch.

Maybe in prison I could finally kill myself and be forever beyond his designs.

But I also wanted Ordé. I wanted to hear his tempered logic. I wanted to think about a future world where I was welcome in the hearts of stars.

Life beckoned me while Death waited down in the street. The confession hung in my throat. Somewhere in the back of my mind I realized that I was bleeding.

Then I began to cry.

I hadn't cried like that since I was a small child. It was a deep shuddering wail of helplessness. The two cops tried to lift me onto the chair, but I was a big man with the coordination of an infant. All they could do was prop me up against the wall.

All I could do was cry.

I tried to confess, but not one word was coherent. Miles Barber was holding a handkerchief against my scalp, trying to staunch the bleeding. But I was moving my head from side to side, seeing death in one corner and something beyond life in the other. I wanted Castro to hit me harder. Miles was talking to me in soft tones intended to pull me out of despair.

After a while it worked.

"Tell me about it, Lester," he was saying.

"I'm sorry," I whispered.

"Tell me what happened."

"I'm sorry," I said again.

"Sorry for what?"

"I'm sorry I didn't, I mean, I'm sorry you can't kill me too."

They put me in a locked room by myself. It had an aluminum toilet bowl and an iron cot with interwoven leather straps for a mattress. I crawled under the cot and faced the wall. Almost instantly I fell into a deep sleep. My dreams began as faintly colored visions of corpses at various stages of decay. Long lines of death in shallow graves. As time passed, the landscape of death decomposed, fading to earth tones and then draining toward gray. The world became dimmer and dimmer until there was only a flat gray earth under only slightly lighter gray skies. A soft buzzing filled the air.

I had come to Gray Man's peace. I saw his world, and then all of my own trepidation vanished.

In my dream I was sleeping.

I awoke on the shore of an infinite beach. There were great white gulls floating lazily in the sky above me. Pulverized quartz in the white sand glittered under a bright sun. I was alone and fully rested, a dreamer awakened from his nightmare into a vision of peace. I went down to the water and watched skinny starfish amble among the rocks, searching for food. They knew nothing of me and my dreams. They simply felt hunger, imagined themselves moving, and lived.

"Time to get up," someone said.

I was lying on my side at the seashore.

I was lying on my side in the cell.

A shod toe nudged my butt.

I rose up, knocking the metal cot onto its side. The heavyset guard looked down on me. He had a clipboard in one hand and a yellow pencil in the other.

"Get up, Foote."

The guard walked me down a long concrete corridor. The walls and low ceilings were corroded and painted a pale lime green. The guard was short and fat. I wondered why he didn't have help moving me, why he wasn't afraid of me. Then I glanced back over my shoulder and noticed that he was holding his pistol down at his side.

"Keep your eyes front and your arms down, Foote," the guard said.

At some other time I might have been afraid, but with Death tracing the pathways of my veins, there was little I feared.

"Hold it right there," the guard said after a minute or so.

To the right was a heavy metal door.

"Face the door," the guard commanded.

I did as he told me.

"Okay, now lace your fingers behind your neck."

He reached around me, slipping a round key into its keyhole. He pushed the door inward.

The room before me was smaller than the cell I'd come from. It was further diminished by a wall of bars that dissected it. On the other side sat a smallish white man in a dark blue suit.

"Go on in, Foote," the guard who was ready to kill me said.

I did as I was told, and the heavy door slammed at my back.

The moment the door closed, the little man stood up. He was taller than I expected him to be, but he was also exceptionally thin.

"Mr. Foote?"

"Uh-huh."

"My name is Howard Weissman. I'm your lawyer from Legal Aid."

I didn't have anything to say, so I sat down in the metal chair provided.

"Do you know why they arrested you, Lester?" Weissman asked. "You don't mind if I call you Lester, do you?"

There was a large cockroach on the wall behind the bony-faced lawyer. If I remained perfectly still, I could *hear* slight orange vibrations coming from the bug. The way the lawyer looked at me, he was probably worried that I might have received a concussion during "questioning."

"Can you hear me, Lester?"

"What's going to happen now?" I asked.

"They have no case. There's no evidence. Detective Barber just brought you in for questioning. Did they hit you?"

"So can I leave?"

Weissman nodded. "The papers should be processed in about half an hour. We can sit here and wait until then. Maybe you can tell me why they're after you for these poisonings. That is, if you want me to help you in the future."

"There is no future," I said.

That was the end of our conversation. I spent the next thirty minutes or so watching the cockroach pulsing red and yellow while Weissman watched me.

I went out the front door of the Berkeley police station on the lookout for Gray Man, but he wasn't there. The sun was shining, bursting with secrets that it wanted to tell me, but I didn't care to hear them. I walked around the streets, gaping at all the men and women, white and black, old and young. I was thinking about starfish and how I wanted to go down to the ocean and watch them—for days.

"Hey, brother," a black man in black leather jacket and pants said.

"Hey, brother," I replied.

My words seemed to have more meaning than they ever had.

"What's happenin'?" my new friend asked.

"Nuthin' to it," I said.

"All right," he agreed and then walked on.

I walked for hours. The police had released me in the early morning. They had released Addy the night before.

I didn't care what happened to me. For years suicide had been my final solution. No matter what I felt, no matter what anybody did to me—I could always end it, I could always throw down the final card.

And then I had died. Died from a dead man's touch. I was neither the vision nor the mind that understood. I was merely a window through which events could be seen. Just a window even unto my own death.

And now, resurrected, I was free for a few hours. I didn't need anything or anyone. I was no more concerned about truth than the starfish that still navigated somewhere in my mind's sea.

I was Buddha and Mr. Natural. I was naked to the world, and nobody cared—not even me.

At about noon I found myself in Garber Park. I was hungry and enjoying the gnawing feeling in my stomach. I climbed the dirt path up toward Ordé's rock. It wasn't until I heard the murmuring of the Close Congregation that I remembered it was Wednesday.

That's when my reverie broke. I wondered what had happened to Julia. I wondered about Gray Man and if he had killed again.

I was walking, even though I didn't want to, toward the place I feared most. Nobody made me do it. Nobody asked me to. Ordé had left me alone in his house while he pursued his own ends. I didn't have to warn him or protect him. There was nothing I could do, and I felt that helplessness. But still I walked toward the Close Congregation because my life had its own path to travel; I was the witness, the invisible chorus of a tragedy far older than the Greeks.

Ordé stood atop his park rock. He surveyed the Close Congregation with something like love in his eyes. He glanced from one face to another and then finally caught sight of me as I came up toward the back of the audience. Among them I could see many of the Blues. Reggie was there holding his little sister's hand. Eileen Martel, Myrtle Forché, Gijon Diaz, Zero Friend, and

Claudia Heart were among the Congregation. I looked at Claudia, trying to recall the passion, but could not.

When Ordé caught sight of me, he nodded and started his speech.

"Death comes among us, my friends," he said softly. "Death and life."

He looked over to his left, and I saw Addy standing there, looking haggard, with Julia in her arms. Julia smiled when our eyes met.

"This is my daughter," Ordé said. "Alacrity."

There were ahhs and nods among the crowd. I thought that the name fit her well, and I understood why she said that Julia was not her name.

"She has come to bring us joy while Death nips at our souls," Ordé said. "An abomination of blue light has come among us. A man who should be dead but who is not. A Gray Man. A man who died but who came back among us. He wants to kill all the Blues. He has already killed Phyllis Yamauchi. He wants to and plans to kill us all. He has great powers and has no debt to the body of life. He only wants death, silence, nothingness."

Everyone listened. Most of them, I believe, thought that Ordé was speaking in metaphors, images, symbols. They didn't believe in a Gray Man. Who would?

"This is the last day of our meeting," Ordé said. "It's time to get on with life. We must spread out to the larger world and disperse the music as best we can. We must sing and we must survive because the future of everything depends on this struggle. Death cannot take us if we move beyond his knowledge. The world is wide and he is but one man, not even a man, just half a man. His will is indominate, but we are like air."

"You don't really mean that we can't meet again, do you?" Alice Rodgers asked. She was one of the Close Congregation, a citizen, a human.

"Not you, Elan," Ordé responded, using his name for her. "You can keep on meeting. You should. Only the Blues have to go. But we'll send a messenger to you later on. Someone who will lead you on the journey."

"No!" a man shouted.

And then another.

Soon almost all of the Close Congregation were chanting no. Meanwhile, the Blues, hearing the word *death* and fearing it, had gathered up around Ordé's rock. The crowd seemed almost hostile, almost as if they were going to attack Ordé and his brethren.

Over the heads of the angry crowd I could see Alacrity begging me with her eyes.

And then the simple, almost silent word "yessssssss" hissed in everyone's ears. It was a word and it was spoken, but it was as if it had been whispered to each one of us.

He was right behind me, the torturer of Horace LaFontaine. His suit was black and his shirt red. I moved out around the crowd and made my way toward my teacher's side. The rest of the Close Congregation turned to the soft-spoken refutation of their demands.

"I am Grey Redstar," he said. "It is time for death."

The first man he reached was Ordé's bodyguard Jason Feldman. Jason reached out to stop the skinny black man. We all heard his arm snapping. No one believed it when Jason's body went flying over the mob at Ordé.

The teacher ducked, and Gray Man plowed into the innocent mortals, breaking bones and rending skin.

"Halt!" Miles Barber shouted. He had jumped out of some hiding place in the trees and approached the zombie. He wore a straw-colored suit with green, red, and black lines sewn crazily through it. He held a large pistol with both hands.

As Gray Man broke the neck of Ordé's second bodyguard, Alexander, Miles Barber fired. Gray Man turned. All I could see was his back, but the fear that blossomed in the policeman's face told the story.

Ordé shouted, "No!" and ran toward Gray Man. He was fast, but not quick enough to save Barber's face from becoming pulp.

Ordé jumped upon Gray Man, followed by Gijon and Zero.

My teacher was torn in two. I saw his back as he fell upon Gray Man and then I saw him come apart, giving off a shower of blood and dying blue sparks.

The Close Congregation scattered, shouts following them down from Ordé's rock. I looked around for Addy and her daughter. They had moved back toward the trees. By the time I turned to see about Gijon and Zero, they were both dead, just bloody pieces on the ground.

I considered whether I should try to stop Gray Man or help Ordé's widow and child.

Then I realized that Gray Man was closing in on Wanita, Reggie's little sister whom Ordé had nicknamed Dreamer. She had her hands out in front of her like claws. Gray Man smiled and prepared to destroy her, but just then Eileen Martel stood before him. She grabbed him by both wrists and stood her ground.

With my vision I witnessed the towering blue flame above her. The darker blues of Gray Man rose also. The lights burned no longer than ten seconds. People were still shouting and running. Paula McDunn, an unemployed RN from San Francisco, ran past me, her face covered with blood.

Suddenly the lights vanished and Eileen fell to her knees. I yelled to bolster my own confidence and ran at Gray Man. I was more than forty yards from them. I knew that Eileen would be dead before I got there, but I ran anyway.

I leaped over Eileen and grabbed Gray Man. He fell to the ground and I froze. It was when he screamed that I realized that our enemy had fled.

"Lemme up!" Horace LaFontaine, Gray Man's dead host shouted, "lemme up!"

He scrambled out from under me and ran, fell, and tumbled away from the scene.

Most of the Close Congregation had also fled. Myrtle Forché and Claudia Heart were gone. Reggie and Addy came up to Eileen, Wanita, and me. Wanita was crying over Eileen, who had fallen on her side. Her face was the color of ash. I could see that she was trying to rise, but it was as if her body weighed a ton and she just couldn't lift it.

She opened her mouth, which, along with her eyes, was flooded with blue light. Then everything was dimmed.

"We gotta go!" little Alacrity said.

And we did.

Two

Interlude

After Ordé's death, and the deaths of so many others I'd loved, I took Adelaide and the children and ran. We found our way to the forests north of San Francisco, living off the checkbook I'd kept for Ordé. We were running for our lives, but sadness, not fear, was our common companion.

Whole days were spent when Addy and I never said a word. We were horrified and numb. The children played or watched TV, when the motel we stayed in that week had a TV, but they cried before going to sleep every night. Wanita had nightmares about losing an eye or a limb. Reggie ran in his sleep, jittering in his bed like a dog, remembering some fright from the day before.

Alacrity called out for the father she'd known only a few hours. The only way she'd go to sleep was for me to sit next to her and stroke her shoulders.

I read the newspapers every day looking for news about Gray Man or Horace LaFontaine. But there was no news about the massacre after the first couple of weeks. Miles Barber had survived Gray Man's attack, though he was badly disfigured and severely injured. One account that described his condition said that he had to be held in restraints to keep him from tearing the flesh from his face. He was in constant pain and ranted continually about the devil roaming the world.

The police labeled the Close Congregation a cult and blamed the episode on drug use. The public dismemberments were called the "culmination of a series of sacrifices," which, they said, included all the poisonings and the murder of Phyllis Yamauchi.

Arrest warrants were issued for various congregation members, including me. Because of the police I spent much of my time hidden in the back of the used VW van we purchased. Addy did the driving and checked us into cabins and motels.

We moved around a lot, rarely staying more than a week in any one place. Our nomadic routine continued for months. The depression that filled up our days was punctuated now and then by high points of fear. Fear that the police would arrest us and keep us in one place long enough for Death to come.

Nothing happened. We just moved around the woods, sighing and crying, hiding in efficiency cabins and hoping for some kind of sign. Reggie was always on the lookout for the perfect hiding place. There was someplace to hide, he was sure, but its location was always just beyond his perception.

But we weren't the only part of the story. Gray Man hadn't stamped out light or life yet. Others were grouping and regrouping on different sides. While I was hiding in backseats or bathrooms, Claudia Heart and Nesta Vine and Juan Thrombone were plotting, gathering, and evoking the words that spoke God. There was the police investigation and the perversions of love. A lot happened before our story continued and so for the sake of the continuity of my *History* I shall tell first about the events that occurred while we hid in the woods.

I learned these stories from newspaper articles and secondhand sources. Every now and then I gleaned my knowledge through blood. And for a while there, I learned while sharing the dreams of the closest friends I ever had.

It doesn't really matter how I learned what I know, not now anyway. Maybe in some far-flung future, when science is not estranged from the soul, someone may find this text and know how to believe in it.

NINE

Winch Fargo lay in his cell, eyes closed, arms and legs bloodied, pale and incoherent. Every once in a while he'd mutter, "Cunt," thinking about Eileen Martel, about how she hadn't been to see him in months. He lay back with his teeth clenched, trying not to hear the music that played only half the melody, trying not to see the small part of what he could never become. In his dreams he'd see himself stalking a man he hates. The man runs scared and Winch falls on him with a knife, but always he turns into the victim at the moment of his thrust, the knife buried in his own chest. The old woman he sodomizes in this dream becomes him. The food he eats, the ground he stomps on. The shit from his ass.

He is everything but himself. A chicken with no head, a planet with no sun.

He groaned on his prison cot but could not move because his arms and legs were tied. He didn't care about the cuts and scars along his limbs. He didn't care about the men who bled him, mixing the blood with powdered milk to drink or inject into their veins.

The blood drug, that's what the brothers called it. One teaspoon, and the prison fell away for a while. One teaspoon, and there was no pain, no sorrow.

"Shit, I'd kill ten motherfuckers just to come back here and get some'a this shit," Mackie Allitar once said while squeezing the blood from a slit in Winch's thumb.

One teaspoon, and an illiterate man could learn to read, a bodybuilder could double his dead lift, a stutterer could recite his family tree without a hitch.

Winch didn't know it at the time, but they called him the Farm. They had to feed the farm and work it. They had to harvest the farm and keep it alive.

It hadn't always been like that. Before Eileen Martel disappeared, Winch discovered the potential of his blood and dispersed it.

But when Eileen had gone, Winch lost his mind again and his customers made him their little acre. They tied him down on a prison cot and got high off his veins.

And all the while Winch stalked himself, ate his flesh, excreted his soul.

He never slept, not really. He felt them cutting him, milking his veins. But the greatest pain was when the iron door to his cell swung open, causing the air to move over his skin like a blanket of white-hot pins.

He yelled from pain, but a hand clamped down over his mouth. His arms and legs were freed from the cot but then were tied together. A gag was shoved into his mouth and then taped over. He was put into a large cloth bag and hoisted over a broad back. The rocking motion of being carried like that calmed Winch somewhat. The snake that lived in his brain was lulled. He couldn't move or speak. It was as if life had not started yet, as if pain was still far off, only a possibility.

Winch Fargo was soothed in the dark trunk he was loaded into. The hum of the motor and the occasional bump in the road felt womblike. He came halfway to consciousness in there. Half sane. He even wondered where it was they were taking him.

He wondered if Eileen might be there sending off those signals like the good songs on the radio when he was a boy in Missouri.

Before they dumped him from the bag, he felt her. He wasn't surprised to see the big blond guard Robert Halston. He didn't care about how skinny he was or how infected his arms and legs had become. All he cared about was the mousy brunette reclining on the couch before him. He wanted to reach for her, but his hands were still tied.

He didn't care. She was his beacon and he'd never be far from her side again in life.

"Winch Fargo," the dazzling image said. "I am Claudia Heart and you are the grandfather to my brood."

The convict stood just behind and to the left of the warden's guest chair. His black skin was ashen, the whites of his eyes were more bloody than bloodshot. Slight jerking tremors went through his body every few seconds or so.

"Where is he, Allitar?" Warden Reed asked.

"I 'ont know . . . sir."

"Mackie, you have to know," said Peter Mainhart, chief of guards. "They say you had him tied to a cot in Detention Cell Forty-eight. They say that you and Halston and some other cons were selling him as some kind of sex slave down there."

"I 'ont know nuthin' about that, sir."

Mackie twitched and the warden stood up from his desk. He wasn't a tall man, but every con in Folsom Prison was afraid when he stood to full stature.

"Where are Halston and Fargo?" Reed asked.

"I wisht I knew," Allitar said, then shuddered so violently that he had to pull the chair back and sit in it.

"What's wrong, Mackie?" Mainhart asked. "You need a fix?"

Mackie raised his ruined face to the warden, ignoring the senior guard's question. He tried to say something; maybe he felt that his yowling groan was answer enough.

"Get him out of here, Peter," the warden said.

"Richards, Weiner!" Mainhart shouted.

Two prison guards dressed in blue came into the room. One was tall and lanky; the other was shaped like two eggs, the smaller one being his head and the larger comprising his body.

"Take him to solitary," Mainhart told his men.

Mackie Allitar fell to the ground, sobbing. He looked up at the four white men and cried some more. When Mainhart demanded that he get up, Mackie did as he was told. He let the guards lead him from the warden's office even though he was still big enough and powerful enough to have killed every man in the room. He didn't think about killing, though. All he thought about was that *bluity;* all he wanted to do was the blood drug.

"There's something wrong here, Peter," Warden Reed said when they were alone again.

The warden was a colorful man. His curly brown hair had red highlights and his blue eyes were almost impossible. His skin drank up the sun in the summer until he seemed to belong on the Caribbean Islands, where he and his family took their vacations.

Mainhart was the warden's opposite in coloring. His white hair had no shine and there was no red under his pale skin. His flat brown eyes were lusterless and could have belonged to a corpse.

"It's a weird one, I agree," Mainhart said. "All this homo drug addict stuff . . . They should line 'em all up at the gas chamber and forget jail altogether."

"You say they had the drug down in Fargo's cell?"

"Yeah."

"Did you bring it?"

Mainhart left the room for a moment and then returned with a plain brown shoe box. He placed it in front of the warden and lifted off the lid.

Inside were a dozen tiny wax paper packets, a few hypodermic needles, a tarnished spoon, and some matches—all on a bed of cotton balls. Warden Reed unwrapped one of the packages, revealing a hard black lump somewhat resembling tar. When the warden squeezed the lump, it turned instantly to dust.

"What is it?" the warden asked.

"Don't know," Mainhart replied. "It's not opium or hash. I don't know what it is."

"What about Halston's family? Has he gotten in touch with them?"

"He moved out four weeks ago," Mainhart said. "Just told Millie that he was going to stay at a flophouse down in Los Gatos and never came back."

"You check the hotel?"

"He never even stayed one night. He just paid the owner to say he wasn't in if somebody called. A couple of the other guards said that he'd met some hippie chick in the Safeway supermarket. He said that she took him out to her van in the parking lot and fucked him right there. Right there in the parking lot, for Christ's sake. In the middle of the day. He said that he was in love with her, that he couldn't even be with Millie after that."

The warden massaged his face with both hands and made a small chirping sound in the back of his throat. "How long now?" he asked.

"Sixteen hours since we realized it. He's probably been gone for two days, though. Thursday and Friday were Halston's weekend. He coulda taken Fargo out anytime. Nobody else went to that cell when he was on duty. It was solitary. It was his detail."

Warden Reed looked at the dark powder. His fingers tingled slightly. He took a paper towel from his bottom drawer and wiped the drug away, but the tingling remained.

"Report the escape," Reed told Mainhart. "Tell them that we're not quite sure when it happened. Tell them we just thought that Fargo had been misplaced and sent someone out to Halston's house. Tell them it wasn't until then that we realized that it was a break. Tell them . . ." Reed's voice trailed off.

"What?" Mainhart asked. "What did you say, chief?"

"Huh?"

"You were saying something."

"Oh." Reed looked at the paleness of his chief guard's features. "Tell them . . . tell them that I got sick and had to go home."

"But, sir, don't you think with the break and all that, you better . . ."

Gerin Reed stood up from his desk feeling like a titan. He had always been a short man and he was still the same height, but it didn't seem to matter anymore.

"You can take care of it, Peter. You can talk to them. Tell them that I'm sorry, but there's nothing I can do about being sick."

The puzzle in the head guard's face tickled the warden.

"Tell me something, Peter."

"What's that, Warden?"

"Did you ever run down a beach as fast as you could, laughing the whole way and then, just when you're going your fastest, want to take off and fly? But you know you can't fly, and now running doesn't seem to be as much fun anymore. I mean, if you can imagine flight, if you can feel it in your arms and down your spine, then . . . how can you go back to running?"

"I think you should see a doctor, Gerry. Maybe that dust can get in through your pores."

"Nonsense. Nothing like that. I'm just sick, that's all. Just sick. Just sick."

Warden Reed walked out of his office and told his secretary that he'd need his car brought to the front of the prison. He waited patiently as the various locked doors were unlocked. He waited for the guards at the front as they searched his backseat and trunk. They were on special alert. The prison horns were sounding, announcing to the world that someone had escaped.

Warden Reed was looking at the foothills on the horizon. He imagined Winch Fargo out there running as hard as he could, wishing for flight.

His Ford's engine sounded as good as it ever would, and the road was smooth. Every once in a while Warden Reed turned on his blinker and changed lanes for no reason. He let his mind wander as he drove a few miles above the speed limit toward his home in the Loma Linda Hills.

He thought about how when he was a boy he wished he could live in a nice house like the one he and his wife now owned. Their children had toys and comforts that he could never afford when he was a child back in Kentucky. Back then all his toys were sticks and thrown-away things that he imagined had magical powers. His red fire engine was a squared-off piece of kindling from the firewood his father cut into cords and sold. His air force was a squadron of leaves taking off every autumn for the German lines.

And when he looked off into the stars at night and asked his father if there was ever an end to all that way out there, his father would say, "I don't have time to think about questions like that, Gerry, and neither do you. Now get to bed."

Lying there in the bed, little Gerin thought about the stars and how they got there and where they came from.

On the day he left work early he was thinking about those stars. The sky was blue now, the stars hidden. Gerin imagined a world that was completely black, no light at all. He was looking out into the imagined blackness, and then slowly a large red rose came into being. Was it there before he saw it? Was it there in the blackness? Gerin didn't know the answer, but he planned to go home and think about it. He knew that the answer to that question was in him. He knew that he'd been asking that question his whole life. And now, with a great sigh of relief, he could go home and sit back and think on it.

He parked the car in the street because there was another car in his driveway. He went up the concrete path through the lawn with the key out, but the door was unlocked.

He could hear them before he rounded the corner from the entranceway into the sunken living room. The young man's sports jacket was thrown on the plastic-covered couch, and her dressing gown was on the floor. His pants were down around his ankles and he was on his knees holding one of her legs high enough to give a clear view of his large erection poised at the entrance of her gaping vagina. Karen's butt was quivering—beautifully, Gerin thought.

"You want it?" the man on his knees asked.

"Uh-uh-uh," Karen responded.

"No uh-uh," the man said. "You gotta tell me if you want this."

"Please," Karen whispered.

"What?"

"Please put it in!"

Gerin thought of magic again when he saw his wife's lover's penis disappear there next to her quivering thigh. And then her loud moaning made him remember the rose coming out of nowhere.

"That's what you been thinkin' about, huh?" The man's voice was huskier now. "That's what you been wantin'?"

Karen barked out half a dozen clear "oh!"s and began to thrash around. When she reached around to caress his testicles, she saw something, a shadow maybe, and screeched as if in pain. She crawled away from her lover, leaving his full erection bobbing in the air.

"Hi, Karen," Gerin said to his wife, and to her visitor, "hello."

The lovers scrambled clumsily, grabbing for their clothes.

Karen donned her special nightgown, the one she took on their trip to Barbados, trying to make it look like normal clothes. She stood in front of the man—protecting him, it seemed to Gerin. Karen's left cheek still had the rough impression of the carpet on it.

"Now don't go crazy now, Gerry. Don't get wild." She was looking at his hands and belt line.

Gerin remembered that he was supposed to be angry if he found his wife of twenty years having sex with someone else. He was supposed to have a gun out. It was one of the few times he could kill in cold blood and get away with it—outside of the prison walls.

The lover was a young man, overweight. He had his pants up and his jacket on. He looked once at Gerin and then ran for the back door through the kitchen. Karen looked after him for a second and then turned back to Gerin, putting out her arms like a mother goose protecting her young.

Gerin saw all of this, but his mind was back at the prison. Back on the times when he'd be brought to the scene of a brutal beating, the corpse of a convict as its centerpiece. He listened to the lies the guards told of suicide or a fight among convicts. He knew when one of his own had murdered. The prison doctor would write up the death certificate. The county coroner would stamp it with his approval. The body was either buried or sent home following a letter from the warden himself giving condolences for the terrible mishap or self-demolition.

"Gerry, he doesn't mean a thing to me. It just happened. I can't deny it but . . . Gerry, are you listening to me?"

"Why don't you put on something, Karrie? Call Sonia to come and sit for the kids and we can go out to dinner."

Ray's Lobster Grotto was painted all in red and looked out over the bay. It was an hour and a half drive from their house, but Gerin didn't mind. He drove down toward the ocean, excited by every shift of hue caused by the setting sun. He kept moving his hands along the smooth steering wheel.

"Talk to me, Gerry," Karen said when they came to a stop in Ray's gravel parking lot. It was still early, so they were the only car there.

"About what, honey?"

"You know what. For God's sake, you found me with another man on our living-room floor."

"What's his name?"

"Who cares what his name is?" Karen said. "What are you going to do?"

"Do," Gerin Reed repeated.

"Talk to me, Gerry."

"You asked me what I'm going to do, baby. What am I going to do?"

"Gerry, what's wrong?" Karen asked with real concern in her voice. "I didn't mean to hurt you. I mean, you've never come home like that; I mean, you don't just come home in the middle of the day."

"It's just like TV," Gerin said. "Just like *Gunsmoke* or *Bonanza* or even *The Dakotas*. You know, like in the real West, but on TV with commercials and station breaks. Not real. Not important or anything. Just something you watch at the same time every week. But it's not like the sunset or the fall. It's not like being hungry. It happens, but it doesn't matter."

"What are you talking about, Gerry?" Karen reached out to touch her husband but then pulled her hand back.

He looked at her. Forty-two but with the same body she had when he first met her in college. Her wide smile still hiding under the concern.

"Going to work. Going to church. Getting my hair cut, buying shoes, listening to the radio, talking to Madge and Dan Hurley about their kids." Gerin reached over, taking her tentative hand in his. "Today I realized that I hadn't ever left early or anything like that. There was trouble up at the prison, but I didn't have to worry about it. Today was the first time I thought about things in years. And then when I got home and saw you with that man. . . . You should have seen your butt, Karrie. . . ."

"Gerry!" Karen pulled her hand from him.

"But you should have seen it. It was up in the air quivering and shaking. You were really happy, all excited. You felt just like I do. You got it from that boy, and I did by walking away from work."

"What happened at work?"

"A prisoner escaped with the help of a guard. They're both gone."

"When did it happen?"

"We found out today," Gerin said wistfully. "But it happened two or three days ago."

"Gerry, you have to be there. You can't just leave like that. They'll fire you."

Gerin looked at his wife and felt happy that she still cared even though she got her magic from other men. He thought about their phone at home and about how Sonia had the phone number of Ray's Grotto.

"I don't want to eat here," Gerin said. "Let's go down to Frisco. Let's have dinner on Fisherman's Wharf."

TEN

Nesta Vine lived only four blocks from Horace La-Fontaine. She worked at the West Oakland library and came home every night with a stack of books in her arms. Novels, biographies, histories, and learning texts, she read everything, remembered everything, but she told her grandparents, "I don't understand what it all means."

"All it means is that you one smart black girl," her grandfather, Lythe Charm, would say.

Then she'd kiss him on the lips and go upstairs to read while he puttered around with the soup her grandmother had made.

Up in her room she closed the doors and forgot all the things that she knew: her mottled brown skin, her sex, the years going by. Nesta thought that she was ugly and that all her intelligence was only in her eyes. She could see things and remember them, but nobody remembered her.

She was reading *The Birds* by Aristophanes when blue light struck. She'd raised her eyes for a moment, wondering if there was a textbook on ancient Greek at the main branch of the library. She wondered what kind of lilts and accents the different Greeks had, when the light came into her mind and illuminated all the millions of words that she'd read.

She inhaled deeply and gazed out over the multicolored three-story houses on Mill Street. She saw equations and plotlines, lies and errors. She imagined building a three-masted schooner and then set up a test model around a hydroponic element designed to extend the girth of root vegetables. And as these experiments unfolded in her mind, she monitored them separately, listening all the while to the music of the Oakland streets. Falling deeper and deeper into her reverie, Nesta changed.

The rooms appeared in her imagination, but they were in every respect real. To the left was a mooring dock above which was suspended her silk and teak and stainless-steel yacht. To the right was a laboratory filled with bubbling bottles and tubes of Pyrex. In this room time passed more quickly to hurry along her experiments.

A mirror appeared at the end of the aisle separating her laboratory and yacht. In the mirror was a taller woman the color of ebony. Her eyes were smaller and extremely white; eyes that seemed to flash when she looked from side to side. Her nose had widened, and her lips were as full as the Nile in the rainy season.

"Nesta."

Her breasts were still small but a little higher. Her feet were much bigger. *For running,* she thought.

"Nesta."

The boat and root plants receded into memory, ready to be called again. She walked into the mirror, merging herself with herself.

"Nesta, girl, did you stay up all night again?"

"No, Grandma, uh-uh," she said. The sun was up outside the window. "I fell asleep in the chair is all."

The books had fallen from her lap around her feet. She stood up among them and looked at Felicity Charm. She was tall, like Nesta's image of herself, but sand-colored instead of black.

"How many books you read?" Felicity asked.

"None."

"None? When's the last time you didn't read even one book at night?"

"I don't know," she said, a little distracted. "But I don't think I'm going to read very much anymore."

"Why not?"

"I have to talk to people now, Grandma. I have to go out and talk to people. I have to make up my own mind about all this stuff. You know?"

"You mean, you gonna start datin'?"

Nesta had a little more than six thousand dollars in the bank from a dozen years of saving. She bought a used camper and a Dodge truck. Then she traveled out across the country, meeting people and talking.

She collected ideas and people's expertise. She learned more than a thousand recipes for chili and how to drive a big rig. She learned 38,263 names, more than

9,000 body odors, and well over 500 shades of skin and eye colors.

In college towns she listened to lectures by scientists, men of letters, and artists. She always asked questions, never giving an opinion. She never took notes, nor did she forget a word. The only thing she ever wrote were letters to her grandparents. Long letters that were probably the most important documents on Earth. These letters told of what Nesta thought about the nature of light in the eyes of our science and philosophies.

She took a winding route around the Midwest, North, and South. Then she traveled to the East Coast, covering Maine to Florida in her studies.

After that she sold the camper and truck and went to Europe. There she continued her cataloging. She learned German and French and Italian; she spent a month in the major libraries of each nation. Then she moved on.

She was in Hong Kong, wondering whether or not to go into Vietnam, when one night she had a dream. It was a simple vision. She was seated at the table in the dinette of her grandparents' home. Off to her left the back door was open. Lythe Charm, her grandfather, was in the doorway, in his wheelchair, basking in the afternoon sun. The light was so strong that his back was enveloped in shadow. There was a ruffled newspaper on the table. A partially obscured headline spoke of murder.

She was with a man named Kai in a small room on a footpath that had no name that she was aware of. She loved being there because all she had to do was to lie on her back, and all the sensations, sounds, and odors of the city came to her. And Kai was a wonderful man who liked to talk while making love. He was asleep, his strong and slender back turned to her.

She sat up and went to the small window. As the gray-red sun rose over the city, she began to think.

ELEVEN

Hidalgo Quinones drank wine only on Saturday afternoon. He worked six days a week in the gardens of
North Berkeley and then he'd stop wherever his last job
was, drink a quart of red wine, and take a nap. He always napped in the back of his truck, thinking about his
seventeen brothers and sisters, counting how many
cousins and nieces and nephews he must have down
around Ensenada by now.

"What an Easter festival they must be having," he
said to himself.

He didn't have any children yet, even though he was
already fifty. He did have his little bushes and big trees,
his seeded lawns and bright roses. Hildy had a girlfriend
named Rosa, but she couldn't give him children.

But the thought of a hundred relatives fully grown
back home made Hildy feel that he didn't have to make
a family too.

"It's sad for Rosa," he said to himself. "But it would
be even sadder if I left her because she was barren."

That was when the first shaft of light hit him.

Fertility was on his mind. Fecundity and growth. Huge plants wandering as roots under the ground, then coming forth as giant woody trees headed for the sun— like those astronauts. Cow shit and milling flies, bees and birds and burly clawing bears.

His life was set in fifteen seconds.

And then the second shaft hit.

The landscape so delicately created was blasted from his mind. Trees uprooted from the ground slammed into animals and grafted with them. Volcanoes of blood erupted under the hapless creatures, who immediately caught fire. Hildalgo screamed and clenched his fists.

He dreamed of blood and death under the blue light. . . .

Until the third shaft of light struck.

Some months after the day that blue light struck, dozens of different kinds of birds were gathering in the northernmost reaches of the King Canyon National Park. Stags and wolves, night crawlers and mosquitoes passed that way again and again. They seemed to find comfort on or near the bark of a great sequoia redwood that had grown there for a thousand years.

Along the bark of the tree butterflies of all kinds spread their multicolored wings.

A forest ranger, Esther O'Halloran, was standing next to the great tree, obviously perplexed. She had taken off her brimmed hat to massage her head and ponder. She didn't know that a bright pair of eyes was watching her wonder.

She tried to frighten a few of the butterflies away, but they barely moved as she waved her gloved hand around their papery wings.

The ranger knelt down to study the ground around the great tree. There were ants milling and caterpillars and walking sticks moving in their long and rigid dance. There were vole holes all along the ground. Spiderwebs were everywhere except on the tree itself. A blurred, furry flash moved quickly across her peripheral vision and she turned, catching sight of the foxtail as it disappeared into the thicket.

She smiled at the fox.

Esther pulled away a few monarchs to place her palm against the bark. She smiled again, tickled by the slight vibration that sounded out like a kettledrum to the one that watched her.

"You should be more careful out in such a wild place," the watcher declared.

She turned to see a short man dressed in a one-piece garment that was a patchwork of cloths and furs, metal and wood, and, in places, bone and clay.

"What?" Esther demanded. "What are you doing here?"

The fox darted out of hiding, running straight for the strange man. Arriving at his feet, she started licking his fur boots.

"I was asleep," the man said. "In the flatbed of a truck. And then I had three dreams, all in a row. The first one was my mother, the second one was my father, and the last one was me."

The man smiled and walked toward the forest ranger. The fox scuttled along, licking and yipping. The man came to stand before Esther. They were about the same height.

A black-and-gold monarch lit on his red-brown forehead.

"I woke up," he said to her, the slightest trace of a Mexican accent rising like vapor between his words. "And looked in my pocket. I found a card for driving that had my picture on it and the name Hidalgo Quinones. But that's not me."

"Who are you, then?"

"My name," the man said, watching her eyes, "is Juan Thrombone. Thrombone with an aitch."

More butterflies landed on Juan's head and shoulders. He smiled at her.

"What do you mean 'dangerous'?" Esther asked, taking a step backward.

"Dangerous?"

"That's what you said."

"No. I didn't say dangerous. It is dangerous. Yes, it is. But I didn't say that, no, I didn't. I said 'wild.' This is a wild place. A place too strong for anyone who cares more about living than they do about what they might find."

Esther looked closely in the little man's eyes. *Maybe,* he thought, *she thinks I'm crazy.*

A raven flew up, landing on the ground near them.

"You see, this is a strong place," Juan said. "It's a very, very strong place, but it is dying. Soon it will be gone. Destroyed. That's why I'm here."

The crazy-quilt man reached into a makeshift tarp bag that hung from his shoulder. He opened the bag to show Esther an egg-sized cone that bore the seed of the great tree.

"She wants them to grow, but they will not. Not until the true equations move her. But she called and I came because it is only the forest and I who can live without hunting. But even these seedlings will go off to war one day, I'm afraid," Juan said. "Until then I will treat them as my children."

"You can't take them."

"Why not?"

"This is government property. I'm a ranger. You can't take my trees." While she spoke, Esther watched the Mexican's eyes. They were black at first but then came to be blue. Bright blue. The kind of bright that glass gets on a sunny windowsill. I have never spoken to her, but I've also seen those eyes.

He left her standing there, looking out where he'd been. There were butterflies all over her. White cabbage butterflies on her cheeks and hands. Down her collar. Up under the cuffs of her uniform pants.

TWELVE

He never slept more than a few minutes at a time but was rarely tired. He was in constant pain, but that was the least of his discomfort. His lower lip was now a leather flap, and his right eye had a patch instead of a lid. The flesh of his face had been shredded and scarred, but he didn't spend long enough in the hospital to find out about plastic surgery for his bones and skin.

Miles Barber had gone from detective to freak in an instant, but he didn't appreciate the change. The last thing Barber remembered was crouching down among the shrubs of Garber Park and hearing a loud scream.

In the hospital the doctors and police told him that he was the victim of a brutal ritual performed in the park by a drug-dealing cult, the Close Congregation. They told him that he'd been butchered and left to die.

Miles Barber didn't remember getting up that morning, but he knew that there had been no ritual.

"Bullshit," he said to the doctors.

"Are you crazy?" he asked his old cop friends.

As soon as he was able, ex-Detective Barber checked himself out of the hospital. Family, friends, and physicians tried to stop him. But he didn't care about health or what people saw when they looked at him. He didn't care about what they saw, because the images in his mind were so much worse than disfigurement or physical pain.

Gray Man had laid the imprint of death, in the darkest blue imaginable, upon Miles Barber's soul. I had felt the same thing when Death jostled me, but I had Ordé's blood to buffer the pain. Barber had nothing but innocence.

He rarely slept, but whenever he let his mind drift he fell into a cold gray swampland of entropy and despair. If he wasn't careful, he'd drift all the way into a coma. This happened twice while he was in the hospital, and he had to be revived with powerful amphetamines.

But Miles Barber didn't spend much time daydreaming after leaving the hospital. He tracked down the Close Congregationalists and interviewed every survivor, hoping to find out the devil's name and address. Because Barber was on a hunt for the evil that destroyed all the hope and heart in him. He had taken it as his mission to kill the man who had touched his soul.

During the months that he shadowed the congregation looking for Mack the Flask, he never paid much attention to our philosophies or beliefs. "Blue light, white elephant, or Christ on a fuckin' cross," he once said to me. "It's all the same nonsense." But now he understood that what we believed had drawn Gray Man.

While I was hiding in the northern woods, he was gathering almost as much information as I had on blue light, its chosen, its acolytes, and its meaning.

He had taped accounts of most of Ordé's speeches from these interviews. He had gotten nearly all of the Blues' names. He wanted to interview one of the chosen, but they had all died or disappeared.

Neither could ex-Detective Barber find another person who had been touched by Death. All the rest who Gray Man had touched, on the day he murdered Ordé, had died in their sleep within the first week of the slaughter. The newspapers called it a virus that drug users got from sharing needles.

When Barber was through with his interviews he had four primary names on his list. There was me because of my close relationship to Ordé and my ramblings about death on the day they took me to jail. There was Claudia Heart (née Aaronfeld, married name, Zimmerman), who had started a commune out in the desert somewhere. There was a man whom no one had ever seen named Winch Fargo. Roberta Garcia remembered Eileen Martel mentioning him, about going to see him in jail. And there was also Gray Man, the devastator. Gray Man was the ultimate goal, the blood clot, the inoperable tumor. Gray Man was a reason to murder. The reason for a man who lived by the law to break that law finally and forever.

Miles Barber was a good detective when he was with the Berkeley Police Department. He was better as a civilian, no longer needing proof or facts or reasonable cause. He carried with him a small thermos full of gasoline and a box of wooden matches. This was because in his interviews he'd learned that he had shot Gray Man, at point-blank range, to no effect. The moment he caught sight of the deceptively diminutive black man with the two fleshy bumps on his face, there would be no need for handcuffs or jail cells, civil rights or judges.

But as good as he was, Miles Barber was grasping at air.

Claudia Heart had repaired to her desert hideaway, taking with her everyone who knew its location. The rest of the Blues, along with me, had vanished completely.

The only lead was a jailbreak. Winch Fargo had escaped from Folsom, with the help of a prison guard. A day or two later the warden, their suspected accomplice, disappeared with his wife and children—leaving no trace.

Ex-Detective Barber went to Folsom but was not admitted even to present his questions. He had to satisfy himself by buying drinks for off-duty prison guards at the Top Tank bar in downtown Represa.

He spent three months and a good deal of his life savings in a flophouse next door to the bar. Over the ensuing weeks he told the prison guards his story—or at least a part of it.

"Yeah," he'd say with a bitter sigh. "Up there tryin' to keep the city safe while you got hippies burnin' their draft cards. They did this to me and nobody even went to jail for it. I'm discharged on disability, but I haven't even seen the first check yet."

No one wondered, or at least they didn't ask, why Barber moved to the town of Represa. The off-duty prison guards accepted the free drinks and humored the freak. He gained their confidence, bided his time. He knew many of the inmates they guarded and told the guards what he knew. They laughed about how stupid some thieves had been and whistled their respect on the magnitude of some unsolved crimes.

It went like that for many weeks before Miles got to buy drinks for the acting warden, Peter Mainhart. Mainhart was just a guard at heart and would never be the permanent warden. That's why he still stopped by the Top Tank now and again. Because he missed the company of real workingmen. Barber learned this after the second round of drinks. By the fourth rye they were talking about blood and bluity. By the time they had come to the bottom of the bottle, Mainhart confided that the whole case had been turned over to the SIB, the State Investigations Bureau, in Sacramento.

"Goddamned state," Mainhart said, a little south of sober. "Chief Inspector Bonhomme goes right in there and takes all the records and asks questions up your ass. What the hell does he think it's like up here? It's hell, I tell ya, Milo. It's hell."

That was twelve minutes past midnight. Ex-Detective Barber was on the 2:42 bus that would make connections to get him into Sacramento by 8:23 the next morning.

"I don't understand," Inspector Christian Bonhomme of the SIB said to Miles Barber at 10:44. "You were fired from the Berkeley Police Department?"

"No," Barber said for the fourth time. "I received a disability discharge after they did this to my face."

"Who did it?" Lonnie Briggs, Bonhomme's partner, sergeant, and friend, asked.

The sergeant had a bald head with no eyebrows. Whereas the inspector was tall and gaunt, Briggs was wide and powerfully built.

"The members of the Close Congregation," Miles said. "You musta read about it. Four people were killed in the park that day."

The sergeant and the inspector glanced at each other across the desk, but Barber kept cool.

"Yes," Bonhomme remembered. "The massacre. You were there?"

"I was."

"Then why weren't those cult members put on trial? I mean, an eyewitness account from a homicide detective should at least put somebody in front of a judge."

"I was there but I don't remember. . . ."

Lonnie Briggs rolled his eyes and sighed.

"I don't remember, because of this," Barber pointed at his ruined face. Then he lifted the eye patch, showing the lidless socket that I saw many months later. Just a naked eyeball permanently bloodshot, hardly human, and dazed by the light. Miles lowered the patch and then took out a squeeze bottle of a sanitized solution to put a few drops in an opening at the top of the patch.

"There was trauma to my head," he told the SIB men. "I was behind some bushes, I heard a scream, and then I woke up in the hospital. But since then I've been investigating on my own. I've talked to everyone who was there and I've got a pretty good idea of what happened and who was responsible."

"Who?" Bonhomme asked as he brought a cherry pipe to his lips.

Bonhomme struck a match over the small bowl, and Barber stalled. Instead of answering immediately, he rubbed the excess moisture away from the bottom of the hard leather eye patch with his finger.

Finally the ex-detective said, "They knew what he looked like, but nobody knew his name."

It was a hot day in Sacramento. The window behind Bonhomme was open, and a large black fly floated noisily into the room. That fly struck fear into Miles Barber. He felt the sweat on his head begin to trickle down behind his ear as he watched the insect hover and then bang its body violently in a vain attempt to escape through the upper panes.

"Where are you staying, Mr. Barber?" Bonhomme asked.

"I just got into town . . . from Represa."

The name of the prison town grabbed the attention of both the inspector and his sergeant. But Barber barely noticed because he was watching that woolly fly.

"You were up at the prison?" Briggs asked.

Miles jumped up and slapped the fly right out of the air. The stunned creature bounced against the gray-green wall and fell on Bonhomme's blotter. Before the fly could recover, Barber smashed it with a powerful open-hand blow.

When he lifted his hand all that was left was a mess of fly fragments and blood.

"I hate flies," Barber said lamely.

"What were you doing in Represa?"

"Winch Fargo," Barber replied. "Could you close that window?"

Briggs moved to slide the window shut.

"What about Fargo?" Bonhomme asked.

"The woman who died in the massacre, Eileen Martel. She visited Fargo every week up until she was killed. This Fargo had murdered her husband."

Briggs nodded at Bonhomme.

"What about her?" the inspector asked.

"As far as I can tell," Barber explained, "she was smuggling in some kind of drug. The cult members told me that there was something wrong with this Fargo, like some kinda nervous disorder, and their leader, William Portman, also known as Ordé, gave Eileen something to give Fargo to keep him calm."

"Did they say what it was she gave him?" Briggs wanted to know.

"Everything with them is blue light. The Blues, blue light, blue gods. If she brought him anything, it would have been called blue somethin'."

"Did they ever talk about blood?" Bonhomme asked softly.

Ex-Detective Barber knew, at that moment, that he was back on the inside. All he had to do was choose his words carefully, omit some of the truths as he knew them, and he would have what he wanted.

"Yeah," Barber said. "That fella Portman was always talkin' about blood and blue light. He was always talkin' about how the chosen ones, the Blues, kinda like priests, had different blood. We found four of his followers poisoned with some kind of toxic mixture, which had been combined with blood, in their stomachs."

"We should try to get a look at those files," Bon-homme said. "Call down to the Berkeley PD, Lonnie."

"No need," the ex-detective said. "I've got copies of all the files right here in my suitcase."

"You do?"

"Yes, sir. It was my case. I had taken them home to study them before the massacre."

Christian Bonhomme put down his pipe and leaned forward on his elbows.

"What are you doing here, Mr. Barber? What do you want from us?"

Miles first took out his squeeze bottle and pressed a few drops down the top of his patch to soothe the naked eye. He reminded himself not to drift into the fear and hatred that was always so near the surface of his feel-ings. The hatred and fear of the man who had laid down the imprint of death upon his mind. He couldn't let them suspect the killing he had in store for Gray Man. He'd already gone too far by killing that fly.

"I want . . ." he said, "I want the people who did this to me to pay for it." Barber closed his good eye and saw the afterimage of a gray cloud that always hovered there. "They took everything from me. They made me a freak."

"And you think your own police department can't handle the investigation?"

"They have the same files that I do, Inspector. Did they come to you? Did they go up to Folsom?"

"They would if you went to them now." Bonhomme was trying to sound reasonable, but his eyes were intent.

"Claudia Zimmerman is in the desert somewhere. Lester Foote has disappeared from the Bay Area, along with three minors and a woman who may have Portman's child. Fargo escaped from jail. There's nothing the Berkeley police can do." Barber suddenly felt a wave of calm come over him. He told me, much later, that he realized that it was fate for him and the SIB agents to work together. He was sure that they had no other choice.

"Listen," he said. "I know these people. Anyone you run across from this cult and I'll recognize 'em. I know the names and crazy talk. I even understand what they mean. Fargo's escape has something to do with the killings in Berkeley. Probably somebody from the congregation got to this Robert Halston. I can help you. And if you find out what happened, it will lead to their boss—and that's the guy I want."

"I thought you said that Portman was the boss?" Briggs said.

"Uh-uh. I don't know the big boss's name, but you better believe that I intend to find out."

In the weeks that followed, Miles Barber became a fixture at the fourth-floor offices of Christian Bonhomme and Lonnie Briggs. The SIB was completing its first central building at that time, so the bureau was still spread out in individual offices all around Sacramento. So no eyebrows were raised when Miles set up in the receptionist's space outside Agent Briggs's office.

Briggs wasn't bothered, because he divided his time between fieldwork and conferring with Bonhomme in the larger back office.

No one complained about ex-Detective Barber. On the contrary, Bonhomme was very pleased. Not only did

Miles take the secretary's space, he did the secretary's work. There were dozens of boxes of handwritten files and reports that dated back to the beginning of Bonhomme's career with the SIB. He was supposed to have typed, classified, and filed each document but never had. Now the new director wanted everything turned into input cards for the new IBM-360. Barber agreed to take on the task. He told Bonhomme that he wanted to look for leads in the Blues case amid the mass of paper. Each morning when Bonhomme came in to work, he found Miles, his one eye scanning a scrawled report that was tacked to the wall, his ten fingers battering the old Royal typewriter. Every evening when the inspector left, Barber was still typing and squinting at the wall.

Bonhomme must have wondered if the one-eyed ex-detective freak was living in the temporary office. But there was no suitcase in the cloak closet or bedding or even a toothbrush to prove it. That was because Miles Barber never slept. He kept his toothbrush in his pocket, stowed his suitcase in a locker at the bus station, and did his latrine with a washrag, a bar of soap, and a ceramic mug. Once a week he took his clothes to a French laundry on Spring.

Barber spent every night working on Bonhomme's files. He typed and filed, ordered and reordered until the inspector returned. He worked because that kept him from heeding the changes happening on the inside.

Miles Barber, while he pecked and hunted, was going through a metamorphosis. On one hand, he was dying, fading out just as his best friend, Brad Sanders, had after a chest wound at Anzio. But on the other hand, there was a life growing from the inside. This new life was coming out of what he had always known as himself, but it wasn't him—at least, it didn't have to be. Barber feared that if he fell asleep for long, he would die and this *bean sprout* in his heart would take over. So he stayed awake, working, playing the radio, and denying the changes that were trying to take hold.

He went on like that, working twenty-hour days and talking to Bonhomme and Briggs now and then about the Close Congregation and their possible relationship to Fargo. Miles had almost finished with the files when he began to worry that Bonhomme had meant to keep him only till all the work was done.

But the ex-detective had a plan. There had been nothing of interest in the files he copied. He would, instead of working on his typewriter at night, break into the inspector's active files in the back office. He'd transcribe all the information that had to do with Winch Fargo, so when he was released, he'd be able to shadow the SIB investigation until they led him to his prey.

Then one afternoon Lonnie Briggs returned from a four-day field trip.

"Hey, Patch," Briggs said to the ex-detective secretary. It was a nickname Briggs was fond of using. It bore no enmity. "How's the filing coming? You almost finished?"

"Not quite."

The smile Briggs gave was wide and insincere. At least, that's what Barber thought. He made up his mind to break into the locked files that night.

Briggs went in to confer with Bonhomme. They talked for a while and then Briggs came out.

"Come on in here a minute, will ya, Milo?"

"What for?"

"Just a couple'a things."

Miles felt something enter his mind. It wasn't a thought, but an overwhelming excitement that bordered on fear. He couldn't explain then that it was a power coming over him, the ability to receive emotional and other, more obscure impressions from people around him.

"Take the hot seat," Briggs said, indicating the chair before his boss's desk.

As Miles lowered himself into the chair, Briggs said to Bonhomme, "He's gonna need a hat."

"What?" asked Miles.

"A hat," Briggs repeated. "With a big brim too. I mean, if we're gonna go out with these crazies in the desert, then we're gonna have to be inconspicuous. No offense, but it would take a blind man not to notice you."

Miles Barber laughed. The three deep single-syllable tones that burbled out of his chest were odd enough to arrest the agents' attention.

"You okay, Barber?" Bonhomme asked. He even put down his pipe in case he needed both hands to lend assistance.

The ex-detective wanted to answer; he tried to. But first he had to figure out what that bullfrog laugh was.

"It was like looking for my long-lost father," Miles said to me much later next to a campfire. "Instead, I found the devil. But in the back of my mind I was thinking that the devil was my old man. You see what I mean?"

I did get his meaning. That laugh was the annunciation of the new life that had been growing since Grey Redstar's will had touched Barber's soul. In that office he was a new man being offered the old man's obsession. And in that moment the will of the man who should have passed on was soldered onto the detritus of Gray Man's rage.

"I'm fine, Christian," Barber said at last.

"You sure? You sounded a little funny."

"Is this about Fargo?"

Bonhomme winced in a final moment of indecision, but Miles knew that it would pass. He'd soon be on the trail of the man who had killed him and then brought him back to life.

"There're three avenues of investigation that we could follow," Bonhomme said a little too loudly. "There's Fargo. He's the reason we're on the case. There're the guys in the prison that were torturing Fargo. And there's this guy Halston. He was the guard on duty who disappeared at the same time. The warden, Gerin Reed, is also under investigation, but we're not sure about his role yet."

"Yeah," Sergeant Briggs added. "He's pretty hard to find too."

"I see," Miles said. He acted as if he were following the conversation, weighing the options. But he already knew the answers. He already knew what they were going to do.

"I'm interested in that guy Allitar," Briggs said.

"Who's that?" Barber asked.

"He's one of the four guys who kept Fargo tied to a bunk in his cell. Halston had to be helping them, but Allitar was the ringleader."

"What kind of name is Allitar?"

"It's an alias."

"Well, then, what's his real name?" Barber asked the burly sergeant.

"His father's name is Brown, a con artist. Took retirement accounts from old ladies starved for love. He went under the alias Conrad L. Allitar for fifteen years. Married under that name. Had kids under that name. Mackie's legal name is Allitar even though it was just his father's alias."

"What's his story?"

"Allitar is in on a multiple homicide committed during the robbery of a pharmacy," Bonhomme interjected. "He claims that there was some kind of drug in Fargo's blood. They used to bleed him for it, he says."

"To sell it?"

"No, not if you're to believe him. Fargo sold the drug himself, even though no one but his cellmate, Allitar, knew the source, that's what Mackie claims. They told everybody that the Martel woman was a mule that smuggled the stuff in." Bonhomme stopped and stared at Barber for a moment or two.

"Yeah?"

"You told us about this Martel woman independently of Mackie."

"So what?"

"What do you think it is with this blood stuff?"

"I couldn't say. They all talk about blue light and blood the way Christians talk about the cross and blood.

I don't know. Did you get any of this stuff that Mackie and Fargo made? Send it down to a chemist?"

A professor of mine used to tell me that a well-placed question is a scholar's best shield. You could use a question to imply an idea that you had but could not prove. Or you might want to seem open to a line of inquiry that you had no intention of following. Miles's question was designed to tell Bonhomme that he had no knowledge, no agenda, and a cop's objectivity about any hocus-pocus that might be presented as fact.

"Yeah, we did," Lonnie Briggs said when his boss went silent. "Milk and sugar, blood and baking soda. But there's something else too. Something they can't analyze. Maybe that's what the broad brought in."

"Like a culture or something?" Barber asked.

"Maybe," Bonhomme replied. "Maybe."

"Maybe if you let me talk to him, I could make some connection he might have with the people in Berkeley," Miles offered. He wanted to meet the blood addict. "Or maybe one of the others that helped him bleed Fargo."

"All dead but Mackie," Bonhomme said. "He's dying too. Wasting away. I don't think you'd get much out of him. Anyway, we couldn't get you into a penal facility. You don't have any certification. No. We'll let the lab worry about the blood. We want you to try and help us trace Bob Halston. We have some information about him and a communal cult in the Haight."

THIRTEEN

In the farthest eastern corner of the Mojave Desert is the abandoned Jacobi gold mine. In a subterranean room off the central shaft Winch Fargo sat on a cold stone, laughing. The thrumming in his body told him that it was the right time.

"She's comin'," he said to himself, sniggering. "She's almost here."

The rocks were cold, and there was only a candle for light and warmth. But that was more than his mother gave him. When she locked him in the closet, when he was a child, there was no candle or room to walk around. There was no promise of somebody coming to love you. No promises at all.

Fargo wore only a loincloth fashioned from a big man's T-shirt. He was skinny and his nose ran freely, but still he tittered merrily.

"She's comin' to get my blood, yes sir. She needs me and I need her. And it's almost time. Yeah, yeah."

The thick oaken door groaned as it was pulled open. Fargo leaped to his feet and lunged for the lamplight that appeared. The chain around his left ankle kept him from reaching the door.

Stanley Brussels, recently a carpenter from Indio, fell back as soon as he pulled the door open. He had seen Fargo's incredible strength before. When Fargo was free to walk among the others, aboveground, he had gone insane, breaking the necks of three of Claudia's chosen. Claudia Heart had told them that he could somehow sense the men who had most recently been her lovers, that he had to kill any man who had been with her.

"You should stay out of reach," Stanley told Claudia.

She was standing, shivering and naked, behind her lantern-bearing acolyte.

"Don't worry, Stan," she said. "Hurting me is the last thing on his mind."

Fargo giggled like an insane child.

Claudia Heart entered demurely, carrying a shallow wooden bowl in one hand and an ornamental dagger in the other. Stanley put down his kerosene lantern and pushed the heavy door shut.

"Hi, princess," Winch said, rising to his knees.

She put down her knife and bowl. "Hello, Winch."

"How's the sunlight up there?"

"I could have you tied up and brought up top if you want, honey. You know it hurts me to see you down here so sick and cold."

"No, no, don't . . . don't take me up there. I couldn't take it, smellin' your pussy on all them men." Fargo stood up suddenly and violently. "Goddammit!"

Claudia rose with him, but not in fear. She drew close to his chest and stroked its long, skinny muscles.

"Shhh, baby. Don't be like that. Come on, let's sit. Come on. Yeah, honey. Don't you think of anything but me right here with you."

They both sank to their knees in an embrace.

"I want you, princess."

"You know we'd both get sick if we did that, Winchy."

"I don't care. I want you. I need to have you."

Claudia stroked his skinny, heaving chest and purred, "You will be the father of my children. You will."

The moan that issued from Winch's lips would have broken the hardest of hearts. But Claudia simply disengaged from the embrace and lifted her dagger.

"Put out your arm, Winch."

"But it hurts," he said, looking as coy as pure evil can.

"Put out your arm now."

She etched the sixth cross on the underside of Winch's left forearm. Then she held the bowl below the wound while he massaged out the blood.

"Six times on one side and six on the other," Claudia chanted. "It's our own alchemy, father. It is the blood of our children."

When the bowl was a quarter filled, Claudia rose, saying, "It's time," and the door behind her groaned again.

When Winch looked up and saw that she was gone, he laughed loudly and for a long time.

* * *

While Claudia Heart and her Special Chosen had gone to the Jacobi mine, her remaining acolytes—men and women—stayed in the commune off Haight Street in San Francisco. They were waiting for Heart's return, but she had already decided that she was never going back. Her servants had served their purpose; they had already gotten all of her that she would give.

Bonhomme, Barber, and Briggs interviewed many of the depressed followers but found no answers. It wasn't that they didn't want to help. They would have done anything to find their lost love. They would have turned her in to the police just to see her again.

Now Claudia lived in the former gold mine's cafeteria with her dog, Max. Her Chosen, originally fifteen virile young men, and Bob Halston, lived in the bunkhouse.

In the cafeteria Claudia Heart cooked up the blood biscuits for her Chosen, only twelve after Winch Fargo's slaughtering rage.

Claudia spent chaste days gauging her ovulation.

He'd come in wearing a long trench coat, taken off one of his human victims, to cover the blood. He staggered up the stairs and shoved the bloody clothes in the bottom drawer of the dresser. Then he lay back, near death from the harsh shine of Eileen Martel's final moments.

"She was strong," Gray Man thought. "The strongest of them all."

Gray Man had killed all the hard ones. Now it was just the children, the strumpet, the other two women, and some things not human. One, probably a tree, a couple of hundred miles to the south, would wait for him. He'd track down the coyote and the dog last.

And then there was that other one. The one who had somehow gotten their light leaked into his veins. The one Gray Man had divined from Phyllis Yamauchi's dying blood. The one Gray Man had hoped would give up his masters. Chance. But he was nothing, hardly worth the notice of Death; except that he had brought the girl.

"Alacrity," Gray Man mouthed in his bed. "I've got a real treat for you, child."

He lay back in Horace LaFontaine's old room, weakened to the point of real death. Gray Man liked the feeling of being so close to expiration. He wanted to die. He was Death. He almost let the final shade come down on him. Almost let the light out of the box.

But there was the child, Alacrity. The passion he felt for her was beyond anything he'd known, beyond anything Horace LaFontaine had ever experienced. Her life beat so strongly, completely free from human frailty, and as powerful as the moment of death when the struggle is its greatest.

Gray Man wanted her.

But first he had to rest.

He closed his eyes and descended into the depths of death without dying. He sighed deeply and an instant later, when those eyes opened again, Gray Man was gone.

Horace looked around the room, feeling weaker than he could ever remember. Even when he had been dying of cancer, he could lift a finger, moan from the pain. But now all he could do was to look out and see the room he'd died in years before.

It's like I'm a ghost, he thought. *Like I ain't even here, but I never left.*

The sun went down while he lay there in darkness, remembering all the things that he'd done in his wasted life. Then he thought of all the things he hadn't done. He'd never learned a thing on purpose, never helped a soul without helping himself. He'd never even done a single thing because it was the right thing to do. Even Death, old Gray Man, did what he thought was right. It was right, Death thought, to kill. He risked his own life to achieve his goals.

A knock came on the door.

A voice, probably the girl, Joclyn Kyle. Horace didn't understand the words.

She must have gone, he thought, *probably thinks I'm out prowling around like he does.*

Horace tried to lift his arm but was still too weak. He could feel Gray Man's presence way down in his mind. He knew how drained the devil was and hoped that Gray Man would die. Even his own death would be worth that.

Horace thought of the man he killed in prison. Prescott Jones, a Brooklyn fence. Horace's best friend, Vinnie the Cat, had gotten the contract from his girlfriend. She told Vinnie and Vinnie told Horace that a man called Beldin Starr needed Prescott Jones silenced before his trial in June. Prescott was going to testify against Starr.

The deal was worth ten thousand dollars and the best lawyer in New York to get on Horace's appeal, which was botched by the prosecutor but also ill represented by an uncaring public defender.

Horace was on the good-conduct program. He had a lot of places he could go in the prison with his mail wagon. He was in for armed robbery and assault, but he'd never got in trouble once they locked him up.

Prescott had a job in the lower kitchen. He washed the big pots and prepped vegetables and fruits, anything that needed cutting. Usually he had a partner, Willie Josephson, but Horace found out one day that Willie was sick, or pretending to be, and Prescott was alone.

The lower kitchen was a big room with a lot of waist-high counters piled with pots and bags of raw fruits and vegetables. All Horace had to do was to put his canvas cart in a broom closet, squat down in the rear corner, and wait.

Horace, lying there in the dark of his sister's old house, remembered squatting down on that slimy wooden floor. He could almost smell the insecticide and detergent. The aluminum counters were cold against his arm and cheek. There was a round metal knife sharpener at his feet. The sharpening steel was maybe fifteen inches long and just thick enough. The perfect weapon to crack bone efficiently.

Horace's heart fluttered when he heard the door open. He reached for his weapon and held his breath. Somewhere in the back of his mind he railed against killing this man. But it was already too late. There was only one way out of that room.

He waited a few minutes and then rose. He couldn't see Prescott above the pots and pans, so he went down the aisle, looking. In the fourth aisle he saw the small white man. He was squatting down as Horace had done. His back was partly turned, but Horace could still see what he was up to.

Prescott was down on one knee masturbating, making little grunting sounds.

Horace knew what was going on. Prescott had a cellmate and was too shy to be heard enjoying a little jack-off. It was a pleasure to get alone and make some noise, maybe even call out the pinup's name.

"Oh, yeah!" Prescott moaned.

Then the knife-sharpening rod cracked his skull open.

Horace tried to stop thinking about it. He actually got out of prison and collected $2,500 from Beldin Starr. Starr said that he had used the rest for the lawyer.

Horace didn't argue about the money. He couldn't sleep for weeks without thinking about the sound when he cracked open Prescott's head. He just wanted to spend a few moments with a whore without thinking about Prescott's last orgasm.

Finally he just wanted his fix. A little brown powder, and he was all right. He was just fine.

"Mr. Redstar," Joclyn whispered. "Mr. Redstar."

Horace opened his eyes to see the dark young woman. It was morning, and Horace was happy that he'd awakened in his own body.

"Mr. Redstar, are you okay?"

"My name ain't Redstar," the dead man uttered. "Not Redstar. LaFontaine. Horace LaFontaine."

"That was old Miss Elza's maiden name," Joclyn said. "LaFontaine."

"You knew Elza?"

"She used to own this house and she rented out rooms. She rented to my uncle, but she was already real sad because her husband died and her brother disappeared. My uncle took care'a her and when she died, she left the buildin' to him." Joclyn reached out to touch Horace's tear. "Were you related to her? You know Miss Brown across the street says that you look a lot like Miss Elza's brother, but she knows that that couldn't be because he had bad cancer and even though he disappeared, he'd have to be dead by now."

"I am her brother, Joclyn. But I'm somebody else too."

"Huh?"

Horace felt strong in the morning. But the task of telling his story seemed impossible.

"Do you believe in the devil, Joclyn?"

"I don't know. I guess I do. I mean there sure is a lotta evil, and I cain't see where it makes no real sense."

"The devil is in me, girl. He's in me." Horace lifted his right hand and tapped the fingertips against his chest. "Right in here."

"Uh-huh." She nodded but still looked unconvinced.

"Did you hear about what happened in the park in Berkeley yesterday?" he asked.

"You mean the killin's?"

"Look in the bottom drawer, honey," Horace said. "Look in the bottom drawer down there."

Joclyn went to the dresser and pulled open the bottom drawer. She took out the bundle of clothes. Horace turned his head to watch as she unfurled the trench coat. She gasped when she saw the bloody jacket and pants, the shoes covered in dried gore. Then she looked up at him and slowly rerolled the parcel. She stood up with the armful and left without saying another word.

"Mr. Redstar. Are you awake?"

It was night again and Horace felt almost strong enough to sit up. Joclyn was sitting on the bed beside him.

"How are you?" she asked.

All day he had been dozing, coming awake at every sound, expecting the police to come. Horace thought that it would hurt Gray Man's pride so much to be jailed that he might die, or kill himself, from the humiliation. But they hadn't come.

"What happened?" he asked the girl.

"I burnt your clothes in the backyard. You don't have to worry."

"You what? Why?"

"You were just sick, Mr. Redstar. That's all. But now you're okay. I'll take care of you. You don't have to be scared. They said on the radio about them killin's, but nobody knows what really happened. All I know is that you couldn't have done it. You ain't even strong enough to pick me up. You just got confused, Mr. Redstar. You just thought you did bad 'cause you was there an' saw all that blood." She had taken his hand in both of hers. She had dry hands, working hands.

Horace forgot about Gray Man for the first time since his resurrection. He was thinking that no one had ever loved him outside his mother and sister. He felt a tear run down to his nose. Joclyn, smiling, brushed it off with her hard fingertip.

"I ain't gonna give you up, Mr. Redstar."

* * *

At that moment Gray Man came awake deep down in Horace's mind. He rose quickly to the surface, pushing Horace aside.

"Mr. Redstar?" Joclyn asked, seeing a change in his face.

Gray Man sat up and reached out for the girl.

Watch your little toy die, Horace, Gray Man thought. He put his hand on Joclyn's neck and smiled.

No.

Gray Man's smile turned to puzzlement.

"What's wrong, Mr. Redstar?" Joclyn asked.

No.

Gray Man tried to increase his pressure but could not. Horace tried to make him put down his hand, but that too failed.

"Are you okay?" Joclyn wanted to know.

Let her be, devil, Horace cried.

Do you think you can order me?

I think that Joclyn's a friend and I'll fuck you up if you thinkin' 'bout messin' around. Horace felt his mind inhabiting the same body as Gray Man. He knew that the devil was still weak, still recovering from his fight with the old lady. He was risking his own life by trying to kill the girl.

"I have to go," Gray Man said to Joclyn.

"But you're sick."

"I have to go away for a while. I have to go but I'll come back soon." He took his hand away from her throat and smiled. "Go on now, let me get dressed."

When she had gone Horace let out a shout of life in the chambers of the death master's mind.

FOURTEEN

Nesta Vine returned to the Bay Area four days after the massacre in the park. She went back to her grandparents' house and was met at the front door by a familiar-looking black woman, somewhere in her forties.

"Yes?" the small woman asked of the girl.

"Who are you?" Nesta asked.

"Renee Ferris."

Renee Ferris, of course, Nesta thought. Renee was from a group of her mother's cousins who lived down near La Jolla. She hadn't seen Renee since she was a child. And Renee would never recognize her, because Nesta had become the image in the mirror. Taller and jet black with bigger feet. Her hair had taken on a coarse straw color and her eyes were bright amber. Her face, which was once round and sad, had lengthened and thinned.

"What are you doing here?" Nesta asked Renee.

"Say what, child? Who are you?"

"Oh," Nesta said, remembering herself. "I'm sorry, ma'am. My name is Ebony, Nesta's friend from Back East."

"Oh. Oh." Mrs. Ferris looked down the stairs and then up the street. "Is Nesta here?"

"No, ma'am. The last I heard from her she was in Korea. But she said that if I ever came to Oakland, I should look up her grandma and granddad," the tall woman said.

Renee Ferris looked unaware into her cousin's face and said, "My auntie, Mrs. Charm, died six months ago."

Nesta couldn't keep the tears out of her eyes. "What happened?"

"She was just old, child," the cousin said. She put out her hand and touched the dark-skinned girl's forearm. "Why don't you come in for a while and rest."

The house seemed smaller but smelled the same. Nesta walked in past the staircase, into the living room, where her grandfather sat in his pitted chrome wheelchair. He was looking out the window at the hummingbird feeder on the back porch.

Nesta saw the pair of green hummingbirds taking turns at the honey water spout. She knew their approximate weight in milligrams and the rate of speed at which their wings fluttered. But all she cared about was her grandfather's eyes on them.

"Uncle," Renee Ferris said. "This here is one of Nesta's friends—Ebony."

Lythe Charm had been an old man as far back as Nesta could remember. But his face was always like a child's, inquisitive and ready to laugh. Now even his eyes were old and sad. Nesta thought of a senior citizens home she worked in for a few weeks outside of Boulder, Colorado. She worked there while attending a series of lectures on Shakespeare that were being given at the university.

The lectures were nothing compared to watching, hearing, and smelling the ever encroaching specter of death among the aged.

She'd sat one evening with an old woman dying from collapsing veins. Nesta was telling her a story that she'd heard in Selma, Alabama. A story about an Indian down there who, centuries before, had first brought snakes to the territory. It was a wild tale of stealth and intrigue, but in the end everything worked out all right. The snake found his hole near a cultivated field, and all the deer and rabbits steered clear from then on.

Somewhere during the story the old woman died. Nesta felt it like a sudden vacuum in the room. Somewhere things felt empty, and Nesta realized how much space the human soul inhabited.

She could feel the sadness in her grandfather's soul.

"Hello, Mr. Charm," Nesta said.

"You know my baby?" he asked, looking hard at the tall and beautiful woman.

"We traveled together around a whole lot of the world," Nesta said. "I got to know her pretty well."

"Where is she now?"

"In Korea," Nesta lied, and then sat down on the corner of the sofa nearest her grandfather. "She told me a lot about you."

"Oh?" The old man smiled. "What she say?"

"She talked about how much you liked blackberry tea—"

"I sure do."

"—and about how when you were younger you drove two hundred and forty-six cattle across Texas on horseback and how you didn't lose one of them."

"She remembered that, huh?"

"She told me all about you, Mr. Charm. She told me a story to tell you when we saw each other. A story that she heard in Alabama."

Lythe Charm smiled with broad anticipation. "And what story was that?"

"Excuse me, Ebony," Renee said.

"Yes, ma'am."

"Is that little bag your suitcase?" She was referring to the beat-up leather bag, the size of a school satchel, that the young woman carried with her.

"Yes, ma'am. I just got into town. I was going to find a Y to stay at, but I wanted to drop by here and say hello first."

"Well, you take that bag upstairs and put it in the third room on the right. That's Nesta's room. You put it down up there and clean up, and I'll make us all some supper."

"But I wanna hear Nesta's story she sent me," Lythe Charm complained.

"Don't worry, Uncle," said the dutiful and dour Renee Ferris. "Ebony'll spend the night and tell us everything about your girl."

"Was it a planet?" Lythe Charm asked the young woman who called herself Ebony.

"No, no, that's not what they called it," she answered. "It was more like a giant stone that was once alive but then became the home to its own children."

"Like a shell," he said.

"Yes."

The black woman's smile was brilliant and white. She had been telling Lythe Charm a story that she said she'd learned from his granddaughter who had, in turn, learned it from a little-known tribe of American Indians called the ArShoni. The story Nesta was telling was a fragment of the creation story that she had inherited from the blue light that infused her with knowledge and power.

". . . for more years than man can count," Nesta continued, "bright forms of life that were like animals and flowers and insects and fish all in one grew out of the ground and bathed in the light of a rainbow-colored star—"

"Were they on a planet then or was that on the big rock?" Lythe Charm asked, hungry for the words of his long-gone granddaughter.

"That was on the planet, before things changed," Nesta said. "The life-forms grew and intermingled and multiplied and changed. Because on this planet the fish and beasts could speak and mate; all life there was equal and respectful."

"What did they eat?" the old man asked slyly. "If they all respected each other, even the flowers and the trees, then what could they eat?"

"They lived on the light from the rainbow star," the young woman said. "The radiant energy of the star fed them. And for eons they grew and multiplied and changed. After many millions of years they began to fly and grow higher and higher until some had completely left the planet and flew closer and closer to the sun, looking for more and more energy because the great joy among these far-off folk was to bathe in the light of the sun and to grow.

"These great flying beasts had within them chambers of quartz that stored light in patterns that held all of the wisdom of all the life-forms that were once planet-bound. Then they began to multiply by placing the seed of their physical being on lifeless chunks of matter in space and then bathing those seeds with the light from within their deep quartz caverns."

"And why was that?" Lythe Charm asked. He was feeling younger and stronger just talking to the strange-looking woman. There was something about her that was familiar, but Lythe couldn't seem to put his finger on it. "Why would they have to shine light on their own seeds if there was a sun still shining?"

"Because their light contained memories and instructions on how to grow. The seeds had the power of life, but in the light was their souls' purpose."

"Kinda like Sunday school in a flashlight, huh?" Lythe asked.

"A little bit. But as time went by, the space creatures got larger and larger. Soon they were as big as moons and there were millions of them. They absorbed all the energy of the star and then floated out toward new stars. By then they were as large as planets. Their hard external shells covered mighty engines that they had for both their heart and brain. Millions of years passed, and the planets of life spread out across the universe. And as they moved, now and again, they would deposit their seed on likely-looking planets. Emanating—"

"Say what?" Lythe Charm, whose eyes were looking younger, asked.

"Emanating. That means 'coming out from.'"

"Oh, yeah. Uh-huh, I see."

"Anyway, emanating from the seed was a soft music, and if another of their celestial brethren would pass by, they would hear it and shine their light where the seed had fallen. That way, information and life could pass between the stars and new life could evolve."

"But what if the seed was dropped, but nobody heard the signal and no light came?" Lythe asked. She could tell that he didn't believe a word of the story but loved hearing it. It was just as if Nesta had never gone, as if she were still there telling him about what she had learned in her late-night reading.

"We are the seeds, Mr. Charm," Nesta/Ebony said. "Just seeds waiting for water in order to grow."

"You mean, we aren't the top ones in the animal world?" the old man asked. He seemed a little sad.

"No, Gramp," she said softly. "We're just empty husks, like, waiting for the light of life to enter us."

"You are my little girl, aren't you?"

"I love you," she said. Then she bit hard into her bottom lip and kissed her mother's father in a way that he had not been kissed in many years.

FIFTEEN

The view from the mountaintop was all that Gerin Reed ever wanted. Whenever his eyes chanced upon the deep blue Pacific or down the steep valley of pines, he stopped whatever he was doing, forgot where he was going to, and stared—sometimes for up to an hour. Many things distracted him. His children making up games based on how fast they could run or how well they could remember, the bottle of urine rotting and congealing on the back porch, the static between stations on the radio.

Karen had gone down with the children to Jason and Bridgette Sandler's place. The Sandlers were their closest neighbors, two miles distant. Jason worked for a lumber company, and Bridgette took care of their kids. Gerin had seen his wife and Jason in the woods together. He knew that he couldn't satisfy her needs and didn't mind too much. All he wanted from her was her company and her laughter with the children. Sometimes he would wake up in the night and watch her sleeping. He once counted 3,700 of her breaths.

Aspiration, he thought while she slept, maybe dreaming of her lover down the hill.

Gerin had a slender paperback book in his pocket, *The Prince* by Machiavelli. The ideas didn't mean much to him, but the words being read out loud made a kind of music that Gerin liked to set free in the forest.

He sang out in the woods, hoping for an echo. He wanted to hear something. Something that vibrated in his own heart and mind. He felt like a child in those woods, sure that there were other children laughing and playing there too. But they were hiding from him. It was a cruel game of hide-and-seek but Gerin never lost his hopeful heart. He knew that they would come out for him someday.

He could hear a car coming up the dirt road. Gerin worried that it might be Bridgette. Sometimes she came up to seduce him while Jason and Karen took care of the kids. She liked to go skinny-dipping, pretended that it was innocent enough, that she and her husband did it with people all the time. Gerin did what she asked but was continually distracted by cloud patterns wrapped in the ripples of the pond. He liked to look at Bridgette's round belly and swirling pubic hair, but he was never aroused.

Karen never excited him either. It wasn't that he didn't want sex. He sometimes woke up having powerful orgasms, dreaming of a woman who, while they were in the act of lovemaking, would talk to him about her shopping that day, the smell of tomato leaves and the thunk of ripe melons.

The car came into sight. It wasn't the Sandlers' Jeep. It was a tan-colored Chevrolet. Three men in hats sat inside.

The sedan came right up to the front door of the log cabin that Gerin had bought with his life savings.

"Warden Reed?" the gaunt pipe smoker asked.

"Yes?"

The driver was shorter than the pipe smoker but looked bigger owing to his swollen muscles and big gut. The third man wore a wide-brimmed hat that hung down a little like a Mexican sombrero. But Gerin could still make out the red scars on the stranger's face.

"I'm Inspector Bonhomme from the State Investigations Bureau, sir," the pipe smoker said. "This is Sergeant Lonnie Briggs and Miles Barber, uh, our assistant."

"Hello."

"Your wife has already agreed to come with us, Warden Reed. She claims that you've been keeping her and the children against their will up here. The Sandlers contacted us for her."

"I'm under arrest?"

"Yes, sir."

"For what? I haven't done anything."

"That's not what your wife says."

"She could have left. I didn't stop her from going down to Jason and Bridgette's. She could have just kept on going."

Lonnie Briggs shrugged his big shoulders even though the plea had been addressed to his superior.

"She says that you used psychological cruelty to keep her and the kids up here," Bonhomme said. "She said that she was afraid of you coming after her and killing the whole family."

Gerin Reed looked at the bluish smoke issuing from the agent's lips. He wondered whether it was true. Was he crazy? Was he ready to kill Karen and little Jason and Anne-Marie? Was he insane?

He remembered Karen complaining that the money was running out. She'd asked him how they would survive if there was no money.

Was that crazy?

Gerry had thought that he could ask Jason about a job in the logging camp down in the valley. He'd been a cook in the Pacific Theater. He'd killed men in the war. He'd killed children too. But all that was before he'd been wounded and been made a cook.

At that moment Gerin saw Miles Barber assessing him. There was neither sympathy nor accusation in that one hard eye, simply the desire to know.

"Warden Reed?" Christian Bonhomme asked.

"Yes?"

"I'm going to have to ask you to come with us."

"Are you taking me to prison?"

"No, sir, I'm not. But we need to have some questions answered and you're a hard man to find."

From all accounts Claudia prepared the sweet oils herself. She used store-bought extracts of cinnamon, almonds, rose petals, and vanilla to scent them. The oils, which came from cottonseed mainly, were heated to body temperature and placed around the room in wooden bowls. The walls and ceiling were draped with deep red cloths. Every corner housed a cluster of a hundred or more lit candles. In the center of the room was a pile of mattresses decorated with silken blankets, sheets, and pillows. Naked, Claudia Heart reclined in the middle of the mattresses and silk. Max the dog stalked the perimeter while her Special Chosen surrounded her. They were also naked and, to a man, erect. Each one had greased himself with the warm oils and now waited, listening to a song that had no words or sound. The music emanating from deep within their love goddess.

She leered with anticipation at their lust.

"Sing to me," she said loudly. "Sing to me."

Lonnie Briggs got that on his tape recorder. He and Miles Barber, backed up by eighteen state troopers, watched through an obscure window.

"We gotta wait until they do somethin' illegal," Briggs whispered to Barber. "Otherwise, the goddamned lawyers'll get the arrest and everything we seize thrown outta court."

But Barber thought that it was the spectacle of all that sexuality that had arrested the SIB sergeant's attention. After all, the SIB usually went after less flamboyant suspects. The rare case of police corruption, construction scams against the state of California, or some bureaucrat using state resources illegally—these were Briggs and Bonhomme's staples.

Barber also felt something from the naked woman. Whatever it was felt raspy and unpleasant on his sinuses and eye.

It was Barber who brought them to this abandoned mine. He used her husband's name to do a title search on desert properties. William Zimmerman had put a down payment of $175,000 on the played-out Jacobi mine in the eastern Mojave Desert.

Claudia Heart's Special Chosen let out groans and guttural pleas. They begged and demanded. They stroked themselves and posed.

At first she called forth a small Asian man who sported an exceptionally wide erection. She made him lie beneath her and rode him while Max bit hard into the flesh of his thighs and arms.

The next lover was a tall and virile Mexican man. She was happy simply to swallow his sperm.

The next three men approached at the same time.

Max's eyes flashed as he moved among the Chosen and howled. Claudia wailed with him.

Lonnie Briggs was breathing heavily. The uniformed state troopers, who couldn't see what was happening in the room, were beginning to get restless. Miles Barber was wondering why he didn't seem to care about sex or even if there was a crime being committed.

Then a man skulked into the room. He was different from the rest, inasmuch as he was fully dressed. But Barber could see that he too was greatly aroused by the woman. He avoided Claudia's line of vision. Barber knew somehow that he was breaking Heart's command, that he just needed to see her.

"Hey, Briggs," Barber said.

"What?" the state agent answered in a husky voice.

"Ain't that one in the pants Halston?"

Lonnie Briggs broke into the room with his uniformed state police force. The prone woman, barely larger than a girl, looked up and shouted, "Stop them!"

Briggs and his men found themselves set upon by twelve naked men. W...

"I was talking to the police, Inspector," Claudia Heart-Zimmerman said to Christian Bonhomme.

He had been feeling a little light-headed ever since he'd entered the interrogation room with the suspect.

"You ordered your followers to attack Sergeant Briggs and his men, Mrs. Zimmerman," the inspector replied.

"No. No, not at all." The love goddess smiled. "I was yelling for your sergeant to stop them from raping me. They'd been raping me for weeks, you know."

Claudia peered intently at Bonhomme, and he felt a vague pang of fear.

"Yes," he said. "That's what you say. But Mr. Briggs calls it murder. He says that you ordered your men to fight to the death. The police officers were forced to respond with deadly force. . . ."

It had been in papers all around the country. STATE POLICE FORCE ASSAILED BY NAKED ZOMBIES OF LOVE. Four of Claudia's acolytes had been shot to death. Five others fought so hard against arrest that they were killed, or died later, from wounds they received while being subdued. The survivors were now locked up in a medical facility in San Francisco, suffering from some disease or withdrawal and committed to their escape and reunion with their queen. Claudia Heart and Robert Halston were arraigned in absentia because of the wounds they sustained.

Halston was subdued in the cafeteria. Claudia had run out into the desert with a dog. When the police approached her she fell, hitting her head on a stone.

She was captured, but the dog, after biting three policemen—who now were hospitalized with undiagnosed ailments—had been too fast for the law.

"I am innocent, Inspector," Claudia said with a shrug, staring intently at the wavering Bonhomme. He noticed the sweat on her forehead.

"You are not, Mrs. Zimmerman."

"Call me Claudia Heart," she commanded.

"I don't know what power it is that you think you have over men, Mrs. Zimmerman. But I am going to have you up on charges of assault and murder." Inspector Bonhomme turned quickly and went through the interrogation-room door. He knew that if the woman had stood up and approached him, he would have gladly let her go.

"Should I have her transferred to a holding cell, Christian?" Lonnie Briggs asked.

"No. No. Leave her right where she is. Open that door only to bring her meals. Don't talk to her. You hear me, Briggs? Don't say a word to her."

"Yes, sir."

After snapping his ankle chain, Winch Fargo slammed his hard and skinny body against the ironbound door in the darkness. No one heard the dull thudding deep under the desert floor.

SIXTEEN

Gray Man walked through the towering forest, unconcerned with the beauty of the redwoods, unconvinced by their grandeur. His leather dress shoes were broken, his black jacket torn. Gray Man's clothes were spattered with mud, but he didn't care. He was waging a war in his mind with Horace LaFontaine, the first soul he'd ever met that he could not easily destroy.

He'd built Horace out of leftover memories, scraps of a wasted life in the shell of a body that had died. The persona, a loose association of thoughts, had been useful when Gray Man wanted to understand what humanity demanded of its citizens. Humanity—like rutting shrimp in a shipwreck at the bottom of the sea. Humanity—globs of self-referential fats and amino acids that couldn't know the source of existence even if they were spoon-fed that knowledge in the lap of their own pitiful God.

Horace was a perfect example of this primitive lifeform. He'd absorbed the inaccurate language, shared the mindless lusts. He was seen as nothing even among the useless, and still his will had stymied the great Gray Man.

Grey Redstar, the Gray Man, the reaper of lost light. The one creature destined to cleanse the soul of its body. The harbinger of a newer and higher form of being.

But as powerful as he was, he could not stop the disease within him, this vague alliance of memories attached around the name Horace LaFontaine.

He'd crucified Horace, stripped his flesh down to the bone and crushed out the cells that remembered him. But every time, Horace had risen out of the depths of Death's mind—whole again, though broken and afraid.

"Please let me alone," Horace cried.

"Then die," Gray Man answered. "Let your life stop and leave me to accomplish my own ends."

"I cain't die," Horace cried. "I mean, I keep comin' back. I don't know why. I'm sorry. But if you leave Joclyn be, I won't have to fight wit' you no more."

"You would threaten me?"

"I cain't he'p it, man. I cain't. It didn't bother me when you kilt all them other ones. But I like Joclyn, and whenever she's around, I just come up in your mind, like. An' even if you wanna do sumpin' bad to 'er, I still like 'er an' don't want that."

Gray Man screamed in his mind, and for a moment Horace faded out of existence. But he was still there, there in the fabric of cells and light. Horace LaFontaine was like a mutating virus that had lodged itself deep in the cells of the god of death. The only cure would be to divest himself of the body and release the beautiful deep blue light into the heavens.

*   *   *

In the yawning space between earth and sky and the bright sun, she had stood for 734,906 mornings. From a sapling bole to branchling finger. From a straining prayer for light to the crashing death of her mother. And then that straight run upward and outward. Not even the black bear's raking claws could stop her. Not gnawing worms or lightning bolts or shifting soft earth could hinder her stretching, yearning ascent. . . .

. . . and then the different light, knifing down on her needles and sinking below the bark. Not for a year did she even feel it. Not for three did she know that she knew anything, and then she knew more than even the longevity of trees can witness. The tickling wings of butterflies and the nuzzling snouts of deer and lion and rat. She felt and knew the scrabbling claws of birds in her branches and among her leaves.

And then there was the sun shining. The pulsing story of creation humming again and again through her inner timber. So beautiful that it called a song from her depths, a song that flowed out through the atmosphere and deep into the soil and stone of the earth. She was calling to awareness the very atoms that composed the world. She purred and rumbled out the song of awakening that only a patient tree could know. She called and counted butterflies; she bathed in morning fogs and knew her sisters even though they were still unconscious as she was on the day before the light.

She reached down farther in the earth and stretched her leaves upward. Her seed fell barren to the ground, and she knew that she was merely a beacon. I say that she knew, but it was not knowledge as we hold it. The green cell is the engine in plants where blue light is purely mind. And blue light is knowledge, the truth before it is warped by perception of eyes and solitary minds. Plants, and some simple animals, are best suited for holding and sharing the light.

The unity of living flesh and divine light is still more a dream than reality. The light strains to reach the flesh that stretches toward it. But they are not yet one, not even for that woody giant. To reproduce herself, then, she could only sing, waiting for a mate to come. Waiting for the moment when she reached maturity.

He approached the ancient tree with no more concern than a woodsman.

"What are you doing here?" Esther the park ranger asked Gray Man. She'd just come from around the tree and was startled by the appearance of the hobo.

Ever since the day she came awake before the great tree, covered in butterflies, with the memory of those bright blue eyes in hers, she came to visit the tree at least once a week. She came to listen to a nearly subliminal thrumming and to watch the wild animals that came in almost religious obeisance. *There is magic near that tree,* that's what the ranger thought.

Gray Man ignored her question, craning his neck to see the full height of the towering column.

"Excuse me, sir, but I'm doing research in this area and it's off-limits to visitors. If you want to see trees, you have to stay on the paths as they are marked."

Gray Man raised his hands and laughed. Sparks leaped from his fingertips.

"What are you doing?" Esther asked in a trembling voice.

Somewhere inside the tree the trembling was echoed, though not in fear.

Gray Man's laugh died at the challenge, and suddenly Horace came back to life. He could see what Gray Man was doing, but he had no power to stop him. He had no desire to save a dumb tree.

"Stop it!" cried Esther O'Halloran as she ran at Gray Man with a dead branch for her club.

The electrical shock was enough to shatter the branch and throw the woman down a small incline into a stream. Gray Man gazed upon her with anger that he'd not felt toward a human before. But he was upset, upset by Horace LaFontaine.

Horace looked at the woman and thought, *Fool, why you wanna go messin' 'round and gettin' yourself kilt like that anyway? I don't wanna see you die, but I ain't gettin' skinned alive again just 'cause you a fool.*

The timber of the redwood groaned, and Gray Man knew that this frail being meant something to the tree. He smiled at the possibility of inflicting pain before death and turned toward the park ranger. Her eyes were rolled up into her head, but still she struggled to rise.

Horace watched with fatalistic fascination. He was less than a ghost, no more than a common cold to his demonic host, and he, in his powerlessness, didn't feel much for the doomed woman. But then the groaning of the tree became louder and more strident. The ground began to tremble. Esther O'Halloran, who had risen upon unsteady feet, danced away while trying to keep upright.

Gray Man and Horace turned to the tree just as it exploded in a shower of splinters and bright blue light.

Horace, fully aware, felt the brunt of the explosion and then ran down a dark asphalt alley under a heavy downpour. Blue streetlights were placed at uneven intervals down the lane. He ran into walls and trash cans and old rotted fences. He fell and stumbled back to his feet, ran and collapsed, all the while followed by the silent specter of pain. It came after him like a flood of thick blood. He ran and fell tumbling right out of Gray Man's life.

But Gray Man didn't see Horace go. He was running himself. The splinters and timbers didn't hurt him, but the light of the life of that tree went down to his marrow. He caught fire from the vitality and sanctity of the tree. And all he could do was run with the curse of the tree etched deeply on his soul.

Beneath the desert, at the same moment of the explosion, Winch Fargo's door broke open. Wild-eyed and impossibly skinny, the black-toothed felon staggered up the mine shaft into the clear desert twilight. As he climbed to the surface, the sun disappeared and the stars slowly winked to life. Thousand and thousands of stars. Each one, he knew, like a flower for the honey bee gods who left him here long before there was time or love.

Winch Fargo sought her in the air. There was a trace and a direction—and many fewer steps ahead than there were years behind.

SEVENTEEN

After two weeks Christian Bonhomme decided it was time for him to enter Claudia Zimmerman's cell again. This was no light decision. He had put it off until the day before the inquest. The only men that had been allowed in to see her were Miles Barber and Felton Meyers, the ex-detective and the court-appointed attorney. And Felton was thoroughly searched before he was allowed into her cell. She fired Felton after their first meeting, however, and spent the next two weeks alone.

Bonhomme was not a religious man, nor did he believe in magic or voodoo or any other such nonsense. But he had seen the depraved survivors of the zombie sex camp. One man, a carpenter named Stanley Brussels, stayed on his knees begging from the time he awoke to the moment he collapsed into sleep. He had to be force-fed through a rubber tube the hospital attendants shoved down his nostril once a day. Others mutilated themselves or became so violent that they were restrained twenty-four hours a day.

Each man wanted only one thing: to see Claudia Zimmerman, to be put in a cell near hers. They begged and cajoled and threatened.

"If that's what you call love," he'd said to Briggs and Barber the day he was to go into Claudia's cell, "then you can have it."

He wasn't the same man that Barber remembered. Outside the detention room Bonhomme stalled, clenching his pipe between visible teeth.

"Did you ask the judge for an extension?" Bonhomme asked Lonnie Briggs.

"You know I did, Chris. They said that they have to see her for the indictment as soon as she's sitting up straight. I don't know what'll happen if they find out that she hasn't seen a doctor."

"Don't worry, I'll take care of it," Bonhomme said through his pipe. "Is Clemmens out there?"

"I told you he was."

"Then go get him, I guess."

When the sergeant went through the door Bonhomme was left with Barber and a guard in a special detention wing of the Sacramento jail.

"She scares you, huh?" Barber asked softly.

"Yeah. Yeah, I never felt anything like it. Nothing. It was like pure sex. I went home and my wife, she . . . well, she went to visit her mother after two nights with me. I was all over her. I couldn't help myself."

"That doesn't make any sense."

"I know it doesn't. I'm no sex maniac."

"No, not that," Barber said. "Everybody we interviewed about Zimmerman said that her effect was to make them love only her. No one in the Haight slept with anyone but her—if she allowed it."

"What are you talking about?" Bonhomme was angry. "Some kinda hocus-pocus? I don't think the woman has some kinda power. What happened to me was what you call *suggestion*. All this talk about sex and perverts brought on a sorta temporary anxiety, that's all."

"Then why're you scared to go in there?"

"I'm not scared. I'm just waiting for Briggs to bring Clemmens."

Miles allowed the lie to go unchallenged. He knew that the small woman had power. He felt her presence, but not like other men did. There was something obscene in his experience. He didn't hear a silent siren's call. The dark place in his heart responded with distaste and anger.

After a few minutes Lonnie Briggs returned with George Clemmens. Clemmens was tall and heavy, Barber once told me, with loose flesh that fit him like a suit a size or two too large. He also had big shiny eyes and nearly no chin.

"Okay, Lonnie," Bonhomme said. "Let's stop acting like kids and get this thing over with."

Lonnie Briggs pulled open the door with a solemnity that made him blush. George Clemmens, who was the state prosecutor, looked from one agent to the other with an uncomprehending frown on his face.

Barber was introduced as a special consultant on the case.

"What's wrong with you guys?" George asked. "You act like you got an *armed and dangerous* in there. I mean, you know this is late for me to be talking to someone we're about to indict."

"You trust me, George?" Bonhomme asked.

"Yeah, yeah, I guess."

"Then hold on to your hat and don't touch her, no matter what you do."

Claudia was sitting on a three-legged wooden stool, her legs crossed and lips red. Her skirt was hiked up to her thigh, and she was smiling.

There was the look of hunger in her small eyes.

Miles found that his distaste had grown nearly into hatred.

"Claudia Zimmerman," the prosecutor said.

"Claudia Heart," she purred.

"You know you should have a lawyer present. These are serious charges you are facing."

Bonhomme and Briggs watched the prosecutor closely.

"I don't need a lawyer, Mr. Clemmens," Claudia replied. "And if there are too many people in the room at the same time, I sometimes lose my concentration."

A dog howled outside. Claudia looked up with the light of recognition in her face and smiled.

"All you have to concentrate on are the concerns at hand, Mrs. Zimmerman," George Clemmens said. "We would like to know how you plead to the charges, if charges are brought, and it would be better if you had a lawyer on hand to do that for you."

"I don't plead to anyone." The love goddess tossed her limp brown hair back out of her face.

"Has your attorney explained to you the charges?"

"What color are your eyes, Detective Bonhomme?" Claudia asked.

Later the inspector told Barber and Briggs that he was surprised not by the question but by the simple fact of how plain she was. "Just a plain-looking woman in her thirties. Not ugly exactly, but homely, unattractive, you know?"

"Answer the questions, honey," Bonhomme said with the harshest tone he could muster. "You're going to be indicted tomorrow for second-degree manslaughter and inciting to riot."

His manner struck Claudia as if it were a bucket full of ice. She got up from the stool and went into her little water closet, half closing the door behind her. The men could hear the retching grunts and then the toilet flushing. A few minutes later Claudia came out of the stall pale and uncertain.

"Has she been seen by a doctor?" George Clemmens asked the agents.

Neither Briggs nor Bonhomme would answer.

"Have you seen a doctor?" the prosecutor asked Claudia.

Claudia went from nausea to a bright smile in an instant.

"Of course," she said, not to Clemmens's question. "I'm pregnant, and all the power has gone to nourish them."

"Excuse me?"

"Leave me," Claudia commanded, a goddess again. "I must rest."

"Mrs. Zimmerman—" George Clemmens said.

"Leave me."

"Come on, George." Bonhomme patted the lawyer on the back. He was smiling. "Let's leave her to boil in her own soup."

The indictment was easy to obtain. Claudia Heart refused to recognize the court or to speak to the attorney that the court appointed. She didn't mind the jail cell or the green-and-white striped dress she was given to wear.

George Clemmens asked for an extension to prepare his case and was granted six weeks. In the meantime, Bonhomme and Briggs plotted with ex-Detective Barber to find the whereabouts of Winch Fargo.

Gerin Reed was already under arrest and being held on various charges, including the unlawful detainment of his wife. Robert Halston also awaited trial. Bonhomme had Mackie Allitar transferred from the prison infirmary, where he was dying, to a secured room in the city hospital in Sacramento.

"It was all me by then, Chance," Miles Barber said. "That bitch had scared all of them. The men that had been her studs were dying. All of Allitar's friends were already dead. All they had left was Allitar, Reed, Heart, and Halston. They had them together for a trial that would never be, but I knew that Gray Man would be there if Heart was. I knew it."

He sounded like a good cop on the trail of an exceptionally hard-to-catch crook. But the sweat on his face and the glaze on his one eye told me that all he'd really felt was fear. He was compelled to hunt. Compelled by his previous life. He couldn't help himself, and so he created a lie and a false faith. He had convinced himself that he could conquer Death—but somewhere, just below the surface, he knew that it was all a lie.

Miles Barber fooled himself that he was the puppet master, that the forces brought together were working for him. But much more than he knew was to unfold.

Nesta Vine had read an article in the *San Francisco Chronicle* about Claudia Zimmerman and her arrest. Even though the journalist, or her editor, played down the power that Zimmerman's followers claimed she had, Nesta felt something from the article, from the words that were missing. She went to visit the lovelorn remnants of the commune in the Haight. The empty structure, which was once a small appliance store, was filthier than the worst crash pad or drug den. The members at first glance seemed as if they might be related. But it was the glassy eyes and emaciated bodies that made them kindred. They lived on corn bread mix and beer. Not one of them ever ventured farther than the supermarket. They didn't bathe or groom, speak or dream. All they did was huddle together in threes and fours in the low, dark room.

"What's wrong with you?" Nesta asked a small cluster of forlorn lovers.

"Just sad," one of them said.

"We'll be better soon," another added.

One doe-eyed and acned acolyte looked up and said, "She said that we had to wait until she came back. But that means she's comin' back, don't it?"

On the upper floor Nesta found three bodies that had been piled in a closet. It was the closest thing to a burial that the love cult members could muster.

"They're dead." The woman's voice startled Nesta.

"Who are you?" Nesta asked, addressing the darkness of the larger room.

A young woman came from the gloom. Her large eyes and slender form marked her as a member of the cult, but she seemed to have more life to her.

"I'm Trini." The girl spoke clearly but slowly.

"What happened here?"

"Without Miss Heart they don't wanna live," Trini said. "She was all they wanted and now she's gone."

"Why didn't the reporter write about this? Why haven't the police come?" Nesta found her humanity pulsing in the wake of this destructive blue light.

"They been gettin' worse. At first they was just sad, but now it got worse and they started to die." Trini was a white girl. Nesta classified her accent as coming from Tennessee.

"Why aren't you sad, Trini?"

"I am. Just not so sad. She balled all'a them. But she said that I was her special girl 'cause'a how it was when I was a girl back home. I crashed here with my boyfriend, Lloyd. He's in there." Trini looked at the six bare feet sticking out of the closet door. "But she liked me. Every morning she'd give me a French kiss and I'd follah her just like a dog. And when she left I was sad, but not like everybody else."

Nesta was sure then that the woman who'd abandoned the commune was her sister in blue light. The notion disgusted her.

"Come with me, Trini."

"Where to?"

"I'm not sure yet."

"Okay."

Miles Barber thought that he was pulling the strings when he was no more than a tick grasping on to a lion's mane.

EIGHTEEN

The deficient Blue, the dog, and Death all converged on the state capitol for their own special reasons.

Gray Man bit on a bath towel in the Transient Hotel, eleven blocks from the state building where the prisoners were being held. The fires still burned in him, pained him. Redwood had transferred into his fiber all her placid memories of water and light coming together—life. This light heightened the death god's senses and his pain. Gray Man felt two Blues, maybe three, maybe four, barely a mile away. He had come to kill them, but somehow the perception of their strong blue light brought even more pain. Life was trying to grow in him even though Horace had finally dissipated and gone.

If he closed his eyes, he could see it like a brilliant red-and-blue tumor growing inside. He conjured up an army of maggots to eat away the fibrous heart. They set at it, gnawing and squirming, but then flew outward, having become crystal-winged butterflies. Gray Man sent sharp flying blades to lacerate the flesh and sinew.

But the rich blood flowed out as flowers that fell to the ground and grew.

Gray Man opened his eyes and bit the towel. He took a step toward the door but fell to the floor, moaning.

Winch Fargo walked, on faltering feet, the length of the 700 block of Proctor. His body caught between the music of love and death. The closer Winch got to one, the more the other one seemed to wane. He'd get to the end of the block and then, feeling the fading of light at his back like the cool breeze from a dark closet, turn to follow that.

Back and forth Winch Fargo staggered, between love and death. His skin was rough and burned from the desert sun and wind. His found pants were too short, revealing thin ankles—one of which was bruised and bloody from its manacle. The overcoat he wore was too warm, with sleeves that went down well below his fingertips.

His senses were assailed by the murmurs of dreams that the people walking by had had in the past few days. Snatches of serene beaches on crisp, cold mornings, of rude rituals, and of sex—not the act of sex, but the feeling of it in their chests and arms and genitals. He eavesdropped not only on human dreams but also on the feral dreaming of cats and rats and dogs. His mind fluttered with the insanity of fleeing birds and the complex geometric flight patterns of flies. Winch Fargo's perception surpassed animal life and went into the deep serenity of the granite beneath his feet and the confusion of bricks, seeking only dissolution.

Winch Fargo, riding the space between the delicate vibrations of blue light, for a moment in time became a conduit for the soul. The soul: what Ordé had called that energy which binds the tiniest pieces of the universe, that force which seeks to unite and dissimulate. For those few hours Winch Fargo was the black hole of all feelings, beyond life and weight and space.

All he wanted was her, his queen. But so much bombarded him that he couldn't recognize her signal or even remember what she looked like. He was a wild animal pacing in his cage, looking for a way out and ravenous to the point of rage.

Nesta and Trini had taken a room in a boardinghouse for women. They spent their days at the state building where the state detainment facility was housed. They asked about Claudia Heart/Zimmerman but were told that information about prisoners was private and confidential.

Nesta considered applying for a job in the building; she almost did it. She needed a job while waiting for the chance to see her blue sister. This curiosity about Claudia Heart was the most powerful urge she'd ever felt.

One day she left Trini in the room and went down to the state building to fill out a job application. She was walking up the broad granite stairway when she felt something.

Max the dog ran out from behind the shadows of a stone column, snarling and wagging his tail. Everything about him sang in her mind. The wave of vibrations going through her abdomen and breasts almost made her cry out. She bent down intending to pet Max but ended up sitting on a stair. The dog crawled up, laying his belly across her lap and whimpering. Nesta cried too.

"He was the first," Nesta said about that meeting. "Like you'd been waiting on a deserted island for years, for your whole life, but you never knew it because you never knew that there was anywhere else. But then he crawled up on me and I held him. I felt his loss. He'd followed a scent there that then turned into a memory. He howled as I held him, and I held him for hours. With my eyes closed I was gone from here. I was out in space with millions just like me, singing the same song that Max did."

"Were you still human?" I asked. "I mean, when you closed your eyes?"

"This body is like a uniform, Chance. I'm like a soldier. I'm proud of the colors and buttons, but they are only vestiges of the spirit that wears them." Her amber eyes glowed in the cathedral we called home. I felt a strong anger because of the love she felt for a dog.

So while Miles Barber played the puppet master inside, the real story was elsewhere, in Claudia Heart's womb and the streets of Sacramento.

Gray Man rose to his feet, shivering like a cold dog. He looked at himself in the mirror. His ungroomed hair looked wild. All the years that Horace LaFontaine had straightened it had killed most of the crinkling, but it was still coarse. When Gray Man brushed the clumps back his head resembled a dark brown porcupine whose quills were only half at rest.

He pulled on a T-shirt and a pair of jeans. He rubbed his hand against his chest, feeling for the pain of life that the redwood had cursed him with. Then he left the room.

He walked out the flophouse door and into the street. The sun grilled down on his bare head. He wore only one black-and-white tennis shoe, the other foot was bare.

"I am Death," he chanted under his breath again and again. "I can kill. It makes me strong." He uttered the words, only barely understanding them. This because the redwood's life had taken root in the soil of his dead soul.

The moment Gray Man stepped out of his door, Winch Fargo was free. The emanations from the death god got clearer as he came closer to Fargo, and Winch knew that it was not his woman's song. He walked out from the dream of everything, giving it up gladly for the mother of his grandchildren.

He stalked forward, dreaming now only of her feet where he could curl up and worship. Winch didn't know that her music had dried up. He was following the scent and sound of the dog now. A dog who had also licked and whimpered at the feet of Heart.

Gray Man was walking fast. Two blocks away Winch Fargo broke into a hobbling run. They felt each other, hated each other. Gray Man despised the passion that drove Fargo, while Fargo knew that Death's light wanted to burn his soul away.

NINETEEN

Nesta felt their approach and dreaded it. Max jumped from her lap and began to pace in front of her, stopping now and again to sniff and growl.

Suddenly he grew still and stared down the concrete stairs.

Gray Man was there half barefoot in a T-shirt and jeans. He was looking at Nesta with a friendly smile, the smile of a hunter at the end of a long chase.

Max scooted behind his new protector as Winch Fargo turned the corner.

In his bulky coat and short pants Fargo looked like a cartoon sorcerer, down on his luck but still with a trick up his sleeve.

Gray Man, the pain of Redwood pulsing in his temples, turned again. He regarded this new creature with confusion and disdain.

"I'm not concerned with you, half-thing. Go away and suffer what little light you have."

"Fuck you, man," Fargo replied. "Fuck you two times. Mess wit' me an' I go to war on your butt."

Nesta wanted to run but was transfixed with the rage and pain down below her. She had never imagined that the light in her eyes could be so twisted and ugly.

"I'll kill you with just these hands," Gray Man said on a slender breath. Then he ran at Fargo.

"Hey, you two, stop that," said a man selling newspapers from a wooden crate on the street.

A woman wearing white pants and a fuzzy pink sweater let out a little scream.

No one but Nesta and Max knew the threat of those skinny arms and legs.

Gray Man, sitting astride his foe's chest, tried to get his hands around Fargo's throat, but the ex-con held those hands away while cursing and foaming at the mouth.

As people began to gather, the men, Evil and Death, struggled against each other. They looked like street denizens, prematurely aged and demented by wine. No one moved in to stop them, more from an unwillingness to touch them than from fear of being hurt.

"Die!" Gray Man screeched.

"Fuck you, nigger!" Winch Fargo spat back.

Max the dog paced behind Nesta and then sat back on his haunches, letting out a great howl.

Two policemen came running down the stairs toward the scuffle.

"Stop!" Nesta cried.

"All right, that's enough of that now," one of the officers said.

He was a large man with close-cut brown and gray hair that stood straight out from his head. He grabbed Gray Man by the shoulder. Gray Man shot out with his left hand, taking the policeman by his lapel, and yanked down hard, slamming the unsuspecting man into the concrete curb.

With one hand free Winch Fargo threw Gray Man off him and rose. He was panting, almost exhausted from the incredibly strong hands of Death. Winch Fargo planted one foot behind him and looked around for a weapon while he waited for the second attack.

Gray Man was on the ground, but he didn't look tired. He rose smiling at his adversary. But before he could attack again he was struck from behind by a police stick. It was a hard blow that might have laid out a professional boxer. But Gray Man was only stung. He turned on the second policeman, and the woman in the pink sweater yelled louder.

A crowd had gathered now.

Gray Man broke the second policeman's neck, but when he went for Winch Fargo again, he found the now barechested savant armed with a police stick.

Fargo used his weapon well. He struck again and again, going backward as he did. Men and women were shouting all around them, but no one tried to interfere.

One man, standing up from the corpse of the first cop, yelled, "Someone get the police!"

Fargo kept striking with deadly accuracy, turning Gray Man's head around to his shoulder with each blow. And Gray Man advanced, seemingly stronger for every blow that was struck.

Fargo backed up the stairs to get better leverage with his swings. Finally Gray Man bent low and caught Fargo by his legs.

And again Gray Man was trying to get his hands around Winch Fargo's throat.

Fargo felt the closeness of blue death for the first time since he'd witnessed Philip Martel's demise. Only now, the death approaching was his own. The snake in his brain writhed and thrashed against the inside of his skull. His hands were failing. Gray Man was beginning to breathe hard too.

Unexpectedly Winch pulled Gray Man toward him, butting the black death god with his own tortured skull. Gray Man sat up. He released Fargo and smiled. Before Winch could react, Gray Man grabbed his left arm and stood up. Placing his foot in Winch's armpit, he wrenched and tugged.

The arm came out of the socket and ripped away from the shoulder with a sick tearing and sucking sound. Winch cried out and Gray Man laughed. People in the crowd began to run and scream.

A blur of brown fur went for Gray Man's throat, knocking the little man down the stairs.

Nesta pulled off her denim jeans and wrapped them around Fargo's narrow shoulders to staunch the bleeding. His blood came fast, but not as fast as a normal man's blood. Then Nesta Vine grabbed the dismembered arm.

Gray Man had gotten the dog by his front legs, but before he could do any damage he was assailed by the meat-and-bone club.

Nesta's image of herself was powerful and strong. She wailed at the weakened personification of death. She clubbed him while Max snarled and snapped.

Gray Man finally ran away, feeling Redwood attack him from the inside even as Nesta and Max struck from without.

The frightened mob parted before Gray Man. Max pursued him to the end of the block, then came back to Nesta, who was holding Winch Fargo in her lap.

"Am I dead?" he asked her, coming to consciousness for a moment.

"I don't know yet," Nesta Vine replied.

A dozen policemen were pressed into action for the disturbance that had broken out on the state building steps.

They found two dead cops, a seemingly mortally wounded Winch Fargo, a feral dog, and a blood-spattered black amazon.

It took six hours for two dozen police detectives to question the witnesses.

Miles Barber, Briggs, and Bonhomme arrived after the violence was over. When he was told of the battle with Gray Man, Barber suffered a seizure that left him unconscious and hospitalized. His coma was short compared with mine, only fifteen days. And it wasn't really even a coma, because he remembered a dream. He was still a policeman, with two eyes. He walked out of the state building onto the scene of the murders. There he came upon a pool of blood left by Winch Fargo's wound.

"But there was something odd," the ex-detective said, remembering the dream. "The blood wasn't drying. It was still wet and had blue veins all through it. I went over to inspect the blood, but it flowed away from me, down the stairs. At first I had this crazy thought that it's 'cause of gravity that the blood is flowing downward. Can you imagine that? Havin' a scientific reason in your dream?

"So I followed the blood down to the curb, but it keeps on going down the street. The faster I chase it, the faster it goes until I'm running after this blue-veined pool of blood that's rushing down the street." As it always was with Barber, he began to experience what he was telling. His breath came quickly and there was visible strain in his body and hands. "I was runnin' so fast that I couldn't see where I was going. I ran right into him. He stayed on his feet, but I tumbled to the ground. And when I looked up I saw that it was him; all black and big, real big. He was naked and his eyes were red. And then he bent down over me and he was whispering. Everything around me turned black like him, and all I wanted was to hear the words. I concentrated as hard as I could and then, just when the last of the light was gone, except for his red eyes, I heard him say, 'It's never over,' and everything went black. And then I was coming out to see the blood again. It all happened all over again. Everything was the same except that I knew it.

"When I regained consciousness, they called Bonhomme. He told me that the court had appointed a lawyer for Claudia Zimmerman and she convinced the judge that her client's rights had been violated. The judge let her go. Mackie Allitar was just down the hall from me, dying from drug abuse, they said. I asked Bonhomme about the black man, the killer.

" 'Oh, him,' Bonhomme said. 'They think he's a judo expert. Add that to the fact that Fargo obviously has some kind of leprosy, and it looks pretty crazy out there. We don't have anything to do with it anyway. We got Halston and Fargo. They let the warden go. Thanks for your help.'

"And I lay back, ready to die, Chance. I swear. I was ready. I lay in that bed for two days. Doctors and nurses came in and frowned at my charts. They stuck me with needles and put soft food on my tray, but they knew I was on my way out. But then the music came. It was like all the horns in the world all at once in a thousand tones, but they were all playing the same note. I was up and outta that bed as strong as I had ever been, stronger. That was about two in the morning. I met Allitar in the hall. We looked at each other and grinned like boys who just climbed over the school fence to check out the big world outside."

The feral dog escaped from the dog pound the night they caught him. He had been knocked out by a tranquilizer dart, but when they tried to carry him from the cell to the gas chamber, he sprang to life suddenly and made a dash for it. No one could ever remember a dog with the will and intelligence to break through a glass windowpane and dash away.

They said he was badly cut, though, and was probably dead within minutes.

Claudia Zimmerman left the Bay Area. No one knew where she went.

Winch Fargo had escaped from police custody a week after Miles Barber and Mackie Allitar, with the assistance of some unknown friend. The hospital doctors, like the dogcatchers, said that Fargo was probably dead a few hours after he escaped.

Gray Man crawled back toward his desert hole, bruised and pulsing with pain. He felt his heart thrumming as if he had been frightened, but he wasn't actually afraid. He felt the blue coyote pup following him and wondered if he would have been strong enough to fight him off.

He finally arrived and crawled down into his hole, burying himself once again. But this time his sleep was disturbed by unnamed night terrors; this time his sleep was more alive than it was dead.

THREE

THREE

TWENTY

"I love you, Chance," Alacrity said to me.

We were looking out over a vista of spiky pines and cloud-rifted blue skies. I carried her in the crook of my arm while she nestled her head against my shoulder. I carried her as if she were a small child. She was young. But Alacrity had begun to grow quickly in the woods. She was more than three years younger than Wanita, but already she was a foot and a half taller than her friend. She looked closer to twelve than three.

She and her mother, Reggie and Wanita, and I were living at the Bear Lodge Country Cabins in northern California. We stayed in California, albeit many miles from the Bay Area, because Addy and I wanted to be near at hand if the remaining Blues somehow made a stand against Gray Man. We were pretty confident that he couldn't find us easily and that we would escape as long as we were free. Also, Reggie kept saying that he felt the safest place in the world for us was close by. He spent many days scanning the countryside for our refuge, but the direction for some reason eluded him.

"I know," I said to the young girl. "I love you too."

I did love her, as a child who was frightened and headstrong, who was inquisitive about everything, and who needed a story before she could go to sleep at night. But I also knew that she was the daughter of a strangeling god who had prophesied the beginning of an era heralding the end of mankind.

"I don't mean like that," Alacrity said. "I really love you. When I grow up I'm going to marry you and give you a big house and you can read books all day long and we'll get a telescope and look at the people in the dark stars. The ones that Wanita said don't have no bodies except just great big eyes in a cave."

I sighed deeply and kept my silence. It was always disturbing for me to hear the child's dreams for the future. She had inherited some of her father's ability with words. I had to fight the nagging sense that her desires were my destiny and my marching orders.

"Reggie an' Nita comin'," she said.

Far up the sloping hill behind us the two other children were coming out of the woods. It seemed as if Reggie was skipping adolescence altogether, going straight for manhood. He'd grown almost as tall as me, and his shoulders were amazingly wide. His sister, Wanita, was still a child, though, round-faced and always serious. She and Alacrity were as different as playmates could be. While Alacrity climbed towering pines, Wanita would curl up by the roots and *dream of Alacrity way up there in the wind an' stuff.*

Adelaide and I never questioned the children's powers. It all seemed natural. This was not only because of our blood experiences. We had both been lost souls before we drifted into Ordé's orbit. You've already heard my story, I learned of Adelaide's experiences while we were on the run. It wasn't a long tale, but it had trailed her for years.

There are many circumstances and minor characters in Addy's story, but I don't have to bother with them. The elements are a white Christian family, a girl becoming a woman, a boy with a black leather jacket and a knife, and a dark night in an alley off Ventura Boulevard where two boys struggled over their hormones and only one survived. Adelaide never told anyone about her knowledge of the killing. She closed up her heart, opening it only to those men who cared so much about their future that they would never be concerned with her past. I was the first person she had ever confided in. But we were on the run from Death, and very little else seemed important or worth questioning.

The children and their survival had become our purpose; their abilities were our religion. Believing in them, we erased our own suffering.

"It's over that way for sure, Chance," Reggie said, pointing south.

"You sure, man?"

"Yeah. It's over that way."

"How far?"

"I can't tell exactly, but it's pretty far. It's hundreds of miles, but it's definitely over that way."

"And if we get there, you think we'll be safe for a while?" I asked the young man.

"We'll be safer. We'll be safer, but that don't mean we'll be safe."

The memory of Gray Man scuttled under my scalp. But lately the kids hadn't seemed scared at all. All that time in the woods had healed the fear in their hearts. Reggie knew the safest place to be, or at least he thought he could find it; Alacrity just wanted to play with each of us in turn and run wild in the woods; and Wanita dreamed.

Adelaide and I thought that if Wanita had any powers of godhood like the others, it must have been the power of dreams. She often came to us in the morning with elaborate tales of visions from the night before. I started to get them on a toy tape recorder when I realized that she was somehow reporting on stories that were not of this Earth or maybe not even this galaxy.

Sometimes the little brown girl would wake up in the morning hardly remembering who we were. Even her brother was as unfamiliar to her as some far-off memory. After she'd come back to us, she'd say that her dream took so long that she'd forgotten who she was for a while.

That very morning she had stumbled out of her bunk bed bleary-eyed and confused. She sat at our rough-hewn table and ate her hot bowl of Wheatena in silence. Adelaide noticed the sleep in her eyes and bent down with a moist towel to rub the sand away. Wanita looked at the green-eyed redhead with bewilderment. She touched Addy's hair, put her fingers to her own cheek. Then she began to speak as if she had already been in the middle of an explanation.

". . . they started out really big, like that tower thing on top's that hill—"

"Coit Tower," Reggie said as he ate.

"—and they get smaller and smaller, but then they come awake and start to sing," the dreamer said. "It's like they was purple glass at first with hot stuff inside, but when they get real small, like a little Christmas tree, then they's pink with little tears runnin' down they sideses."

"Who are they?" Adelaide breathed in the softest possible whisper.

"Like glass," Wanita said again. "An' they sing when they get little. Tinkle-like, humming-like, an' nobody could hear it but them an' me. All the animals and bugs that drink the little tears think that the glass sticks is just sticks, but they not. They be singin' an' laughin'. An' you could hear 'em everywhere."

"Where?" I asked gently, but I should have been gentler still.

By the way Wanita looked up, I could tell that she was coming out of the dream.

"Wanita!" I said sharply.

"Huh?"

"Where were the pink sticks made from glass?"

She shrugged and said nonchalantly, "In a place where the sun is blue and the sky is red. Not anywhere that we could go. Except if you dreamed it."

"Can you go there in your dreams, Wanita?" Addy asked.

"I did last night. Can I have a apple?"

And so went the way of Wanita's dreams. She traveled the universe at night while we slept. Her mind was gone for what must have felt like weeks or more overnight. Sometimes we worried that she'd be gone so long that she'd forget who she was completely, or even what she was. But that was the way of godhood, I supposed. All Addy and I could do was feed them and listen to them, groom them with our love and respect. And keep them safe from Death.

"There's something out there, almost like it was music," Reggie said. "But . . . but it's something . . . it's something else. Like safe. Safe."

As soon as Reggie said it, I could *hear* it. Like a whole orchestra of brass and silver horns so far away that I couldn't even tell what direction they were in. But when Reggie pointed I believed that sound might be coming from that way.

The extra senses I'd gained from Ordé had quieted over time. The stars still sang to me, the bands between the rainbow still revealed new colors, but it had become so normal that I hardly remembered what it had been like to have common senses. And my time around the children had disoriented those perceptions because I could always feel the Blues when they were near. It wasn't a hard sensation, more like the feeling of a cloud partly blocking the sun.

Their light had hidden the music from me.

"Uh-huh." Adelaide nodded while closing her eyes, holding her face up as if to feel the wind. "Yeah, I do feel something. It's like sunlight through water."

The children and I had gone back to the cabin. I was excited to tell Addy about what I felt. Addy's senses had been altered by carrying Ordé's child. She and I had somewhat similar powers, only she couldn't hear and see things as much. Addy's ability was more in intuiting what the children were feeling and thinking. They could come to her for advice and she'd interpret what they felt even though the needs of those small blue gods were often things that she had never known.

"Mr. Needham didn't feel it," I said.

Needham was the camp handyman. He was an older white gentleman who didn't mind having an interracial family on the grounds. It was late in the fall and we were the only paying customers. Maybe he would have felt differently if it were the height of summer.

"We can't hear it either," Alacrity added. "We just said we could 'cause we were so happy."

"Uh-huh," Reggie said. "It's like I know it's there, but I can't really hear it."

"Probably because it wasn't meant for normal people or the Blues," Addy responded, opening her eyes. "This is probably meant for people like Chance and me. It's like a beacon for the half blind. Reggie probably figured it out because he was looking for someplace safe but it just happens to be where that call comes from."

"How far away do you think it's coming from?" I asked.

Addy closed her eyes and held up her face again. After a few moments she shook her head and frowned.

"We gotta go there," Reggie said.

"Uh-huh," Alacrity agreed.

"What do you think, Wanita?" I asked our round-faced dreamer.

"'Kay,' she answered, as if I had been trying to force her to go.

"I don't mean you have to go, honey," I said.

"But we do," she said softly while fingering her pink sweater. "Like them fishes."

"What fish?" asked Alacrity.

"The blue ones," Wanita replied.

Alacrity nodded, making a rare serious frown.

"Then we better get some more campin' stuff," Reggie said. "'Cause we gotta go way up in the woods an' I don't think the road will go all that far."

We spent the week buying nylon tents and rugged shoes, powdered packets of food and sleeping bags. We had gloves and bug repellent, a shortwave radio, hard candy and chocolate bars to energize little girls. Ordé's account felt the drain.

We were all happy at the prospect of refuge. But the morning we were to leave, the signal—brass horns, the liquid air, whatever it was—was gone. Reggie was disoriented and uncertain; Addy and I couldn't hear a thing. We waited for another week for the sensation to return. It came while we were sleeping on a Tuesday night, late. I got everybody up and hustled them into the van, and we drove without stopping except for gas stations and food stores. Addy and I alternated driving and sleeping. We traveled for eighteen hours on highways and secondary roads going south. Two hundred miles or so past San Francisco we hit dirt roads. For another two days we bumped along back roads.

The last drivable road finally came to an end on Friday afternoon. It didn't end exactly; there was still a clearing there, but it had fallen into disrepair—recently, as far as I could tell. There were trees fallen across it and great upheavals in the ground. We decided to camouflage our VW van and explore. The feeling that came from that way was neither stronger nor weaker. None of us knew how long the trek would be.

Reggie had almost half our gear on his broad shoulders. The pack he carried was impossibly large. He was straining under the weight, but there was something about him when he got on the trail of an idea or imagined destination—he kept on going no matter what.

He mouthed soft drumlike sounds, *pom pom pompom pom,* as he went. Now and then he'd make verbal notes about our passage. "Heavy foot on the right turn. Slashing lines on the left." Sometimes he'd stop and look around like a small child who has temporarily lost sight of his mother in a crowded supermarket.

"You okay, Reggie?" I asked once when he seemed a bit lost.

"Yeah, man," he replied. "You know what, Chance?"

"What?"

"My sister's been here."

"Wanita?"

"No, uh-uh. Luwanda's been here," he said.

"You mean you were here with your sister before she died?" I asked.

"I was once, but she been here since then. She been here 'cause this the place where we come together."

Alacrity carried a pack almost as big as she was. She didn't seem to mind the weight, though. She moved playfully up and down the path, over fallen trees and down into woods to explore. She wasted more energy than the rest of us used, but she was never tired. Her blond hair knotted on itself, and dried mud clung to her boots and jeans.

As I watched the child of my teacher dart in and out between the trees, I got the first glimpse of her purpose among us.

I had begun to believe that there was purpose to each light that began these creatures. The visionary, the dreamer, the pathfinder, death. Alacrity I could see was simply a hero. She was brave and foolhardy and the best friend anybody could have.

As I watched her move so deftly between pines, I wondered whose hero she would become: mine or theirs?

It was the first time I'd realized that there would one day be sides drawn and a conflict ahead.

TWENTY-ONE

That night we made camp in a clearing of fallen pines. We set up two tents, one for Addy and the girls and one for Reggie and me. The moon was three-quarters full and the air was cold. I could hear Wanita and Alacrity laughing in the other tent while Reggie snored next to me. He was sleeping outside of his down bag, wearing only briefs. I could still feel the heat pouring off him from his exertions leading our journey.

Addy and I could see the change in the boy that day. Somehow the walk in the woods had made him into the man that he was destined to be. All along the walk he would turn to his sister and ask, "Do you remember this, Wanita? Do you remember when we were walking here before? It was the night that the light came, the night Luwanda died."

The girl said nothing but kept close to her brother, touching him every now and then. When she tired he took her up in his arms and pressed forward with great concentration and force.

Reggie's face became more angular, and his eyes lost their wandering and distracted air. It was as if he had been born to take this hike in these woods.

I loved those children. They seemed perfect together with Addy and me. Part of me, the part that was active and engaged, was only there for the children. But that night another part came alive. I was a link between natural enemies. I was the flotsam that Ordé preached about, but now I was partly aware, partly alive. I was spineless and mindless like a jellyfish, but still I had an instinct for survival. And survival, I knew, was the possibility of a bridge between these gods and my small race.

Maybe some pink crystal far away was dreaming of me, imagining the dignity of my partial awareness. The dignity of fungus stuck to a rock, depending upon the sun for life. At any moment we might be robbed of our single-note pleasure, procreation; a shadow could rise between us and the sun, could end our whole history. And even if that shadow never appeared, even if we did not meet annihilation, still, mindlessly, we would just multiply one on top of another until we covered the entire planet with our bones.

But now there was a different light, the blue light. It was, I believed, my job to conserve that light and to help my people feel its brilliance.

While Reggie snored and Wanita and Alacrity giggled in the tent next to ours, I found a direction for my life. I had been following the path for some years, since Ordé saved me from suicide, but now I was aware. Now it became my choice. I could feel it in my heart and lungs and liver. I knew that my duty was more powerful even than the visions I was allowed to see. Even the thought of Gray Man could not deter me. I would give everything to make my blood count for something beyond rutting and the piling of bones.

In the morning nothing seemed the same. I was lying next to a full-grown man who had been a child two days before. But as much as Reggie had changed, I had changed more.

The girls made breakfast for the camp with Addy's help. I ate the baked beans and canned black bread with no taste or hunger. I ate because I needed strength.

The numbness that followed my convictions left my mind unencumbered. Freed as I was, I could remember what we saw without being overwhelmed by the trappings of fear or awe.

The first five or so miles through the woods that morning were not very different. The road had been torn up and blocked by trees, and we hoped that this was why Reggie had deemed the place safe. I couldn't see how, but maybe the inaccessibility made it partially secure from Gray Man.

By afternoon, however, the changes became more spectacular.

"Look at those leaves up there," Addy said, pointing to the roof of pine forest. We were in a large clearing. "They're like a rainbow."

And big. Some of the blue and yellow and orange leaves were as large as serving platters. They seemed to be blowing in the wind, some floating on currents of air and others falling lazily to earth.

"Them's butterflies," Wanita said matter-of-factly.

"Oh, God." That was me.

The cavernous roof of leaves above us must have held hundreds of thousands of them. Many had wingspans of nearly two feet, some even larger. We were all stunned into silence by the beauty. In that hush we heard the soft fluttering of their wings. The sound was like the thrumming of a fast-pumping vein. It was exciting and a little bit scary.

A giant orange-and-black monarch with iridescent blue eyes etched in its tail sailed down, landing on Reggie's shoulders and back. Its wingspan was almost a yard. The impossible insect unfurled its tubular tongue, gently lashing the young man's small Afro.

"It tickles," he said.

Alacrity giggled, and Addy and I smiled.

"We better run," Wanita said.

Just then the butterflies overhead formed into a great multicolored blanket that began to descend.

"Let's go!" I shouted.

Reggie took off, leading us down a corridor through the trees.

The thrumming of butterflies became so loud that it was almost a rattle. They were very fast, coming quickly and intently through the leaves and branches.

We made it through the corridor and into a dense stand of pine. The butterflies kept coming, though. Three ivory-colored ones grabbed on to Wanita. They seemed to want to lift her off the ground. She screamed, but Alacrity killed them with a branch.

The children were beset by butterflies.

We all took up branches, swinging about our heads as fast as we could, smashing the rainbow fliers into the same trees that impeded our escape. Addy and I could more easily kill the creatures because the butterflies didn't want us. Once in a while one would land on me with feet that felt like grasping Brillo pads. But as soon as that long tongue tasted my skin, it was off after the kids.

The touch of the butterflies' tongues had the tickle of mild electricity or the beginning of an acid burn.

We kept swinging and trying to run. The butterflies died easily enough. Their wings ripped from the slightest touch and their soft bellies came open, shedding thick green blood.

We were overcome by the crush of butterflies. Choking on the dust that rose from their battered wings. They came on in a flood of color and dust. The girls choked and cried. Reggie fought hard but was covered by tongue-lashing insects. I jumped on top of the boy, using my body to crush the insects as well as to protect him.

The butterflies' touch seemed to sap the children's strength.

The thrumming rattle of insect wings overwhelmed our cries. The crush of bugs stopped our advance completely and slowly pushed us downward. The children and Reggie were already on the ground. Addy and I stood above them, on our knees, beating off our attackers with thick branches.

And then came a thump in the air. It was the sensation of a sudden and powerful vacuum. I lost my balance and consciousness at the same moment.

"Chance! Chance, wake up."

Alacrity was shaking me by the shoulder. Reggie was trying to prop up Addy into a standing position. She was unconscious, or mostly so. The forest floor was littered with the bodies of brightly colored butterflies. They weren't dead, only stunned like I had been. Their giant fanlike wings waving slowly. A few of them were standing on weak, shivering legs.

"We gotta go, Chance," Reggie pleaded.

In my stupor I was still amazed by the size and nature of the beautiful predators.

"C'mon, Chance!" Alacrity yelled.

Her voice was strained and commanding. I jumped up and took Adelaide from Reggie. If anyone was going to lead us away, it was him, and his pack was already large enough.

As soon as I hefted the swooning woman over my shoulder, Reggie was off. When I turned to run, Addy's head slammed into a tree. It was a hard knock, but there was no time to stop.

He took the lead, zigzagging through the trees ahead. The waist strap of his pack had loosened, and the load pounded up and down loudly against his back. Alacrity ran behind Reggie, wielding a long branch like a sword. She turned full around every now and then, still running, looking for danger.

Wanita shadowed Alacrity, moving more like a normal child, slipping and wavering as she went.

We didn't have the strength to run for very long—no more than ten minutes. I fell to my knees, exhausted. When I laid Addy out on a bed of pine needles, I saw that her head and face were lacerated. She was bleeding pretty hard.

"Come on, Reggie," Alacrity said, throwing him a branch the size of a cartoon caveman's club. Then she pointed to where he should stand for defense.

I took the gauze bandage from my first aid box and pressed it hard against the long cut down the side of Addy's face, cursing myself for being so rough and careless.

"I don't hear anything coming," Reggie said.

"Nothing?" asked Alacrity.

I was trying to hold together the flaps of Adelaide's skin under the bandage. The thought of the butterflies' coming through the dense woods and the feeling of the blood slipping between my fingers somehow increased my feeling of numbness. The breath in my chest felt like a cold breeze through a deep cave.

For the next hour we sat there: Alacrity and Reggie on the ready for any attack; Wanita hugging on to Reggie's leg; and me pressing on the big white bandage that I had tied around Addy's head.

The forest was unnaturally quiet except for an occasional moan from Addy.

"I don't think they're gonna come," Reggie said.

"Are you sure?" I asked.

"No, I'm not sure," he said petulantly. "What do you want me to do?"

*　　*　　*

Night fell and Addy became delirious. She went out of her head with fever and nightmares. We huddled around her in the tent, trying, I guess, to press her back to health. I dissolved aspirin in water and made her drink, but she was still burning up.

"Why not?" she begged some unseen torturer. "Why can't we? No. No. We love the children. We love them."

She begged all night, thrashing and crying.

I stayed up as long as I could, but sometime in the early morning hours I dozed off.

In the dream I met a man who wore a one-piece suit that sheathed him from head to toe; only his red-brown face could be seen under a hood of woven branches and fur that had flowers nestled within. The flowers, asters and small yellow daisies, seemed to be rooted there, growing out of the man's head. The rest of his costume was no less unusual. It was a loose-fitting patchwork of cloth and skins, metal and wood, ceramic and bone. From the belt looped over his shoulder hung a large wooden knife, a dark quartz crystal, a small hide sack, and a handmade wooden mallet with a tree branch for a handle.

His eyes were small and very dark. His smile was permanent. And he smelled of the forest: strong, acrid, and sweet.

"Chance," he said. "Is that your name?"

"Who are you?" I asked.

"I call myself Juan Thrombone, but don't ask me why. I don't have use for names much. They seem like the juggling balls in the circus."

"What?"

"I throw you the yellow ball that I call Chance and then you throw back the red one—Thrombone." He grinned and I did too. I had to.

"Like a baby duck," he said.

"Excuse me?"

"Like baby ducks," he said. "All of you here are like baby ducks following their momma up into the woods."

"I don't know what you mean." I was nearly in tears at my own stupidity.

"But I'm not your momma, little one," Juan Thrombone said. "I'm the Big Bad Wolf and you were just dreaming about your mother. You're lost in the woods, Last Chance. Go back."

"I can't," I said. "I have to save the children."

"Save them? You can't even see them. Can't you see that, little man? Can't you see?" With that, the many-textured man held his hands over his head.

His gesture compelled me to look up.

Suddenly I was in the center of a dark web. All around me there were large spiders slowly moving closer.

"They aren't coming for you," Thrombone, now disembodied, whispered. "Jump, little man. They'll bite you just to spit out your blood."

I thought that they'd have to swallow a little bit of that blood. I thought it, but I was too scared to talk. The spiders were big and scaly; they smelled like the foulest infection.

TWENTY-TWO

I awoke to the sun shining brightly on the yellow fabric of our tent. My senses were alive with the world around me. The crystal-clear cold of the morning waited right outside. I was happy, ready to jump up and go exploring.

But when I sat up I saw the girls and Reggie sleeping. In their midst was Addy. She was pale and fragile-looking. I moved as quietly as I could, reaching around the sleeping girls to remove the day-old dressing.

The wound underneath was a spectacle as amazing and terrifying as the butterflies the day before. It was a long and jagged gash, white down the middle, bordered with bright red. The skin around the sides was darkening, not the blue of bruises but the black of deep infection.

"How is she?" Reggie asked. I could hear him stirring behind me.

"We've gotta go back, Reggie," I said. "She's real bad, man."

He leaned over to see the deep cut down the side of her face. His eyes, I knew, were looking for some kind of path even down that infected valley. He saw none, though, and nodded.

When he stood up I noticed that he had an erection straining underneath his boxer shorts. He might have been inhabiting a grown man's body, but he was still a boy who had to pee bad in the morning.

We left everything that wasn't absolutely necessary. The second tent, two sleeping bags, pots, pans, books, and extra clothing. Reggie and I tied Addy's arms to his shoulders. He carried a leg under each of his arms and hefted her as if she were a living backpack.

Alacrity and Wanita were quiet. Alacrity walked close behind Reggie and stroked her mother's leg now and then.

"Will my mom be okay, Chance?" she had asked that morning with tears in her eyes.

I said that she would be, that I'd make sure of it. And for the rest of the morning I found myself, now and again, wondering if it was a sin to lie to that child.

"Reggie, are you sure this is the way we came?" I said.

It was about noon and we were descending a fairly steep hill toward a quiet stream. The pine needles were slick under my hiking boots, and I was trying to remember having scaled the side of that particular valley.

"I don't know," the boy/man said. He was breathing hard. "I'm not sure."

"What do you mean?"

Reggie was always sure of where he was going. Ask anything that had to do with a direction or a place, and Reggie knew it. He could walk through the deep woods blindfolded and never hit a tree.

"I mean I'm lost."

"Lost?"

"Look, Chance," Reggie said. "I don't know what's happening. It's like I'm not anywhere at all, like there aren't any rules anymore."

We stopped at the bottom of the valley. The stream was burbling and sunlight winked down through the branches and needles. We were lost in paradise and Addy was dying.

"Well, you can see by the sun that we're on the west side of the range," I said. "So that means if we follow the stream down, we'll get to the lake sooner or later."

"What difference does that make?" Alacrity asked.

"At the lake is a road. We can get a ride and get your mom to a doctor."

It seemed like a good idea. Reggie hunched his shoulders, hitched his living load up a few inches, and groaned. Addy was deadweight; she hadn't opened her eyes that day.

We made it about a half a mile before coming across the bear. Big and black, he reared up in the middle of the stream and roared. I moved quickly out in front of the children. I waved my hands and yelled, "Ho! You big ugly bear! Get! Get away!"

As if he were mimicking me, the bear waved his great clawed paws and roared again. Then he charged.

"Run!" I yelled, pushing my arms behind me as if I were performing some underwater swimming maneuver.

Then I was flying. Up in the air and in a small arc until I hit the stream, and the hard stones therein, with a loud splash. The girls were screaming. Reggie had pulled a large stone out of the stream and was ready to throw it like a medicine ball.

"Drop it, Reg!" I shouted. "Run!"

And that's what we did. Straight up the valley. The bear growled and came from behind but didn't catch up. He just threatened and kept close enough so we couldn't consider running up into the woods.

The girls were ahead of Reggie and me, screaming. The bear kept coming on.

Over the next hour our retreat slowed to a fast walk. The bear always behind us.

Finally Reggie fell to his knees.

"Take Addy," he said. "Take her with you."

I looked around for a weapon. Alacrity was already armed with a yard-long branch that she held like a baton.

But the bear had stopped too. He held back a few steps and sniffed the air. He let out a great bellowing roar that made Wanita scream and cry.

"Shut up, you ugly bear," Alacrity said.

Reggie was lying on his side, Addy tied to his shoulders and still unconscious.

I struggled with the double weight of Addy and Reggie, pulling them both up a few feet from the stream. Alacrity stood guard with her stick, shouting at the bear now and then. Wanita stood close by me.

"Alacrity, come on back here to me," I said in an urgent but muted voice. "Come on. Leave that bear alone."

"Tell him to leave me alone," she said, more to the bear than to me.

"Come back here," I demanded.

Slowly she obeyed. You could see that she hesitated to back down from her attacker. She was ready to go down fighting.

"Come on, now."

We huddled together on the steep sloping bank of the small mountain stream. The bear watched us closely from the other side. He alternated between sniffing the ground and standing on his back legs, surveying the full area.

"You can go to sleep, Chance," Alacrity told me. "I'm not tired. I'll watch him."

I laughed to myself at the maturity of the child. I would have told her to take a nap herself, but before I knew it I was in a deep sleep.

"Hello, little man," Juan Thrombone said.

He was sitting on a big stone set alone in a wide desert. The sun was already down, but there was enough light to see the receding field of sand and rock.

"It's all in our mind, little one," Thrombone said.

"What?"

"The things you count and calculate. The numbers of colors, the weight of light on a lawn. It's all in our mind. I know because I have seen it. I have seen it. And it's not really there."

"I don't know what you're talkin' about, man."

"The smallest one can tell you." Thrombone's smile grew large with something he was thinking. "I tried to talk to her, but she drew me away to a place where stone moves within stone, thinking deep rocky thoughts and singing to the stars. I never knew that a stone's voice could be so high."

The man of stone and bone, cloth and flowers, stood up. It took a long time for him to attain his full stature. He was a short man seeming to be a giant. He stretched, and this made him laugh. The laugh was a musical tenor with a twang and a whine around the edges.

I thought that I probably couldn't kill this man; he probably couldn't die.

"No, little man. No. We can all die—and you"—he looked at me with intent yet benign eyes—"you could kill anyone. That's what makes you human. You're the best at it. You're the cream of the killers."

I didn't like his knowing what I was thinking.

"But let's not worry about that now," Juan Thrombone said. "You can kill me whenever you want, Chance. But first we should drink something and eat something. First we should sing, little man. My friends will bring you to me."

"What friends?"

"You'll know them," he said. Night was descending on the desert. I strained to glimpse the odd Mexican man, but he faded away.

"Chance." Wanita was tugging at my arm. "Chance, wake up. Wake up. Look, look."

I sat up quickly but got dizzy and fell back.

"Chance!"

I sat up again. The green canopy of leaves was spinning around in my head, but I stayed up. Wanita was still pulling, wanting something from me.

We were surrounded by bears. They ranged in color from cinnamon to black. Some were very large, others were less than three feet in length.

We weren't actually surrounded. There was one path, up away from the stream, to the east, that we could take.

The bears, some of them, were yowling and standing up on their hind legs. The big black bear that chased us at first was already halfway across the stream. He was telling us to move on—there was no doubt about that.

I hefted Wanita in my arms. Reggie groaned and rose. Addy was still tied to his back. Alacrity naturally took up the rear guard even though I told her to go ahead of us. She walked backward behind us, swinging her staff as the bears herded us upward.

They flanked us, big woolly shepherds bringing their flock to a man in a dream. I was sure that these bears were Thrombone's friends. I was sure that he'd changed his mind and, instead of chasing us away, was calling us on.

I would have dreaded the destination if it wasn't for those bears. I counted more than sixteen, but I think that there were even more. Smelling strongly of bear musk, roaring and barking. The deep growls sent fear through me, fear for the children and myself. If we slowed down, snapping jaws would urge us forward. And if a bear snapped, Alacrity cracked it with her staff, which sent out a communal bear complaint that was deafening.

They drove us all day long, into the moonlit evening.

Wanita sobbed on and off in my arms. I wanted to check on Addy, but the bears wouldn't let us slow down. We moved deeper and deeper into the woods until late in the evening.

Reggie, who was the strongest of us, finally gave out again under Addy's weight. He went to his knees, and the big black straddled him, snarling dangerously.

I put Wanita down and went for the bear. But Wanita grabbed on to my foot and I fell.

Alacrity, however, was surer of foot. She jumped at the big black, yelling. He swung at her but, amazingly, she ducked under his swipe and came up delivering a powerful blow to his snout. The bellow was enough to knock me over, but Alacrity just swung again. The bear backed away from Reggie but then reared. I had my footing and my knife out by then. I was up beside Alacrity, half believing that the girl and I could down a giant bear.

We were surrounded on all sides by pacing, angry bears. Reggie was down. Wanita was holding her brother's head.

The big bear bellowed again.

"Come on!" Alacrity challenged.

But he didn't charge. Instead, he leaned backward and walked away until he disappeared into darkness. The rest of the angry bears did the same.

At that moment it started to rain. The moon had been covered over just that quickly, and drizzling rain began to fall. Alacrity and I huddled around Reggie and Addy. We all tried to fit under the plastic tarp I had kept. The girls were crying. Reggie's eyes were open, but he wasn't saying anything.

Addy burned under the cold rain.

* * *

We were all sneezing and coughing by morning. But with the light Alacrity regained her courage. Wanita didn't seem afraid either.

"You think they're still out there?" Reggie asked.

Alacrity lifted the tarp to let us see.

There were bears everywhere. The big black with his bloody snout was foremost, not five feet from us.

"Gimme your knife, Chance," Alacrity ordered.

I almost obeyed.

"No," I said. "I think we better keep going."

"Gimme your knife," she said with emphasis.

I found it hard to resist her will.

Alacrity raised her staff, and for a moment I was sure that she was going to hit me.

"Nooooo!" yelled Wanita. "No, Alacrity. It's okay. It's gonna be okay."

Alacrity lowered her pole, looking deeply into the smaller girl's eyes.

"It's okay?" asked the little self-styled captain.

Wanita nodded.

"Okay then, come on, everybody," Alacrity said. She shooed us up ahead and took her position at the rear. It was yet another change in a moment. Alacrity had proved herself a leader and a general, a hero—and maybe a fool.

The bears drove us hard all morning long. There must have been a hundred of the creatures. You could hear the shuffle of their hides against bark as they went. Fights broke out among them. They roared and broke down small saplings for sport.

I took Addy for a while to give Reggie a break. She was heavy. Not dead, just deadweight. I carried her for only an hour and was already exhausted. I marveled, in my pain, at how Reggie had carried that load for a whole day.

The bears wouldn't let up. Alacrity was our biggest problem because she had begun to pick fights with our burly shepherds. More than once we heard the thwack of her staff and the roar of ursine rage.

I was getting weak, intent upon walking until I passed out, when we came to a dead end.

It wasn't really a dead end. It was more a thick wall of woods. The white firs blocked our way as efficiently as a brick wall. The bears hung back, pacing and growling in a low, purring call.

"Maybe they want us to rest here," I said hopefully.

"Maybe now I can have your knife," Alacrity said.

"Come," said a voice off to the left.

The bears were gone just that quickly, and before I turned around I knew that he would be standing there.

TWENTY-THREE

Juan Thrombone stood in a solitary gap in the wall of trees. He stood in a space that had not been there before, surveying our tattered, half-dying group with a smile.

"Come quickly," he said, gesturing with the fingers of his left hand. Then he was gone, back into the thick woods.

Wanita jumped from my arms and followed Alacrity into the breach. Reggie staggered after them.

I stood for a moment between the vanished army of bears and the impossibly thick woods. I felt Addy's nose and mouth to be sure that she was still breathing. The only choice that I had, the only choice that was mine, was to stand still. It felt good to be standing still and in control of my fate, if only for just a moment. I wanted a PayDay candy bar and to hear the Chambers Brothers song "Time Has Come Today."

It was mostly shaded there before Juan Thrombone's terrain. A single shaft of light fell not three feet from where I stood.

I took a deep breath of freedom and then carried my friend, heavy as a sack of sand, into the dark doorway of a land I came to know as Treaty.

The path between the trees was large enough for three to walk abreast. A glowing, golden light filtered down from above. The trees stood so close together that they seemed to be the logs in a western stockade's wall, or at least a great thicket of bamboo.

Juan Thrombone led the way crazily, skipping and dancing like a child. He sang to the trees and ran and climbed. He even did cartwheels and flips now and again. Alacrity tried to keep up with him, but he was too fast and changeable even for her.

No one asked him who he was, because all of us had met the man in our dreams.

After an hour or so I passed Addy over to Reggie again. We were all stronger following that golden path. Our sniffles were gone. Addy groaned and complained when we secured her arms around Reggie's neck. It was the first sign of life that she'd shown in more than a day and a half.

"Come quickly," Juan Thrombone said again.

We kept coming for hours.

The brown needles and leaves on the path glowed under the softly broken sunlight. The air was warm and comfortable. A breeze blew from the direction in which we were headed. It whispered slightly in my ears. It was the call. There was something so wonderful in the whispering tones that I had to consciously slow down, to keep from wearing myself out cutting capers like our host.

I realized that I was no longer headed for the music but that I was in the center of it. Many of the trees that surrounded us were singing like musical instruments that were almost human.

"This is what I was looking for," Reggie said to me.

"What?" I asked, irritated that he had distracted me from the melody.

"This road," he said. "This is the road I was looking for. But it's not really here."

"What are you talking about? Here we are on it."

"But if you went backward," he said, "it would be gone."

"Why are you men wasting the air with words?" Juan Thrombone said.

He was standing there next to us, hands akimbo and eyes alight. Wanita and Alacrity were going on up ahead.

"Plenty of time to talk and chatter. Plenty of time to drink and drool later on when we get there."

"Where?" I asked.

"To our destination, little man, tender fool, Last Chance."

"What destination is that, Skin and Bones?" My retort made Thrombone smile wider.

"Treaty," he said. "Treaty."

He ran backward toward the girls, leaving me to wonder if he was jokingly asking for a truce or informing me of the name of our destination.

Treaty. We came to it by way of a rise in the path. At the very top we looked across a field of grasses and brush into a great forest chamber. A place like none I had ever seen before. Twelve giant sequoias stood like pillars. The largest of these trees was the exact center of the great space. From it, and from the surrounding trees, hung large man-made netting that held shingles of leaves that angled down; they made a loose roof for the spaces right under the trees, making houses without walls under each giant redwood.

"The wind swirls around the roof and the rain rolls out and away," said Juan to me. "You can see the sun and the stars, but no one can see you. Here the war is over, Last Chance. This is Treaty."

"Do you live here?" I asked.

"I am wherever I am," he answered.

"But do you have a house, a bed even?"

"My bed is where I lay these bones. My home is what I survey. I stay around here mainly because of the puppy trees. But I have been elsewhere."

Talking to him tired me. As soon as he started to answer, I wanted to stop listening. It was as though his voice was in my head rather than in my ears. It was hard work to listen.

"Anywhere," Thrombone said as if giving me a respite from the exhaustion he had induced.

I wondered if I was still dreaming.

"The things you left behind," our host said, "are under a pile of leaves over that way. You will find your blankets and things there."

"How'd you do that?" Reggie asked.

"Under blue light things simply are, Pathfinder. Don't waste our time with mudbound questions."

"We can't stay," I said.

Thrombone looked at me.

"Of course," he said. "Adelaide."

"We have to get back down to a hospital. She's real sick. There's nothing in our first aid box that could help her."

Reggie had put our companion down beside the great trunk of the main tree. There she languished between sleep and despair. The crazy-looking man knelt down and bent over her. He moved closer and closer. First he was looking at the wound, then he was smelling it. When he ran his tongue down the length of the laceration, I jumped to pull him off.

I jumped but Reggie grabbed me.

"Let him alone, Chance."

"Look what he's doin'."

"He's one of us. He knows what he's doing."

I watched him. His hands on either side of Addy's head. Lapping at the cut made him look like a forest creature licking moss from a stone.

"Come on, Chance," Reggie said. "Let's go over to the stuff. We can make a fire to keep her warm when he's through."

I wasn't going to be dissuaded by a child. I pushed against Reggie, but he didn't budge. I was considering a right hook when Wanita grabbed hold of my fingers.

"It's okay, Chance," the dreamer said. "Else, she gonna die."

A high-pitched moan escaped my throat. It was as if a man next to me had finally succumbed to despair. I knew this man's pain, I felt for it, but I was also removed from his feelings.

"Okay," I said. "All right."

The little woodsman was working his head and tongue vigorously against the side of Addy's face. I watched for a moment and then left with Reggie. Wanita came with us, but Alacrity stayed there next to her mother.

More than a thousand feet away from the main tree was the smallest. A redwood less than twenty feet in diameter. This was to be our home for many years, there under the bark of Number Twelve.

Reggie and I broke out the tent and the cooking utensils. I built a small fire from the kindling Wanita gathered. Every once in a while I'd glance over to see Juan hunched over Addy.

"He's okay, Chance," Wanita said. I turned to see her looking up at me. "He's just crazy, that's all."

"What do you mean?"

"He's all mixed up. Too much blue in him. It's not even a color no more. Just real bright, like pins in the window when the sun shine on 'em."

"What do you mean, honey? What do you mean he's crazy?"

"All'a the rest'a us just think one thing, y'know? I mean like Reggie. He like t'get losted but then he finds his way back. He don't never have dreams. But I do." Wanita looked into my eyes as if to say, You see?

"So does Juan Thrombone do more than just finding or dreaming?"

"Only me'n Reggie do them."

"But what—"

"He do a lotta things. But now he don't think like we do no more because when all them things come together, they stop bein' blue-like."

"How do you know this, Wanita? Did he tell you in a dream?"

The little girl shook her head. "Nuh-uh. I can see it. Where it was."

At that moment Reggie, who had been sitting on the other side of the fire, eating oatmeal, rose quickly.

"Here she is," Thrombone said at my back.

He was standing there, carrying Addy in his arms. Seeing him in relation to Addy's long body accented how small the man actually was. He brought Addy next to the fire and laid her down. He rubbed the sleeve of his right arm across his tongue and spit into the fire.

"She was almost dead, you know. You wouldn't have gotten her down to the cities in time." With that, the little madman lay next to Addy and fell into a deep slumber.

I moved next to Alacrity's mother. The wound looked the same, only dimmer. The blood red was now brick red. The white center had turned gray. Addy opened her eyes for a moment and looked up. She smiled and said, "Where's Julia?"

"I'm here, Mommy," Alacrity said just as if she were still a small child.

Adelaide smiled and then fell back into unconsciousness.

Juan Thrombone snored loudly.

He slept like that, next to our campfire, burning or dead, for the next two days. Addy was up the next morning and, though weak, was well on the way back to health.

I wanted to leave, but Alacrity and Wanita said that it would be bad manners to leave Mr. Thrombone sleeping after he had saved Addy's life. Reggie said that he had no intention of leaving the woods anyway, because it was the safest place he could imagine.

"It's the only place that's safe from Death right now," Reggie said. "Anywhere else is like being out in the open where he could see us if he looked hard enough. But there's cover here. That's why I was lost, because Juan made it impossible for us to see or hear or feel."

So we stayed in the deep woods that Juan Thrombone had called Treaty. And as each hour passed, I was more and more lost to the place.

The forest seemed to generate heat. It was cold enough to have to build a fire at night but not too cold. More than enough light filtered down through the leaves. The space was like a great cathedral, a place to worship and give thanks for.

I worried, though, because I didn't know how we could survive up there.

"Mr. Thrombone live up here okay," Wanita said.

"But he's crazy," I answered.

"Maybe he could show us how to be crazy like him."

TWENTY-FOUR

Two days later Juan Thrombone awoke from his deep slumber. He rose and stretched, yawning loudly. The girls were out exploring while I tended the fire and watched over Addy. She was still tired, and I feared, in spite of Thrombone's treatments, that she might relapse into fever.

Reggie was behind Number Seven, masturbating. He'd grown from his early teens into manhood in less than a week. This brought on certain hormonal tensions. He went behind Number Seven nine times, and maybe more, a day to slake their pressures.

I realized what was happening when I saw that Alacrity spent much of her time climbing high into Numbers Five and Six to look down behind Seven. When I asked her what she'd been looking at, she replied, "Reggie's trying to go to the bathroom but he can't."

"It's a good morning, Last Chance," Juan Thrombone said. He looked at Addy and added, "First Light."

"So you're back among the living," I said, using exactly the words and the tones of my uncle Oscar, the only black relative I knew coming up.

"Never left you, friend. How do you like it here among your brothers, the trees?"

"It's okay, I guess," I said. "But how did you find this place?"

"It was waiting for me just like it was waiting for you. There's a place for everything, you know." He brought his hands together in front of his face as if in prayer and rose. "I have to go tend to my forest, friends. I'll bring you some supper when I get back."

He moved gaily into the woods across from Number Twelve and was gone.

"He's funny," Addy said.

"I don't trust him."

"He's okay. He did save my life."

"Maybe he did. I don't know, Addy. I don't know." It was the first time we were alone, really alone and talking, in days.

"What's wrong, Chance?"

"Nothing," I said, actually saying much more.

Addy nodded and smiled. She reached out her hand and I moved closer to hold it. The fire threw out a brilliant heat, but there was still foggy condensation from our breath. I don't know that I felt better then, maybe just reconciled to my fate and happy that I didn't have to face it alone at that moment.

Reggie was coming back from behind Number Seven. I could hear the girls laughing not far away in the woods.

The golden and yellow light from the cover of leaves winked and glittered. I left myself open to the half-told tales of where they came from and where they hoped to be. Each sparkle of light entered my mind, humming a forgotten tune that my heart tried to beat for. A dance took off within me. I was swirling to the fragmentary music of light. I was soaring and stationary like the giant pillars of my new home. I was decaying and dying but still full of life. I was decomposing the lies I had always believed defined me and my skin.

The children came back around the fire to eat and talk to us. Every now and then Reggie would wander off to Number Seven. I may have heard them. I might have even said a few words now and then. But mostly my mind was in the trees, in the light in the trees, swirling and capering to melodies older than life down here. Ordé's blood moving in mine was a refuge from all the vacant fear that had gathered in my gut, clouded in my skull cavity.

I was dizzy with meaning that I did not understand. I tried to be brave in the face of immensity that dwarfed even my wildest dreams of expanse.

I fell asleep after an hour, maybe less. I was unconscious but aware of the scent of earth and decaying foliage. I listened contentedly to the girls playing and Addy cooing to them. It was a sleep with no dreams, as refreshing and as clear as water from a cold spring after a long long walk in July.

The visions of light had started to subside. I woke up thirsty just as the sun was throwing her last rays on the ground around my body.

"So you're back among the living," my uncle Oscar said.

When I looked, I saw that it was Juan Thrombone mimicking my words to him.

"It's just in time too." The little man giggled.

The fire had been expanded to three different units, each separated by and surrounded with similar-sized oblong stones. Over each fire was a pan or a pot. There were trout simmering and mushrooms and some kind of forest green too. Everyone was sitting around the fire. The flame seemed to echo the visions of my afternoon nap.

"Time to eat," Juan said simply. "Eat first and then to tell stories, I think. Stories are good when you live out with the trees and bears and butterflies. Here, sleepy," he said to me. "Have some sap and water."

He handed me a carved wooden mug that was tall and thin. Instead of a handle, it had a leafy branch sticking out from one side. The mug was filled with water that smelled of sweet sap. There were bits of branches and leaves floating about in the drink. I tasted it and then couldn't pull the cup away from my lips. It was the best-tasting water I had ever had. It was water and also the dream of water in a thirsty's man's desert.

The fish were from a nearby stream. The mushrooms were hacked from the sides of trees with homemade wooden knives, and the greens were small leafy plants that grew in the clearing between the forest and our cathedral of trees. Everything was delicious. I felt satisfied from the back of my mind down into my toes.

When the dinner was over, Thrombone came out with honey wine for the grown-ups and honeyed water for the girls. Reggie drank his wine too quickly and got drunk. He pulled himself up and declared that he was going out to find a drum.

"Now is the time for stories, my friends," Juan Thrombone said in a singsong voice. "Telling the tales keeps them from sneaking up on you when you're not looking. When you're not looking."

The girls laughed. Alacrity held Wanita in her lap. All her heroism and command had faded now that she didn't need it. She was our charge again, her mother's little girl.

Thrombone went to a hollow below Number Three and retrieved a dozen homemade beeswax candles. The candles were thick shapeless globs encrusted with gravel. We placed them around our campsite, letting Wanita light them because Addy wouldn't let her play with the campfire.

We all settled in on one side of the fire, with Thrombone squatting down from us on the other side.

"What will it be, Chance? What do you want me to tell?"

"Why me?" I asked. "I don't know your stories. You could just make one up."

"Come on, Chance," Alacrity said. Her head in Addy's lap, she shoved her feet under the tent of my knees. Wanita leaned on me from the other side. Addy draped a sleeping bag over our shoulders.

Juan Thrombone's eyes were like two more candles in the night.

I was fearful that he might really answer any question I had. I was tired of knowledge and truth.

"What is the blue light?" I asked finally.

Juan Thrombone laughed and rolled on his back. He rocked on his spine while grabbing his knees and let out a howl.

"Ho-ho, Chance the gamesman. Chance the check-mater. Chance the opponent till the end."

The children laughed and Addy smiled.

I didn't find his childishness funny.

Thrombone rolled to a squatting position in an agile move. He looked at me for a long time before speaking again.

"You think to ask me a question you already know the answer to, hombre. You think you know how the light traveled, how it bonded and took. You think that I will just repeat the words of your dead teacher. You do not want to know anything more, but you lost the gam-bit and so I will tell you more.

"Your question, my friend, should have been another. Because asking about blue light is like asking about blood when you have never seen an animal. How can you know about a man's blood, its magic, if you have never seen him laughing and you've never heard him cry?"

Juan Thrombone settled easily on crossed legs and held out his hands as if to say, Isn't that true?

"You must, it is clear, ask about life and not light or blood. Because life holds them both like the canvas holds paint."

I was completely in his spell by then. The words and their rhythm charmed me like the sunlight had that day.

"Blue light or yellow or red, it doesn't matter. They're all like blood. Blood that sustains you, blood that builds. But blood in a bottle, or blood on the ground, is not a man, can't be, but only a promise without an ear to hear."

Holding up an educating finger, he said, "All the world is music, you see. There is music in atoms and music in suns. That is the range of a scale that you can see and read. There is music in emptiness and silence between. Everything is singing all the time, all the time. Singing and calling for what is missing. Your science calls it *gravity*, but the gods call it *dance*. They dance and fornicate; they listen and sing. They call to distant flowers when buds ring out. Because, you see, it is not only atoms and suns that vibrate in tune. Rocks sing, as do water and air. The molecules that build blood and men also build the wasp; these too sing a minor note that travels throughout the stars. Greedy little ditties that repeat and repeat again and again the same silly melodies. They change, but very slowly, chattering, 'me me me me me me me me me. . . .'" He repeated the word maybe a hundred times, lowering his head to the ground as he did so. He smiled when he was finished and shook his head sadly. The next instant he was on his feet holding his hands out in the question Why?

"So much boring chatter for one so deep. Of course, the iron atom will say only his name. Water too and even granite or glass. Because iron has only one note; water two, maybe three. But you, my friend, make the violin seem simple. You are a song of the gods in the mouth of a fool. You can't help it. So much promise in one so weak attracts disease."

Juan Thrombone sat again and smiled. We looked at each other, and even though my head had begun to ache from the words, which seemed to go directly into my mind, I asked, "Are you saying that blue light is a sickness? That one who sees the light is sick?"

"Sick?" Thrombone said, chuckling softly. "No. But weak as kittens in a cave full of stones. They feel mighty, but there is no strength in them. Only ambition and youth. They cannot hunt or mul-ti-ply. Only can they play like the big cat who has left the den carrying their milk in her udders."

"What do you mean? Alacrity was born from Ordé and Addy."

"First Light," Thrombone's eyes filled with fondness. "Her child is rare but no different from the rest. The next generation is coming, but not yet. Maybe never. Maybe not at all."

By then I wanted to know everything that the little madman knew.

"So this isn't what Ordé said?" I asked. "This isn't the beginning of the change of the world?"

"It might be some kind of start," he answered. "But this is storytime and not school."

"But—" I started to say.

"I have answered your question, and now you need to ask another. Not about blue light, though. With that I am through."

"Why didn't you want us to come here?" Alacrity asked. "Why'd you send those butterflies to hurt us?"

"Because, little one, I was afraid. I was afraid that Death would sniff at you even here and come to kill the puppy trees as he did their big mama redwood. I was afraid and so I sent my butterflies to sting you with their love." Juan Thrombone almost lost his benign smile for a moment. "But when you fought so hard and killed so many I"—He held his palm to his lips and sucked suddenly, pulling his hand away from his mouth. This caused the same thumping in the air that had rendered the butterflies, and me, unconscious. This sound, however, wasn't as violent as the first—"so you wouldn't kill all of my beautiful friends."

"What did those butterflies do to the children?" Addy asked.

Thrombone smiled again, holding up the baby finger of his left hand to the point at his left eye.

"You mean to ask," our odd host lectured, "what are those butterflies that they could do what they did? But the answer is no story. I made water every day in a clearing of rotten wood. In a year there were wild flowers everywhere. In another year there were butterflies. From butterfly to worm, and then from the worm rose the creatures that suckled on blue."

Thrombone smiled to himself.

"Maybe it is a story," he said.

Wanita asked, "Then why did you let us come if you was scared? Ain't you scared no more?"

Thrombone was looking into Addy's eyes at that moment. She stared back while running her finger down the healing wound on her face.

"I can hear people's dreams also, Dreamer. I can hear all living things when they dream. Dogs and trees and fish and bears. I can speak to dreamers. I spoke to all of you. I knew in our talks that you were not bad—at least, not yet. And I was lonely, but that's not why I let you pass."

"Why then?" Wanita asked again.

"To sleep with you, Dreamer."

"Say what?" That was me. "Hey, man, I know you livin' up here with the bears and shit, but down the hill, in civilization, no matter if you got blue light or Thunderbird wine, men sleeping with little girls is just not happenin'." I was angry and used street talk like a hapless frog puffing up his throat to bluff his way.

"I'm sorry, my friend," Juan said. If he was in any way intimidated, he hid it well. "You are right, of course. I've been up here so long that I forget how to talk. I don't mean sex. I like sex. I want sex. But for Wanita, it is only her dreams I wish to share. I can hear dreams, but she—she can travel in them, she can see with them. Her dreams are the most beautiful I have ever seen."

I was not convinced. I made up my mind right then to tuck Wanita in every night—and to sleep close by.

Bomp bomp bomp resounded in the air. *Bomp de bomp. Bomp de bomp.*

"It's Reggie!" Alacrity cried.

The sound came closer and closer. Finally Reggie emerged from the woods with a big hollow log in his arms. He beat the drum with a thick branch.

Thrombone leaped up and so did Addy and the girls. They all danced and laughed happily. No one else seemed to feel that the world was falling apart. No one else seemed afraid of what might happen in the days to come.

I fed the fire while my friends and Juan Thrombone danced. Reggie beat his drum with an amazing ear for someone untrained. They were all wild and abandoned, but Alacrity was by far the most primal. Her movements were like nothing except maybe the flames I fed. She leaped and gesticulated, bounced and sang out. Her whiteness was fearful to see. Her intensity, I feared, was the future of the world.

The dancing went on for quite a while longer. Finally Addy tired, and Juan followed her back to the fire. Smiling and happy, they sat there next to me. I felt more lonely than ever.

"The trees are not only a wall of wood and root," Juan was saying later on, after much honey wine, "but they sing a dull song I taught them. That song hides the puppy trees and you and me. They also call for people like you, First Light"—he was referring to Addy, he was holding her hand—"humans half dipped blue. I wanted them to come help me tend the trees and the forest."

"Why would the trees need tending?" I asked. "It is a forest, isn't it? The trees can get along on their own."

"But these are special trees," the little woodsman replied.

"What kind of special trees?"

Juan Thrombone turned his full attention upon me then. In his eyes I saw a vastness across which, I imagined, a strong wind blew. His smile didn't seem relevant to the power in those eyes, but he smiled anyway and said, "There are two kinds of trees that are special. One because they can sing and the other because they roar."

"What do you mean?"

"You heard a call, did you not?" he asked.

The storm in his gaze seemed to grow in power.

"That call," he continued, "was from a thousand trees whose parents were white firs. I grafted them so they could sing so sweet and high. They sing like the wind, only higher. They sing like the sun before dawn."

"The wind and the sun," Addy said. "Are those the two kinds?"

"No, First Light," Juan said gently. "The white firs sing of the sun and wind. And then there are the puppy trees."

"What are they?" I asked.

"Deep bass rumblers. Children of what you call blue light but, like Alacrity, born here. They are orphans and I tend them. They rumble like bullfrogs and tickle Earth's soul."

"And we're here to tend them?" I asked.

"No," he said. The tone of his voice would have knocked me down if I wasn't already seated. "The puppy trees, the deep rumblers, might mistake you for dinner and suck the life from your bones. Stay away from them. You were summoned here to tend the special white firs, the high singers, the maskers of blue. The ones that called you. They called and you came."

"We did," I said. "But you didn't want the children. You wanted Addy, but you wanted her to leave Alacrity behind."

I wanted Addy to see him for what he was.

"I never expected that those of such power, even so young, would follow those so weak. I didn't know if I could protect them and the puppy trees too. The thing out there, the one you call Gray Man. He wants only to kill. I thought that all of us together here would make too much noise, would bring him here."

"And so he could be on the way here right now?" I said, happy that I now had a way to get my friends to leave.

"He might be. He might." Juan cocked his ear upward. "But I don't hear him coming. No, I don't."

"But he could be coming," I said. "He could be, and you just don't hear it yet. He could come on us in our sleep up here. He could kill us in our sleep. We've got to get out of here. We've got to get out of here now."

I looked around at my companions and friends. The children had stopped their dancing to listen. They were all looking to Juan Thrombone. It was he who they turned to for answers now. It was he whom they trusted.

"You can leave if you want to," Juan said to me. "You are welcome if you care to stay. The Gray Man may not know where we are; he may have changed also. This could well be true."

"I'm staying," Reggie said. "It's nice here. It's the safest place in the whole world."

"Me too," Wanita said.

"Please stay, Chance," Alacrity whined. "Please stay with us here. Please."

I looked to Addy. Her fingers were laced with Juan Thrombone's. She held my eyes a moment and then looked away.

"I'm staying for a while at least, Chance. I'm tired and sick still. And I can't think of anywhere else to go."

"And there will be others," Juan said. "More people will come to us over the weeks and days. The song you heard goes like a ribbon on the wind, blowing here and there. Some will hear it. A few will come. And when they get here, there's an old town down by the stream. It's a ghost town now, but soon they will come and we can be happy, Last Chance, for a while more."

Addy snuggled down and put her head against Juan's shoulder. That's what broke my will. He had taken everything that I had left with his funny way of talking and his eyes like forever.

"Okay," I said. "All right, I'll stay for a few days more. At least until Addy is better. Then we can talk about it again."

And with that, something eased in me. A pressure, a weight. I gave in to the spell of Juan Thrombone and his magical wood. Reggie began playing his drum again and we all danced. Somewhere in the early hours of the morning Juan and Addy disappeared. I found them the next day naked and wrapped in each other's arms under the hanging shingles of Number One. They were together from that day on.

TWENTY-FIVE

At first I stayed because of the children. But within the first month I knew that they were safe with Addy and her man. After that I just didn't know where to go. Juan offered to walk me out of the wood if I wanted to leave. But the truth was, I wanted *him* to leave. Sometimes he'd go away for days at a time. I'd begin to hope that he'd hurt himself or maybe just decided to go elsewhere. I'd try to comfort Addy at those times, telling her that she didn't have to worry.

I wanted Addy then. It had never crossed my mind before. She was Ordé's woman to begin with, and later, while we fled the threat of Gray Man, I was too worried even to think about love. But once we were settled in Treaty, I wanted her to choose me over Juan. I wanted her to see that he was unstable but that I was constant.

But she never worried when Juan was gone.

"He'll be back, Chance," she'd say with a dreamy look on her face. "He'll come back to me and he'll have great stories to tell."

Not only had her wound healed but her skin had soft-ened, the little red veins in her eyes had cleared. She started singing songs and working with strange leaves, tree needles actually, and barks that Juan brought for her to cook in a huge stone tub that appeared one day next to Number Nine.

"My friends brought it in the night," he told me when I asked how the big hollow rock got there.

Juan taught Addy how to cook the leaves and wood and how to pound the mixture with a pestle the size of a baseball bat. She worked at it for days until the result-ing green paste was thick. Then she spread out the mix-ture on a big stone that lay in the field separating the cathedral of Treaty from the surrounding woods. The paste dried into an extremely thin and seemingly deli-cate blue-green material. It was like rice paper, only it wouldn't tear or decompose. From this cloth Addy made our clothes. She didn't sew the seams but used wooden buttons with bearhair ties that Juan collected for her.

"There's what you call blue light in those leafies," Thrombone said to me when I marveled at the fabric Addy made. "I harvest them from the puppy trees when they're rumbling content. They have power in them plenty."

He also made tea from those leaves. He would let them steep over a low flame in a stone pot for weeks at a time. Then he'd pour the liquid into one of his few precious glass bottles and let it cool in a stream. The brew was strong-tasting, sweet and pungent. Whenever I drank that tea I felt a momentary elation followed by an hour of unutterable calm.

* * *

One day I awoke to deep drumbeats playing somewhere out in the woods. I remembered something and went looking for Alacrity. She and I were going to look for straight branches from which she could make arrows for the bow Juan and Reggie had made. I couldn't find her, so I went to Addy, who was naked next to Number One, making pants for either Reggie or me.

"She left with Juan this morning," Addy said.

"When are they coming back?"

"Not for a few days."

"A few days? You let your daughter go off into the woods with a man like that overnight? What's wrong with you, Addy?"

"It's okay, Chance. He's going to help her. You know how restless she's been. He found her hacking away at tree bark, and Reggie had to stop her from tormenting Wanita. Juan said that he's going to take her on a walk to discover her true nature."

"How could you just let her go like that?"

Addy looked up at me, putting down her work. Like I said, she was naked. She was a very beautiful woman, and I was especially aware of that when she peered into my eyes.

"Sit down, Chance," she said.

I did so.

"You have to stop this now. You have to accept Juan and his life out here. I know that you love us and that you want to protect us, but fighting him isn't going to help. This is his home and we're his guests. I don't know what he's doing with Julia out there, but whatever it is, I know it's for the best." Her green eyes held on to the light like dusky quartz.

"But how can you say that?" I said. "You don't know him. You just met him. He can get in your head. Maybe he's hypnotized you."

The way she shook her head crushed any hope I had left.

She brought her hands to either side of my head and kissed me, softly at first.

I wanted to give her the best loving that she had ever had. I wanted to make her sing out my name and forget all about Juan Thrombone. But I hadn't made love to a woman in many months, so it was the most I could do to call out her name once before I came.

She gave out a loud *oh* and then wrapped her arms and legs around me, to comfort my distress. She cooed in my ear, "It's all right, Chance. It's okay."

I sat up and away from her.

"What's your boyfriend gonna think about that, huh?" I asked.

"Juan doesn't love me for that," she said. "He'd know that I was just sharing the love around us with one of our friends."

"Like he's doing right now with your little girl?"

Addy rose and walked away. I made to go after her, but instead I went another way, the direction from which the drumming was coming.

I followed the deep vibrations until I came upon Reggie, who now called himself Pathfinder, and Wanita in a small hollow. He was beating his big log with hardened hands while Wanita lay down before him absorbing the music with her bones.

"Reggie."

"Yeah, Chance?" he answered, still rolling the rhythm out from his drum.

"I need you to help me find Alacrity. There's something wrong, and I need to go find her."

"What's wrong? Somethin' wrong with you, Chance?" the boy who had become a man asked.

"No, with Alacrity. She's disappeared and I want to find her."

"She's wit' Bones," Wanita said. Bones is what she called Juan Thrombone.

"But I've got to find her."

"She'll come back, Chance," Reggie said. "We don't have to go looking for her if she's comin' back."

"But I need to find her," I said again.

"For what?"

"All you need to do is help me and not ask all these stupid questions." I was mad and hoping that my anger could still overwhelm the child that lingered in the man.

"I'm stayin' here," Reggie said. "I'ma play drums out here and that's all."

I left them in the clearing and went out to find Alacrity and Thrombone myself. I wandered in the woods around Treaty and then I went farther away. I started calling for her after midday. That evening, when my voice finally gave out, I returned to camp. Reggie and Wanita were already asleep. Addy was sitting by a fire under Number One, but I didn't feel like talking to her.

The next morning I went out again. For the next six mornings I searched and called. But I couldn't find her.

In among the regular trees (firs, incense cedars, yellow pine, even a hemlock here and there) were the special white firs of Juan Thrombone. These trees had a different kind of life to them. They were trees like any others in most ways, but they also gave off a low-level emission—a sound that you couldn't quite hear, a song. And though I had never actually seen one move, I was often disoriented by parts of the woods that were sometimes crowded by white firs but at other times were sparse or even bare.

During that week I am sure that the firs conspired to stymie my attempts to find Alacrity. Sometimes, when I thought I heard a child's strained voice, I'd rush to get there, but the firs were too dense and I couldn't make it through. Sometimes the path I followed went in circles leading me away from my destination.

Addy refused to talk to me about it. Reggie thought I was crazy, and Wanita kept telling me stories about dreams she'd had. I think she hoped I would forget about Alacrity while listening to her tales.

I was young and stupid then. I don't remember most of the dreams. I was too worried about Alacrity, or more accurately, I was jealous. Alacrity treated me like her father and her best friend. I knew that Juan wasn't abusing her. But he was taking her from me. Just like he'd taken Addy.

The one dream of Wanita's that I remember was about the Tusk Men. Big men with hairy bodies and lower jaws that jutted out sporting long saberlike teeth. They carried clubs and wandered up and down the streets of a bombed-out city. They were meat-eaters. They ate people. People, Wanita said. Whatever place her dreams took her that time, there were people there, not pink crystals or rolling sentient fogs.

The Tusk Men knew that Wanita was there. They looked for her but she ran. She ran across the sky to a big stone fort where people gathered to fight off their enemies. These enemies were Tusk Men and wolf women, crawling worm people and fat bottoms who weighed almost nothing, floating on poisonous gases like flatulent balloons.

The dream had frightened Wanita, that's why I remember it. I put her on my lap and hugged her and told her that all of that was far away and she was safe now in Treaty.

"Why don't you like it here?" Wanita asked, rubbing her tears off on my shoulder.

"I like it, honey. It's just all so different."

"Different from what?"

"I don't know," I said. "You and Reggie, Alacrity and Bones. I can't keep up with it all. Sometimes I just want to go home."

"Don't leave us, Chance," the little girl said.

"Chance," someone else called from a distance away.

I looked up because it was not a voice that I knew. It sounded familiar, but I couldn't quite tell from where or when.

"Chance," she called again.

Across from Number Twelve, out of the trees, came Juan Thrombone accompanied by a tall woman. She had short-cropped blond hair and fair skin. As they approached, I could see that she had a nasty-looking scar down her jawline. She wore only a fur cape that didn't

cover all of her body at once. She was calling my name
and waving at me.

"Alacrity" issued from my lips.

The next thing I knew, I was running. Addy and Reggie and Wanita were behind me. I was the first to reach
her, though. I picked her up and hugged her hard. The
squeeze she gave me nearly broke my spine.

She hollered in my ear and threw me around.

"Hi, everybody!" she yelled.

We all cheered and capered, a lost tribe of primitives
secreted beyond the reach of sanity.

"Bones made me fight with the bears," Alacrity said as
we sat around the fire that night. Clothed only in her
bearskin robe, she sat at my side, holding my arm, lac-
ing her fingers with mine. A dark circle of dried food
was etched around her full lips. "First it was just a little
one. We wrestled for an hour almost, but then I pulled her
ears so hard that she ran away. I wouldn't have done
that, but she clawed me on my jaw and that made me
mad."

Juan Thrombone was snoring under Number One
while the rest of us sat around the fire under Twelve.

"But then," Alacrity continued, "after I would fight,
I'd get real tired and have to go to sleep. And all the
bears were growling. And when I'd wake up there'd be
another bear, only a little bigger, and then I'd fight
again. But every time I was stronger and knew how to
fight better. Sometimes I'd get a broken leg. Sometimes
I'd get cut real bad. But the only scar was from the first
time. Bones said it was first blood, and he put special
dirt in it while I was asleep so it wouldn't go away. He

said that I should always remember first blood because I was a warrior, and warriors had to remember that they could be hurt too.

"Finally I had to fight Brutus."

"Who's that?" Wanita cried.

"Brutus was that big black bear that chased us here. He always hated me because I broke his nose. He's always been waiting around here to get me, only Bones wouldn't let him until we had the contest. 'Cause, you see, Bones said that I had to grow in order to feel my power. He said that I was always so restless because I needed to be big to do what I need to do. And so after each time I'd sleep, I got bigger. And when I was all grown up, I had to have a fight to the death with Brutus because that would be my bap . . . bap . . ."

"Baptism," Addy said.

"Yeah," Alacrity agreed. "Baptism."

"Uh-huh." Wanita nodded and looked into her friend's eyes. "That's 'cause you gotta be fightin' an' stuff. I seen that. I seen it, Alacrity. You were beautiful and real mad."

"He came at me real fast," Alacrity said. "But I jumped high and landed on his back. Then I pulled his ears and jumped off when he tried to crush me on a tree. And then I got me a stick and he kept comin', but I'd keep jumpin' outta the way and hittin' 'im on the neck and stuff. One time he caught me and pushed me down with his paws and he cut my chest, but I rolled away when he got offa me for a second. And then I hit him across the face and he couldn't see nuthin'. And so then I hit him on the head with a rock and he fell down and rolled around 'cause he couldn't see and his head hurt."

Alacrity stopped for a moment then and looked very serious.

"So you beat 'im," Wanita cried. "You won."

"Bones said that I had to kill Brutus if I was the winner," the warrior said. "He said that I had to be able to kill my enemy, and then we would eat his liver for a feast."

"Did you kill him?" Wanita asked fearfully.

"I dug my fingers in his neck and tore out his windpipe, uh-huh, yeah."

I looked closer at the dark circle around her lips. What frightened me was that she hadn't washed off the grisly trophy.

We were all quiet after that. The only sound that could be heard was Juan Thrombone's snoring more than a thousand feet away.

TWENTY-SIX

Alacrity's change had a strong effect on Reggie. He began stalking her from a distance. When she'd go down to the stream to bathe with Wanita, Reggie could always be found somewhere nearby—watching. He brooded in her presence and said almost nothing to her directly. Sometimes he'd say things to Wanita while Alacrity stood there.

"She better wear a shirt if she gonna be climbin', else it's gonna be tittie trees," he said many times, laughing thickly to punctuate his bad joke.

Alacrity was confused by Reggie's behavior. They'd always been friends. She looked up to him. He showed her about pathfinding and made her little toys and trinkets out of wood.

Of course, Alacrity's behavior didn't help things any. She was still a child in many ways, moving around and dancing with no sense of shame. She liked her tree-cloth dresses short so that she could move easily and often went naked, or nearly so, like her mother.

Reggie spent even more time behind Number Seven.

The tension in the air was unsettling, and I found my-self leaving the cathedral during the day to go out among the trees.

The special white firs around Treaty gave off a sense of deep calm. Juan had said that he planted many of them and helped them grow quickly, as he'd done with Alacrity.

"I got 'em all over here. They're kinda like you, Last Chance—half-light and free."

I learned not to ask about his pronouncements. What-ever he knew about me, he could keep to himself.

"I know about the song trees, the white firs, but where are these puppy trees that you keep talking about?"

"Where they belong, my friend. Where they belong."

One day I left the camp early to go out among the trees. It was easy to pick out a tree that Juan had brought along because of the slight *singing* vibration it gave off. Sitting under the boughs of one of those young firs, I had the feeling of motion and peace. It was the opposite of being in a convertible racing down a straight road on a flat plain; even though I was standing still, there was the illusion of moving.

I was sitting in a grove of those special trees, wishing that I had brought my *History* along, when Alacrity came up. She wore a short dress of tree cloth with wooden buttons down the side. She bent down to lay her bow and arrows against the tree. You could see most of her powerful, long legs, and her breasts seemed to point wherever she happened to be looking.

She turned to me then.

"Hi, Chance," she said. Then she moved close just like the child she still was.

"Hey, Alacrity. What's goin' on?"

"Nuthin'," she said.

We sat for a few moments, looking into space.

"When I was out there with Bones," Alacrity said, "I could hear you calling for me. I could hear you when I was sleeping and I could feel myself gettin' bigger and stronger. And I could hear you calling for me, and all I wanted was to come back here to you."

She put her hand on the inside of my thigh.

"I wanted you to do it to me," she said.

"Oh, yeah?" I tried to sound nonchalant.

"Uh-huh." Her hand moved up slightly. I was very aware that the fabric of my tree-cloth pants was no thicker than skin.

"What do you want now?" I asked.

It was a first kiss for her. A first kiss as a woman, that is. She pushed her lips against mine and shivered. I wanted to believe that she was just a young woman coming to a man she thought she could trust.

It was a sweet kiss, and I needed love.

But Alacrity had been like a little niece to me only a few weeks before. I wanted her but had no intention of giving in to that desire. I'd like to say that I pushed her away and told her that there would be other men for her. But other circumstances separated us that day.

"You guys better stop that!" he shouted.

Alacrity was on her feet, nocking her arrow in the direction of the shout. Through the dense tangle of leaves, maybe sixty yards away, I could see a form that I knew had to be Reggie. With the impossible speed of a dream, Alacrity pulled and let her arrow fly.

The body through the trees lunged for cover more quickly than I would have imagined possible, but the shout of pain told me that Alacrity's speed had been greater.

Reggie was up in a moment, hobbling away.

"I'll kill you!" Alacrity said. She had nocked another arrow.

Reggie screamed.

I jumped, grabbing the bow and throwing my body weight against the enraged girl. The bow snapped and I fell. Alacrity started running in the direction that Reggie had fled, but I managed to grab her foot and topple her.

She went down but was up in an instant. I grabbed her again; she turned and threw me up against a tree. With one hand against my chest, Alacrity hefted a large wooden knife in the other. The killing rage that shook her dampened any possibility for love. I could see that this was the passion sex brought up in her.

I was used to wildflowers and red wine, not arrows and knives.

"Fuck!" Alacrity shouted in my face.

She turned away from me and stalked off into the woods. I wasn't worried about Reggie anymore. It looked as though the arrow had only caught him in the thigh, and I knew Alacrity wouldn't be able to find him once he got out of sight.

The surrounding white firs hummed a sweet counterpoint to my panic. But the music was no balm for my pain. I was flesh in the face of iron blades; I was a Christian at the mercy of lions. I was at the center of history and paying the price. I shivered when I thought of how quickly Alacrity had decided to kill her friend. I tried to think of something to do about it, but nothing came to mind. The aftermath of my fright left me drowsy. I closed my eyes, and sleep followed me into the dark.

When I returned to the camp that night, Reggie had been there but was gone again. Addy said that he claimed his wound had come from a fall. She hadn't believed him, but he was gone before Juan or I had returned.

Alacrity was back late. She was sullen and went to sleep soon.

We didn't see Reggie again for days. He made his presence known, though, through missing food and the disappearance of his sleeping bag.

Silence prevailed over those days. Wanita was quiet, not even talking about her dreams. Addy sat for hours with her daughter, cooking and working with tree cloth. Only Juan Thrombone seemed unaffected by the mood. He spent most of his time preparing for the new citizens of Treaty.

He kept saying that people like me and Addy—half-light and free—would soon be coming.

Bones was always returning from or going to the abandoned town about five miles away. It had been a mining town, just three broken-down buildings on one side of a creek that must have once been a road. There was a hotel, a church, and what might have been a barn or a dance hall. Juan was working on them, filling in cracks, bringing bear pelts and big granite pots.

I once saw him moving a great pot by using bears as beasts of burden. He led them with simple reins made from various animal hairs and deer leather. The ropes he used were also from hair and of thickly braided tree cloth. It was quite a sight, seeing a team of six huge bears working in unison pulling the four-foot-high oblong stone bowl.

That particular morning I had been out looking for Reggie. I hadn't seen him since the day in the singing grove. I heard sounds pretty far away and followed them. When I got there, I saw the team of bears pulling the stone bowl down a gully of small trees. Juan Thrombone sat atop the bowl, driving the grunting bears. All around them were butterflies. Thousands of butterflies. Some were big like the ones that attacked us, but many were small and normal-looking. They seemed to be urging the bears and Thrombone on.

"Hurry up, bears!" Juan Thrombone barked. "The sooner we get there the sooner you get your honey!"

I followed them for the rest of the morning. There was nothing else to do. They pulled and yanked, growled and roared for more than three hours until coming to the town of Treaty deep in a cedar grove.

When they got the big bowl out in front of the barn-like structure, Juan laid out six big wooden bowls, filling each with honey from a large deerskin pouch. The bears went at the sweet liquid and were instantly carpeted with butterflies.

"Pretty, huh?"

The voice startled me. I gasped just like a frightened starlet in a bad western.

"Hey," Alacrity said.

"Hey," I whispered back.

We watched for a while, and then she jerked her head to indicate that we should leave. I followed her down a path that I hadn't noticed before. She was wearing a pair of her mother's jeans and one of my plaid shirts.

We walked for a long time, saying absolutely nothing. For more than an hour we made a gradual climb but then began to descend. The terrain was pretty rough, and through most of it there was no path. Every footfall was a different motion, a new gesture. Following Alacrity through that rough terrain was like going through the motions of some primeval prayer and dance.

After maybe two hours more she stopped.

"It's just up there," she said.

"What?" I was breathing hard and didn't want to take another step.

"You got to get ready now, Chance," she said instead of answering my question.

"Ready for what?"

"Just try to keep calm now; it's just up here. Right after we go between these trees."

We were in a grove of Juan Thrombone's singing firs. They formed a blockade and a doorway. Alacrity pushed her way through the sapling trunks. Actually, the trees themselves seemed to move apart for her. We went up through into a large space, a grove of young sequoias. Young, but what trees they were.

There were two dozen forty-foot sequoias spaced out around the clearing. Each one was magnificent in its own birthright, but what dazzled me was something else. Where the singing trees of Juan Thrombone chanted in high-pitched tones like castrati, these great trees hummed out a psalm so deep that I was forced to my knees. They were, I was sure, the choir of Earth. Their deep rumbling melody told me everything. They were the hymn of unbroken history back so far that they predated the light that illuminated them.

I was there on my knees outside of the circle of trees. I named them instantly—the Bellowing Trees of Earth.

"Come on, Chance," Alacrity said to me. "I wanna show you the throne."

"No," I croaked.

"Why not?"

"I can't." I swallowed the words. I didn't think she understood me. "I can't," I said again.

"But it's a throne. You'll really like it."

I sobbed but couldn't say any more. Alacrity knelt beside me and put her arms around me. Instinctively she brought my head to her breast. Her strength and warmth, the powerful beating of her heart, revived me some. I held on tight and her embrace tightened too.

As sad and suicidal as I had been in San Francisco, I never even once thought that there could have been too much beauty. But there with those trees, in that beautiful warrior woman's arms, I felt too small to enjoy the pleasure offered me.

"Come on, Chance," Alacrity said again. "Come with me."

She pulled me to my feet, and we walked through the chorus of gods. The music that emanated was less sound and more a bone-shaking vibration. A deep longing for friction was satisfied somewhere that I hadn't known existed. My balance was shaky, the ground seemed to shift now and then. The trees didn't appear to be limited by space at all. They were everywhere at once.

Alacrity walked with her arm around my waist. She led me to the largest tree toward the other side of the grove. There was an opening shaped like a frozen black flame in its bark. The slit was large enough for a man to go into, but not far.

"Sit in it," Alacrity told me. "Sit down in it."

I did as she said, going to my knees and crawling into the space.

As soon as I was seated, the chorus ceased. It was as though the vibrations all came together, negating one another, or maybe complementing one another. Then, instead of hearing them, I saw their music as the intricate interlacing of multicolored lights. It was like sitting in the middle of a giant gem, experiencing its formation over the millions of years. The trees were building themselves and the world around them. An exquisite and invisible edifice of possibility arose in the forest, and I was the only witness. It was a conspiracy of the trees. A grand design. I wanted to be a part of that design. I wanted to lay down roots right there in that hollow. I wanted to be a deep note in their ululation.

My human senses closed down inside the tree. Instead, I was a root sensing water, a cell sucking on light. I could feel my body reaching and reforming.

A lazy tendril root caressed my cheek.

"Come on, Chance," Alacrity said again. "That's enough. You're not supposed to stay in there that long. Come on."

If I had had any strength left, I would have fought her. That tree had more hold on me than Claudia Heart ever did.

Alacrity pulled me to my feet and made me run out of the grove. I could hear the trees calling for me, calling. Once we were among the simple singing firs of Juan Thrombone again, I relaxed. An exhaustion came over me that I had never felt before. Every cell was tired. I took in a deep ragged breath like a man who'd been drowning.

"I'n'it cool?" Alacrity asked, excited by our adventure.

"What happened to me?"

"I don't know, not really, but the tree wants you. It calls out and then, if you go in, it tries to pull you down with it. It's so cool."

Alacrity was very excited by it all. She tore my shirt open, popping all the buttons, and then she pulled my pants down. When she stood up, shucking her own clothes, I watched with only one thing on my mind.

Alacrity, and her breasts, were looking at my erection. I realized that she brought me there because she knew somehow that the song of the redwoods would arouse me.

I brought my hand to my hardon, and Alacrity gasped. When I reached down to pull up my pants, she frowned and I hoped that her new bow was not around.

"Sit down, Alacrity," I said. "Come sit down here next to me."

"Why?"

"Just sit down, honey."

She waited a moment or so and then did as I asked.

I took her hands in mine. She relaxed a little.

"Baby," I said. I was tired and the deep song of the trees was still playing in my mind. "You're my little girl. I was your father's student, and his blood runs in mine. I'm like your uncle or older brother. I'm your family, honey. I can't be your boyfriend."

"Why not?" she asked. "I love you. I don't even think about anybody but you. All the time."

"That's just because you've grown up so quickly. You love me, and all of a sudden you've come to be a woman. It's confusing, but don't worry, there'll be men for you."

"When?"

"Not that long. But you've got to remember that you can't settle your problems by fighting. You are a fighter, but you should go to war only when nothing else will work."

"But Reggie was wrong to be spying on us," Alacrity said.

"Yeah, but, you know, he's grown up almost as fast as you have. And you're beautiful, Alacrity. If you covered up some more, he wouldn't get so excited. You know, if you run around naked, men will follow you—and that's not good. I mean, most of the time women have trouble when men go after them like that. But in your case I think it's the men who will have it bad."

"If he leaves me alone, I won't bother him," Alacrity complained.

"I can't tell you what to do, honey. You're a woman now—ready or not. But do me a favor, okay?"

"What?"

"Go easy on us poor men. Give us a break."

I don't know what it is that I said exactly. I don't know what she heard, but Alacrity threw her arms around me and hugged so hard that I had to put off breathing during her embrace.

"I love you, Chance," she whispered in my ear.

I heard in her words the song of the trees. They were still calling for me.

TWENTY-SEVEN

One drizzly day not long after my talk with Alacrity, we all heard a weak scream from somewhere not too far away. Juan was sitting beneath Number One with Alacrity, skinning a deer she had taken down with her bow and arrow. He was the first one to raise his head.

"They're here," he said. "They're here."

He jumped up and ran for the singing wood, followed by Alacrity and Wanita and, finally, by Reggie the pathfinder. Addy and I walked up to the edge of the cathedral and waited. I strained to listen, but there were no more screams. All I could hear was the patter and hiss of the light rain.

"There they are," Addy said.

Through the trees, twenty or thirty yards to the left of where they had gone, came the whole crew, including a smallish man with thick eyebrows and a brown woman who was crying and wailing about something.

Addy and I ran out in the rain to see what we could do.

"The bears," the woman was saying. "The bears are after us."

I knew then that these were the first new residents of the town of Treaty.

Not many strangers wandered into Treaty. A couple of campers now and then. A park ranger every once in a while. But most would-be intruders were daunted by the thickets of Juan's special trees or by the bears. Even if someone happened to stumble upon us, it didn't matter much. Bones would greet them, shake their hand, and look deeply into their eyes. After a while whoever it was that disturbed us just turned around and left, a corridor of trees opening before them and closing in their wake.

"It's okay now, my dear," the small man with bushy eyebrows said. "We're here now and we'll never have to worry again."

His name, I learned later that night, was Gerin Reed. Once a warden at Folsom Prison, he was now a sort of nomad, a hippie even, who took pleasure in everything he could see or touch or hear. His girlfriend was a Pakistani woman named Preeta. She had come to America with her parents when she was an infant. But they died and she became a ward of the state. She was also a drifter. She and Gerin had hooked up in Bakersfield only a month earlier. Gerin had heard the call of Bones's singing trees—not the bellowing sequoias, but the ones that Thrombone had cultivated to mask the god trees' song.

Gerin moved into Treaty just as if it had been meant for him. He and Preeta stayed with us for a few days and then moved down to the town. They took a room at the back of the hotel. Preeta was doing laundry in the creek before the day was through.

Over the next few months Gerin Reed and Juan Thrombone grew very close. They took long walks in the woods and went fishing together often. Gerin spoke little, but he never seemed to tire of Thrombone's riddles. Juan called Gerin Pride of Man. It was through seeing their friendship that I understood how wrong I had been about Bones.

Three days after Gerin and Preeta moved into the town of Treaty, I was out walking in the woods. It was a few hours before dark. I was wondering about my mother. Did she think that I had died somewhere? Was she crying over me? I decided to ask Bones if he would walk me to a mailbox somewhere and then show me the way back to Number Twelve. I planned to tear two of the back pages out of my *History,* one for the letter and the other for the envelope. My writing had become tinier as I kept the account; I still had more than six hundred blank pages left.

I was about to turn around and go back to the cathedral when I was grabbed from behind and thrown to the ground. Two men stood over me. One held my legs while the other sat on my chest. The one on my chest was badly scarred and wore an eyepatch. He hefted a stone about the size of an ostrich egg in his left hand.

"Scream or fight, and I crack your head," the scarred man said.

"Okay," I said. "Fine."

He stood up off my chest then, and the other man released my legs. I stood up to meet my attackers. I wasn't afraid. I hadn't known fear since coming to Treaty. Not the fear of being hurt, anyway. I was more curious to know who had come so far into Treaty without being expelled by bear or tree or butterfly.

They were an odd pair. The one who held my legs had the frame for a powerful build but had no meat on his bones. He was of medium height with shriveled black skin. His nose was running, and the whites of his eyes were bright pink. Even though it was cold, he wore only a T-shirt.

His companion was a race of his own. He wore black leather shoes and a long gray trench coat that had once been black. The scars across his face were in a cross-hatched pattern almost regular enough to be a grisly design. He had a hard leather cone for an eyepatch over his right eye and a leather strap across his lower lip. There was something familiar about his good eye.

"Chance?" the scarred man asked.

"Who are you?" I replied.

"Miles Barber."

My skin went cold. The thought that the detective could have traced me all that way, when I didn't even know where I was, disoriented me. For the first time in my life I considered killing a man. Murder tightened my jaw and clenched my fist. Barber could hardly see, and the man he was with seemed weak and sick. It had taken the two of them to topple me unawares.

The muscle in my right forearm twitched violently.

"Why are you here, Detective?"

"Ex-detective. I was *retired* because of my . . ." He finished the sentence by gesturing at his face. "But we're here because we heard somethin'. Mackie and me heard it."

"You?" I couldn't hide the shock. "How? You thought that Ordé was an idiot and a criminal. How could you hear anything?"

"I can feel pain," the ex-detective said. "I feel it every second of every day. I feel it on my skin, in my bones, and in my soul, whatever that is."

Barber then produced a .38 pistol, ending any lingering thoughts of murder.

"Where is he?" Barber demanded.

"Hey, man. Point that somewhere else." I looked over to my fellow black man for support, but Mackie's wasted face held no hope and little interest.

"Don't play with me, son." Barber gestured dangerously with his pistol. "I don't have a shield anymore, and that means you don't either."

"Who?"

"No name. Just Gray Man."

Laughter was the best answer I could give.

I brought Barber and Mackie Allitar to the cathedral. No one there was very surprised to see new citizens for Bones's town. Wanita even knew their names before she was told.

"Why didn't you tell me they were coming?" I asked the dreamer.

"You already knew people was gonna come," she said. "And it's not polite to tell people's names. They like to do that themselves."

"Did you see any bears?" Reggie asked Mackie.

"Huh?" the escaped convict asked. He was looking at Wanita with his nostrils opened wide.

"Did you see any bears?" Alacrity repeated the question.

"Nuh-uh. I mean, we heard some shit like that but we ain't seen nuthin'."

"But the bears chase everybody," Alacrity said. She stood up, which by itself was a threat.

"Don't be killing him if the man is not your enemy, child," Juan Thrombone said, appearing from somewhere out past Number Ten. " The bears know the scent of our friends now. They can move unmolested. They come for gardening, not for gutting."

"But they look bad." Alacrity always told the truth and had never even heard of manners.

Bones walked up to her and cupped his hands around her face. "And you look like an angel. But we all know to be afraid when you do not smile."

Alacrity's blush and grin put us all at ease.

"I am Juan Thrombone," Bones said to his guests. "And you are Mackie and Miles. I will take you to your lodging. The rooms are ready, and you even have some neighbors."

Bones looked deeply into the eyes of the ex-detective and smiled.

"One need not look for death, Miles and Miles. He is forever seeking you."

The policeman shuddered.

"Come," Juan said. "Let us find your new home."

I followed the three without being invited. On the way Mackie was silent, Barber was sullen, and Bones was full of incomprehensible puns and jokes. He had good laughs at the expense of pine needles and sunlight and winter winds out of the sea.

Mackie was startled to see Gerin Reed, his old warden, at the doorway of the ramshackle hotel in the makeshift town of Treaty. But he was put at ease when the warden smiled and shook his hand.

"Mackie, isn't it?" the warden asked.

"They got the blood drug here?" were Mackie's first words.

"Come on," Reed said. "Let me show you guys to some rooms. Everything's going to be okay."

TWENTY-EIGHT

Six weeks after the ex-detectives and the escaped convict came to Treaty, I saw Gerin Reed and Juan Thrombone picking their way through the deep woods. This was not an unusual sight. The onetime warden and the gardener were fast friends from the first day they met. Gerin could listen to Bones for hours without getting tired and without needing any of Bones's odd phrases or jokes clarified.

Just a few minutes of the little brown man's words and telepathy left me gasping for silence. But not Gerin Reed. He basked in the power of Juan Thrombone. And I suspect that the little gardener was lonely for someone, a friend, to hear him. Maybe that's one of the reasons that he brought so many half-lights into his presence.

Full Blues didn't understand Bones any better than I did. They struggled trying to decipher their nature, procreate, and change the world to fit their image. But they rarely laughed or played. At first I thought it was because they were no longer human, that they had become in some way the Platonic ideals. These ideals, being beyond human idealism, had turned in on themselves, and so you had the philosopher without humanity, the lover who felt no love. Of course, there were Blues like Eileen Martel and Phyllis Yamauchi who were friendly, but even they seemed to be following some complex inner compulsion, some drive that seemed to be more instinctual than it was enlightened.

But Juan Thrombone did laugh and play. He capered and was, it seemed, haphazard about what he believed and said. He was more human than the other Blues. Instead of a mere concept like Love or Death, he had a personality. He loved Addy as any man would a woman.

Bones was a secret beyond the secrets held in blue light. He was the key and that, finally, was why I stayed close to him. I might have stayed anyway—because of Death. I believed Reggie when he said that Treaty was the safest place on Earth. I believed him mainly because of Bones and his great bellowing sequoias.

One day while thinking of those trees, I asked Bones if he had made the great redwood's seeds into trees because most of the Blues were infertile and he wanted to change that.

He answered, "No, Last Chance. I am not a midwife. I loved the song and I knew that it would end. I was a man who became light and then a light who became man. I don't like the sting of death, but neither do I need to see the world transformed. A little song and a good laugh, a dream of far away and I am satisfied."

I could have fallen down on my knees and asked him for the truth for me right then, but I knew that he would only leave me there.

The only way I could learn what I needed to from Bones was to observe him. I decided to follow him and Gerin Reed on the way through the thick brush and woods that day. The smaller Thrombone was moving fast, making it hard for his friend to keep up. Bones wasn't laughing or joking either. As a matter of fact, he wasn't saying anything at all.

They covered ground quickly and, after quite some time, entered a part of the forest that was familiar to me. This was unusual because of two things. One, I'm a city boy with no woodlore. Two, my second sight makes everything I see different no matter how many times I see it. I could see a tree a thousand times, and in every encounter, the tree would have something new to say to me.

But that particular grove of white firs was different. As Bones and Gerin Reed made their way, I began to feel dread. It wasn't until a colorful wing flitted past my face that I realized we were under one of the deadly canopies of Blue-killing butterflies.

Above me were tens of thousands of brightly colored wings. They moved continually, resembling a masterfully created kaleidoscope that never repeats an image. I was captivated by the undulating blanket of their wings. For a moment I was lost in their performance. The wisp of blue in my veins seemed to flutter along with them. If I hadn't heard the plaintive note of human despair, I might have died there watching the colors.

As it was, I tried to turn to see where the cry had come from and found that I was on my knees. Bones and Gerin were nowhere to be seen. I tried to get up, but my first attempt failed. The second try got me to my feet, but I was unsteady.

A loud moan could be heard through the woods.

I stumbled off in that direction.

Upon reaching the source of the wail, I found Bones and Reed hunkered down over two butterfly-encrusted bodies in a clearing. Juan was picking off the deadly fliers by their wings. He tossed each insect into the air and blew on it. That was enough to make the creature float away.

When I came out from the cover of trees to approach my friends, a woman's voice called out in wordless surprise. I realized that there was a third person there, a young woman who had also been on her knees and hidden from my view by the two men.

"It's all right, little one," Thrombone crooned, putting a comforting hand on her shoulder. "He's our friend."

By then I had reached them. The two bodies looked to me like corpses. The man had white skin with straggly long dirty blond hair and only one arm. The woman, the taller of the two, was lean, strong, and very black. Her coarse hair was straw blond. She opened her eyes as I gazed upon her beauty. I don't know if I was more surprised by the fact that she was alive or that her eyes were the color of blood and gold.

"Nesta!" the hysterical young woman cried. "Nesta!"

"She's alive, little one. And full of stories, if I'm not mistaken," Bones assured the skinny girl.

"Nesta knows everything," the girl I came to know as Trini said. She was a sixteen-year-old runaway whom Nesta had saved from Claudia Heart's dying commune.

"Everything." Bones's eyes lit up in mock surprise. "Then it is good to have her here. You see, I know nothing—at least nothing important. Maybe we can share secrets and seed trees together."

Trini seemed to enjoy the little madman's words. She giggled and ducked her head in a conspiratorial gesture. That's when the one-armed hippie sprang to life. "Whoa ho!" he shouted and sat straight up.

He aimed a fist straight for Gerin's head. At the time I wouldn't have believed that that fist could have dented a cardboard box. Later I realized that Winch Fargo's fist could kill any mortal man. But Bones blocked the blow and pushed Fargo down with what seemed to be a gentle shove.

"You are safe now," Thrombone said while looking into Winch's eyes. "No more darkness. No more running in the night. You are home now. You are free to stay and lie around all day long."

I don't know what I expected to issue from that wildeyed and depraved visage, but the tears surprised me. In the months and years to come, I had little love and less concern for Fargo but I never hated him. I didn't because of his sad and total abandon at Bones's promise of sanctuary.

"The children will be happy to be among others like them," Bones said.

"But you are like us?" Nesta's statement was more a question than anything else.

"No," the tiny woodsman replied. "Everything you believe I have forgotten. All you'll see in me is heart and bone on stone in wood. I am free of your destiny."

The beautiful black woman frowned and then stood straight up as if she were rising from a nap rather than from near death. She wore a blue-checked work shirt over a black T-shirt with cutoff jeans and heavy hiking boots. Fargo was wearing soiled and torn hospital pajamas that were light green. He was barefoot and smelled strongly of himself.

"I released him because he was in pain," Nesta Vine said to Miles Barber under the shelter of Number One in the cathedral of trees. It was raining, but we were dry under the man-made shingles of leaves and warm from our fire.

Miles had accepted Mackie Allitar, even helped him to escape police custody, but he took an instant dislike to Winch Fargo, challenging the amazon's right to help such a man.

"He's a mass murderer. With him here no one will be safe."

"You better watch it, prick pig," Fargo said. "Or I'll put out that other eye."

"You see?" Miles turned to me for support.

But before I could think of anything to say, Juan Thrombone spoke up.

"You will respect life and limb in my domain," Bones said to Fargo. "And in return I will show you how to make your own light. But if you harm anyone here, I will put you where you will never know peace again."

It was the only threat that I ever heard Bones make. Fargo alternately cowered and glared, but Juan wouldn't look away.

Finally Fargo said, "Okay. All right. I was just jokin' anyway." And then, "Can you really help me keep the shakes down on my own?"

"We are all family here," Thrombone answered. He stood up and looked at each of us in turn. "Yes, you will receive what you need. You will sleep with the stars and moon and the sun so bright that never again will you cry or need to put out eyes."

Somehow it seemed that we all came to a solemn agreement to put aside all differences for a time. It was not that we would like or even trust one another but more that we had agreed to become a small nation committed to our little turf.

TWENTY-NINE

For a long time no one new came to the town of Treaty or to the cathedral of trees. Preeta and GR (that's what everybody but Bones called Gerin Reed) pretty much stayed to themselves, but they were friendly.

Reggie was over the moon for Trini. She was hungry for a young man to love her. He no longer had to go behind Number Seven. They spent long hours in the woods running naked and making love. Reggie adored her. He even learned how to make clothes and jewelry to give her.

Trini wasn't a loud kind of person. She didn't want to lead and never complained unless something was really wrong. She knew that Nesta and Winch had brought her to a magical place with powers as great as Claudia Heart's. And so Trini was more deeply moved by Reggie's protestations of love. She told me that every morning she had to find our Pathfinder and look at him a long time to believe that it wasn't all just a dream.

Nesta wanted to educate them and the rest of the "children." She insisted, with varying degrees of success, that they all spend three days a week learning how to read. Reggie and Wanita, Trini, and Alacrity all had to go.

"The written word is where we can all come together," Nesta said before each class. "Words are thoughts, and thoughts are dreams, and dreams are the dawn of change."

I asked Bones how two more Blues had gotten to hear his special call.

"Winch Fargo is more like you, Last Chance. A crooked light, a dim light. A creature between here and not. He heard my call and came running like a dog on Teacher's leash." Teacher is what he called Nesta Vine. "But now I have changed the call. Now all that the singing trees hide is the blue spoor of the puppy trees and the ones you call Blues."

"So, no more will come?"

"No. Not so many, I think."

"So now that we're here, what do we do?"

"Eat and sleep," the little brown man said. "Drink and dream, tell stories and kiss. Tend the gardens that we need."

"What gardens?"

"The puppy trees are growing now. They dream of devouring the sun and tickling the tonsils of Earth. They're not yet grown-up, but they'll be loud enough to hear unless we can grow a whole chorus of singing firs to drown out the sounds of hunger."

"How many trees do we need?"

"Hundreds and then thousands should do."

"All that? We can't do all that."

"Then we'll do what we can and hope for the best. I can make you stronger, make you work longer. I have ways to make you a tree farmer." Bones smiled at me but didn't share his secret plans. And I didn't mind waiting to see what he meant.

While I waited, a society had begun to form among the citizens of Treaty. Alacrity fell in love with Nesta Vine. She followed the black amazon around, hanging on her every word and gesture. They ran in the forest together, executing great and small projects, like building a raft or making exotic clothes from the wings of the killer butterflies. They'd often disappear for days at a time. Whether they were lovers in the physical sense I never knew. But next to the looks they had for each other, any passion I'd ever felt was pale and insignificant.

I was a little jealous of that love, but not in the way you might think. I was happy for Alacrity, happy that she had a close friend. But that meant I could rarely see Nesta alone. And being alone with Nesta was what I dreamed about every night.

A few days after she'd arrived in Treaty, Nesta and I took a long walk in the woods together. She was full of stories about places she'd been and times she'd read about. And she was accomplished in dozens of disciplines, arts and sciences. One was the Chinese medicine called acupuncture. She said that the Chinese needle-and-flame doctors could cure many symptoms that the drug-and-knife doctors of the West couldn't begin to treat.

"You mean these guys could treat with a pin one of the headaches I get listening to Bones?"

"Give me your left arm" was her answer.

She took me by the upper half of my left arm and applied pressure to two nerve points. It started off by tingling like flesh receiving blood after the circulation had been cut off for a while. I wasn't even aware of my erection until I looked down and noticed the bulge in my pants.

Nesta smiled while keeping the tingly pressure constant.

"You like that?" she asked.

"I don't know," I said, really trying to answer her question. "It's like I don't really feel it."

Nesta then released the pressure from one point, touching me lightly with her free hand somewhere on the right side of my neck.

"Do you want to feel it?"

When I nodded she pinched a nerve on my neck, which caused a great deal of pain. I thought that I was going to scream when the ejaculation started. She didn't keep the pressure on my neck constant. After a painful pinch she'd release for a second or so, then pinch again. And every time, I tensed and ejaculated more.

After the seventh or eighth time I stammered, half laughing, "S-stop. I can't—"

She gave my neck one more hard nip and then released me with both hands. This left me quivering on the ground at her feet.

Nesta got down on her knees next to me and put her lips near my ear. "Those are pressure points doctors give to women who have not conceived or whose husbands are impotent. It drains the man. Do you feel drained, Chance?"

I nodded, grinning like a fool.

"Then come by and see me night after next and I'll show you some points that you can pinch on me."

I spent as many evenings as I could under the tutelage of Nesta Vine. There was never what I'd call love between us, not like the love between either of us and Alacrity. We were more symbiotic in an intellectual and physical way. To be blunt, I needed sex and I needed her knowledge to write my *History*.

Nesta wanted children and she loved to talk and tell stories. I wasn't much help, but it wasn't from a lack of trying. She was childless in the years we were acquainted, and I learned more about blue light from her than from any other source.

"In one sense," she once told me, "the light is the motivation while blood is the machine. Like gasoline and a car engine. That's one way to look at it. Bones says that light is more like the chemical reaction needed to motivate a seed, which is the blood. At this point you and I are the root jutting down from the seed."

"But Bones also told me that blue light is like disease," I said.

"Or maybe it's just magic," Nesta replied; then she kissed me.

I liked her kisses very much. The kisses and pinches. It was a sorrow to me that we never conceived a child.

I also lamented the days on end that she and Alacrity would go off together. Sometimes I would catch glimpses of them running naked in the woods or sitting on opposite sides of a small stream from each other speaking in low tones and gazing into each other's eyes across the distance.

I wasn't the only one who was disturbed by the friendship between the two young women. Wanita had been Alacrity's closest friend before Nesta showed up. They had been girls together. When Alacrity had been miraculously transformed into a woman, she still shared her deepest secrets with the Dreamer. But after Nesta showed up, Alacrity either ignored Wanita or treated her as an adult would a child.

Often when I'd be looking after Nesta and Alacrity, I'd see Wanita watching them too. I found myself searching her out sometimes just to say hi to someone who shared my bruised feelings.

This self-pitying concern for Wanita is what made me aware of the threat to Treaty's only child.

Often when I'd find Wanita I'd also see Mackie Allitar somewhere in the vicinity. I began to worry about her safety and so made it my business to always be aware of the whereabouts of either Mackie or Wanita.

But whenever I stalked Mackie I found Bones there too. Once when I was watching Mackie watch Wanita playing down by the stream, I looked up and saw Bones high in the branches of a tree.

It comforted me to know that Bones was guarding her, but I was afraid that one day he'd be off with his bears or stone pots, that one day I'd wake up late and Mackie Allitar would have raped and murdered my last charge.

I was sure that Mackie wanted to kill Wanita. We all knew that he'd been a convict under ex-Warden Reed.

I followed him all day long. Reluctantly Addy promised to keep Wanita with them at night. She didn't think there was any threat. I guess she figured that keeping Wanita with her would help my sleep.

Mackie looked old and withered, but I saw him as a threat as great as Gray Man.

No one would listen to me. Reggie and Trini couldn't see past their own love for each other, and Addy trusted in Bones. Miles Barber was morose and sad most of the time, and when he wasn't he was in terrible pain that was both physical and in his soul.

"If he breaks the law, I'll take him in," the ex-detective told me once. "But until then it's a free country."

Nesta sympathized, even worried a little, but she wasn't a woman of action, at least not the offensive action I thought it would take to save Wanita.

I finally decided to tell Alacrity my fears. I knew that if she thought her little friend was in trouble, she'd kill the offender. There was no law in Treaty. Juan Thrombone for the most part made no judgments over our moral behavior. And even if he did, I didn't think he would have wanted to go up against Alacrity.

By that time she was an amazon. More than six feet tall and as strong as the bears she ran with. Alacrity practiced with weapons and in hand-to-hand combat continually. She was an excellent archer, and her ability at throwing the wooden knives she made was frightening.

I was sure that Alacrity was the greatest warrior in the history of the world. She was bold and kindhearted, savage and ruthless. The killing stroke was her caress, but her smile could break your heart.

Alacrity had become a hero—no heroine she—and I found myself thinking of her as the solution to the problem I faced. But then I thought that I should be looking out for her, not the other way around. So I hesitated for a few days more, following Allitar while he shadowed Wanita. Juan Thrombone was always somewhere nearby.

One morning Wanita was sitting under a big rock, watching water cascade into a stream. It was a glittering bright day and warm, almost hot. Mackie sat in the shadows, watching her. I sat in deeper shadow, watching them both.

We stayed that way for hours.

The day grew hotter and I started to nod. I worried that I'd wake up to find Wanita's small body floating in the stream, so I got up and strolled down to where the child sat.

"Hey, Wanita," I said.

"Hi, Chance."

"What you doin'?"

"Watchin' the water."

"You see anything I don't see?"

"I don't know. I guess. I mean, we all do, I guess."

"You mean, you and Alacrity and Reg and them?" I asked. I was thinking that my being there must have upset Mackie.

"I mean everybody see sumpin' different," the child answered. "People an' bears an' everybody."

I sat down next to her. She tossed a pebble into the stream.

The water was very clear and full of the sun. I could feel my second sight, my blood vision, kicking in. There were trails of light beginning to arch and explode in the center of the water. The water itself began to expand. I could feel the beginning of a tale. I let go of the images I beheld, open to the real story, or at least the part of that story I could comprehend.

"You been followin' me, huh, Chance?"

"Huh?" I realized that there was a big fish taking up the whole inside of my skull cavity. There was a flop in my head, and the fish seemed to swim out through my eyes.

"You been followin' me," Wanita said.

"Did you see me?"

Wanita nodded. "In my dream. In my dream I saw you. I saw you followin' Mackie a'cause he was followin' me. An' I seen Bones studyin' you."

"Me?"

"Uh-huh. He was studyin' you 'cause you gotta go to school."

"But you saw Mackie following you, right?" I asked.

"Uh-huh."

"Then why didn't you tell anybody?"

"Why should I?"

"Weren't you scared of him?"

"Uh-uh. I wasn't scared."

"Why not?"

"'Cause I could see that nuthin' was gonna happen t'me. He wasn't gonna hurt me. He just wants my blood, but he's too scared to take it."

"He's scared'a you?" I asked.

"Uh-uh. He's scared'a my blood. He want it, but he scared'a it too. He used to take Mr. Fargo's blood, but now Mr. Fargo's too strong an' mean. An' everybody else is too big. He's more scared'a all'a them, so all he could do is look at me."

Whenever Wanita talked about her dreams, there was a certainty to her, a truth that was undeniable. If she said that Mackie would not bother her, I knew that it had to be true.

The fish came back into my head. My brain was the water in which he swam. I was the stream and then the sea. I was experiencing the wild ecstasy of evaporation when a thought came into my head, displacing the water that I had become.

"Wanita?"

"Uh-huh?"

"Can you see the future?"

"Uh-huh. Some I can."

"And you can travel to other places in your dreams?"

"Mostly them places come to me. I mean, they happened a long time ago but they still there."

"All you have to do is look at them?"

"No," she said a little impatiently. "It's not lookin'. You got to close your eyes. It's more like music that you feel through your skin. It's like music that you feel."

"But the things you dream were a long time ago?"

"Yeah, yeah, but they right now too. I mean, nothin' ever goes away. They just move but they always there."

*   *   *

And so we sat there while the clipped music of the stream played almost unheard. We were watching the water, and Mackie was somewhere watching us. I was being watched. The whole universe was on automatic replay and no one could hear it but a small black child who wasn't worried about a thing.

THIRTY

Early one morning, not many days after my talk with Wanita, I was approached by Juan Thrombone beneath the shingles of Number Twelve. Wanita was out hunting with Nesta, Alacrity, and Reggie. The tension between Alacrity and Reggie had disappeared since Reggie had taken up with Trini.

"Last Chance," Bones said. It sounded more like a warning than a greeting that morning.

"Bones."

"You remember that job I told you about?"

"About growing more singing trees?" I asked, trying to stave off the pressure in my mind, the pressure I always felt when Bones's attention was on me alone. "I was wondering when you'd get around to that. I mean, sometimes I think I hear the bellowing sequoias in my dreams. And if I can hear them, maybe someone else can."

He smiled and nodded. "Up high in the mountains. Near a stream in a clearing. There's a place to make woody songs about just plain old trees. Just cell and seed and decay."

I winced. "And you want me to go there with you?"

"You," said Thrombone, "and one or two others. Those who need magic that makes things, magic that you can see."

"Are we gonna have to talk a lot?" I asked the little woodsmaster. "'Cause, I swear, if you talk to me much longer, every blood vessel in my head's gonna pop."

Bones brought his finger to his lips, winked, and turned to walk away—I followed.

It was a pleasant summer's day. Down out of the mountains it would have been hot. But where we were was just perfect. White clouds, blue sky, and the dappled shadows of the sun winked around us as we made it down the tree-covered path that had been blazed by bear and deer and Juan Thrombone. My second sight never worked well in Bones's presence, but my human senses were good enough on that day.

After a while we came to a small hollow. Therein we found Gerin Reed, Mackie Allitar, and Miles Barber. I thought at the time that it must have been an important moment. A gathering of men with no law but themselves. Each one of us had been exposed indirectly to blue light. Each one of us was crazy in his own way. Here and there in the surrounding woods were singing trees, the trees designed by Juan Thrombone to hide the blue music that emanated from the great bellowing sequoias and the human Blues who lived in our forest hideaway.

Mackie was pacing back and forth across the rough circle of the clearing. Gerin was crouched down, examining a line of large black ants as they followed their tiny destinies. The ex-detective was the only one of the three seated. He was applying pressure with a small twig to various points on his neck and face that Nesta had shown him to ease his constant pain.

When Juan and I entered the circle, they turned their attention to us. Juan raised his hands, and we all came together around him in a tight arc. It was a kind of attention and proximity that I hadn't felt since my days with the Close Congregation.

"You are more than you think, and we are less," said Juan Thrombone, a bit more earnest than usual for him—maybe that's why he stopped and giggled. "We can tote and drop, burn and build, laugh and even war—together. You will all find what you are missing and give what you have taken and save the precious seconds that you throw away on pain.

"Not you, Slender Reed," he said to Gerin. "All I need from you is what help you can give. But for the man who hurts and the man who cries and the one who guards the doorway, but has never seen the throne room. From all of you I want help, and I will give you in return space and time."

I had no idea what he meant or which of us suffered which affliction, but I was convinced that he wanted to help me, and I wanted that help.

Bones turned abruptly and began a quick march through the thick woods. We all followed. Nobody talked. After a half an hour or so I had a pretty good idea of our destination. I didn't know many places in the woods of Treaty, but the path to the Bellowing Trees of Earth was burned into my memory.

Sometimes at night I would lie awake listening for the rumble of the throne tree in the ground. I'd promise myself that once I heard it, I would go back to the throne and plunge my body into its depths. It would be my "Thanatopsis," my becoming a part of the earth and sky, root and bark. And the rumble would come, but only in my sleep. When I awoke, ready to heed the bass call, there would be nothing but clicks of night insects and the rustle of the breeze through the shingles above my head.

We marched for another couple of hours before entering a grove of singing trees. Their vibrations were like laughter, like the tittering of small children just beyond sight in the woods.

"No longer the siren's call," Juan Thrombone said to Gerin Reed, just ahead of me.

"Now they're laughing at Papa Shortribs," Gerin replied. He loved making fun of Bones only slightly more than Juan liked being made fun of.

The white firs seemed to gather around us. Behind us the wall of trees was impassable while ahead was always open and even beckoning.

And then we were in the open grove of the young sequoias. The first deep note of the Bellowing Trees sounded. All of us half-lights, even Gerin Reed, were struck still. Bones smiled and indicated with his hands that we should sit.

No one complained. We'd been walking for a long time, and that deep note had taken what little energy we had left. Bones passed around a water bag that was made from deerskin and filled with a tea brewed from the leaves of the singing trees. It was the best thing I had ever tasted, clear, sweet, and somehow dense. Juan's teas always brought vigor and a sense of well-being.

"Today is the day that your lives begin," Juan Thrombone intoned.

These words combined with the power of his thoughts and the high-pitched laughter of the white firs behind us. Then came the reverberations in the damp and grassy earth. It was far beyond any lecture Ordé preached. Those were ideas held in a voice that captivated and elated. But Bones's talk was a symphony that by turns amazed and frightened us. No one of his audience of four could sit still. We couldn't stop fidgeting there on the ground; every now and then one of us would grunt or laugh.

He retold the story of blue light, saying that it was "no more than a seed in the history of a forest." He told the story of the great redwood and her death. About how he saved her seedlings so that the world would still have music.

"And now we must begin the work of the world," Bones said in a hushed tone. Everything else went quiet too: the trees, the earth, even the low continual chatter of my senses and the history of my life inside my mind. All that was left was me hearing his words.

"In Dreamer's dreaming the worlds fall apart," he said. "But of faith and future there is no clear sign, only the blunt clubs of death and love, of fire and freezing, and the highest and lowest animal—man."

A low moan issued from my chest. My three companions also sang.

He had stopped talking, but I listened still. His words washed over me again and again. The words turned to images. Fires and men who walked like dogs, slithered like snakes, who killed for death and not survival. I saw an army of trees holding back the tides of killing man-animals. And I heard the music of death in the ears of Grey Redstar, and I almost laughed his laugh and felt his glee.

"Rise" came a voice.

Whether it was Bones or one of his puppy trees, whether it was word or thought, I was not sure. But I stood along with the murderer, the one-eyed ex-detective, and the cuckold. We walked together into the presence of the greatest creatures the world has ever known.

They welcomed us with deep bass notes that trailed off into one another. A different color was set off in my mind with each note, and the ground, which was flat, seemed to undulate beneath my feet. We were all staggering and squinting at Bones, who led us.

I realized then that these trees of Juan Thrombone's were a company of gods. They were only whispering right then so as not to demolish our small group. Bones was one of them. I had become so familiar with his laughter and jokes that I'd half forgotten his true nature.

The journey between the trunks of those trees was like walking through an earthquake. Halfway through I was sure that I wouldn't make it, that I would fall and be consumed by the roots I could feel reaching up and tickling the soles of my boots.

Then we were on the other side, and it was over.

Out of the presence of divinity and onto a grassy field about a hundred yards in diameter. A plateau looking out over a panorama of California forest. The sky was completely covered in high clouds, and a breeze was the only sound.

My heart was thumping and sweat poured down my face.

We were all silent and scared.

"Damn!" Mackie said at last. "What was that?"

"The heart," said Juan Thrombone. He held up both hands, clenching them into fists and releasing again and again in way of instruction. "The throbbing heart of life. Where the blood of our souls goes for cleansing before the day begins."

"Why did you bring us?" I asked.

"I've already told you."

"But there aren't any trees here to tend."

Instead of answering, the little man walked to the right, all the way to the edge of the field. We followed.

Down the slope there was another clearing that was at the base of a small waterfall. The fall was no more than a trickle, its water slapping down dark mossy rocks into a large stone cistern.

"It's like a big bucket," Gerin Reed said.

"What's it for?" asked Miles Barber in a rare show of curiosity.

A herd of white-tailed deer wandered around the field beneath the stone water tower. A few were licking the water spilling down the sides.

"Gather your buckets," Bones said to us. He pointed to a small patch of bushes a few feet away.

I was the closest. Nestled under the bushes were four rough-hewn wooden buckets fitted with covers made from a thicker version of the fabric Addy made for our clothes and with handles made from the same material.

There was also a long pole, maybe eight feet long, that had a flat wooden disk attached to one end with wooden dowels.

"Come on, come on," Bones urged.

We each grabbed a heavy bucket and followed Bones down the steep slope toward the deer and water tower.

One or two were startled to see us approaching, but they didn't bolt. When Bones stepped down among them they took turns nuzzling him with their snouts in greeting. He scratched ears and thumped on their sides. He crooned to them and they seemed pleased.

When the greeting was over, Bones rummaged around behind the water tower and came out with a ladder made from tree-fabric rope and thick branches. He set it up against the side of the stone container.

"Ho, Last Chance," he cried. "Climb up there and make yourself useful."

As I scaled the rickety ladder, the deer became agitated. They ran back and forth with excitement. Some even reared on their hind legs with anticipation.

Upon reaching the last rung, I could see down into the big container. It was at least nine feet deep. The sides were blackened, but the water was crystal clear.

"Pass up the first bucket, Miles and Miles," Thrombone said.

The deer were running back and forth across the small clearing, stopping at the end of each circuit at the cistern before dashing away again.

The heavy bucket was passed up, and I removed the thick green fabric cover. It had certainly been used as a chamber pot, but it also contained tree needles, bark, and fist-sized globs of thick golden tree sap.

"Pour it in," Bones said. "Pour it all in."

I emptied the contents as well as I could into the water and then I submerged the bucket, washing out whatever was stuck to the sides.

"Now hand it back down! Come on! We don't have all year!"

I was passed up all four buckets in succession. After they were all emptied, I was given the long pole and told to agitate the water as though churning butter. I'd never used a churn before, but I'd seen it done on TV.

We each took a turn mixing the concoction, and then we each took another turn.

I was afraid that the deer would lick the foul substance from the sides of the cistern, but they did not. They kept up their running, though more slowly after a while.

After a couple hours of churning, Juan climbed up the ladder to examine our work. He nodded and told us to pass up the buckets one at a time. He filled each one and passed them back down to us.

We carried the buckets to the upper clearing, spilling a good deal along the way. Juan led us to a spot near the edge of the plateau. He took from his pouch a tiny seed and a small twig, maybe eight inches long. He poked a hole in the soft earth and dropped in the seed. Then he stuck the twig in the ground to mark the planting.

"Keep pouring until I tell you to stop."

It was hard work carrying buckets of water from the lower to the upper clearing. While we did, Bones planted more seeds and marked them. Each seed was planted about fifteen feet from its nearest neighbor.

After about two hours we'd poured twelve buckets of water on each seed.

"Aren't we going to drown them?" Gerin Reed asked.

"Can you drown a mackerel with the sea?" Thrombone replied.

A half-moon crowned the night by the time we were through. Bones had made a fire that was hot and bright from some tarlike substance that I didn't recognize. We were all glad to sit after our exertions of the day.

"I have your salaries, gentlemen," Bones announced.

During that whole day of work not one real discussion occurred between us. There was no feeling between us. Just separate bodies and solitary minds going through the motions of our lives. No one knew what we were doing there, or anywhere.

Then Juan Thrombone produced four small tree-cloth pouches from his larger one. He handed us each a pouch.

Inside mine I found a small dark stone that was cold and slightly moist to the touch. An orange lichen or fungus of some sort was growing along one side.

"A drop or two of water each week and keep it in the pouch. When the moss covers the whole of the stone, scrape it into a bottle of water and let it sit for at least a year." He pulled out his canteen made from hide and continued, "And then this strong brew have you."

He passed the bottle around, admonishing us to take only a mouthful. He needn't have bothered with the warning, though. It had to be at least 150 proof. It was so potent that I had a hard time keeping it down.

The evening had been cool before that sip. But the warmth of the liquor along with the heat of the tar flame warmed me from the inside out. The moon itself seemed to be a source of heat. I loved that moon and I loved the men I'd worked with that day.

I smiled at Mackie Allitar and he saluted the gesture.

My vision began to play tricks on me. The woods around us, lit by the flickering fire, were as bright as day, but the shadows were impenetrable black. In and out of this absolute dark and light moved deer and bear and Juan Thrombone. I had the urge to join them, but when I tried to rise I ended up flat on my belly—laughing.

For a while I struggled with gravity. I was about as coordinated as an infant. I called out and my friends did too. I remember looking up at the moon. I saw the silhouette of a hand reaching for the orb but couldn't tell then whether it was my hand or not. And then I was asleep.

The dreams were not mine—not completely, at any rate.

I was the poor boy from Kentucky coming in on his cheating wife, offering her a rose. I was a cop branded by the pain of death, sitting in the dark with a man whose name was an alias. Mackie was sitting next to me in an otherwise all-white classroom. He scared the kids so much that they left us alone.

We moved thus back and forth between one another's memories and desires until we were the best of friends, brothers beyond blood.

I cried when I felt the jangled pain in Miles Barber's face.

Gerin sat with me as I bled on the floor of the People's Warehouse.

We climbed mountains together and cried over our greatest losses. We shared our inner fears and lusts. We weren't alone for the first time that any one of us could remember.

When I felt the light of morning on my face, it was with disappointment. Never had I felt the intimacy of that night of dreams. I didn't want it to end.

I was covered with a thick tree-cloth blanket, as were the rest of my friends. Juan Thrombone was gone.

I sat up. I could see that my friends were rousing also. Beyond them was the beginning of a new forest. Fifteen young firs had grown at least eighteen inches in the night.

"Hey!" I shouted. "Get up! Get up!"

"How could this be?" Miles Barber wondered out loud.

Gerin Reed was shaking his head.

We were all chattering and amazed when Juan Thrombone appeared among us. I guess he just came out of the woods, but none of us noticed because we were too busy sharing our new friendship and our surprise.

"No more talk, chatty boys," Thrombone said. "Man your buckets, water your trees. You'll have no breakfast until their roots are satisfied. It is the future of civilization you hold in your silly dreams."

Gerin Reed taught us a coal miner's song that he'd learned from his grandfather. We alternated singing and talking about our dreams.

We doused the saplings, and they grew just that fast. By the end of the day they were five feet apiece. By the end of four days they were twenty feet high.

While we worked, Bones fueled us with venison stews full of wild mushrooms and greens from the woods. Each night we drank stone liquor and passed out and into one another's dreams.

On the fourth morning we went back through the grove of god trees. It wasn't nearly so hard, because we held hands and sang.

Everything changed in those few days. Ex-Detective Barber's pain subsided and his scars, though still there, lost their red rawness. Mackie Allitar gained at least forty pounds, and every ounce seemed to be muscle. Gerin Reed's eyes became clear and focused, and his perpetual melancholy lessened until it finally disappeared.

I was different on the inside also. I was happy. For the first time I had real friendships. For the next week or so the four half-light men of Treaty were always visiting and talking, playing catch or just taking walks in the woods. Gerin taught Mackie how to fish, and Miles Barber showed me how to write in shorthand.

After ten days we returned to our tree farm. The plateau was empty again. The trees had disappeared, leaving no trace that they had ever been there. And so we replanted. This became our ritual in all seasons and all weathers. We dressed in the blue-green material that Addy and her friends made and grew sentient singing trees and dreamed.

That was the beginning of the groupings among the citizens of Treaty. The primary separation was between half-lights and Blues. But there were more divisions than that among us, among the half-lights especially.

To begin with, each of the half-lights had found what little ability he or she had in very different ways. I had imbibed the whole living blood of Ordé, whereas Mackie had burned out much of his humanity with the crazy and deficient blood of Winch Fargo. Gerin had only tasted the same tainted blood. Addy, on the other hand, had actually shared the living blue blood of her daughter. Of the half-lights only Miles Barber had been transformed by the arcane emanations of Gray Man. No blood had been exchanged, but somehow Gray Man's dark blue soul had been impressed upon Barber's mind. Trini had been kissed by Claudia Heart, and Nesta assured us that even a kiss from one of the Blues, under the right circumstances, could afford change. Preeta and later Woolly (the child Gerin and Preeta would have) gained whatever toehold they achieved through the teas and waters, potions, and brews of Juan Thrombone. Bones was a sort of alchemist. He made tars from tree sap and spit that kept insects from biting. No wound could fester under his leaf poultices. He enlightened bears, trained deer, enchanted butterflies, and orchestrated the singing forest.

The whole of our woods, five miles in any direction from Treaty, was deeply touched by Thrombone's hand. He was the tri-light, as different from his brethren as Gray Man or Winch Fargo.

"I am the forest warden," he once said. "I tend to the trees and sleep next to First Light."

Among the half-lights men and women were divided. The four men spent four days out of every fortnight planting trees, drinking stone liquor, and having one another's dreams. The women worked together also, making tree cloth and cooking, following the recipes given them by Juan Thrombone. About twice a year Addy, Preeta, and Trini would go off with Nesta to perform some ritual in the woods. I don't know what they did or where they went.

In the hierarchy of the Blues, Bones came first. He was the most powerful (with the possible exception of Gray Man) and knew the most. Not that Juan saw himself as a leader or king.

Everyone loved Juan. He was our patron and protector. After that we looked to Nesta, who seemed to know anything worth knowing. Nesta was concerned and cautious, and her effect on Alacrity calmed many a situation that might have otherwise led to bloodshed.

Winch Fargo, as I said before, had deficient awareness, having seen only the last second of the divine message. Alacrity had not seen the light but had been born of a witness's blood. And even those that witnessed a single shaft of blue were as different from one another as anyone else in the world. Wanita lived in dreams, Nesta in ideas, and Reggie looked for signs and portents of things that are hidden.

No one actually liked Winch Fargo. He was profane and obnoxious. His nickname for me was Big Nigger with the Woodbook. He called Trini and Preeta Cunt Number 1 and Cunt Number 2. He didn't have a name for Addy because his respect for Bones was actually fear.

The Blues didn't like Fargo but did pity him. For them his deformity was not the loss of an arm but a deficiency of light. They allowed his company because of his pain.

But they were all Blues, even Winch Fargo. They convened from time to time to discuss their nature or the nature of the universe or Grey Redstar and the ultimate clash of life and death. I tried to eavesdrop on those meetings but I could never take it for very long. The Blues communed with words and also the power of their minds or souls. I could listen for a few minutes, but soon my head would start to ache. If I weathered the pain, a buzz would start in my ears and then my vision would begin to blur. Finally I'd be forced to run from their presence. After that I'd sleep sometimes for a whole day.

Such was Treaty. A congress of outcasts sitting on the precipice of infinity, under the threat of death and living each day more primitively and more magically than the last.

THIRTY-ONE

The years passed like so many moments. Nothing changed much among us. Preeta was the only woman to bear a child—they called him Woolly because he had thick hair like his father. Every seven days Gerin Reed would give a talk on whatever it was that he'd been looking at that week. His sermons covered ants and rocks, the rhythm of the singing white firs, or the bellowing of the puppy sequoias. We'd meet in the clearing, outside of Number Twelve, in the early morning as the sun rose. Warden Reed's wisdom grew in the forest. Bones said that Reed heard the songs of the trees more clearly than even the Blues did because they took the music for granted but Gerin listened with all his heart. Bones was almost always present at these talks, but other than that, you never knew when he'd be around. He was off *minding his forest* most of the time. Sometimes he was gone for days.

Alacrity also took to leaving Treaty for long stints. She had a boyfriend; she said his name was Eric Beauvais. Eric lived in a cabin sixty or seventy miles distant. She'd found him with a broken leg in the deep winter and nursed him back to health. They became lovers, and so she went to him every spring, when the sap began to flow.

Wanita remained a child, but that didn't keep her from becoming our counsel and guide in most things. She interpreted dreams and told of important events. She settled disputes on the strength of her wisdom. Even Juan Thrombone came to Wanita for advice now and then.

I divided my time between the four days it took us to cultivate a crop of fifteen singing trees and ten days of solitude. The hard days of working and imbibing the stone liquor made me strong, stronger than any normal man. And the friendships I forged with my fellow half-light workers were worth all the pain and loneliness of my childhood. But I still craved the peace and privacy of the deep woods. Walking the hills and valleys around Treaty, I was in a daze most of the time, high on the vision granted me by the blood of my teacher. We all had different abilities. Mine was like a drug. Over the years my hallucinations became more vivid. The visions that came to me I could not describe in words. I did not understand their purpose or origin. Some days the sunlight would speak in colors and sound. The texture of trees and earth had their own tales, meandering and unfocused.

Whenever I could, I slept with Nesta. She made time for me when she wasn't teaching or off with Alacrity. We spent a lot of time together in the spring when Alacrity was off with her woodsman lover. Sometimes after a whole evening of passionate lovemaking I'd realize that Nesta and I hadn't said five full sentences to each other.

But I wasn't sad. I caught fish and slept in the shadow of Number Twelve. I hummed the song of the singing trees and plotted out the day that I would end my life by sitting in the hollow of the great tree that grew in the bellowing grove.

How can I explain to you what it felt like over the months and years? Looking back on it now from my cell, there seems to be very little to say. We cultivated more than eleven thousand firs to protect, with their songs, the twenty-four bellowing sequoias that were also gods. We grew the saplings and they moved away. I never recognized a tree after it had gone from our gardening place.

Nothing happened in the way that events of a life usually occur in the modern world. No heartbreaks, job promotions, goals met. Only one child was born.

There's no way for me to impress upon you the passage of time in the ordinary sense. It was just one long day and one long night passed in the presence, if not the concern, of God. Not the God of organized religion, but the amazing vitality of existence.

It was like sitting before a simple granite boulder every day, seeing in that plain surface more variation than is possible to comprehend. Every night is spent dreaming of that stone, wondering what amazing differences lay beneath the small surface that you have failed to perceive.

Now and then, while contemplating that boulder, comes a magic moment when you catch a glimpse of an image or phrase that increases the smallest possible increment of not only your knowledge but also the sum total of possibility in the universe.

Looking back on it now, I am unutterably sad with loss.

The years passed. Woolly, who aged at a normal rate as far as I could tell, was about fifteen.

And then one night I had a dream:

Gray Man was sleeping fitfully in a dark cave blocked by a huge boulder. He groaned and there was the smell of redwood in his nostrils. In my dream he dreamed that he was in wide wood dressed formally and swinging an ax against the greatest, tallest sequoia that I had ever seen. I knew that this towering giant was the parent of the Bellowing Trees. I understood then why Bones had called them puppies.

Gray Man was swinging his ax to great effect. Large chips of the giant tree were flying off. But she was wide. Thirty feet or more in diameter. Gray Man was more than halfway through the thick trunk. He was standing inside the wound, hacking away. Hacking, hacking.

Somehow I realized that when the tree fell, Gray Man would be freed from his cave.

Near where I stood a man was crying. A black man. The spitting image of Death. He was different, though; he was the man I'd seen in my room before Gray Man came out of him. Horace LaFontaine.

"Who're you?" he asked.

"I'm Chance."

"What you doin' here?"

"I think I must be inside your head," I said.

"I ain't got no head, man. I'm dead. It's his head. I was gone up till a couple minutes ago. That tree there done blowed up an' I was dead. I thought he was dead too; that Grey Redstar, that Gray Man."

All the while the hacking continued. And as it went, I became more anxious and afraid.

"You have to be alive, Horace," I said.

"How you know my name?"

"I know it from Phyllis Yamauchi's blood."

Horace's frightened visage became sad.

"Yeah," he said. "I remember her. But you know I couldn't do nuthin' t'stop him. He's the devil an' they ain't no God."

The chopping had stopped.

"How is she?" hissed a voice from behind.

I turned and Gray Man stood there, the ax hanging from his right hand. I didn't respond, so he asked the question again.

"Who?" I asked.

"The little girl. The one who escaped me by jumping out the window. Alacrity."

"Why're you cuttin' down that tree?" I asked to mask my fear for Alacrity.

Gray Man smiled. "So I can get at you, little man. So I can kill your perverted friends. So I can shed that one standing there with you and leave this place."

Horace tittered in fear. I can't say that I blamed him.

"Now tell me what I want to know," Gray Man said.

He swung his ax before I could react, and my left arm was severed at the shoulder. Blood spurted from the wound, and I went down on my knees. Horace screamed and ran away.

"Chance!"

"Where is the girl?" Gray Man shouted.

"Chance!"

Gray Man raised the ax high over his head, poised for the killing stroke.

"Chance!" Wanita shouted.

I jumped. I was pulled. The ax blow fell. I found myself being yanked by the arm that had been severed. I was in my tree-cloth sleeping bag, and Wanita was there in my tent—saving me.

"Chance, wake up!" she shouted.

"Wanita," I said. "What happened to me?"

"You had my dream," she told me. "You had my dream and you almost died because he didn't want to let you wake up."

"Gray Man?"

"I came an' slept next to you because I knew you had to have my dream. I saw you dreamin' but I wasn't there. You had it 'cause I was sleepin' next to you. You was my dream, but you almost died."

I called a meeting. I told them about Gray Man and how he wanted to kill everybody.

"But he doesn't know where we are," Reggie said. "He told you that."

"He gonna know, though," Wanita told her brother.

"I don't care if he comes," Alacrity said. "I'm not afraid of him no more."

"Yeah," Winch Fargo chimed in. "Let the nigger come and get it."

Wanita stayed silent. Addy sat hushed next to Juan Thrombone.

"Can we kill him?" I asked Bones.

"Can you bring a stone to life?" Juan asked in return. "Can you set a star on fire?"

Nesta took in a sharp breath as if the words jarred some deep memory. Maybe it was a phrase from some prayer that the Blues knew before they had bodies.

We sat for a while pondering his questions. I wondered if they were riddles that actually had answers.

"What should we do?" Gerin asked Juan Thrombone.

"I am staying here, my friend," Bones said. "But you and all of the half-lights should go." He looked at Addy then, but she turned away.

"But you and the rest are going to stay?"

"Together maybe we can fight him off," Juan said. He didn't seem worried. "But divided, he would kill the children. Divided, he would kill me or Nesta or Winch. And if you were here with us, we would have to worry about you. He would use you and make us weak."

"I don't want to go," Trini said. She laced her fingers with Reggie's.

Mackie hunched over on his tree-stump and covered his face with his hands.

"The half-lights have learned how best to use what they have," Juan Thrombone said. "You can see if shown, you can run if chased. There are glimmerings in you, and that may well be enough even if the rest of us die here."

Enough for what? That was the question in my mind, but I did not ask it. That might have been my greatest mistake.

Juan shed his unique overalls. He was naked except for the thick mane of hair and beard. His body was thin, but I knew the strength that lived in those limbs.

"It is over," he said. "Now Treaty has become War."

"Are we gonna fight?" Woolly asked. He was short like his father but had inherited the golden skin of his mother.

"No, Woolly," Gerin said. "We're going to go now."

"Go where, Dad?"

We all knew that Bones would drive us from War if he had to.

All of us but Adelaide.

Addy told Juan that she was staying, that she would kill herself if she had to leave her daughter or her man. She promised that she would kill herself if her life threatened the war against Gray Man. But she would not leave.

Juan Thrombone did not argue with her.

Gerin and Preeta left with Woolly within the week. They were headed for his mother's house in San Diego.

The morning of the day they left, the sky was cloudless and pale. Everyone from Treaty, now War, gathered in the clearing beyond Number Twelve. Gerin was waiting when I got there with Reggie. Preeta and Woolly were the last to arrive.

Gerin Reed was the only one standing. The rest of us squatted or sat in a half lotus. A solemnity hung over us, making the talk seem more like a eulogy than a goodbye.

"I guess this is my last talk," Gerin Reed began. "At least, the last talk here. It's been a long time, and I was thinking just last night that I'm going to miss this place and you. Bones and Wanita and Chance and everybody. I'm going to miss drinking and dreaming with my friends. I'm going to miss the trees' voices and, I guess for a while, I'll miss death. Or Death will miss me. Or will he? That's what I was thinking this morning. I can hardly remember the last time I missed anyone in particular. All I've done for years has been to think and speculate. I got some blood on my fingers and I stopped caring, because when I cared I also hated. I hated black men and rich men too. I never even touched my wife, couldn't stand the smell of her sweat or breath. I hated going to work and hated coming back home. I even hated the grass growing because all I had was a push mower and I couldn't stand the work.

"I was angry when I had feelings of love because it only reminded me of how much I was going to be hurt and disappointed. And so when I touched that blood drug, I forgot all of that. I didn't love my children but loved the idea of children. I didn't care about the men in my prison, so I left.

"But last night I realized that I care about you guys. All of you. I love you. You're my family. And it's not blue light or anything like that that moves me because I love Woolly and Preeta too and I'm happy that they're coming with me. I'm worried about them and I'm thinking about all of you even when the rain is falling, even when the bright orange termites swarm out of a dead log. Even when the air is frozen and the wood duck breaks the silence that the trees make." Gerin stopped speaking for a moment. His rapt expression took all of us in.

I was completely caught up with his words. Not in the way that the Blues could charm me, but with my mind.

"And then I knew," Gerin Reed said with a show of wonder on his face, "that not only can we see but we can also change. We are not trapped or locked up in these bones. No, no. We are free to change. And love changes us. And if we can love one another, we can break open the sky."

It was the only time I ever saw Bones with tears in his eyes. He stood up and hugged his good friend, kissed him on the lips.

That night, after Preeta and Gerin and Woolly had gone, was my loneliest night in years.

Mackie and Trini wanted me to join them. They were going to Miami as soon as they could raise enough cash in the Bay Area. By late spring they were ready to leave.

The night before they left, Trini came to me. She was scared and heartbroken at the prospect of leaving Reggie. Mackie had promised the Pathfinder that he would take care of his childless bride until the war was over.

I tried to console her. I told her that everything was going to be fine, that Gray Man would have trouble with either Nesta or Alacrity or Bones alone.

"He certainly can't beat all three," I told her.

"Come with me and Mackie," she pleaded. "Come stay with us."

I looked at her, noticing, maybe for the first time, that she still looked like a very young woman; twenty but no older. None of us half-lights had aged, except for Woolly. Mackie and Gerin, Addy and I actually appeared younger than when we'd arrived. Juan Thrombone with his green elixirs had given us a fountain of youth, and we barely knew it.

"I can't, Trini. I gotta stay until the last minute."

Reggie kissed Trini good-bye the next morning. Bones gave Mackie a small mask carved from the wood of one of the Bellowing Trees.

Ex-Detective Barber just wasn't there one day. He didn't speak or even tend to the trees for the last meeting. He was simply gone.

"You have to go soon too, Last Chance," Juan Thrombone said to me that night under the hanging shingles of Number Twelve.

"I know, Bones," I said. "I know. But I can wait until he's coming, can't I?"

"You should get on with your life," Juan said. His tenderness touched me.

"I don't have any life outside of here. The only friends I have ever had are in Treaty, and now you tell me that Treaty is gone. What can I do now that all I had is gone?"

For a moment Juan's permanent smile faded. "I don't know, my friend. But you have to find something."

A week later I was walking down the fishing stream toward the again-abandoned town of Treaty. I came upon Alacrity. She was naked, standing in the middle of the stream, bathing, I suppose.

"Hi, Chance," she said.

There was never any shame in the child or woman. Her body was the perfection of any human standard. I remember being surprised that her nipples were enlarged. The pleasure must have shown in my eyes because she smiled and looked down at her body before returning her eyes to me.

"I been wanting to talk to you," she said.

"'Bout what?"

"I want you to do something for me." She walked to my side of the stream and up onto the bank. A few feet from the water she had set up a pallet of woven grasses. She sat down there and I sat beside her.

"What can I do for you, little girl?" I asked.

"Not so little," she said.

"No, I guess not."

"I want you to go down to my boyfriend, Eric, when you go away. I want you to tell him what's happening here and that I'll be down to see him when we finish this."

"Where is he?"

"Reggie can make you a map. He knows where it is."

"Okay," I said. "I'll do that for you."

"Will you do something else?" she asked.

Making love to a warrior like her was a muscular thing. It was hugging and kissing on the friendliest terms I have ever had with anyone. Her smile and sweet breath were like hands holding me up.

When she asked me, later, if I loved her, I broke down in tears.

We stayed by the stream all night, keeping each other warm. I told her everything that I had ever felt about anything that was important to me. She kissed me and rubbed me and told me over and over again that I was the only man that she had ever loved or ever would love. I held on to Alacrity for her warmth and her strength. There was nothing else I wanted from her, nothing else I needed.

The next day we went to Reggie, and he made me a map with charcoal and tree cloth. Then he and Alacrity went out hunting.

I was alone in the cathedral when Juan Thrombone came upon me.

"Ho there, Last Chance," he said in his unusual but formal way.

"Hey," I said.

He scrutinized and smiled more broadly.

"I have to go do something," he said at last. "You would honor me with your company."

I stood without thinking and followed him into the forest.

THIRTY-TWO

We went quite a ways into the woods. Every now and then a bear would pass us. The bears were set like sentries around the cathedral of War.

"They will warn me," Bones said. "Warn me when he gets near."

We went at a good pace, finally coming to a slope of granite that went a far way down to a stream that was rushing in the melting snows of spring.

Far down at the base of the slope came a pack of what looked like six dogs. Not dogs, but coyotes. Well, there were five coyotes and one smaller dog that kept pace with the leader of the pack—the one-eyed mother.

The largest of the canines raised her nose and sniffed at the high ground where Juan and I stood. She yipped and gave out a small howl.

I had another friend in the grove of Juan Thrombone.

"Did you feel their approach?" I asked Bones.

"With them our strength is almost doubled," he said instead of answering my question.

* * *

The afternoon of the arrival of the coyotes and Max, Claudia Heart's blue dog, Juan Thrombone called a council under the trees of War. Everyone left in our woods, except for Addy, came. It wasn't a meeting for humans, but I was intent on attending and recording for the ages what might have been the last council of the gods.

I got my skin of stone liquor from under Number Twelve and took two deep drafts. I hoped that the strong drink would brace me against the symptoms I usually experienced when trying to eavesdrop on the Blues.

The meeting came together slowly. Nesta Vine appeared with Alacrity. They were hand in hand. Winch Fargo skulked in behind them. Alacrity was naked except for a quiver of arrows and a long bow slung crisscross over her shoulders. Reggie came wearing tree cloth with a mesh of leaves over it for camouflage. Wanita seemed to have wandered in playing with Coyote and her pups. Max and the coyotes huddled on the ground with the twenty-six-year-old who still had the appearance of a child less than ten years of age.

Juan Thrombone was seated on a high stump, watching as the clan settled in.

Nesta sat near the animals and child. Reggie's eyes were searching the perimeter. He caught a glimpse of me but said nothing.

"It is time," Juan Thrombone said in an uncharacteristic somber tone.

The reverberation of his solemnity nearly slammed me to the ground. I gritted my teeth and leaned against Number Three.

"Coyote has heard the call of the puppy trees, and she has stalked Death at our borders."

"I thought you made the singing trees block anything from people like them?" I shouted.

Everyone turned to me. They seemed slightly surprised that I was there.

"I opened it up a few weeks ago, Chance," Bones said. "When I heard him stirring in his desert cave."

"Gray Man?" Winch Fargo's eyes narrowed and his one fist rose.

"I'm not afraid of him," Alacrity said. She was looking into Nesta's eyes. The two young women had moved close together.

"Maybe he won't find us," Reggie said.

"He's already on his way," his sister replied.

"Death has clawed his way out of the grave," Juan Thrombone said. "It is time for you, Chance, to leave."

"Where?"

"Far away. In three months' time you can return. Maybe we will be here. At any rate Death will be gone."

It was an odd council of two madmen, a child, an amazon, and a beautiful egghead. There was the coyote pack too and Reggie, who was so well camouflaged that I almost forgot that he was there. All of them were of one mind.

Juan Thrombone turned from me and *communed* with the other Blues. There were no words spoken. I'm not sure if there was any sound at all. There might have been some grunting or humming. A coyote might have howled. Or maybe it was just the nature of my small brain trying to decipher their thoughts. Their congress was not painful to me. I didn't experience the pressure that Bones's attention usually caused. It was like a choir practicing pieces of songs that gave hints of great meaning only to break off midway.

It was the last moment of pure beauty in my life.

After a while things broke down. Nesta and Alacrity held hands and stared into each other's eyes. Juan Thrombone took Winch for a walk through the woods. Coyote reclined and Wanita rested her head on the canine mother's chest. The dog, Max, seemed to remember me from our evening together with Claudia Heart. He stayed near me while watching Coyote. Reggie began sharpening stone arrowheads. Then the rest of the coyotes came around me, playing like they had in my hospital room years before.

After a while I lay down with the beasts and slept.

I dreamed of scents. Sweet water wafting on the air and the musky odor of desert rams, the sharp, stinging smell of the bobcat and the stench of humanity. But those creatures could smell much more than their earthly brethren. They could smell the moon and stars and the spaces between the stars. Their howling song was an intricate equation honoring the placement of gravities they sensed.

A long crying note came into my dream. For a while I thought that it was the baying of my sleepmates. Then came a flat thumping, a deep rumble, and then a song.

I awoke to see Alacrity working a small hand-sized bow along the taut string of her longbow. The sound was a pure distillation of all the possibility of a violin in a varying note. Reggie followed her with a slow beat. And Juan Thrombone gave voice to a wordless song. The coyotes joined in, yipping and howling. Wanita slept on and Winch Fargo, who had gotten into Juan Thrombone's honey wine, made toast after toast.

The music was too powerful for my halfwit senses, so I made my way out of the cathedral of War knowing that my time among the Blues was short.

"He's coming close," Juan Thrombone said to me a week later. "He's almost here." He had found me in the abandoned town of Treaty. I had gone there hoping that I'd go unnoticed, that I might be able to stay and help in the stand against Death.

Thrombone was accompanied by Winch Fargo. Fargo had made himself a giant two-bladed ax from a metal plate that had covered a broken generator Reggie had found. It had a rough hemlock haft and was more than three feet in diameter with blades that were perfect crescents as sharp as razors.

"Nigger come up here and he's gonna lose some head," the felon said.

I had always tried my best to stay away from Fargo. He was rude and insulting to everyone but Nesta.

"Let me have a little while with Chance," Bones told the axman. "I have to send him off."

Fargo hesitated a moment. He hated ever being alone. But he finally moved off.

Before going he said, "You tell that nigger that I'm waitin' for 'im up here if you see 'im, Chance."

When Fargo was gone Thrombone turned to me.

"It's time for you to go," he said.

"Tomorrow."

"Now. There is no more time. You have to go."

"You're not making Addy leave," I said.

"She will die if I do."

"I don't mind dying," I said. "People die. They die all the time. But this is my home; it's where I live."

"It's easy for you to die, Last Chance. As easy as the red leaf falls. But you have a job to be doing."

"What job?"

"I cannot say except that you must leave now."

The small man's eyes turned blue. I blinked and found myself alone in the town.

My backpack had been ready for days. I retrieved it from Number Twelve and set out on the path for Eric Beauvais's cabin in the woods. I didn't say good-bye to anyone. I was angry and hurt that I had to leave. I blamed them for not running with me. No one had ever explained to me why they had to stay or why I had to go. We could have all run away and made our home elsewhere. Bones could have planted new trees.

I stomped away from our Eden without a friend or a future. All I had was another set of memories of people who were lost to me. I ignored the whispering secrets in the sun and sky. I hated what had been given to me because all it did was accent my loss.

I traveled hard for three days before reaching Eric's cabin. It was a small fallen-down affair atop a bald hill. The walls were reminiscent of Juan Thrombone's multifabricated suit, composed of plasterboard and wooden slats, tar paper and thatch. On one side there was an aborted foundation of stone, or maybe the house was built with a broken-down stone fence as one of its sides. The roof was rusted metal, and no smoke came from the black stovepipe at its center.

There was no porch, just a front door that opened to a yard. In that yard lay the wreckage of one man's life. There was an old Dodge that couldn't possibly have worked, a broken-down washing machine, an animal pen with no life in it, a half-tilled garden, and a dead goat flung in the path to the door.

I gazed upon the scene for a long time before acting. I tried to think of some reason why a dead goat would be left to rot outside one's front door.

Eric wasn't dead. Blinded by Death's talons, hands and feet crushed by Death's weight, but he wasn't dead.

"Who is it?" he cried when I pushed the door open.

"Friend of Alacrity's," I said.

He was crouched down in a corner, ruined hands held up in front of his face.

Eric Beauvais was a large blond man in his late forties. He was powerful and handsome except for the red gashes he had for eyes. Gray Man had left him blinded and unable to flee or fight. I was sure that Eric had been a brave man before his encounter with Death. Maybe he had never known fear. But Gray Man left him cringing and broken. I could almost hear the death god's laughter lingering in the room.

"Help me," Eric begged.

He had soiled himself. The room smelled strongly of the man. I washed him off with water from his rain barrel and changed his clothes. I wiped the blood from his face and cleaned the wounds. All the while he cried and moaned.

"He just came in and and and . . . ," Eric whined.

"Was it a black man?" I asked.

"Yeah, yeah. I never did a thing. He was little and I wasn't scared at first, but he was so strong."

"Did he tell you why?"

"He said that it was a surprise. He said that it was a present for a friend. Why did he do this to me?" While Eric cried, I held him in my arms.

I got him into the bed and set his hands and feet as best as I could. Then I opened some canned beans and put them on a chair next to his bed. I put water there and set up the door so that he could push it open to go outside to piss and shit.

While he slept, I searched the cabin. I found a .22-caliber target pistol, a good-sized hunting knife, and a box of Hershey candy bars. These I took for myself.

Gray Man had passed Eric's way a day before, maybe a few hours more than that. He must have passed me on his way toward Treaty. Either he didn't see me or, more likely, he felt that I was beneath his notice. I was intent on making that his big mistake.

"Eric," I said, shaking the ruined man.

"What?" He started awake, thrusting his hands out in fear. When the hands touched me, though, he recoiled in pain.

"I've got to go for a while," I said. "You have food right here and I jammed the lock on the door for you to go outside if you've got to go."

"How'm I gonna get back in?" he cried.

"There's a big crack at the bottom," I said. "It'll hurt but you can get your foot under there and pull it open like that."

"Don't leave. Please."

"I have to, Eric. Alacrity's back there."

"She has friends there. You said she did. Please take me with you."

"The man who did this to you will be there. You don't wanna get near him again, believe me."

"Please," he begged. "Don't leave me."

"I'll be back."

"He'll kill you and then I'll die here." Eric tried to grab me, but his hands were useless.

I left him crying there on his bed. He was calling out to me like a lost child. I knew he was right, that I might not return and that he might die, but I had to go back to War.

THIRTY-THREE

I thanked Juan Thrombone for all the years he had me working on his tree farm. Toward the later years we'd sometimes work through the night, pushing the growth rate of the trees until they were almost completely mature by the fourth day. The extra-large buckets we fashioned held fifty pounds of water at least. We carried a bucket in each hand, trotting from the lower field to the upper without a stop, for eighteen hours and longer. It was the tea we drank that gave us such strength, that's what Juan told us.

"Brewed from the dead leaves of the blue sequoias. It is just weak enough not to hurt your delicate natures."

I jogged for ten hours straight before having to rest. It was deep night and the moon was exactly half full. The candy bars were all gone, so all I could do was sleep. The sun was far into morning by the time I woke up.

My feet hurt as I went, but I kept thinking of Eric and his ruined and bloody feet.

By midday I could hear the trees screaming. It was the singing trees, not the bellowing ones. They were keening a solitary note of fear.

I ran harder. The pistol in my pocket had five shells in it. I kept thinking about stars going nova and stones breathing life. I hoped that I could create miracles with what little I had.

The woods went suddenly quiet when I was no more than a mile from the cathedral of War. It was an abrupt silence in my mind that came on so quickly, it disoriented me. I fell to the ground feeling the deep exhaustion of my day-and-a-half run. I lay there on the damp earth thinking about standing but nowhere near the act. Every muscle and cell in my body screamed for water, for oxygen, and for rest. My lungs couldn't take a deep enough breath. My fingers and toes were numb. And even though I was thinking about rising, my head was hanging down. It came to me that I was dying, that the exertion of my supermarathon, coupled with the sudden extinction of the singing trees, had depleted me. My eyes were open but the midday light faded still.

Then came the rumbling. The Bellowing Trees in great anguish began their bass song. It wasn't fear but disgust and anger. It was the outrage of the earth against the abomination of Gray Man. I saw him in my mind, and strength flowed back into me. I was called back to life by the trees.

It was not only me but bear and butterfly, bird and gnat. The life of the forest around the cathedral, which had been so silent, surged. A large copper-colored bear lumbered past me. I stood up under a current of broad-winged black-and-white and red monarchs.

We all raced for the grove of Bellowing Trees. Along the way I saw the corpses of two of the coyote brood. Bloody and broken, they lay like Eric Beauvais's hands and feet.

When we came into the grove of singing trees, it was as if we had come into a wood after years of blight. Black fungus hung from their limbs, the once green needles were brown and fallen. As quickly as they had grown, Juan Thrombone's trees died. Sickly and brittle, the whole grove was dead. Not one note of life or calling was left.

Death had taken their souls with him into the valley of the Bellowing Trees.

I took the lead in the headlong race toward Death. My longtime flirtation with suicide was now a reality. I had no illusions that anyone could stand up to Grey Redstar. But I would not let him frighten me; I would not let my friends die without help.

Before I noticed that the bears and butterflies had stopped, I was almost on top of him. Gray Man. The rush and chatter of animals around me, coupled with the rumbling of the blue sequoias, had masked his presence. I suppose that was a stroke of luck. I say this because the recognition and anticipation of Death's approach is enough to shatter the bravest man or woman's resolve. But to sense Death and approach it is contrary to the very notion of life. I do not know that I would have had the courage to go on if I had sensed Gray Man.

He was leaning over Coyote, bearing down on her throat as she clawed at his groin and chest. Max was on Death's back, tearing viciously at his neck and head.

Blue light emanated from all three. A vibrant yellowish light came from Coyote. Max's dull blue aura was almost erased by the indigo coming from Gray Man.

I moved deliberately from the wood and held Eric's pistol to Gray Man's head. I pulled the trigger many more times than there were bullets to fire. Every shot entered the dead man's brain.

He stood from the now inert form of Coyote. He slapped Max from his back, sending the poor dog flying.

"Pity," he said. Then he reached out, brushing my forehead with his fingertips.

I fell to the ground, nothing but mindless weight. From my side I could see Gray Man moving toward the grove of Bellowing Trees. He was naked and skinny, hunched over and stalking.

I took aim with the pistol and pulled the trigger. The chamber was empty but I would have missed anyway. The thought of my lying on my side, shooting at a man who was already dead made me laugh. My weakness, combined with impotent courage, seemed to be the funniest joke anyone could tell. And once I started laughing, I couldn't stop. I laughed so hard that I convulsed and writhed, tittering like Horace LaFontaine and choking on my tongue. I rolled up on my knees, trying to get away from that black humor. I lurched to my feet, no longer dying, coughing on the ridiculous nature of my mind.

My second encounter with death in ten minutes and I was moving again. I was stalking him now, looking for a mistake, an opening, a chance to end him.

He stopped at the edge of the grove of Bellowing Trees, leaping suddenly behind the ruined trunk of a ruined singing tree. He appeared again with Addy in tow. She buried the blade of a large wooden knife in the side of his neck, but he was unaffected.

He went into the grove then, dragging Addy in his wake.

I followed him to the very edge of the grove, but then I could go no farther. The deep tones coming from the Bellowing Trees hit me like ten-foot waves at the shore. I couldn't penetrate their power. Even Gray Man was struggling against their incredible strength. Addy was knocked senseless, but Death pulled her on.

It was all I could do to hold my ground.

Toward the center of the grove stood Juan Thrombone and the rest of the Blues. Alacrity was naked again, her bow drawn and notched. Reggie wore his camouflage, and Fargo wielded his ax.

"To your trees!" Bones commanded loudly.

"I wanna fight!" Alacrity cried out.

I could feel their struggle in the center of my brain. It was wisdom versus rage.

Gray Man laughed.

Alacrity was still young, and the derision of Death unnerved her.

"To your trees!" Thrombone cried.

Five trees surrounded the great throne tree. Each one was attended by one of the Blues. As soon as each one stood next to a tree, white tendril roots crawled out of the ground to fasten them to the trunk. Alacrity and Winch struggled a bit, but Reggie, Wanita, and Nesta were resigned to the ritual.

"I am too strong now," Grey Redstar said. "I can kill you and your whole forest with the strength released from the old redwood. No alliance you can achieve is more powerful than death."

His words were confident, but he did not press forward.

"Join me, Three Lights," Gray Man said in a tone that approximated friendship. "You can see that this desire, this plan to sire, is foolish and wasteful and weak. Join me. Tell your trees to drain their lives, and I will leave you to your forest. You can even have this woman."

For a long moment Juan Thrombone stared into the face of Death. Maybe for an instant he considered the promise of life for his trees and his First Light.

"Never," Bones whispered at last.

"Then watch her die, abomination within an abomination," Gray Man said. "Watch her die."

"Come, Death," Thrombone replied. "Come to *my* embrace." He held out his arms. "Take me to your cold heart."

No sooner had Bones spoken these words than the waves of energy from the trees ceased. Gray Man lurched forward and so did I.

Next to the helpless Winch Fargo, on the ground, was his big metal ax. I hoped that it would be more deadly than the small pistol. I hefted the ax and ran, yelling like a fool, at Gray Man's back. I swung, aiming for his head, but he was faster than me.

He reached back with his free hand, grabbing the haft and pulling me off balance. I fell between him and Juan Thrombone.

Gray Man looked down on me and smiled. He bent forward to take me by the shoulder. It was the strongest grip I had ever felt, but it was colder than it was strong. For the third time that day I felt the life draining out of me. Gray Man was leaning toward me, smiling.

"Come," he said, almost kindly, the anticipation of my death somehow bringing out what little love his evil heart housed.

"Got ya now," Juan Thrombone said. He leaped and grabbed Gray Man by the arm, dragging him back to the throne. Gray Man released Addy and me to struggle with his attacker.

There they stood before the throne tree, a black man and a brown one, though they had both given up the human race long ago, flexing muscles that could have easily felled one of the god trees that were now all humming a deep and frightening note. My friends were all unconscious or dead. Addy was as cold as stone.

Gray Man and Juan Thrombone fell into the hollow of the throne tree. Gray Man cried out and pushed Bones down. The roots of the big tree flailed helplessly at Death while he closed his icy fingers around Thrombone's throat.

My left side was numb, but I rose up and threw myself on Death's back. The three of us fell deeply into the hollow. It seemed much deeper than it could have possibly been. I put a headlock on Death and pulled with all my might. From behind I was aided by someone. I dared a glance and saw a man who was the image of Gray

Man but I knew by the fear in his eyes was really Horace LaFontaine. I didn't understand, but there was no time to think anyway. The roots surrounded us, and suddenly Gray Man yelled with frustration. I saw a root of the great tree press into one of his eyes.

"You can't kill me!" he shouted.

Juan Thrombone laughed. Then, suddenly, my headlock was on Thrombone, though not from behind. Our embrace was like an adolescent attempt at a first kiss. I released my hold, and Thrombone pushed me clear of the hollow.

"Last Chance," Thrombone said and then winked. "Not yet."

He threw himself back on Gray Man, who was struggling with the roots. They were pushing into his sides and chest, but he was breaking them off faster than they took hold. Horace LaFontaine was in there trying to wrestle Gray Man down. Juan Thrombone jumped in and grabbed Gray Man's hands. The roots ate into Bones and Horace then. They seemed to be rejuvenated by what they found in those men's blood. The attack against Gray Man was redoubled, and they all were lost in a tangle of writhing roots.

A screaming shout that started at the edge of the grove of god trees made me turn. It was Miles Barber, running and holding something above his head, something that was burning. Miles shouldered me aside and threw his burning missile into the tree. Flames jumped high into the air, and a concussion threw the ex-detective backward. He flew into me, knocking me down and nearly unconscious.

Over the years I've wondered about Miles Barber and that last desperate act. In our time together as friends, sharing a whole dimension of mingled dreams, I never perceived this plan. It is true that he once carried a container of gasoline that he intended to use to incinerate Gray Man, but that had been a long time before. All I can figure is that the approach of Death rekindled the hatred that dwelled in Barber's heart. He didn't want us to keep him from his vengeance; that's why he hid from us the moment this dark desire returned.

When I came to my senses all the Bellowing Trees were burning. Wanita and the rest had been freed from their bonds. The whole company of gods lay unconscious under the burning woods, them, Addy, and Miles Barber. I got myself to stand and dragged them, one after another, out of the fire.

Wanita was first and Winch Fargo was last, but I saved them all. The whole wood was blazing by the time I pulled out Fargo. The heat on my skin spoke to me and for once I understood, but I have since forgotten the truths revealed at that time. They're hidden from me in a charred and smoky place in my soul. I lost consciousness then. The last thing I remember was rolling downward.

When I came to, I found myself beneath a mass of prickly vines. I was burned pretty badly along my left side. Everyone was gone. Bear and butterfly, friend and foe. The Bellowing Trees were burned black. I made it to the throne tree, walking over hot embers and ash. There was a sticky mass of hot tarlike stuff in the hollow. That was all that was left of Gray Man and Juan Thrombone.

I stumbled out through the silent woods. Every once in a while I'd come upon the blackened remnants of a singing tree. Gray Man's fingers sought out and destroyed every one of Bones's beautiful trees. I feared that maybe the other Blues had suffered the same fate. I looked everywhere for a sign of their survival or demise but found nothing.

I was badly hurt but I treated the burns with poultices and salves that Bones had given me. If I had rested a day or two, the burns would have probably healed, but I had made a promise to look after Alacrity's boyfriend and intended to keep that promise.

The forced march brought me to his cabin door in two days' time. But the cabin was empty. The clothes from his closet were gone, along with the trunk that sat at the foot of his bed.

I don't remember much of what happened after I got to the cabin. Distraught over the disappearance of my friends, I rushed out, hoping that they had only recently been there. I don't remember how far I got. The infection from the burns must have overwhelmed me. In the hospital I was told that I was found by hikers. I guess with all that had happened, I went a little out of my head. The doctors had me in a straitjacket and had been injecting me with powerful tranquilizers every six hours.

The next few months are only spotty in my memory. I remember a man, Dr. Lionel, who told me that I was under arrest for setting fires in a national forest. But be-

cause of my burns and irrational behavior, I was re-
manded to the hospital for recuperation and observa-
tion.

That conversation was just a small island of clarity.
Other times I was in Treaty making love to Addy or
fishing with Gerin Reed. Sometimes I was in darkness
and Alacrity was calling to me. I wanted to go to her, but
my arms were tied and I couldn't get to my feet.

At one moment I faded into consciousness, finding
myself dressed in an ill-fitted tan suit and talking to a
middle-aged woman, a judge I believe, about Treaty and
blue light and Grey Redstar, who kept Horace La-
Fontaine in an Attica cell behind his eyes. When I finished the sentence, I could see that the henna-haired
woman thought I was crazy. I yelled and leaped at her,
but strong men grabbed me by my arms and legs. I was
strong enough to throw them off, but before I could get
my balance, someone injected me with the tranq. The
last thing I saw were the judge's frightened eyes.

I've been at the state mental hospital at Camarillo since
then. I came in diagnosed as a paranoid schizophrenic,
but they changed that diagnosis to borderline psychotic
with a new administration in 1988. I explained to the
doctors that I was proof of my own story because I
looked like I was twenty but my driver's license said I
was forty-three. After a week or so of that tack, a kindly
orderly allowed me to see my reflection in a handheld
mirror. My hair had gone completely white and the left
side of my face was roughened by small scars left by the
fire.

That's when they started to brainwash me. I don't mean on purpose like they did to those POWs in North Vietnam. They thought that they were helping me. They just could not believe in blue light.

It was impossible for light to contain consciousness, they said. I looked my age and should be thankful that I was in such good physical health. They threw away my lichen stone while I was out of my head, so I couldn't prove my claims with the stone liquor.

At least they let me keep my *History*. When I sit down and read these words, I know that it all must have happened. No one could make up all of that.

After a year I found out that my mother died in 1976. I think that hurt me worst of all. I never got to see her and apologize for all the years that I ignored her letters.

It's been more than seven years now, and I'm learning how not to use my second sight. All the drugs they give me help dampen the visions. They keep me sedated and in isolation because I'm so strong and I want to get away.

But they let me use a computer, and I have mail privileges to take out materials from state and local libraries. I guess they know that as long as I can work on my book, I won't get too violent or wild.

My hope now is that they'll release me, that they'll find me sane and let me go, so I can go looking for my friends. I am sane but I know more than the fools who keep me here. I know too much. That's why I'm trying to close my eyes to the history of light and matter. Because if I stop seeing things the way the Blues do, I'll become less like them and more like regular people.

I've almost done it. I've almost stopped seeing. The only problem I have now is at dusk, when I'm drawn to the high window of my cell and I search the twilight skies for colored lights that I know to be the teardrops of God.

WALTER MOSLEY is the author of the bestselling Easy
Rawlins series of mysteries, the novel *RL's Dream*, the
story collection *Always Outnumbered, Always Outgunned*,
for which he received the Anisfield-Wolf Book Award,
and a second collection starring Socrates Fortlow,
Walkin' the Dog. He was born in Los Angeles and has
been at various times in his life a potter, a computer pro-
grammer, and a poet. His books have been translated
into twenty languages. He lives in New York.

WALTER MOSLEY is the author of the bestselling Easy Rawlins series of mysteries, the novel RL's Dream, the story collection Always Outnumbered, Always Outgunned, for which he received the Anisfield-Wolf Book Award, and a second collection, Walkin' the Dog. Born in Los Angeles in 1952, he was formerly a New Yorker and has been dramatized. His books have been translated into twenty languages. He now lives in New York.

Rascals in the Cane

What I wanna know is if you think that black people have a right to be mad at white folks or are we all just fulla shit an' don't have no excuse for the misery down here an' everywhere else?" The speaker, Socrates Fortlow, sat back in his folding chair. It creaked loudly under his brawny weight.

Nelson Saint-Paul, the undertaker known as Topper, cleared his throat and looked to his right. There sat the skinny and bespectacled Leon Spellman. The youth was taking off his glasses to wipe his irritated eyes. The irritation came from Veronica Ashanti's sweet-smelling cigar.

"Is that why you had us come to your new house this week?" Veronica asked.

"It sure is a pretty house, Mr. Fortlow," Cynthia Lott cried in shrill tones.

Chip Lowe sat back in his chair glowering, his light gray mustache glowing like a nightlight against the ebony skin of his face. His hands were clasped before him. They had turned almost completely white with the creeping vitiligo skin disease that was slowly turning the skin of his hands and face to white.

"How long you been here?" Leon asked.

1

" 'Bout two months." Socrates took a deep breath to keep down the nervous passion that had built up before he asked his question.

"You need somebody to help you pick out some more furniture," Veronica Ashanti said. Her eyelids lowered and her hand moved to cover her small bosom. Almost everything Veronica said seemed to contain a romantic suggestion.

But she was right. Socrates' living room was empty except for six folding chairs and a folding table, all of which had been stored in a closet before the Wednesday night discussion group had arrived.

"I like it spare, Ronnie," Socrates said. "I like it clean."

"But you need some kinda sofa," Cynthia Lott screeched, her stubby legs dangling from the sharp-angled wooden chair. "Some place soft for a woman to sit comfortably."

"I use these same kind of chairs at the funeral home," Nelson Saint-Paul said. "We meet there all the time and you never complained."

"But that's not a house, Topper," Veronica explained. "You expect more comfort in a house. Here Mr. Fortlow got this nice new place and a yard with flowers and fruit. He should have a nice big sofa and a chair and maybe some kinda rug. That's what you expect to see in a house."

"I like the yard, man," Leon said. "It's fat."

"And if you had some lawn chairs . . ." Veronica began to say.

"What kinda shit you mean by that, man?" Chip Lowe, head of the local neighborhood watch, blurted out.

"Excuse me?" Veronica did not like the interruption.

"I said what the hell does he mean by that question? Do black people have the right? Do I have the right? Who is he to question me?" The anger rolling off Lowe's voice was like a gentle breeze across Socrates' face.

2

"I was talking about lawn furniture," Veronica said icily.

"I don't care 'bout no damn furniture," Chip said. "What I wanna know is what he mean questioning me?"

"He didn't say nobody in particular, Mr. Lowe," Leon quailed. "He just said black people."

"And what the hell you think I am?" Lowe said.

"That's why I asked you, brother," Socrates said. "I asked you 'cause you the one know. If you don't know then who does? I mean you read the paper an' you got white people writin' about it. You got white people on the TV talkin', on the radio, they vote on it too. You got white people askin' black people but then they wanna argue wit' what those black people say. Everybody act like what we feel got to go to a white vote or TV or newspaper. I say fuck that. Fuck it. All that matters is what you'n me think. That's all. I don't care what Mr. Newscaster wanna report. All I wanna know is what we think right here in this room. Right here. Us. Just talkin'. It ain't goin' on the midnight report or the early edition or no shit like that."

Silence followed Socrates' declaration. A police helicopter passed overhead but it could not have suspected the conversation unfolding below. And even if the policemen knew what was about to be said they wouldn't have wondered or worried about mere words.

"Wh-wh-what do you mean, Mr. Fortlow?" Nelson asked after the loud rush of the helicopter passed on. "I mean we all know what's been done to us that's wrong. We all know what we got to do to make our lives better."

"We do?" Socrates stared hard at the middle-class mortician. "We don't all look the same. We don't all talk alike. We ain't related. The only things we got in common is what's on the TV an' in the papers. And ain't nuthin' like that made from black hands or minds."

"But we know," young Mr. Spellman said.

3

"What is it you know?" Cynthia Lott asked the boy.

"I know I'm a black man in a white world that had me as a slave; that keeps me from my history and my birthright." Leon spoke proudly and loud.

Tiny Cynthia waggled her dangling feet angrily. "First off you ain't a man you're a boy. You wasn't never a slave. And as far as any birthright, you live wit' your momma and play at like you tryin' to go to school. As far as I see it you ain't got nuthin' to complain about at all. I mean if you cain't make somethin' outta yourself with all that you got then all they could blame is you."

Cynthia sucked a tooth and looked away from the young man.

Leon was trying to think of something to say but he was trembling, too furious to put words together.

"But I didn't ask if he could blame somebody, Cyn," Socrates said. "I asked if we got the right to be mad. All of us is mad. Almost every black man, woman or child you meet is mad. Damn mad. Every day we talk about what some white man did or what some black man actin' like a white man did. Even if you blame Leon for his problems you still sayin' that there's somethin' wrong. Ain't you?"

"Only thing wrong is that these here men you got today ain't worth shit." Cynthia curled her lip, revealing a sharp white tooth. "Black men puffin' up an' blamin' anybody they can. He say, 'I cain't get a job 'cause'a the white man,' or 'I cain't stay home 'cause Mr. Charlie on my butt.' But the woman is home. The woman got a job and a child and a pain in her heart that don't ever stop. I don't know why I wanna be mad at no white man when I got a black man willin' to burn me down to the ground and then stomp on my ashes."

Cynthia's high-pitched voice always made Socrates wince. He swallowed once and then prepared to speak.

But before he could start Leon opened up again. "I don't know why you wanna be like that, Miss Lott. Some man musta hurt you. But I'm doin' what I can. I am. I got a job . . ."

"What kinda job you got?" Cynthia demanded.

"I work at the drugstore on Kincaid on the weekends."

"That's a child's job," the tiny woman shrilled. "Come talk to me when you doin' man's work."

"Come on now, Cyn," Veronica Ashanti chided. "You know Leon's a good boy and he tryin'. And you know ain't no man start out perfect. No woman either. I know a lotta black women out here mess up just as quick as a man. Quicker sometimes."

"Yeah," Chip Lowe said. "Leave Leon alone. I got a job and a family. I live at home with my wife and my daughters. I work hard. Harder'n any white man do the same job. That's why I got the right to be mad. I come in early an' leave late and they still pass me over for some lazy motherfucker don't know how to tie his shoelaces."

"No need to curse, Chip," Topper said. "But you are right. We all have difficulties that are incurred by our skins. We all know that we have to work harder and longer hours to be recognized. We have to be extra careful and honest not to be fired or even arrested. And if one black man commits a crime then we are all seen as criminals. All of us share that legacy."

"But do you have the right to be mad?" Cynthia Lott asked. It was rare that Cynthia would dare to question Topper and she seemed to take pleasure in the grilling.

"Certainly," Saint-Paul said. "We are held back not because of worth but because of prejudice and racism. That is reason enough."

Socrates looked at his friends with harsh satisfaction. He had been thinking about the question for months. It

5

had been on his mind for years. Every time he saw a white man he'd get mad. Sometimes he had to leave the room so as not to yell or even attack some man who was just standing there. His ire was as natural as the sunrise. It was more like an instinct than like the higher faculty of reason that supposedly separates people from other creatures.

Socrates had long wanted to ask the question but he couldn't get out the words in the Saint-Paul Mortuary. He was afraid of the big room and the many doors all around. Somebody might be listening; he knew that it wasn't true and even if it was that it didn't matter. But Socrates' throat was clamped shut. So he had decided to invite the group to his new home in King Malone's back-yard, next to the sweet-smelling lemon bush. If anyone came around, the two-legged dog Killer would bark.

In the nearly empty rooms of Socrates' home he felt his heart beating and the air coming into his lungs. There he could believe that he was the master.

He had made lemonade and ham sandwiches, bought two fifths of Barbancourt Haitian rum. He had put the small bounty on his folding table and set up chairs for his friends as they arrived at the door. But even with all of that he could barely get the words out. When he started to put his question into words his face had flushed with fever and the room seemed to shake.

"But I know what you mean, Miss Lott," Leon said in a voice that was devoid of feeling. " 'Cause when it come to tearin' down a black man it's a black woman the first one on line. Like when I come here to talk. You always be ridin' me even though I ain't never done nuthin' to you. Even though I give you a ride home every week an' you never say thank you or offer me somethin' like a drink of water or maybe a dollar for all that gas. There's a white woman work at the pharmacy speaks nice to me

6

every day. She treat me better than half the black women I ever meet."

"Well if you so hurt then why you come here?" Cynthia Lott said. Her voice was less angry than it was strained. "Why you give me a ride? I don't ever ask you. I don't ever ask you for nuthin'. I don't ever ask no man for nuthin'."

There were tears in Leon's eyes but he didn't seem to notice. The muscle and bone at the hinges of his jaw bulged out. "I come here 'cause I wanna be around black people who talk about stuff other than just complainin' or lyin'. I want to be somebody other than just some nigger or gangbanger."

Cynthia almost said something but then she held back. Socrates thought that this silence was an answer to the boy's hurt feelings but that he would never know it.

"My aunt Bellandra," Socrates began, "used to tell me a story."

Everybody in the room seemed to understand immediately that this was the real beginning of the Wednesday night talk, that everything up until then was just like an introduction.

"It was a story," Socrates continued, "about slaves that were set free by a freak storm down on a Louisiana sugar plantation a long time before the Civil War. She said that it was a big wind . . ."

". . . that blew out of the Gulf of Mexico." Bellandra's words came back to him. He was a scrawny child again rapt in the frightening tales of his severe auntie. "And it tore down the ramshackle slave quarters and tore out the timbers that their chains was bound to. Many of the slaves died from the crash but some of them lived. They cut away the corpses from the long chain that bound them all together and then moved like a serpent toward the overseer's hut.

7

"This overseer was a man named Drummond and he was evil down to the bone. He heard the slave quarters crash but he didn't do nuthin' to help because the wind scared him and so he stayed in his hut. He didn't know that the chain gang was movin' toward him. He just laid up with Rose, a slave girl that he took to his bed sometimes. Outside the wind was howlin' and the trees were scratchin' at his roof. It was like hell outside his do' an' he wasn't goin' nowhere."

Bellandra, Socrates remembered, paused then and glared down at the boy. He felt as if he had done something wrong but didn't know what it was.

"An' then the knockin' started on his do'. It was a loud thump and then the drag of chain and then another loud thump. Rose called out in fear and her master cringed. But the knocking got louder and the chain sounded everywhere all around the house. Then there was the angry cry of men. If it wasn't for the storm that cry would have reached the plantation owner's ears. He would have called out his men and his dogs but the wind ate up the slaves' voices. Only Drummond could hear them men and he wasn't even sure that it was men. He was afraid that ghosts from some shipwreck had blown in on the winds of that storm. He was tryin' to remember a prayer to send them ghosts away when the do' shattered and so did the shutters on his windows. And then four men came into his shack one after another, manacled hand and foot and chained in a line. There were two empty shackles that were bloody from where the dead men had been cut away.

" 'Carden, is that you?' the overseer cried. ' 'Cause if it is, you had better get ret ta die. Ain't no slave gonna come in on me in my home!' The overseer stood up to thrash Carden the slave but another slave, Alfred, raised his chain and laid the overseer low. Drummond lay on the ground bleedin' while Rose cried from his bed. 'Give us the keys, man,' Alfred said. He held the chain above the overseer's head and that broke him down. He took the key to the fetters from a string on his neck. And when he freed them they set on him with the loose chains and while they beat him, do you know what he said?"

"Uh-uh," little boy Socrates said to his auntie.

"He said, 'Why you killin' me? I freed your bonds.' But the slave Alfred said, 'You just dead, white man.' And he was dead even before he could hear those last words.

"And they took Rose and freed whatever slaves there was left alive in the wreck. And then they set fire to the master's home and ran out into the sugarcane fields and hid. There was twenty-two escaped slaves. Man, woman, and child. They went up into the swamp-lands and laid low. And after a day or two they got strong on fish and birds they slew. Small groups of white men came looking for the escaped slaves but they died and their weapons went into the hands of Alfred Africa, the leader of the runaways.

"Everywhere in the parish white folks was scared of them slaves. Bounties was put on their heads, but after the first search parties disappeared most folks were too scared to go after Alfred and his gang. But the runaways was scared too. Scared that if they ever left the swamp-lands and the cane, they would be hunted down and killed for their sins. Because they knew that killin' was wrong. They knew that they had murdered old Drummond and Langley Whitehall, the plantation owner, and his family and men. So they stayed in the wild and went kinda crazy. They attacked white people that traveled alone and burnt down houses and fields of cane. Nobody was safe and they started to call Alfred and his gang the rascals in the cane. And it wasn't only white people that was scared. Because if Alfred's crew came up

9

on a slave and he was too scared to go with 'em then they would say that that slave was their enemy and they would kill him too.

"They called the state militia finally but they never found Alfred's crew. After a while that whole section of farmlands was abandoned because nobody felt safe. Nobody would brave the rascals in that cane. Every once in a while one of 'em would be caught though. If one of 'em got tired of the mosquitoes and gators and he wanted to leave. And if one of Alfred Africa's men was caught they'd torture him for days to find the secret of where the runaways hid. But they never found out. After a long time the attacks stopped and the plantation owners came back. But they still went with armed guards. And they set out sentries at night who had to stay at their posts even in the worst storms. Because everybody said that the soul of Alfred Africa lived in the eye of the storm and that one day he would return and burn down all the plantations everywhere in the south."

Socrates looked up and saw the faces of Cynthia, Veronica and Chip Lowe. He was surprised because he half hoped to see his long-dead auntie Bellandra. He wondered if he had really told the story that he'd only just remembered after more than fifty years.

"It sounds like a true story, Mr. Fortlow," Nelson Saint-Paul said.

"Yeah," Socrates said, still partly in the trance of his memory. "Rose, the woman that the overseer raped, was my aunt's great-grandmother. She was the only one of the escaped slaves to survive. She caught a fever and wandered away. Indians took her in and she wound up in Texas. She had a child and became an Indian but the army massacred the tribe she traveled with and she and her baby were sold as slaves. After the war she came to Indiana with her son. That's where my family is from."

"So what you tryin' to say, Socrates?" Chip Lowe asked. "What's that story supposed to mean?"

"Depends on what part you're talking about," Veronica Ashanti said on a cloud of blue smoke.

"What you mean by that, Ronnie?" Chip asked.

"Could be the storm or the killin', could be that they thought the killin' was sin even though they killed a sinner." Veronica counted out each point on a different finger.

"Yeah," Leon added. "Or maybe that they stayed around and fought against the people who persecuted them."

"They should'a run," Cynthia said. "But no doubt that Alfred Africa wanted to fight instead'a doin' somethin' right."

"Maybe they couldn't help it," Leon argued. "Maybe it was like Mr. Fortlow's aunt said and they couldn't escape. That's like us. We cain't escape. We here in this land where they took our ancestors. How could you run from that?"

"I don't know," Veronica said sadly. "But maybe Miss Lott is right when she says about men always wantin' to fight. Our men always on the edge of some kind'a war. All proud'a their muscles. I mean I like me a strong man but what good is he if he's all bleedin' an' dead."

"Sometimes it's better to fight," Chip Lowe put in. "That's why we got the neighborhood watch. Sometimes you got to stand up."

"But not like no fool," Cynthia said. "Not like them, uh, what you called 'em, Mr. Fortlow?"

"Rascals in the cane. That's what they were called." Socrates was happy to hear his question discussed. He didn't need to say much because everybody else was alive with words.

"Yeah," Cynthia said. "Rascals. That's just like a man.

11

So busy fightin' that he gets killed and his woman and child go back into slavery."

"But what is the storm?" Topper asked Socrates. "What does it mean?"

"Why's it got to mean anything?" Cynthia screeched. "It's just what happened."

"No," Topper disagreed. "No. Every story, everything that happens has a meaning. A purpose. That's why Mr. Fortlow asked that question and then told his auntie's story. The story is the answer. The answer to his question."

"Is that right?" Veronica asked. "Is what Topper say true?"

Socrates looked at the beautiful, black, pear-shaped woman. It was the first time he ever heard her ask something without the twist of sex in her tone.

"I'm not sure," Socrates said. "I mean I been thinkin' about bein' mad at white folks lately. I mean I'm always mad. But bein' mad don't help. Even if I say somethin' or get in a fight, I'm still mad when it's all over. One day I realized that I couldn't stop bein' mad. Bein' mad was like havin' a extra finger. I don't like it, everybody always make fun of it, but I cain't get rid of it. It's mine just like my blood.

"But I didn't remember Bellandra's story until we were already talkin'. It just came to me and I said it. And now that Topper says that the answer is in the story I think he might be right. Maybe not the whole answer but there's somethin' there. Somethin'."

"But why you wanna ask the question?" Chip Lowe asked.

"Because I'm tired'a bein' mad, man. Tired. I see all these white people walkin' 'round and I'm pissed off just that they're there. And they don't care. They ain't worried. They thinkin' 'bout what they saw on TV last night.

They thinkin' 'bout some joke they heard. An' here I am 'bout to bust a gut."

"Maybe they should have left the cane fields," Leon said. "Maybe they should have forgotten all about that fear and guilt."

"Yeah," Cynthia added in an almost sweet voice. "And they sure shouldn't'a killed those black folks that was too scared to run with'em. Sure shouldn't.'"

"Uh-huh," Veronica agreed. "And Alfred should have taken Rose and gone north or south or west. If he ain't had a home to go back to he should have made a new home rather than stayed in the cane fields with them mosquitoes and alligators."

"Maybe that's what Mr. Fortlow's aunt was saying," Nelson Saint-Paul said. "Maybe they couldn't leave the plantation. Maybe they were stuck with those white folks that put 'em in chains and the blacks who stayed slaves."

"This sure is some good rum, Socrates," Cynthia Lott exclaimed. She had taken a small paper cup and filled it. "That's just about the best liquor I ever tasted."

"Made from sugarcane by black hands in the Caribbean sun," Socrates said.

Everyone had a drink and then they all had another.

Socrates felt secure in his secluded home with his black friends and smooth liquor. They ate the ham sandwiches and talked about white people and how they felt about them.

"But do we have the right?" Socrates asked Nelson Saint-Paul.

"We got reasons," Nelson answered. "We got reasons. But reasons and rights ain't the same thing."

"I don't know what it means really," Cynthia Lott crooned, her voice calmed by smooth rum. "I mean so what if you don't have the right? You still gonna be mad."

Socrates smiled and rested his big hands on his knees. He stood up saying, "Well we can't figure all that out in one night anyway. It was just a question been on my mind."

"Oh my it's midnight," Veronica said. "I better be gettin'."

"Damn," Chip Lowe said. "We usually out by ten. That rum loosen up the tongue."

The Wednesday night group gathered themselves up quickly and left Socrates' home. He wondered if Leon drove Cynthia and what it might feel like to kiss Veronica's big lips.

"Bye," he said at the front door.

He noticed a light on in the front house. Maybe tomorrow Mr. Malone would complain about his little party.

After everyone left Socrates went to fold his collapsible chairs but then he stopped and stood there in his living room. He looked at the chairs, imagining that they still held his guests. Snobby Topper, angry Cynthia Lott, and all the rest. He thought about being angry himself. Somewhere in the night he realized that it wasn't just white people that made him mad. He would be upset even if there weren't any white people.

"How come they didn't go down to Mexico?" little Socrates might have asked his stern auntie.

"Because the road wasn't paved," she would have answered.

Socrates laughed to himself and poured one last shot of rum. He left the chairs out for the night because they felt friendly.